BLOODLINES

A JIM LOCKE NOVEL

P.F. HUGHES

BLOODLINES

by P.F. Hughes

For Family.

Blood is blood.

SURVEILLANCE

ONE

"Are you a gambling man, Locke?"

Was I? Not really. I don't think I'd ever set foot in a bookie's in my life. I wouldn't know where to start with placing a bet, couldn't give the slightest fuck about horse racing, not even the Grand National. My poker face was just my usual expression and I wouldn't know a card game if I tried. I never was one for chasing a win, and a tip was something I gave to the barmaid if I thought she was doing a good job at keeping me in beer. I occasionally bought a lottery ticket if it was a big one and I sometimes took risks - dangerous risks as Laura kept reminding me - so that was probably as far as my gambling went. I'd gambled with my life many times, and yet I'd always came out the other side relatively unscathed, except for the seven-inch scar across my abdomen. You could say those gambles mostly paid off. But was I a gambling man? Did I place bets? No.

"Not really," I said. "Can't say I am."

Seamus Connolly looked me in the eye and smiled. His youngest son, Kian, had returned to the table with a bottle of Jameson and two glasses. Grinned as he joined us and sat down. His older brother, Shane, the middle of the three brothers, lifted a Guinness and drank.

"I'm surprised by that," Seamus said. "I really am. But then what's a little bet now and then, eh? This one's just for fun."

"I suppose I could give it a go," I said, eyeing the bottle. "Looks a decent drink."

"Smooth as a baby's arse," Kian said. His accent was pure Mancunian, as was his brother's, when he bothered to speak. Seamus, on the other hand, was a mix of heavy Dublin coated in Manc and somewhere in between. He popped the cork from the bottle and poured two good measures into each glass, pushing one to me.

"What do you say we drink a dram each until this bottle is finished and the last one standing gets to take this home?" He dipped into his trouser pocket and pulled out a large wad of cash in twenties. Dropped it on the table. "A grand. Yours if you can keep up."

"A grand? You'd seriously give me a grand if I'm still standing after this?"

"That's what I said."

"I couldn't, Seamus. It's a lot of money."

"You'll have earned it."

"And if you win? I have to give you a grand. Is that how it works?"

"Ah, we just call it quits. Just for fun, like I said."

"But you're still willing to give me a grand? That's a lot of money to lose, if you don't mind me saying so."

"I don't intend to lose," he said, leaning in. "But I'm a man of my word. The cash is yours if you manage to finish on top. What do you say? Come on, it's St. Patrick's day. Live a little."

I looked down at the whiskey. It was one I knew well. Could I match him, dram for dram? On a night like this? "Are you sure about this?"

"Deadly."

And then the band kicked in, a six-piece fusion set, kind of like a cross between The Pogues and Toss the Feathers. If it wasn't lively enough, it was about to get that bit livelier. When the drums counted in a one-two-three-four, and the tables bounced, Kian and Shane jumped up to join the party, and Seamus and I raised a glass and drank it in one. I poured us another and told him I was planning on savouring this one. I saw him laugh and he mouthed something that I think was meant to be funny, but I couldn't hear him over the noise. Instead, I caught his daughter's eye, a pretty young twenty-something standing over near the bar with a handful of men around her. She looked over her shoulder at me sitting with her old man when Kian whispered something in her ear. Then she turned away and moved into the crowd. I suspected she had no idea she was the reason he'd brought me here in the first place. And I needed to know that reason, too. Last night's phone call had taken me by surprise. "Meet me at Mulligan's," he'd said. "I've got a proposition for you. I'll make it worth your while."

So here I was, feeling drunk, weeks of sobriety falling away like rocks down a cliff. Suddenly, I was back in at the deep end.

Seamus left his seat and joined me on the bench, squeezing in between a fat girl who was half asleep. He nudged me and downed another dram. Urged me to do the same. I did, thinking that this could end messy, and watched him top us both up again. It wasn't a drink to be reckoned with. Best not to treat it as a session whiskey but I doubted Seamus Connolly would agree.

"So," he said. "Like this cash sitting right here," which he pocketed in his shirt breast pocket, "this job I want you to do for me is easy money. I wouldn't even call it work, to be honest, but if anyone can do this kind of thing, I suppose it must be you, eh?"

"What kind of thing?" I said. I'd also have liked to ask him to get to the fucking point, but you don't challenge Seamus Connolly, not if you value your teeth. "How can I be of service?"

"Surveillance," he said. "Just the straightforward kind."

"Meaning?"

"Just keep your eyes open," he said. "And report back to me on a weekly basis or as and when, depending on what you find."

"And who am I watching, exactly?"

He nodded into the crowd, and I followed his gaze. "My youngest daughter. Aisling. You see her?"

How could I miss her? She was beautiful and alluring, dancing away to the band in a short brown dress, her black hair tied up in a green velvet band, her blue eyes sparkling. Slim but curvaceous in all the right places and an arse that wouldn't look out of place in anyone's bed. She was a young twenty-three, a party girl if the rumours were true, and every kid in town was in love with her. It was easy to see why.

She was also untouchable given that her father was the patriarchal boss in the family, a family whose tentacles stretched into every corner of the country. Protection, drugs, loan sharking, prostitution even, if the latest reports were to be believed. I knew Seamus had various properties scattered around, and his eldest son, Connor, was about to invest in the latest skyscraper apartment boom in a big way. Gangsters that even the gangsters feared. It was well known they'd fuck you up if you crossed them. Well known that Seamus and perhaps some of his boys were responsible for far more than breaking fingers. Bodies had shown up just recently that had their stamp all over it, though in this town, Seamus was king. I had no doubt he'd kept the local politicians happy in exchange for their protection from the law. Rumour had it he'd kept the police quiet too, and it didn't surprise me at all. Despite all that had gone down in recent years, the smell of corruption had never really gone away. It was just the faces that had changed.

"So she's your daughter then?"

"Youngest," he said. "My eldest, Siobhan, is settled with her own family back in Donegal. She's thirty-five now. Two kids, a boy and a girl, and her husband, Kevin, has taken over his dad's farm. Pigs, mainly. They never run out of bacon."

If it was meant as a joke, I didn't find it funny. I looked at him, this old man pushing seventy-five but still sixteen stone of raw muscle and hands like shovels. Not a rare breed for an Irishman, but I knew people often wondered why he kept himself in the game at his age. I felt it was because he loved what he did. It kept him young, gave him something to live for. Kept the blood pumping through his veins. He topped us up again, and I saw the bottle was slowly going down. I thought about what I could do with that grand he had in his breast pocket.

"So why do you want me to watch her?" I said. "Make sure she's okay, that kind of thing?"

He shook his head. "She can handle herself. She's like her mother. Soft on the outside, hard on the inside. Won't be taken for a fool, you know? No, she'll be okay, I'm sure. I just don't want her to be taken advantage of, if you know what I mean."

"Not quite."

"A little bird tells me she's been seeing a fella."

"No surprise there," I said. "She's a good-looking woman."

He nodded. "Young lad, about her age. But I worry about her because of who he is."

"You know him then?"

"Know of him," he said. "And the rest of his family. Anyone else and I wouldn't normally give a fuck. But this lot..."

"Sounds like you're not too happy about it. But kids are kids, Seamus. It'll just be a fling, I'm sure."

"If I find out he's fucking her, I'll murder the bastard."

"Who?"

"One of the Poles," he said. "Lukasz. Lukasz Badowski. You may have heard of his father."

I had. Wiktor Badowski was a well-known career criminal around Manchester. He'd done time back in the eighties for manslaughter, but everyone knew he was a murderer. His younger brother, Oskar, had taken over the reins for a few years while Wiktor counted the days inside, making connections and striking up deals in unlikely places. But then Oskar was found dead in a reclamation yard out in Cheshire and it kicked off a war among the Poles and the Irish and the Italians. A few people were killed, including one of Connolly's boys, a young Cork man called James Dunne. Since then, the Connollys have not been best of friends with the Polish, least of all Wiktor and his lot, having long suspected him of being involved in Dunne's demise. They'd found him hanging from the Stockport viaduct, a hundred feet from the ground, on Good Friday in nineteen eighty-nine. Since then, it's said a truce was called and patches respectfully not crossed. The Connollys and the Badowskis had agreed to leave it at that and move on with their respectful businesses. But there had always been the suspicion among both sides that either one was up to no good. So for Aisling Connolly to be romantically involved with the young Badowski kid, Lukasz, things had appeared to have taken a turn in a very different direction. And judging by the look on Seamus's face, I guessed he wasn't too keen on his daughter getting involved with the enemy.

"I find it hard to trust anyone," he said, "let alone a Badowski. See, Aisling likes to think she's streetwise, and she is to a certain extent, but I just don't trust these bastards. Which is where you come in."

"You think he's got an ulterior motive?"

"Something like that, yeah. And if he has, I'd like you to find out what that might be."

"As well as follow Aisling around and keep you informed of what she's up to?"

"That's right," he said. "You'll be well sorted for anything you need. All you need to do is ask. Cars, assistance, whatever."

"I like to work alone in cases like this," I said. "Too many cooks and all that."

"Let's just make something clear from the outset, though. I don't want you to feel like I've got some kind of power over you, you know. You know my reputation, Mr. Locke. I don't want you to feel like you're working for me. I'm your client. I'll pay you an excellent rate. Only fair for what I'm asking you to do."

"Normally I'd charge a straight five hundred per week for this kind of surveillance job. That covers my time, petrol allowances, the spying kit, you name it."

He waved this away like he was swatting a fly. "I'll double it. A grand a week, cash in hand. Shall we say every

Sunday? Just come to my house and we can sort everything there."

It was silly money and he knew it, and I knew I could drag this shit out for as long as it took. A grand a week in cash in my pocket would do very nicely, thank you very much.

"When do I start?"

He finished his whiskey and took the wad of cash from his breast pocket. He put it between my twitching fingers. "You win," he said. "I'm done, anyway. No time like the present. We can iron out any paperwork you'd like me to deal with on Sunday. That's when you'll get your first payment."

"Seamus, this is good enough. Forget the bet, I don't gamble anyway. It feels wrong to just take this money."

"I never shirk on a bet, Locke."

"But I couldn't, really."

"You can and you will." He stood up and I did the same, suddenly feeling high and light as a feather. I was drunk, and the party was kicking in. Someone - I think it was Shane - put a fresh Guinness in front of me, then vanished into the crowd. Seamus and I shook to seal the agreement. It was easy enough.

"We'll look forward to learning what she's up to," he said. "And remember, Locke. She's my daughter and I love her. I want to know everything, for her own good."

"I'll need some details," I said. "About her. Where she likes to go, who her friends are, that kind of thing."

He nodded. "Come to mine on Sunday. I'll give you everything you need."

"Just one thing to start me off," I said. He nodded, but looked impatient. He was ready to call it a night. "Who told you she might be seeing Lukasz?"

"You'll have to speak to Kian," he said. "He knows all about that."

I glanced around for Kian, who was watching from over at the bar. When I turned back to Seamus, he'd gone. I watched him walk away, out the side door and into the night.

I sat for a while, just minding my own business and watching the party get into full swing before the last band was due to come on. It was only just gone ten o'clock and I was beginning to think about one for the road. Thought about the job Seamus wanted me to do and his reasons for it. I suppose he'd do whatever it took to feel better. I just wasn't entirely sure I was the man for the job. If he didn't like whatever I had found out, how would he react? I'd heard my share of bad things about the Connollys over the years. There was no telling what these people could do, given half a chance. I decided right there and then to do the right thing and be cautious with the truth if I knew it would make relations go tits up. My initial thoughts on this romance was that it was destined for disaster, but then what did I know these days? Not much.

My phone buzzed, and I drained my pint and pulled it out, stepping outside via the front door. Two bouncers moved aside as I stumbled into the street. The night was noisy and beyond, the traffic on Deansgate moved like an electric snake.

"Laura."

"You said you'd be home by now."

"When have I ever been governed by time?"

"That's a point. So, you on the way back then?"

I glanced back at the pub. It was bouncing. I felt a temptation - no, more than that - an urge to get back inside and get acquainted with the subject of my new job. Well, that was my excuse. What I really wanted, I knew, was another pint.

"I'm on the way."

"I've been waiting for you," she said. "It's lovely and warm in bed."

I knew what she wanted and was more than willing to oblige. But already a new case had whetted my appetite. It had been a while since I felt the buzz of it again. My last major case had gotten me hurt and had been enough to put me off the job for life... until I got bored hanging around the flat all day. It was time to get back in the saddle. I could only take so much of insurance fraud. Surveillance was my bread and butter and a job that paid as well as this was enough motivation.

"Sounds like an invitation," I said. "How could I refuse?"

"Just hurry up. But anyway, what did Connolly want?"

I told her.

"Seems easy enough, eh? A grand a week would be just fine."

"That's what I thought. Cash in hand as well. Bonus."

"Just make sure you keep him sweet."

I instinctively felt my scar, which was something I found myself doing of late. Since the stabbing, there had been a strange itch, a kind of ethereal pulse. It made me want to move my hand there as if the scar itself was some kind of oracle to forces unknown.

Or maybe I was just drunk. I turned away from the pub, figuring the further away I got, the further from my mind it became.

"I'm gonna walk," I said. "I'll be half an hour, tops."

"I'll be waiting."

I hung up and walked down to the river, lingering on

Victoria Bridge as the night revellers buzzed past. Sparked up. Took that shit in deep.

The Connollys. The Badowskis. Bloodlines that ran deep.

I stared into the murky water as the rain fell. It was dirty, the colour of hell itself.

I took Bob's Fedora from my jacket pocket, a bit crumpled up but perfect in every way, and placed it on my head.

Then I turned away and walked into the neon lights of the city.

TWO

I was looking forward to surveillance. It had been a long time since I'd just been able to follow someone around and sit in my car. It required work at all hours, and things could get very boring with only the radio for company, but it was a lot better than getting stabbed or blown up or attacked with a machete. Of course, it could be lonely work. And tiring. On cold and rainy nights, the drudgery was enough to send you under, and before long you'd have to leave the post just to see something different.

But I didn't expect any of that in my pursuit of Aisling Connolly. Well, maybe some of the boring stuff. But from what I'd heard, she was an active girl in many ways. Seamus wanted everything on what she was up to, and I intended to deliver. I didn't expect a walk in the park. It wasn't lost on me that last night, in the pub, she'd looked directly at me after Kian had whispered something in her ear. Gotta say, I wondered what that was about. She probably knew who I was already, of that I have no doubt. The hardest job for me now was keeping out of her sight. She probably wasn't stupid. If she knew I was following her around, would there be any point in this job? I reminded myself that I served my clients, not the subject of the job itself. If Seamus Connolly wanted to pay me a grand a week for watching his daughter, so be it. I knew I'd have to be cautious, though. I had a feeling this girl knew how to play games.

I left Laura at the office and took the Volvo down to Chorlton. It was a place I knew young Kian hung out, drinking in the bars and no doubt cavorting with the young ladies he had his pick from. The Connollys had a huge house out in the village, hidden away behind a little wood beyond the green, and I'd heard through a few people that Kian was now spending most of his time there and the house was considered pretty much his own. The kid was basically drunk on money and drugs and was practically living a lifestyle of debauchery and infamy. He was barely twenty-five yet had a successful business promoting local bands and DJs and putting on party nights that attracted the coolest heads around. A side business of dealing pills and coke and all manner of uppers kept him in decent clobber and kept the house ticking over nicely. I'd done a bit of research already, not that I'd needed to, and I knew that the drug dealing was sanctioned and supplied by none other than his father and his contacts. In the drugs game, it paid to keep your suppliers sweet. Seamus had made things easy for his son. It was his heavies that had done the hard stuff at the business end, keeping the supply coming in. All Kian had to do was plaster on a fake smile and schmooze the punters into buying his stuff rather than someone else's. He was no fool, though. What he was supplying could be bought from any other dick around the corner or up the road, too. But it was the quality of what he was selling that stood out from the rest. This was no street corner dealing but appointment basis only and you'd better have good money to bring to the table. As the old adage went, you get what you pay for, and with Kian's stuff, what you paid for kept you up all night.

It was around midday when I pulled into a space down a backstreet from the main crossroads at Wilbraham Road and Barlow Moor Road. Got a few dirty looks from some of the locals as I locked the car up and made my way towards the main stretch. It was clear I didn't belong here. Last night, at Mulligans's, Kian had said he'd meet me in the Tap Room, a local bar that attracted the ultra bohemian types that lived here like flies round shit. If I didn't feel out of place when I stepped over the threshold, I certainly looked it. Caught my reflection in a full-length mirror and cringed at how unkept I looked. I had a week's growth on my face and my three quarter length leather coat hung on me like the skeleton I'd become. I'd thinned out significantly since I was stabbed in the abdomen. I'd told Laura it was just because I couldn't stomach my food like I used to. The truth was my mood had dipped dramatically, which I'd tried to keep from her. It took me a while to come to terms with how I'd come so close to leaving this earth. It changed my perspective on things a little bit. I barely felt like eating, but took in just enough to keep my blood pumping. It was the booze that kept me fired up and kicked my arse into gear. I knew I was slowly killing myself and it was a problem only I could address. There was always time, though, and time, I felt, was on my side.

Stepped up to the bar and ordered a coffee, black. Took away the froth and got myself a brandy to top it up. Ah, fuck it. I knew it would be just enough to spark my enthusiasm, which I knew was lacking. I knew I had to put my finger on why that was. A grand a week in cash was more than enough to pique my interest, but perhaps it was the client who was paying me that got me twitchy. Suddenly I felt nervous and got to thinking that Seamus could've sent someone else after me too, just to keep me on my toes. I knew he had enough of his boys to do what he liked. I looked around, saw nothing suspicious other than a bloke in a dress and a room half full of trendy types drinking continental beer. Took that as my cue to step outside into the spraying March rain and sparked up. Took that shit in deep.

There were a handful of people outside, all sitting alone, just like I was. Passers-by must've thought we were a bunch of sad cases, or a group let out of the care centre for the day. I sat and sipped my coffee, looking out over the main stretch and the heart of the place, and took out my phone. I opened the photographs I had stored in there, the bloodlines on the walls, the rifle on the floor, the body in the armchair. The images were calling me daily and I could feel that something didn't add up about Bob's death. Bob Turner, my old friend, former Chief Crime Correspondent at the Evening Chronicle. A man who'd took his own life because he had blood on his hands he could no longer live with.

The coroner had concluded it was a straightforward suicide pretty quickly, and it probably was. I'd read his last words myself in a note he'd left me in a bottle of Bowmore. The cigar he gave me was still sitting in my pocket. I rolled it in my fingers regularly. Even came close once or twice to smoking it, but I always resisted. Keeping it on me somehow kept Bob close, and his fedora, which I'd taken to wearing now and again, somehow kept me ticking over.

I closed the photographs, tried to put them out of mind. I knew it was a lost cause. The night George Thornley and I found him will live long in my mind. I could still smell the dried up blood in the summer heat. Could still taste that sickly sweet air at the back of my throat.

Still felt that something wasn't quite right.

"You been here long?"

I looked up and saw Kian looking down at me. He was smirking. Said he'd get us a pint, but before I could object - knowing that if I had one, I'd want half a dozen more - he was deep inside and at the bar. I checked the time on my phone. It was coming up to one o'clock and I told myself I could justify it. Just the one wouldn't do any harm. Before I could pocket it again, it rang.

"What do you want this time?"

"Morning to you too."

"It's the afternoon," I said. "Been a long night?"

"Something like that."

"Been at the wine again? Something tells me you've been wallowing."

"What makes you say that?"

"The sound of your voice."

"Well, the only thing I've been wallowing in is a long, hot bath. This girl deserves it."

"So, to what do I owe the pleasure?"

"Got some news," she said. "Thought you might like to be the first to know."

"Good or bad?"

"Could be both."

"Spit it out, Fiona."

I heard her sigh and pictured her pacing around her house with a towel on her head and nothing else. Kian appeared by my side and placed a pint of lager before me. I stood and got out of earshot, but he'd taken the hint anyway and took a seat as I edged onto the pavement. By now, the rain had stopped and a few more punters had gathered around an enormous plant pot they were using as an ashtray.

"It's our friend," she said. "Robertson."

"Please tell me he's choked to death on a jam doughnut."

"No such luck. But he has been promoted."

"You're kidding me."

"Wish I was. He's now a DCI."

"Fuck off."

"Told you he was after it."

"They must be fucking stupid."

"We already know that, Jim."

"So I suppose this puts his natural ability to be a total cunt at epic levels."

"Not if we take the plunge, no. Isabella is ready at any time."

But I wasn't. I liked him just where I had him. I knew I could keep him on his toes and take him down anytime I liked, but he was useful. Although his disgrace and downfall would be a joy to behold, I could use him to my liking. The power had shifted now that he knew what we had on him, and he didn't even know Fiona had the red button right at her fingertips. Which proved to me just how useless he was at his job.

"I don't think now's a good time," I said. "He's proving useful."

"I know, but it worries me you'll piss him off so much that it might go pear-shaped from our point of view. All I have to do is release the files and he's fucked."

"So what's the rush?"

"No rush, I suppose. It's just that he's pissing everyone off already, and he's only been in the job a day. I'm worried the power will go to his head."

"Absolute power corrupts..."

"Absolutely. I just want to see justice done, Jim. Isabella

does too, and she's got every right to see the bastard sent down."

"I know, I know."

"Will you think about it?"

"I'll think about it," I said. "I want to see him suffer as well."

"But you want to prolong it for your sake, no one else's. And that's not fair, Jim."

I suppose I could see it from her point of view. "You still want to leave the force?"

"Damn right," she said. "After I've seen to all this. There's no progression for me now."

"But you'll have exposed Robertson and got a conviction. Won't go unnoticed by top brass."

"Come on, Jim. They'll probably have me up for a disciplinary."

"They should give you a medal," I said. "And a promotion."

"I've more chance of winning the lottery. Anyway, I've made my mind up. As soon as it's done, I'm off. I might even go on holiday to celebrate."

"You sound like you can't get away quick enough."

"You know what it's like, Jim. It's just not the career I thought it was."

"So what will you do instead?"

"I don't know. Become a trucker or something. Go back to being a bloody travel agent. Not thought about it, to be honest with you."

"Well, I'm paying you good money to help me out," I said. "That should tide you over for a while."

"I've been squirrelling it away," she said. "Thought it best because I don't know how long I'll be out of work for when I do finally quit."

"Well, it's time you earned your crust," I said. "I need some information. Anything you can get for me would be good."

"What kind of information?"

"I need whatever you can find on a bunch of people."

"This relate to a new case or something?"

"Got it in one. You'll be no stranger to who my latest client is."

"Sounds intriguing."

"Seamus Connolly," I said. "The whole Connolly family, actually."

"Oh, everyone knows about them."

"They're hardly strangers, are they?"

"Do you really need me to help you with this one? You're getting sloppy."

"Your help just gives me a bit more time on my hands. Saves me from getting lost in a digital wasteland. Got better things to do."

"So what do you want to know?"

"Anything and everything."

"And are you gonna tell me what this is about? What does Seamus Connolly actually want?"

"Officially, he wants me to trail his youngest daughter and report on what she's up to. Unofficially, well, we know the Connollys always have an ulterior motive."

"So what's your feeling on this?"

"I don't know. I'm just gonna do what he asks until I find out what's really going on."

"Seems weird him coming to you. Hasn't he got his boys to help him out?"

"His three sons? Yeah."

"I meant his loyal toss bags."

"Them as well."

"So what's she done?"

"Nothing, as far as I can tell. But he wants me to keep an eye on her because of who she's shagging."

"So, who's the lucky man? Footballer or something? Young rock star?"

"Much worse," I said. "It's one of the Badowski kids. Lukasz."

There was a pause as I let this sink in. I heard her catch her breath.

"Shit."

"Exactly."

"But that's like Jeremy Corbyn taking Theresa May up the arse. Unbelievable."

"Not to mention horrific," I said. "I know. It's a strange one."

"They're like polar opposites, aren't they?"

"They have bad blood, going back a few years. You might not remember James Dunne hanging from Stockport viaduct."

"Before my time, I believe."

"There's probably a lot more we don't know about. Which is where you come in."

"Aye aye, Captain."

"The Connollys and the Badowskis," I said. "I need whatever little nuggets you can find. Stuff that might not necessarily be on file or the PNC, especially where the Connollys are concerned."

"I've heard they like doing one or two top brass the odd favour."

"You know more than you think," I said. "And you'd be right. So I need you to keep your ears peeled. Talk to a few coppers, especially some of the older lot. Find out what you can."

"And the Badowskis?"

"Same with them. Anything you can dig up, especially on Lukasz."

"It might take me a while."

"There's no rush," I said. "Just let me know what you can, when you can."

"I'm on it," she said. "But I'm regretting calling you now."

"Why's that?"

"Well, you've just given me a load of work to do."

"It's what I'm paying you for, don't forget."

"Well, it is keeping me in good knickers, I suppose."

There she goes again. Flirting. There was always that pause when I did a double take and she waited for me to catch my thoughts. It was as if she wanted to stop me in my tracks on purpose. Playing games. Pushing the boundaries (and my buttons). I liked the fact that she was a bit cheeky, though it made me a tad uneasy, especially when she was with me in the flesh. Because, although I kept denying it, I had to admit to myself that I was attracted to her. Which made our mutually platonic relationship difficult. The thing was, I wasn't sure if she was just playing around or she meant it. Either way, I knew it was only a matter of time before any professionalism we had went out of the window.

Her cackle down the phone brought me back to reality, and I had one eye on Kian, too. I didn't want him getting bored and wandering off.

"Listen, I'm gonna go."

"Okay, love."

"Keep me updated," I said. "Anything you come across, remember?"

"I'll be in touch as and when."

It was my cue to hang up. I turned to Kian, who was

already halfway through his pint, and sat opposite. Took a long drink and sparked up. Took that shit in deep.

"A woman?" he said.

"How did you guess?"

"They like to chat shit, don't they? So anyway, how did you become a private detective? Police not exciting enough for you?"

"Something like that," I said. "They booted me out, so I had no choice."

"So what did you do?"

"None of your business," I said. "And anyway, we're not here for me."

"Touchy type, eh?"

"Not at all," I said, thinking about how much I'd like to punch the little shite. "Just keen to get down to work."

"So you've summoned me here because...?"

"I want to know more about your sister. It's not lost on you that your dad wants me on her case. So I need a few things."

"Go on."

"We'll start at the beginning. How did you find out she was seeing Lukasz Badowski?"

He laughed and shook his head. Took a drag on his smoke and looked me in the eye. "She told me. One night after she'd had a few. She'd had a row with my dad and later on, when I found her in the pub, she just came out with it. Told me there and then over a drink. Said they'd been an item for a while."

"When was this?"

"About a month ago."

"And they'd been together a while, like a few months?"

"She didn't say. Maybe."

"And how do you feel about that?"

He looked away, then down at his beer before taking the last of it. "It's her life, I suppose."

"So you're not too happy about it then?"

"What makes you say that?"

"Tone of voice. Come on, Kian. Lukasz Badowski? About your age, isn't he? What are you, twenty-three?"

"Twenty-five. He's twenty-three, same as Aisling."

They were just kids, all three of them. No doubt Kian thought he'd seen it all, but I knew, just by sitting here and looking him straight in the eye, that he hadn't. I had years of experience on this kid, was old enough to have fathered him myself, and yet he was cocky. An air of self satisfaction graced his perfect face, and I knew instantly, the moment I first met him, that his smugness reminded me of everything I hated in people. Robertson had the same look about him. And sure, weren't we all cocky at that age? I know I was. And I wish, just like this kid before me, not a care in the world or a weight on his shoulders, that I was twenty-five again.

"Do you think it'll last?"

This time, he said nothing. Which told me everything. The Connollys were worried.

"So, how did your dad react to the news?"

"He wasn't happy, as you know, otherwise he wouldn't have roped you into following her around."

"And what about your brothers?"

"What about them?"

"They feel the same way? I mean, it can't be easy seeing your little sister going out with the enemy."

"You'll have to ask them."

"But what do you think?"

"I don't think Connor's very pleased."

Connor Connolly. The eldest of the five siblings,

pushing forty and just a year or two younger than me. The last I'd heard was that he was about to go full real estate tycoon with the refurbishment of an old warehouse out in Ancoats. Trendy and expensive apartments for trendy and expensive people. The city's Northern Quarter had morphed into a vast bohemian suburb in the middle of the city, once run down and disused, a throwback to Manchester's glorious industrial past. Now it was all ultra cool bars and quirky restaurants, restored facades and revolutionised warehouses. Connor, no doubt representing the Connolly family, had become one of these developers. There was every chance dirty money had been involved in this substantial invest-ment. Refurbished warehouse apartment blocks didn't come cheap. Drug money, blood money, or both. Perhaps Aisling going out with a Badowski was an unwelcome distraction.

"So," I said, changing the subject. "You have a good night last night?"

"Ah, you know. Paddy's day, isn't it? Always a good night."

"And Aisling?"

"As far as I know, yeah."

"You talk much?"

He shrugged. "No more or less than usual."

I nodded. "So, do you hang around together? Some brothers and sisters do, don't they?"

He shook his head. "Not us. We sometimes end up in the same bars and stuff but she's usually with her mates and I'm usually with mine."

"Well, this is the kind of stuff I need from you, actually. If you want me to find out what she's up to."

"It's not me that wants to know, though, is it? It's my dad."

"All right then, your dad."

"What kind of stuff?"

"Just the little things," I said, knowing they could turn out to be big things. "Who her mates are, what she does at weekends, where she likes to drink and hang out, that kind of thing."

"Suppose you've got to start somewhere, eh?"

"That's right." I took out my notebook and pen. "Mates first."

He sighed and fumbled with some cash. "I'll get us another."

"Not for me, thanks."

I watched him head back to the bar and order two more pints. I sparked up and thought about making my excuses. A drink was the last thing I needed right now. Trouble was, it was the thing I needed most as well.

"You don't seem too keen on helping me out," I said when he returned. "I got the impression from your dad that none of you were overjoyed about her seeing Lukasz Badowski."

"That might be true," he said. "But I'm not gonna start dictating who she can and can't fuck either."

"And your dad does, is that right?"

"There's two things," he said. "First off, the family business. We're not too keen on the Badowskis, as you know. Well, I say we..."

"That include you, then?"

He smiled, shrugged, took a drink. "Different generation, you know. Do I really give a fuck? Is that what you're asking? Not really. I'm not one for playing at gangsters. The rivalry is no different to the rivalry with the Montones or the Jewish lot, yeah? But this is the twenty-first century and times have changed. Things have moved on. My generation has a different perspective on matters."

But I didn't quite believe him. "Is that why Aisling and Lukasz can get it together, you think? You know, without killing each other?"

"And what would be the point of killing each other? No, my dad and uncle Jimmy have got this older generation thing going on. Carrying on like it's the Godfather or something."

"And is it?"

"Is it fuck, man."

"All right then," I said. It was my turn to take a drink, and I cringed when I noticed my hand shaking as I lifted the glass to my lips. Swallowed and carefully placed it back down. "What's the second thing?"

He took a final drag on his smoke and stubbed it out. I rolled the Montecristo in my pocket.

"The second thing is the simple fact that my dad is over-protective and can't stand that she's a grown woman having sex and living her own life."

"Seems a bit much to have her followed around."

"It is. But you don't know him like I do. He's not happy because it's him, but he wouldn't be happy, anyway. You got kids yourself?"

I did. A daughter I'd managed to let down too many times. It was something that needed to change. "A daughter."

"It's that father and daughter thing," he said. "Dubious about who she's seeing. He's been like that with all her other boyfriends growing up. He was the same with our Siobhan. I bet you're protective of your daughter as well."

"She's not at that stage yet," I said, although I had to

admit that when that stage came, I'd probably be following her around like a ghost. "Thankfully."

He nodded. "So that's how it is. The older he gets, the worse he is. The fact that it's a Badowski she's seeing only adds to the paranoia."

"So you think he's paranoid?"

He shrugged. "Just a bit."

"Tell me, Kian. I'm curious to know. Have you met Lukasz? I mean, do you know him?"

"I've met him," he said. "Seems okay."

"First impressions?"

"He's just another lad, really. No different from anyone else. He knows I'm not interested in any of that family stuff."

"And him? Is he the same, do you think?"

"Hard to say. I don't know. Maybe, maybe not. Maybe you should ask him."

Maybe I should. But I wanted more on Aisling before I moved any further. "So, are you gonna give me something on your sister? Where she drinks, that kind of stuff."

He sighed. Rolled his eyes. "There's four of them," he said. "Aisling's mates. They all went to school and stuff together, you know. Grew up together, really. There's Kerry Ainsworth. She works at a gym in Castlefield. Lynsey Byrne. Daytime bar manager at Grain. It's in the Northern Quarter."

"Whereabouts?"

"Over near Piccadilly station. Then there's Lisa Browne, she's Lynsey's cousin."

"What does she do?"

"What doesn't she do?"

"What do you mean?"

He grinned. "Nothing. As far as I know, she doesn't

work. Her boyfriend's a top banker. One of these traders, you know. A big cheese in finance. Keeps her well, so I'm told."

"So she basically lives off him, that what you saying?"

"Something like that, though she's known to do favours, you know?"

"What, sex?"

He grinned, like he knew from experience. "If you play your cards right, Jimmy ..."

A flashback of the Angel case suddenly came flooding back to me and I had to take a drink.

"You said there was one more."

He nodded. "That'll be Claire MacGowan. She's the sensible one. A nurse. Works at the MRI."

I sparked up. Tried to picture the five girls, all best friends together. Different, but the same. Girls who'd no doubt shared their deepest secrets over bottles of wine and lines of coke. Probably supplied by Kian himself.

"You got any pictures of them? On your phone or something?"

He shook his head. "No, but I'm sure you'll find them on Facebook."

"Isn't everyone on there these days?"

He raised his eyebrows and nodded. "In terms of where she goes, I couldn't tell you other than she's sometimes out around here. In the bars and stuff."

"She go clubbing?"

"Sometimes, probably. She's just like any young woman, really."

"What, fiercely independent?"

"Fierce is one way of putting it, I suppose."

"Meaning?"

"She can be feisty. Takes no prisoners. Don't be fooled by her soft side."

I nodded. Seamus had said she was soft on the outside, hard on the inside. But did either of them really know her at all?

"What about during the day? Does she work?"

He laughed. "Work? No. She's been playing around with various degrees for about ten years. Dad's kept her sorted for money up until now. You might find her behind the bar at Grain. I think Lynsey keeps her busy."

I had my doubts, though. About both claims. I didn't think Seamus could abandon his daughter financially like that, especially given the power and wealth he had. And he wouldn't see her working behind a bar in a million years.

I thought I might have enough, for now. Except one important thing.

"You got her phone number?"

"Aren't you supposed to be keeping inconspicuous? Why would you need that?"

Why indeed? I thought of Dave, the computer wizard who, along with Fiona, had saved me from being blown up.

"Just think it might come in handy, that's all."

I had no doubts that any under cover surveillance I carried out would last about ten minutes. Kian would be on the phone to her before I even got back to the car. I could see by his expression that he didn't trust me as much as I didn't trust him. There was a game being played here, a subtle one, and I didn't quite know whether to believe anything that came out of his mouth.

He tapped on his phone until he brought up a number and showed me the screen. I jotted it down quickly and pocketed my notebook.

"Anything else?"

"Yeah, you been eating kebabs recently?"

"What?"

I pointed to the chilli sauce stain down the front of his tee-shirt. "I'm not a fan of dealing with the washing, either. Thanks for your time. I'll be in touch."

I looked back at the table as I left and weaved through the traffic. He was already gone.

THREE

I supposed the next thing would be to start as I mean to go on, which meant tracing exactly where Aisling was right now and taking it from there. My guess was that with it being a Saturday, and that she was currently enjoying the honeymoon period of a blossoming new relationship, tonight might be date night. Question was, what was on her agenda?

I reached the Volvo and decided the best place for it now would be parked up at the flat. An early afternoon sun was trying to break through the dense grey, but at least the spraying rain had stopped. I drove away from here and into town through crowded Saturday south Manchester roads until I made the city centre as the clouds had gathered again and a downpour caught me just as I reached home. There were a few things I needed before I stepped out again, not least a shower and a change of clothes.

Laura had left half her wardrobe lying around the bedroom floor, her little basket of make-up scattered across the bed. She'd mentioned she was going out shopping for the afternoon with Maya. Shopping that would no doubt turn into a girlie lunch complete with a bottle or two of white wine.

I showered and changed and stuffed my pockets with hard cash. Then I opened up Laura's laptop and parked myself on the couch with a large coffee, black. Sparked up and opened Facebook. Figured it would be easy enough to find out who Aisling's friends really were and what they looked like. More importantly, perhaps I'd find out what she was up to tonight.

I started with Aisling herself. She made no secret of the fact that she was out there and it took me all of two minutes to find her among a relatively short list. Clicked on her profile and scrolled through what was on her wall, which I knew would give me some indication of her character, though not entirely. There were the usual memes everyone shared, she was a member of a few closed groups that would need further inspection, and like most young women her age, she liked a photograph, especially ones of herself and her friends and the cocktails they were enjoying.

I had a quick look through her friends list to see if Lukasz Badowski was among them, but there was no sign of him. Yet. I suspected it was only a matter of time before I came across their shared connection somewhere online. Everyone did social media these days, even kids from gangster families. Especially kids from gangster families. I had these two down as no different. However long they'd been seeing each other, no doubt it would be documented somewhere online. A photograph here, a tweet there. I'd dig them out or, even better, get Laura or Fiona to dig them out for me.

And sure enough, there it was, right at the top of her

profile page. A meal out 'with the man of the moment', though she didn't say who that was. You didn't have to be a genius to guess. Beside this status were love heart symbols and an emoji of a girl in love and blowing kisses. Another giving a cheeky wink. Several glasses of red wine in a row. Now all I had to do was find where she had a table.

I clicked on the first person of interest. Kerry Ainsworth worked at a gym in Castlefield, Kian had said. Judging by her photographs and status updates, she more than just worked there, but lived the lifestyle that went with it. She didn't appear to ever be out of running gear, as if she couldn't be seen in anything else, except when I found pictures of her in an evening dress and sipping mojitos with Aisling and the others on Lisa Browne's twenty-second birthday night out. Kerry was pretty and athletic, even in a sports vest, and she carried her figure with confidence. She struck me as the obsessive type, perhaps a fridge overloaded with energy drinks and obscure protein shakes instead of a fridge like mine that was full of beer and cheese and not much else. They said you could tell a lot about someone by what was in their fridge. I guessed they'd have no problems with Kerry Ainsworth. There was even a photo of her with her arms full of the weirdo non-food supplements that fitness freaks had for tea these days, her thin smile only spoilt by the stretch wrinkles at the side of her mouth, like this photo had been taken straight after a hard session on the bench press. It was a look I couldn't find sexy on a woman, even a young and pretty one like her.

Perhaps the same could be said about the next person of interest, but for different reasons. Lynsey Byrne had a face like she spent most of her time sucking lemons. Was it really so difficult to crack a smile? Looking into her eyes, her expression hard and cold, it was no wonder to me she'd been bemoaning the fact that she'd been single for over seven years. It was all over her Facebook page, this problem of hers, yet she failed to see the obvious staring her in the face every day. She carried her misery like a comfort blanket, unable to shake it off for anything because she needed it like I needed a drink every day. It was a part of her, it was who she was. But her persona did little to attract this man of her dreams she seemed to spend most of her time looking for.

I quickly moved on to friend number three, the one I was most interested in. The one Kian had suggested moon-lighted as a lady of the night, albeit when it suited her. Lisa Browne could have her pick of men, no problem. She was stunningly attractive in every way, her mixed race skin a pale brown, her naturally curly hair long and buoyant, her curvaceous figure flaunted at every opportunity, along with her fluttering eyelashes and her soft, wet lips. Sure, she was beautiful. On the outside, at least. But as I scrolled through her Facebook page, every opportunity she had of showing the world just how good looking she was, was taken. She came across as the type of girl who knew she was super-model fit but was clueless when it came to personality or how ugly she was on the inside. She seemed to have had a long line of ex boyfriends leaving a bitter trail behind her - or were they clients? - and her current man, a Matt Baker of Coutts Financial, seemed like merely the latest in a long line of suitors. I thought about what Kian had said, implying that this guy kept her in money, no problem. It wouldn't have come as a surprise. Perhaps the two were made for each other. He got what he wanted; she got what she felt she deserved. A rich prick in all senses.

Claire MacGowan was the most difficult to find, which

didn't come as a shock. She, by all accounts, was the most sensible of the five girls, holding down a respectable career as a nurse on the cardiology unit at the MRI. She was probably the one who worked the hardest for the least pay, the complete opposite to Lisa Browne. I wondered just how well the two got along. Was there a resentment there on Claire's part? Here was Miss Browne, quite happy and content to accept her current boyfriend's cash in exchange for whatever he wanted in the bedroom, and here was Claire MacGowan, staring out the hospital canteen windows late at night with a shit coffee and a headache and another resuscitation that had ended in tears.

I had to wonder what it was they had in common, if anything.

But then, of course, they'd all had their past together at school. It was amazing how people could turn out twenty years down the line or, in their case, six or seven. I knew it couldn't have been the only common bond that kept the girls as friends.

I saw that Claire had a Twitter account too, and when I clicked the link that was attached to her Facebook page, it took me straight there. Seemed she was more into tweeting as her social media thing, and I saw she'd done just that several times today, including one to Ais_Con1, our very own Aisling Connolly. A simple message, to the point - Here's a link to that place I told you about! - and an equally swift reply from Aisling, complete with the obligatory emojis she seemed to love using. Love hearts all round.

I clicked on the link and found the place I was looking for. I was lucky in that it wasn't that far away from the office. I could kill two birds with one stone and take Laura along, too.

I took out my phone and dialled.

They'd tried to deny they had a table the minute they heard my accent. I thought times had hit a new low when you couldn't book a table in a restaurant in your own home city. But then this was The Ivy, the exclusive London based eatery that had moved up in the world and had finally arrived in Manchester. You needed top dollar to eat a fine steak, but with the money Seamus Connolly was paying me every week, I didn't expect to find it a problem. When I mentioned I was eating on business with the Godfather Connolly, a table for two was found no problem.

Laura had put on her glad rags, hinting at a night on the cocktails. To hell with it. I loved her and she deserved it, especially with all my shit she'd put up with the past few years. Times had been hard, and she'd been there, a rock. Her sister Sara was still having a bad time of things and was back on the mental health ward at Wythenshawe, a place I still had nightmares about. So what kind of man was I if I couldn't treat her every now and then? I'd not seen her eyes light up like this since our first night in her bed. It was amazing what an espresso Martini could do.

"This is nice," she said. "Want to try it?"

"I'll stick to my beer."

"You're not really the cocktail type, are you?"

"I don't mind a whisky sour now and again."

"Why don't you get one? It's rarely you treat yourself, Jim. You deserve it with all the crap you've been through."

She was referring, of course, to the stabbing. That and the fact that I'd been nearly blown to pieces by a far right nut job. But I knew I needed more than a cocktail to get over that.

"Maybe I will, after dinner. I think I'll go for the porterhouse."

"So when are you expecting them?"

"No idea," I said. I checked the time. Just before eight. "Around now, I suppose."

I'd shown Laura Aisling's Facebook profile so she could know who we were here for and then keep her eyes peeled on the door. As far as Lukasz Badowski went, I guessed we were looking for a good looking Eastern European type with a chiselled jaw. He had to at least be as good looking as Aisling was, no doubt. She wouldn't settle for just anyone. He, I guessed, was to women what Aisling was to men. Irresistible and unattainable. The kind of man - albeit a young man - that would always seem a distance away. Given that he was the son of Wiktor Badowski, it would take a special kind of young lady to make him fall for her, and a brave one to handle his type. Aisling fitted both requirements like a glove.

As the waiter put down my starter, I clocked the main entrance and saw Aisling breeze in like she knew the place well. Lukasz Badowski, ever the gentleman, followed behind, holding her coat, one hand on her waist. It was all smiles as they were led to their table, which was at the opposite corner of the room, still within a good enough distance for me to get a decent view of proceedings. Aisling sat with her back to me, which was fine. It would give me ample opportunity to get a good look at Lukasz, to study his expressions, his mannerisms. How he was with her.

It was busy in here, and too warm. The rain had picked up again outside, lashing against the windows, and every table was taken, which suited me fine. The hustle and bustle and noise I hoped was enough to keep the two lovers distracted from my prying eyes. Already they were deep in conversation, oblivious to almost everything around them. A waitress arrived with a few drinks, a beer for him, a gin and tonic for her. He went at it like he'd not drank all day. I knew that feeling and took a long drink of my own.

"So that's them?" she said, peering over her shoulder.

I nodded. "Just the type of bloke I thought he'd be."

"And what's that?"

I leaned in, keeping one eye on the lovers. "Smartly dressed. Sharp. Not like your average inner city gangster, you know, loads of money but no style. No, he's got taste. I love his suit, the cut of it. It's well tailored. Shirt as well. Must've cost a few quid. And he's wearing a chunky-looking watch. Expensive haircut, very good looking. Well built in an athletic kind of way."

She turned again to look. "He's fit."

"Steady on."

"But like he knows it, you know."

I knew what she meant. Aisling was the same. She revelled in having a swarm of men around her, and I saw it firsthand on St. Patrick's night. They suited each other. They probably would've found each other one way or another, anyway. They looked the perfect couple together, lost in honeymoon period bliss. It'll never last, I thought.

I took out my iPhone and got some random shots, capturing Laura in several of them, but focused and zoomed in on the two. I was really only doing it for Seamus's benefit. Being an old guy, and old school too, I doubted he was the type to mess around with social media. He said he wanted everything on the couple and I intended to supply the goods. I was just giving the old man what he wanted. Perhaps the photographs I'd show him tomorrow were just what he needed, to cement in his own mind that it was really happening.

"So how long do you think this job will go on for?"

"As long as it takes," I said. "He wants me to just follow them around and report back what I find. If that's what he wants, that's what he gets."

"And what do you think you'll find?"

I shrugged. "Not much. The usual stuff young couples get up to. I mean, I don't know what he really expects. It's a bit of an odd one."

"Funny though, isn't it?" she said.

"What do you mean?"

"It can't just be because he's a Badowski, can it? I mean, all daughters eventually end up with someone, right, and even that someone might be considered 'the enemy', but do you really think there would be anything he could do about their relationship? Really?"

"He said that if he found out he was fucking her - his words, not mine - then he would kill him."

She laughed. "What, and you believe him?"

"We're talking about Seamus Connolly here."

"Well, of course he's fucking her! Wouldn't you? Actually, don't answer that. As for killing him, no. No father would risk hurting their daughter like that. You know, murdering their man just because she's slept with him. There's being overprotective and there's taking it to the extreme. I don't think even Seamus Connolly would resort to that."

"Maybe not," I said. "But he'd be giving the orders."

"That would be even worse, getting another man to do your dirty work."

"You obviously don't know Seamus Connolly," I said. "He's made himself a career out of doing just that."

"Well, he sounds," she said, lifting her glass and taking a sip, "like a total fucking dickhead."

"I wouldn't let him hear you say that."

"Well, he's not here, is he?" she said, standing. "So I'll say what I like. And anyway, you agree with me, don't you? He is a total dickhead. I'm going to the ladies."

I liked her when she got angry and half drunk at the same time.

But she was wrong. Seamus Connolly, I knew, wouldn't think twice about ordering the killing of a man who had been having sex with his daughter. But he would think twice about that man being a Badowski, the son of Wiktor Badowski himself, especially given the consequences thereafter. He obviously knew his daughter was seeing Lukasz in every sense of the word. Was he in denial about that? Was she really still his baby girl? So why hadn't he taken him out already? Perhaps he wanted the proof, the firsthand evidence. Was I destined to be the one to give him the ammunition, the one to load his gun?

"You want to see those toilets," she said, flopping into her seat and blowing a strand of hair from her eyes. It was the little things that made me realise how much I loved her. "There's even a girl squeezing the soap out for you."

"I beg your pardon?"

"You know, when you've finished. Puts it in the palm of your hand and expects a tip in return."

"Did you give her one?"

"Did I fuck. Starter not here yet?"

"I think it's coming now."

I was only half in the room as the waitress put our food down. I'd clocked Lukasz leave the table with his phone clamped to his ear and watched him move towards the front door. He left in a hurry and my view was obscured by a blur of people coming in as he was leaving, but I caught him again as he found a spot under a lamp outside and sparked up. It was just a guy having a conversation as he smoked, stepping absently around the cobbles as he chatted away. I got several crappy shots of him through the glass, trying hard to not make it obvious. Then a high end silver BMW pulled up in front of the restaurant and Lukasz stepped up to it. He got inside via the front passenger seat. The windows were tinted and dark. There was no sign of who else was occupying the car. I took more shots while Laura got stuck in to her food. I glanced over at Aisling. She was deep in conversation with a waiter taking her order.

Just what was Lukasz up to in that BMW? A drug deal? Giving instructions to his lackeys? Maybe. I made a quick note of the registration - GU17ADE - and put the phone back down on the table as the passenger door opened again and Lukasz got out. He was smiling as he looked back inside the car and they shared a joke. A handshake and a nod before he stepped back into the road and the BMW pulled away into the night. The whole exchange had lasted less than a minute.

He looked more than happy as he returned to the restaurant. Laura looked more than happy with her beetroot salad.

"This is amazing," she said, mid swallow. "Seriously good. You not eating?"

I came back to reality and dived into my squid. It was perfect. "Just keeping an eye on Lukasz."

"Why, what's he up to?"

"You're oblivious, aren't you?"

"To what?"

"The BMW?"

She was too wrapped up in her food to notice or care, so

I filled her in despite there being pretty much nothing to report.

"Probably scoring some coke or something," she said. "Seems like it'd be his drug of choice."

I couldn't disagree. You could tell by the way he walked that he was a user. He - or at least his family - were probably dealers of it too. Back in the day, before Wiktor got sent down, the Badowskis were high on the list of suppliers of cocaine coming into the UK. Back in the seventies, if you were doing coke, the chances are it had been brought in by them. They were seasoned pros, or at least had been once.

It wasn't the same now that there were other families involved. Seemed these days everyone was either sniffing it or selling it or both, depending on how much money and power you had, and the Badowskis, not to mention the Connollys, had a lot of both.

I'd seen how power can corrupt before, seen how it can quickly go to their heads. Seen the damage it can cause.

I watched them, laughing hard and stealing kisses over the table between courses. By now I was several pints in and thinking about that whisky sour while Laura threw caution to the wind and had moved onto Margaritas. The porterhouse had been worth waiting for, and I couldn't face another bite of anything. Laura got herself an additional crème brûlée - she was really pushing the boat out and I knew this was going to cost me - so I went for the whisky sour after all. It didn't disappoint, but now I had a taste for it and I knew I'd have to leave soon enough before I fell into the trap of sipping cocktails and getting hammered.

"Looks like they're leaving," she said.

I looked up from my drink and sure enough, Badowski was keying in his card pin while Aisling threw a tenner down as a tip. It had just gone ten o'clock, early enough for them to be carrying on somewhere else.

"I'm gonna follow them," I said. "See if I can see where they're staying."

"Probably his," she said. "Can I come?"

"Probably best that you don't."

She sighed. "Scared I'll get in the way?"

"Nothing like that, love. I just work better when I'm alone. If they go back to his or a hotel or whatever, I doubt I'll be hanging around. You think I want to spend the night hanging around these two?"

"I thought we could carry on our own little party back home."

"We can," I said. "When I get back. Maybe you can meet up with Maya for last orders or something?"

She was already on the phone. I quickly got the attention of our waiter for the bill, keeping one eye on the two lovers. Badowski was helping Aisling with her overcoat as I settled up and threw a handful of loose change down. They were heading for the door, but there was no sign of that BMW again.

Laura finished up and got her bag together. "A quick one in the Turk's Head," she said. "She's with Dave."

"That's handy," I said. "Tell him I'll need his services soon."

We left quickly and I put Laura in a black cab at the rank on Deansgate, all the time keeping my eyes peeled on Aisling and Badowski.

The night was lively and full of the hedonistic swinging their way through the city. I watched Laura's cab drive off, having assured her I'd be back at a reasonable hour and that I'd stay out of trouble. I advised her to do the same, knowing what she was capable of with a cocktail inside her.

I caught the two lovers up quickly, falling into step about twenty yards behind, hovering out of sight behind a group of students out on the piss. I watched closely as they stepped through the night, arms around each other, her head on his shoulder. I got a feeling they were up for a good night ahead.

I sparked up and got on their trail.

FOUR

I thought I'd lost them when the students blocked the pavement outside the fried chicken place. I had to step into the road to get around the crowd and almost lost my balance when a black cab skimmed close to the kerb. I glared at him, knowing it was pointless but unable to stop myself. Anything goes on nights like this in the city, and the taxis were notorious for not giving a fuck.

I was splashed by dirty water in the gutter, but there was no harm done. At least I was still walking.

I caught the two lovers up and stayed well back and out of sight when they dipped down a darkened alleyway. There were still plenty of people around for them to not be isolated, and I knew people often used this as a cut through so I didn't feel like I was taking much of a risk. Still, I ducked back and kept tight against the wall when they stopped to kiss. I thought I saw Aisling look directly at me, almost like she did a few nights back in Mulligan's, but then they quickly moved off, skipping out of the alleyway and back into King Street.

I followed, figuring that if she knew I was onto them,

there was nothing I could do about it. And I had my suspicions that she knew the score, anyway. Kian would no doubt see to that.

I hoped they were heading to a bar. I needed a drink and it would be easier to blend into a crowd than follow on the street. As I walked I questioned why Seamus would really be so bothered about his daughter seeing a Badowski, anyway. Like Laura had alluded, it was patently ridiculous that he had such an attitude, especially in this day and age. Kian had said more or less the same this afternoon. It wasn't Hollywood. It wasn't a gangster movie, yet I knew the two families hated each other with a passion and that the scars ran deep. Ultimately, it was really about who ran things and who didn't, who had more power and who had none. Who was top dog. I guessed Seamus's reasons for me doing this job were really down to fear; of what his daughter was getting involved in, of what young Lukasz Badowski was really up to.

Of what could happen if he was the one who lost control. And if I was being honest, I think that scared me too.

They left King Street and walked, perhaps a little drunk or high, across Piccadilly and into the Northern Quarter and into the ever-expanding mix of bars and cafes and nightclubs that lined the streets. The night was busy and noisy, whole armies of punters moving around, either standing outside bars smoking or moving between places, high on life and probably a little something else too.

Saturday night in the city was a lively affair. I was only a few minutes' walk from the office and was more than tempted to abandon the trail and head over there to get my head down. It was hard to get enthusiastic about being out when it was work, even if I was allowing myself a drink. But

I knew I had to get into the swing of surveillance, which I hadn't done in a while, in order to get to know my target better. The girl had me intrigued, Lukasz too, but I knew I would quickly become bored of tracking them if all they did was hold hands and coo at each other all night.

They turned into Lever Street and I tracked them from a good distance back, passing the Roadhouse and a hundred indie kids smoking weed while the live drums pounded from inside. When they took a right onto Dale Street, I picked up pace so I didn't lose them. I caught them just before they were swallowed up by the shadows of a dark and dingy den at the far end across the street from the gay cabaret bar. The queue was forming quickly, and I joined it at the tail end, keeping my head down and out of sight.

Less than five minutes later, I walked straight into Hell.

The worst thing was having to part with twenty notes just to get in. The place was heaving and everything appeared in black and white, the strobe lighting flashing so fast it looked like people were standing still on the dance floor, even though a lot of them were clearly off their faces on whatever drug they'd ingested hours before.

I spent a good five minutes trying to find my way to the bar, which stretched along the back of the club, at least three deep from one length to the other, and full of freaks waving their cash around. I'd lost Aisling and Lukasz in the melee, which I quickly concluded was inevitable in this mess. I told myself I'd give it half an hour, if I could take that much, then leave by the quickest exit. The music was the kind that was not music at all, just a succession of monotonous beats with no melody and no soul. Kind of appropriate for the environment I was standing in, because it seemed like everyone around me had lost their soul, too.

Caught my reflection in the mirror on the back wall and was shocked to see that I looked half dead. Perhaps I'd lost my soul too, just by stepping in here. There was a sign above the mirror, a ramshackle tin number plate starting in 666. Beside that, Welcome to Hell in bold type.

"I'll have a bourbon and coke," I shouted to the Emo girl behind the counter, whose eyes were so black she looked like a panda. "No ice."

She took her time getting it, so I looked down the bar for any sign of what I came in here for. Seemed I'd lost them. It was no big disaster. I'd carry my drink around the club, stumbling in the dark around the perimeter of the place until I'd finished it - which I knew wouldn't take long - before fucking off as fast as I came in here.

After my drink arrived, I tossed the girl a tenner and fought my way back into the main body of the club, a heady mix of flesh and sweat in my face at every turn. The loud drum and bass echoed so deep it made me shiver. I felt like the black sheep in a sea of farmhouse lambs, perhaps the only bloke in here who wasn't high as a kite on coke or MDMA or a combination of the two and more. I could almost smell the chemicals in the air as I shuffled my way around, keeping my eyes moving in the white and black, using the smell of the bourbon in my glass as a kind of beacon to sanity and to light the way and keep me going.

When I finally broke my way through a wall of bodies and found a seat on a blood red leather couch, unsure if the girl beside me was really a man, I threw my drink down my throat so quick, savouring the taste, that I felt like a walking advert for booze. Never have I hated a place as much as this, yet here I was with a job to do. A man had to make sacrifices when carrying out surveillance. I'd forgotten how quickly things could deteriorate when at the mercy and whim of your subject. It was as if I wasn't the one calling the shots but instead having my strings pulled by a puppet master controlling my every move. It was a feeling I didn't like, and I vowed to fight it with every passing moment.

I sparked up. Took that shit in deep. I was about to drain my glass and was more than ready to call it quits when I saw Lukasz, just for the briefest of moments, pass between a group of zombies no less than ten yards away. I stood, stepping back into the darkness, and watched Aisling follow close behind.

Then I left the glass on the seat and followed.

They headed straight for the men's room, a vast place so wide and busy that it was easy to get lost. The difference to the main room was stark, too. It was so bright in here it felt like a laboratory, all clean lines and polished mirrors, and there were plenty of lines being snorted too. I guessed the security, if they even was any, would have their work cut out if they stepped in here, but it was plain the club turned a blind eye to what was going on. The drug taking was so open I wondered if I'd somehow stepped into a parallel universe, one where it was the drinking of alcohol that was forbidden.

Through the crowd, I watched Lukasz pull Aisling into a cubicle at the back. There would be no one giving out prizes for guessing what they were up to in there, but ever the voyeur, and with a clear commitment to the job bestowed on me, I went over to stand nearby, just to make sure they really were in there and it wasn't a figment of my imagination.

I put my head close to the door when I saw a pair of knickers fall to the deck. Heard a lot of laughing and shouting - both in Polish and Gaelic - quickly followed by the unmistakable sound of the two lovers fucking. Their party would go on all night, but mine ended here. My work was done for now.

I fought my way through the crowd and left by the nearest exit, out into the cold and wet Manchester night.

FIVE

"They were a present, you know. Our Siobhan brought them back from Thailand one year. I thought she was taking the piss, to be honest with you. In fact, I'm sure she was."

I tried to tear my eyes from the sight before me, but it was too mesmerising, too... clownish. I was finding it very difficult. It was a good job he had his back turned, fiddling with the combination lock on the safe in his kitchen cupboard. I lifted my coffee and drank in an effort to be normal, to try in vain to ignore what I was looking at. It was impossible.

The Thai boxing shorts were a bright and sparkly red with a yellow band around the waist and pulled all the way up to just beneath his nipples. Seamus Connolly was simply going about his business as usual, like he wore these things every day. I watched him as he took a large wad of cash from the safe, which was stored in a kitchen cupboard, then locked it up.

He turned to me and grabbed his half eaten bacon sand-wich, ploughing into it as he dropped the cash on the counter before me. I pocketed it before he could change his mind.

"So," he said, as he ate. "What's that daughter of mine been up to? Have you even started following her around yet, Mr. Locke?"

"Call me Jim," I said. I took out a smoke and asked if I could spark up. He told me to go ahead. "I'm on her already. And yes, I can confirm that she is courting the young Badowski."

"Lukasz, right?"

"That's right," I said, careful to blow my smoke away from his breakfast. He grabbed his t-shirt from the counter beside him and threw it on. It was red and green and bore the classic emblazoned slogan - Guinness is good for you - a fine drawing of a pelican with a pint of the black stuff on the end of its beak. I couldn't disagree. "Last night, they were at The Ivy. Spinningfields. I followed them there and ate a pretty damn good steak. They didn't stay too long. When they finished their food, they left without hanging around. I went to follow them but they soon disappeared into the crowds on Deansgate, you know."

He was nodding. Swallowed the last of his breakfast and rubbed his hands to get rid of the crumbs.

"She seem - you know - happy?"

The last time I saw her - or rather, heard her - she seemed happy all right. "Oh, you know," I said. "Hard to tell, really. I was sitting a good distance away. But they seemed okay together, you know? She seemed quite comfortable with him."

He couldn't quite hide his grimace. "Aye, well. She's young and stupid, you know. Just a kid. It won't last, I'm sure."

But I didn't have those same assurances. I'm not sure Kian did, either. "Maybe not."

"So talk me through it so far," he said. "Where was she again?"

"The Ivy. A nice restaurant. Afterwards, they left. I don't know where they went because I lost them, but I got some photographs." I took out my phone and handed it over so he could scroll through. Nothing like seeing the evidence yourself. A picture painted a thousand words. The images would bring it home to him, at least. As he took it all in, I wondered why I was really bending the truth, or at least not telling the whole of it. I guessed he wasn't ready to hear the sex part just yet. I feared that if he knew what I had seen and heard in Hell, he would make the call - the call to kill - just as soon as I'd left the house.

I didn't want blood on my hands. He may be standing here in Thai boxing shorts and shovelling a bacon sandwich in his mouth, but I wasn't fooled. Seamus Connolly wielded power, a dangerous power. Not even the law would touch him or his family. It was a game I wanted no part of, so keeping my mouth shut in certain circumstances gave me some power and control, too. I needed that control if I was to continue working this case.

He handed the phone back, looking like he was about to throw up. "Stupid little girl," he said, and poured coffee from a pot that had been sitting in a machine. He asked if I wanted sugar. Something a little stronger would've been better, so I just settled for the coffee, black.

"Is there anything else I can do for you, Jim? Do you need any assistance? Anything at all."

"Thanks, but no," I said. "Probably best to remain as inconspicuous as possible, you know. Too many cooks and all that."

He was nodding, eyeing me up and down. "Well, if you need anything, just let me know."

I assured him I would, but I was thinking the exact opposite. Was best to keep my distance and work this alone. Things could get nasty quite easily with Seamus's lot sticking their noses in. I drank the coffee, still just warm. It was time to go now that I'd gotten what I'd came for.

"It's all there," he said, as if reading my mind. "One thousand in twenties. Hope that's okay."

"It's more than fine."

"Good," he said. "Right then. If you'll excuse me, Jim, I need to get back to work."

Work? He'd barely done a day's work in his life. "No problem," I said, leaving the stool at the breakfast bar. "I'll keep you updated. So far, it's just two kids going on a date. If anything untoward crops up, you'll be the first to know."

"Good man," he said, and clasped me on the shoulder as he ushered me towards the hallway. His dog, a big bastard of a brute - one of those meaty looking pit bulls - was busy gnawing a massive bone by the front door. Gotta admit, it made me shiver.

"Busy day, then?" I said, as much as filling the silence more than anything.

"A few things to organise," he said. "A bit of a boxing match. Kind of an underground thing, nothing major. You know how it is trying to get everyone to pull their weight."

I didn't. "Bit of a promoter on the side, eh?"

"Ah, nothing like that," he said. "But you should maybe come along and take your mind off things for the night. You could meet a few of the boys, you know."

I was nodding my approval, but could think of nothing worse. "Yeah, that'd be great."

"I'll let you know. In the meantime, keep a close eye on that daughter of mine, will you?"

"Of course."

I said my goodbyes, and he watched as I started up the Volvo and drove off the enormous gravelled driveway. Out over the hills of Macclesfield, a storm cloud was gathering. My head was beginning to feel the same way.

Just as I was coming back into Manchester, the phone rang. I had her on speaker as I drove.

"Was hoping I'd catch you," she said. "You'll definitely want to hear this."

"Sounds juicy."

"He's not turned up for work."

"Who?"

"Robertson," she said. "He's been missing since Wednesday."

"Really?"

"Really. No one can get hold of him and the Chief is getting concerned. DCI Crane wants to launch an investigation."

"Fucking hell, that bad? Well, where is he? He gone on holiday or something and not told anyone? Would be just like the silly twat to do that."

"No, no. Nothing like that. There's no record of him going on leave or anything. His phone's just ringing out. We've traced the phone's whereabouts this morning and it's turned up back at his house. His wife's been in this morning as well. You remember her?"

"Which one?" As it turned out, Robertson had been leading a double life. His official wife, Amanda Michelle

Robertson, was married to the Robertson all coppers knew. His secret one, Marie Dawson - married to 'John Dawson' - was still a mystery to everyone except Fiona and me.

"Ha ha, good question. Amanda, of course. She's distraught. But I reckon it won't be long until Marie turns up as well, and then the proverbial shit might definitely hit the fan."

"So where do you think he is? Do you think he's finally realised the power we've got over him and called it a day somehow? You know, fucked off somewhere and done himself in?"

"Wouldn't put it past him, but no. Not how he operates. At least, the doing himself in part. He might have decided to disappear, though."

"Could be on a sun lounger in Acapulco as we speak."

"Or a cabin in the Swiss Alps, that's much more him."

She could be right. I considered if he had any other reasons to just vanish and could think of nothing other than him wanting to escape the tangled web of his double life. It must have been putting considerable pressure on him, unless the two wives were complicit in the arrangement somehow. That and the fact that we had him by the balls.

"Is he working on a case at the moment?"

"Several," she said. "Main one being the murder of a young woman who'd been stabbed by a jealous lover."

"He was busy then."

"Exactly," she said. "No reason to just disappear like that, unless the psycho's had some kind of breakdown."

"Do you think he might have?"

"Maybe."

"And when was the last time you saw him, Fiona?"

"Last Monday at the morning briefing. He seemed fine."

"Anybody else said anything? You know, about where he might be?"

"Well, everyone's coming from the same place, really. No one's got a clue, it's totally out of character, not like him, all that."

"Is he officially declared missing?"

"Not yet, but if he doesn't show up tomorrow morning, yes. You can count on that."

I slowed down at the bottom end of the Princess Parkway and joined the queue. The clock on the dash said 11:33, so the pub had just opened. I couldn't remember a time when my life wasn't governed by the opening times of the beer house.

"Keep me updated. In the meantime, have you managed to get me anything on the Badowskis or the Connollys?"

"Well, there was another reason I was ringing."

"I'm all ears."

"Not much so far, I'm afraid. These people like to keep their business private. But I found out that one of the Badowski lot - guy by the name of Leon Drabek - is a suspect in a murder enquiry. One of DCI McKenzie's, actually. Apparently, he shot a Jewish guy by the name of Gershom Katz. He was shot in the head on a Saturday morning about six months ago as he was on his way to the Synagogue. No witnesses, which is surprising given it was the Shabbat. Synagogues are full, the whole place is carpeted with orthodox Jews."

"Where was this?"

"Prestwich. On the border with Salford."

"Was Katz an orthodox Jew?"

"Yes," she said. "But it's suspected he was also a member of a secret group known as the Silver Tigers."

"What, a gang?"

"That's right. Not a commonly held bit of knowledge when it comes to gangsters, but there you are. You wouldn't think it with the Jewish population, but they exist. Keep themselves well underground. Not much is known about them, but it's believed they're a relatively small group. No more than fifty or so members."

"So the Badowskis had beef with the Silver Tigers?"

"Maybe. Probably. No one seems sure why."

"Territory, maybe. Could be anything."

"Yep. Anyway, Drabek is definitely involved with the Badowskis. We believe he's married to a Badowski, one of Wiktor's cousin's daughters, something like that."

"Interesting..."

"To say the least," she said. "Anyway, that enquiry is ongoing. As it stands, Drabek remains a free man. He's not been arrested, not been charged, nothing. Just a suspect. I believe there are others."

"Anything on the Connollys?"

"Nothing more than what you know, really. Connor Connolly is the big cheese at the minute. Everyone's talking about him, but there's nothing new. I'll keep you posted. But listen, I've got to go."

"Okay, any news on Robertson, let me know."

"Will do."

And she hung up. I drove to the office as the early afternoon rain fell. I wasn't expecting Laura to be there given it was a Sunday, her usual day off. Being a traditional type, she'd be at the flat knocking up a roast dinner, if she wasn't still in bed. The late drinks she'd had with Maya last night after I'd followed Aisling and Lukasz had no doubt taken their toll. One too many gin and tonics on top of the cocktails she'd already had must've left her feeling like she'd beaten her head against the bedroom wall. She wasn't good with hangovers.

I parked up around the back of the office and made my way up the stairs, which was now newly decorated. Aside from making it look cleaner, it did nothing to deflect from the fact that we knew there had been a bloody big swastika daubed on the landing wall not too long ago. Since then, I'd stepped up the security. The window to the fire escape stairs now had a bolt and key lock to keep it shut. The entrance door now had a key pad fixed in, which was connected to the office. Anyone calling would have to be buzzed in unless they knew the code. I'd had CCTV fitted to the front and back of the building and a high end alarm system that was so sensitive it cried at the merest touch. I'd been reluctant about the alarm, reckoning what we had was enough, but Laura had insisted and I couldn't not get it done in the end. She was, after all, present in the office when our intruders strolled in right under her nose. I wanted her to feel safe. She said it had all made a big difference, which pleased me. We both felt a lot more relaxed about the situation.

I crashed on the battered old leather chesterfield and sparked up. Took that shit in deep. The day had well and truly woken up, and out the window, the city hummed with people and traffic.

I took out my phone and opened the photographs, scrolling, as I had done many times, to the pictures I'd taken of the inside of Bob Turner's living room on the day George Thornley and I had found him dead. Stared at the blood on the walls, the face of my dead friend, the scattered photographs on the carpet and the rifle he'd used.

Why, Bob? Why? In his suicide note, he'd told me he couldn't live with it anymore. What he'd done. The fact that he'd killed a man in cold blood. Bob had more integrity in his little finger than most. I could understand him not wanting to live with what he'd done, but I couldn't help but question if he really did do himself in. Had he really been the one to pull that trigger? Did he really have the balls to do that? I could accept him taking his own life, even believed that he could, but not that way.

The suicide note had been typed. It wasn't his handwriting, yet I could hear his voice as I read it over and over. I was ninety percent sure he had been the author, and yet... and yet.

The nagging doubt lingered.

I'd thought about showing the photographs to George Thornley, but I didn't for long. It was too gruesome, too macabre. I wasn't even sure why I'd taken them. I just felt it was something I had to do at the time. Many times, I'd hovered my thumb over the delete button. They weren't stored anywhere else other than the phone, so it would've been easy to just get rid, but I couldn't bring myself to do it. I felt haunted by those images, looked at them every single day, and of course they brought everything back immediately. I couldn't begin to explain why I was keeping them or why I felt I needed to look at them. I just did, that was all.

I switched my phone off and tossed it aside, falling back onto the couch. Closed my eyes. Thought about Aisling Connolly and her new man, Lukasz Badowski. A different generation to their fathers. Perhaps Seamus was right. Maybe she was just a stupid little girl. The relationship wasn't serious. It would be over soon.

Just a fling.

I drifted, let the outside hum wash over me.

Dreamt of blood and light.

SIX

I found Grain tucked away in a little corner of the Northern Quarter, down Brewer street and in the shadow of Piccadilly train station. It was a relatively small bar compared to the others in the area, but it was busy enough. Not surprising on a Sunday afternoon. I could still smell the rain in the air as I stepped in, though it had since stopped. As well as the continental beers and ales, the unheard of gins and the expensive cocktails, they also served coffee and bar snacks and had a short food menu. I stepped up to the bar, debating for the briefest moment about whether to get a coffee or not, and settled instead on a beer and a club sandwich.

I wasn't expecting Lynsey Byrne to be around. Managers rarely worked weekends, though I was ready to be surprised. I knew the girl who'd served me wasn't Lynsey - she was friendly and pretty - whereas I'd suspected Lynsey, judging by her Facebook profile, was a hard case and a misery. I hadn't found anything about her that told me otherwise as yet, but I could be proven wrong.

I sat in the corner on a chair that reminded me of

school. Brought all the memories flooding back. I hadn't spent much time there, thanks to my dad, who had put both the fear of God in me and 'toughened me up', ultimately only causing me to end up like him. Every time I stared into a bottle or thought of mum, out there in the middle of nowhere all lonely and fucked up, I always thought of him too, lying there in his grave, rotting down to his bare bones in the cold, hard ground. Turned out to be a fitting place for the old bastard.

I was brought back to reality when my sandwich arrived, which looked bloody good, but not quite enough to fill a hole. Not that I'd be finishing it, given my current state. The weight continued to drop off. I'd lost almost two stone since the stabbing. Had managed to put a few pounds back on, but that was mostly in Guinness and whisky. Laura continued to nag me about it, and I couldn't honestly blame her, so I'd been trying to make the effort, for her sake. Last night's steak had been the one thing to give me an appetite lately, which was a good thing. I knew if I carried on the way I was going, I'd be living on borrowed time.

I sat and ate, slowly and patiently, and figured out a plan for the day. I'd have liked nothing more than to stay here for one or two before slowly making my way back home via the pubs down the back streets. A warm bed and a good woman would top the day off nicely, but I knew that all that stuff only happened in a fictional world. I had work to do and time to kill. I was going to damn well kill it.

I figured the best way to proceed would be a visit to the gym in Castlefield to sound out Kerry Ainsworth. Then maybe have a casual walk around the MRI to see if I could spot Claire MacGowan. Better to see these people in the flesh, so I knew what I was getting involved in. You never could get a feel for much through photography alone. I'd thought about sounding Kian out again too, maybe pay a visit to his big brother, Connor. Or at least scope out what he was up to.

And then there was Robertson. I couldn't help but wonder what game he was playing. The news of his disappearance had become a distraction, and not a very welcome one. Had to admit, it was on my mind.

"You finished with this?"

I looked up at the girl who'd served me. "I think I've had enough. Listen, is the manager in?"

"No, she's off today. Why, was there something wrong?"

"No, nothing like that. I was just wanting to bend her ear, that's all. Any idea when she'll be in?"

"You'll catch her Monday to Friday, eleven until four. And Saturday mornings. I can leave her a message if you like?"

"There's no need. I'll call in again."

"Was it important?"

"Not particularly."

That seemed to satisfy her and she went on her way. I was getting closer to the bottom of the glass. Told myself one for the road was out of the question. I finished up and left quickly, before I could change my mind.

I walked the long way round down to Castlefield, skirting the canal and letting the fog of the weekend's events clear from my head as I mulled a few things over.

I took my time, figuring there was no real need to rush, and the canal side walk had begun to cleanse my mind as I got nearer to the gym in question, an exclusive club down the end of Liverpool Road and in the shadow of the Museum of Science and Industry.

The entrance to Guy's was a glass fronted, key code affair, but I was eventually buzzed in by a sprightly looking young girl that looked like she'd sprung from the pages of a sportswear catalogue. She came out, all white teeth, flowing brunette hair and toned legs.

"Can I help?"

"I hope so," I said. "I was thinking of finally sorting my shit out once and for all and joining the gym. I mean, look at me."

"Okay." She was nodding as she looked me up and down. "That's not a problem. When was the last time you were in a gym?"

I guessed it was pretty obvious I'd never stepped foot in a gym in my life. I tried to think back to the last time I actually did any exercise. It was probably back when I first became a PC, when I still had that rookie enthusiasm for the job. I never could stand it, and the thought of throwing a fucking medicine ball one more time filled me with dread.

"A few years ago," I said, thinking it was probably closer to a decade, at least. "A friend of mine recommended I join up, so I thought I'd check it out, you know. Kerry Ainsworth? You might know her. Hope you don't mind me just turning up like this?"

"Oh, not at all. Kerry's usually always here, but she's not working today. She started out as one of our gold members and couldn't keep away, so Guy gave her a job in the end."

I smiled. "Never out of the place, is she? Not working, you said?"

"No, she never comes in on a Sunday. It's a quiet day, so you've come at the right time. I can show you around if you like?"

"That would be great, yeah."

She smiled and turned on her heels, leading the way inside. I followed, watching her well worked out arse in those black leggings, an arse that was so tight and perfectly formed it could crack a few nuts, no problem. Probably had.

"Kerry's one of our oldest members, actually," she said. "When the gym changed ownership and had a refit, she was the first at the door. In here every day. Six months later, she was working behind the desk."

"I suppose she's found her calling then, eh?"

"Something like that, yeah."

I spent ten minutes wandering about the place, pretending to be interested in the latest cardio machines and bikes. I nodded in all the right places, but just watching the handful of people in here was giving me the sweats, not to mention my guide's flattering curves. Lydia was a stunning beauty and a fine host, but everything she said passed straight over my head and kept going. As we finished the tour by the sauna and steam room, she tried to entice me in straight away with an application that could be processed immediately and I could be on the treadmill in no time at all. Told her I'd take the form with me and went on my way. Two down, two to go.

Today wasn't turning out to be very productive, yet it was to be expected. Sundays were for chilling out and eating. Was no surprise these first two girls weren't working. I was going nowhere, fast. And after leaving Hell last night without following the two lovers - I didn't honestly fancy staying out all night - I had no clue, so far, of where young Aisling and Lukasz might now be. I needed an address, a focus. Which gave me an idea. But first I wanted to scope out Claire MacGowan's workplace. Figured she was the one most likely to be on duty. Nurses, I knew, very often worked Sundays. There was no certainty, but I felt I needed to be doing something. The grand Seamus had paid me was burning a hole in my pocket. As I crossed Deansgate to find the nearest taxi rank, I instinctively touched my scar. Sparked up as I walked, the nicotine helping me focus, as always.

The Manchester Royal Infirmary was just ten minutes away.

I got myself a strong coffee from a nearby cafe, knowing that the machine versions inside the hospital were neither here nor there. Got the barista, a young and pretty student type with a nose piercing, to add a good shot of espresso too. Strolled around outside the A and E entrance and smoked, casually watching events unfold as I thought about things other than work. Sometimes I forgot I had a life of my own away from all of this, not least my life as a father. I knew I needed to improve my skills in that department and make more of an effort with my own daughter. Karen had been banging on at me for ages about it, especially now that I'd returned from my sabbatical on the streets. Now that we'd patched things up and were back on speaking terms, I knew I needed to do my bit and remind my daughter what it was her daddy did for a living.

Then there was mum. It had been a long, long time since I'd visited her, and for good reason. The woman had begun to lose it years ago, and I really did dread to think how she was coping now. Thankfully, Bill, her neighbour, had been doing a far better job than me at keeping an eye on her, so I at least had some inkling as to how things were. All I had to do was phone him, but it had been a while, a year at least. I hadn't gotten on with mum in recent years and, if I'm honest, it had only been a matter of time before things ended up that way, what with dad's addictions. The last time I'd spoken to her, she'd said I was becoming my father, and I supposed she was right. I couldn't admit it or see it at the time, but now I could see what she meant. Those words had hurt me and I'd told her so. Even though she was pushing eighty, I didn't mince my words, because she was hardly blameless in that regard. I had two parents to raise me, yet sometimes I wondered if I even had one. The pair of them had been a waste of space for the best part of my life. She said I was an even bigger cunt than my dad as I slammed the door on my way out.

Takes one to know one.

I tossed my smoke and headed inside, walking aimlessly for five minutes until I finally saw a sign for the department I wanted. Cardiology was in the purple zone, upstairs. I found a lift down a hidden corridor and punched the button for level two, thinking I was probably wasting my time. Claire MacGowan was just one among several hundred nurses working here, despite the quiet Sunday, and it was highly unlikely I'd find her. Not that it really mattered. As long as I was finding out for definite where it was she spent most of her days, I'd be happy. Just a few carefully considered questions here and there and my work would be done. For all I knew, she could be at home, relaxing in the bath. Or perhaps getting ready to meet her boyfriend for a roast lunch at some rural pub. It didn't matter. I kept telling myself I needed to be doing something, at least, even if it meant wandering around hospital corridors. It wasn't entirely a pointless exercise. It was relatively peaceful here, which gave me time to clear the noise from my head, for a while at least.

As I walked, I took out my phone and dialled Fiona. She answered almost immediately.

"You stalking me or something?"

"Just need something from you if you can help?"

"Go on."

"Anything in the PNC about where Lukasz Badowski lives?"

"It just so happens I'm at my desk now," she whispered, "but the office is pretty busy at the minute. Give me half an hour?"

"No problem."

"Can I ask why? You intending to send him a Christmas card this year?"

"Just need to scope out where he's living. Where they both live, even. I've got a feeling Aisling's currently shacked up with him."

"Most likely."

"Soon as you can. So, any news on Robertson?"

"Nothing. But a lot of people are getting worried."

"Should they be, do you think?"

"There's no sign of him so, yes, I think it's pretty normal."

"He'll turn up."

"I'm not so sure, Jim. Anyway, I'm gonna grab a brew and a smoke, then I'll try and find what I can. What are you up to?"

"Just following my nose."

"So not much."

"I suppose not."

"Well, maybe you can head to the cash machine. You owe me some money."

I'd been paying Fiona for information since my last major job on Trevor Hardy and the E.N.D. Those far right nutters had almost got me killed, of course, and I owed Fiona a lot more than money for information. What she had on Robertson was gold, and we'd agreed that I'd keep her sweet for what she could get me off the Police National Computer, plus any files GMP still held on me, which I was still waiting for. I was looking after copies of her files, but I owed her my life, not just a few hundred quid here and there. It was an arrangement we were both comfortable with, and I could afford it. It was worth it to keep Robertson looking over his shoulder.

"I know," I said. "I can drop by tonight, maybe."

"You could pay me in other ways, if you like. You know, if you're a bit short."

I stopped walking, the silence on the line heavy, the corridor I was on suddenly dark. Did I hear her right? And if so, what on earth could she mean?

"Fiona, I... look, it's not..."

"Jesus, Jim, you're so easy to wind up."

"For fuck's sake, Fiona..."

"I wouldn't say no, though. Just saying."

"What?!"

"Jesus, chill. I'm not gonna seduce you or anything, even though I'd quite like to. I mean, you have got a certain something, Jim Locke."

"Stop it now."

I could hear her giggling on the line, like this was the ultimate wind up she'd never get bored of, but I was beginning to think she meant every word she said, which gave me something else to think about.

"All right, honey."

"Just get me what I need, eh?"

"An address?"

"Whatever you've got."

"Aye aye, captain."

I couldn't hang up quick enough, aware that there was a

feeling in my pants I hadn't felt in a while. Could she be serious? Could she, really?

"Can I help you?"

I looked up to find a woman in a royal blue nurse's uniform clutching a clipboard of pink notes.

"I'm looking for the cardiology department," I said. "And a nurse MacGowan?"

"Follow the corridor all the way to the end, then right, then left, through the double doors at the bottom, then right again. You'll find it on your left. Can't help you with a nurse MacGowan, I'm afraid. Not my department, but can I ask why?"

I tapped my jacket and my inside pocket. "A thank-you card. I wanted to make sure I delivered it personally. Dad made me promise before he died."

She nodded and moved off while I turned and followed the directions I'd already forgotten.

I followed my nose for another five minutes until I came across the double doors of Cardiology and ventured right down a quiet corridor. When I reached the end, I went left until I came to a reception desk and a woman reading a magazine. She looked up as I approached. Got the impression she was bored or frustrated, or both. She was putting out vibes that she didn't want to be here on a Sunday afternoon. Who could blame her? Before I could wing my way through the usual spiel, I glanced down at her badge. Claire MacGowan was a good-looking young woman, the kind who'd think nothing of making you a decent breakfast to go with the other parting gifts she provided. She was curvy and attractive, a homely kind of girl with a cheeky hidden side she only revealed to people she trusted. I knew I had to come clean immediately if I was to win her trust and co-operation. I nodded and took out a business card, handed it over and placed it into her slim, delicate fingers.

"Jim Locke. I'm a private investigator. I hope you don't mind, but I tracked you down because I think you're a friend of Aisling Connolly and I believe she might be in danger."

I suppose I could bend the truth just a bit, and even though I didn't believe it yet, I guessed she could well be in danger eventually, if her father had anything to do with it.

"Aisling? What, really? Well, why? And what do you mean, you're a private investigator? Where from?"

I held my hands up and nodded sagely. I suppose I could've expected questions. It's not everyday you turn up at someone's workplace and tell them their friend is in trouble.

"I've been asked to keep an eye on things since she got involved with Lukasz Badowski."

"What?"

She heard me right, she just didn't quite understand. I decided to make it clear. "Lukasz Badowski, son of Wiktor Badowski. You heard of them?"

"Yeah, but..."

"Then you might've heard that the Badowskis wield a bit of power in this city."

"Years ago, maybe, but not now."

"Then you mustn't quite know them as well as you think. They still have a lot of say around here."

"Yeah, right."

"It's true."

"So why is she in danger, then? What's she done that's upset them?"

"It's more her father she's upset," I said. "The very fact that she's seeing Lukasz hasn't exactly made him ready to walk her down the aisle, if you know what I mean."

"She can handle her dad."

"I'm not so sure."

"He's never given a shit about her. Why would he start now?"

It was a valid point. "Because she's getting involved with a Badowski. The enemy. There's bad blood, going back a long way. Things could get ugly."

"She can handle herself as well."

"So I keep hearing."

"And you're 'looking out' for her because...?"

"Her dad's my client."

"So you're tracking her as well?"

"For her own safety."

She laughed then. Out loud. "Just wait until she hears this."

"Look. Claire. I know this sounds ridiculous and yeah, maybe it is, I'd go as far as agreeing with you on that."

"It's not some shite film."

"But these people... these families... they live in a different world to the rest of us. It's all about power and control. They'd stop at nothing."

"And how long have you been following her around?"

"A few days."

She was shaking her head. She reached for a bottle of water and drank. "So, what do you want with me? Not that I'll take anything of what you say very seriously, if at all."

I couldn't honestly blame her. And what did I want? I didn't really know. She was another pair of eyes and ears I could maybe persuade to help me if shit went down.

"A coffee? When do you clock off?"

She laughed again. "I finish in about an hour."

"Works for me. We need to talk. You'll be doing your friend a favour, believe me."

"Yeah, well, I'm not sure if she's my friend for much longer. There's a place inside the Museum. You know it?"

I nodded. "Okay."

She checked her watch. "I should tell you to fuck right off. But I'll see you there at half four. Could do with a laugh."

J ust as I was getting lost in the ancient Egypt display of the museum, the face of Tutunkahmun staring back at me, my phone rang. I nudged my way out through the crowds of families and made my way to the corridor outside. The noise and bustle meant I had to find a quiet corner just to hear her, and I had to ask her to speak up twice. There were handfuls of kids running circles around me, and I found the whole place dizzying.

"I said I've got an address for you. You got a pen?"

"Just send me a text."

"Fair enough. But Lukasz Badowski, need we be surprised, lives in Hale."

"Plenty of money, then."

"We knew that anyway. The house is worth in the region of two million, give or take a few hundred grand."

"Jesus."

"No wonder she's shagging him."

"She's not short of cash herself."

"Nothing like what he's got, I expect."

"Who's to say."

"Anyway, there you have it. I'll send it to you now. You planning on scoping the place out?"

"Yeah, but I'm not sure why. Just a feeling. Any sign of Robertson?"

"Nothing. Not a peep. DCI Crane's getting seriously worried."

"He'll turn up. He can't have gone far."

"I'm not so sure, Jim."

"Well, if he does turn up, let me know."

"I will. And listen, we need a proper catch up. In the flesh."

"Steady."

"I'm free tomorrow if that suits?"

"I'll get back to you on that."

"Okay. Text incoming. Ciao for now."

I hung up and made my way downstairs to the cafe. If she planned on keeping to her word, Claire MacGowan should be there any time now.

I found her on the table by the door with a flat white and a blueberry muffin. She looked up from her phone and gestured for me to sit opposite.

"I got you a straight Americano. Didn't know how you like it."

"Black," I said. I took a sip, my head slightly fuzzed. "Listen, I'm glad you're willing to hear me out. I know it sounds ridiculous but, here we are."

She shrugged. "They do say the truth is stranger than fiction."

She wasn't wrong. "Yeah, well. Look, I know me turning up like that, out of the blue, seems a bit odd but..."

"Nah, that kind of thing happens all the time."

"Of course it does."

"You don't work at my place."

"I couldn't possibly do what you do."

"And what do I do, Mr. Locke?"

"You know. Nursing."

"Not as bad as it sounds. I actually quite enjoy it,

although it's getting harder these days, no resources, cuts, all that."

"It's a very different lifestyle to Aisling Connolly's, I expect."

"You could say that."

We were silent a moment. Exchanged a look as she waited for me to get down to it.

"So," she said. "What's all this about?"

"Well, pretty much what I said earlier. Seamus Connolly has asked me to keep an eye on Aisling because he's worried about her."

"Because she's going out with Lukasz Badowski?"

"That's right."

"Seems a bit sad, don't you think?"

I suppose it did. "The two families have bad blood. I suppose as a father, he has a right to be concerned."

"He's never been concerned about her before."

"What makes you say that?"

"I've known Aisling a long time. Since we were at school, you know. I don't ever remember her saying anything good about her dad."

"But he's her dad. She must love him, right?"

"She doesn't like him, Mr. Locke."

"It's Jim."

"Jim, then. She doesn't like him, but she might love him. I don't know, he's her dad, isn't he? But she's always talked about him like he's a total arsehole. Which he is."

"You know him then?"

"Not really, no."

"So how do you know he's a total arsehole?"

"I don't need to know him to know that," she said. "Everyone knows what the Connollys get up to."

Maybe everyone did, at least those who were bothered to be interested.

I watched her sip her coffee and pick at her blueberry muffin. She was young and pretty, no older than twenty-five and yet she was wise to the world. I could see that much. I wondered about what she said earlier, about her not being friends with Aisling for much longer. I asked her why. She looked at me before looking away, then down at the table.

"Just, you know. We've never been best friends or anything. And now we're getting older, we're into different things. That's all."

"Growing apart?"

"Something like that."

"But you still care about her?"

"Yeah, I care about her, she's still a mate, but...you know, we're into different stuff now."

"Like?"

"Oh fucking hell, does it matter?"

I held my hands up. "Just trying to get to know you, Claire, that's all."

She tutted and shook her head. "Just little things, you know."

"Little things can turn into big things."

"Music and stuff, places we like to go to, books we read, the shit we watch on the telly..."

"Mates you hang around with?"

"Yeah, stuff like that."

I nodded. Needed a smoke but reckoned it could wait. "So you don't see her that often these days?"

"Not really."

"But you knew she'd been seeing Lukasz Badowski?"

"Yeah, I knew."

"Ever met him?"

"No. Aisling wouldn't introduce her boyfriend like that. She never has done in the past. If I ever meet him, it'll be by chance."

"Really?"

She nodded. "Really. That's just Aisling."

"Not one to show her new man off, then?"

"She'd be too busy wrapped up in the romance to bother with anyone else."

"I see. Any of your other friends met him?"

"Not that I know of. Anyway, not that I care. She's happy. I'm too busy to give a shit."

But it didn't sound like she didn't give a shit. "You fallen out or something?"

"No, for fuck's sake! Why do you want to know all this, anyway? I mean, why care? And why are you following her around?"

"I'm just doing what her dad's asked me to do, that's all."

"He is one sad old bastard."

"He's a bit overprotective, yeah."

"I mean, what does he actually think she's gonna do?"

I shrugged. "I suppose he's just looking out for his daughter, nothing more than that."

"Yeah, well, I don't buy it. And what do you want from me, Jim? You can't have brought me here for no reason."

"I don't want anything," I said. "Just to ask about Aisling, that's all."

"But you seem more interested in me than her."

Not true. "I suppose I need a picture painting. Of Aisling. What she's like, that kind of thing."

"She's just like any other twenty-three-year-old. Likes a drink, likes a party, goes clubbing, likes men, likes to spend her money on shoes and handbags and clothes and shit.

Likes a holiday in the sun and thinks she knows everything about life."

"Is that you as well, Claire?"

She shrugged. "I suppose. I don't see what any of this has got to do with it, to be honest. And if her dad's sad enough to get a private detective to follow his own daughter around, I hope she keeps fucking him until the cows come home."

I couldn't resist a smile. Claire smiled too, then looked away when the mother struggling with the two toddlers a few tables away started glaring at her.

"Look," she said. "That's Aisling, in a nutshell. She's just a young woman, like any other young woman. Likes doing what young women do. I really can't elaborate much more than that, so, if you don't mind, I'm gonna go now."

I nodded. Took a drink of the coffee. "Fair enough. Just get in touch if you need to."

"And why would I need to?"

"I don't know. But if you do, you've got my card."

She stood, downed her coffee, collected her bag, and mumbled something about wasting her time.

"You do realise I'm going to tell her, Jim? About how her dad's got you following her around? I don't think she'll take too kindly to that."

"She probably knows already." I didn't doubt it. "If it's a problem, she can speak to her dad."

"Unlikely," she said, and swung her bag over her shoulder. "It's been a pleasure."

She didn't say goodbye, so I followed her out the door into a quiet Oxford Road and watched her stomp off towards the bus stop. She turned around once, saw me watching her, then gave me the finger.

I reckon she liked me.

SEVEN

Driving through Altrincham at one a.m. was the very last thing I wanted to be doing, especially alone, yet here I was, committed to the job but feeling like I should be committed to an asylum. The car felt cold, despite having had the heaters on for the duration of the journey, but I suppose that shivering I felt could've been caused by my mild anxiety as I cruised down Altrincham Road towards Hale and the address Fiona had sent me. I sparked up as I drove and took that shit in deep. It had been a while since I'd had to carry out surveillance, and I knew all too well it could be a lonesome and tedious affair. The local talk radio show was full of gormless fuckwits jabbering nonsense into the night, and I'd long since grown bored of my blues collection. But the voices and the chatter, however tiresome, provided at least some company, and I was grateful for that. It was going to be a long night.

I turned into the road in question and drove towards the end. It was a road I wasn't at all familiar with, but I'd done my research and knew the house was down the bottom end. I slowly cruised past the gated mansions on either side, evergreens lining the gardens and the pavements illuminated by the lights from both the front garden decor and the security spotlights on many of the walls. Glancing into the front driveways of the houses that weren't blocked off by solid wooden gating, I wasn't surprised to see many expensive super cars sitting proudly under the blue neon luminescence that seemed to hang around the place like spectral fog. Porches, Ferraris, Maseratis and Mercedes. They were all there. Bentleys too. Even a Rolls. I pulled up across the street from number 23 and killed the engine. The night had turned to silence.

I'd come prepared. There were some essential supplies required for a job like this and already I was thankful for my foresight. I opened the glove box and took out the bottle of brandy, half empty. Necked a sweet little shot, just to calm the nerves. Felt the burn. Stashed wherever I could fit it were chocolate bars, smokes and a large bottle of water. I had a handy little pocket torch and a spare mobile phone that was fully charged. I had access to the internet for when I got bored and a blanket if I needed to sleep, which was likely. Although if I could manage to do what I had planned in good time, I didn't fancy hanging around any later than when the birds were starting to tweet.

I grabbed my night vision binoculars from the seat beside me - part of an expensive spying kit Dave had sorted out for me and insisted I started using, despite me feeling like a complete twat - and aimed them at the top bedroom window. Thankfully, all the lights were out, but I couldn't be sure if there was anyone home. The three cars on the drive - an Audi Q7, a Ferrari and a fuck off pick up truck - indicated that someone could be, probably both of them. But there was no movement that I could detect, so if someone was home, I could be pretty sure they weren't awake.

The wall, I could now see, would be easy to climb, and the thick rhododendrons on the other side would keep me well covered if the security lights came on, which I expected they would. I finished my smoke and tossed it. Kept telling myself it would all be easy enough, if I did it quick and God knows I wanted it over and done with.

It was time to rock-and-roll.

In the rucksack I'd dumped in the front passenger footwell, the GPS device Dave had sorted for me in record time was sitting beside a flask of black coffee and a tuna sandwich. I didn't anticipate anyone clocking me sitting here in the Volvo eating my lunch at three a.m., but you could never tell when scoping a place out. Which is why I wanted this done before anyone could bat an eyelid. I'd already removed it from its packaging and Dave had assured me that it was set up correctly. All I had to do was plant it on Lukasz Badowski's car. Trouble was, which one was it?

I pocketed the device in my jeans - a shiny metallic thing with a microchip in it, the whole thing encased in rubber and no bigger than a matchbox. There was a strong magnetic strip on one side that would stick to the metal on my target vehicle. Once it was where I needed it - Dave reckoned under a wheel arch was perfect in order to get a strong signal - my work was done. All that was left was to let Dave know so he could trigger the program that would track it, and get back to the car to drink brandy and coffee and watch the house until dawn.

At least, that was the plan.

I mentally prepared myself for the task ahead and figured the quicker I did it, the easier it would be. I knew I had to focus and take each step quickly and efficiently, like a lion hunting its prey.

I slung on the black body warmer I had sitting on the back seat and put the black wooly hat on too. Making sure the GPS device was safely in my pocket, I took the torch - not that I would be needing it much - from the rucksack and placed it in the top pocket of my denim shirt. All I had to do was step out of the car, cross the street, pull myself up over the garden wall and take it from there.

It was easier said than done.

I took the key from the ignition and pulled the handle on the driver's door. The door unlocked and I stepped out, careful to not make a sound as I shut it behind me. Took a deep breath out there under the light of the moon and the security lamps that were scattered around on the nearby houses. One blinked on as I stepped across the street in my black trainers, then went off again as I moved. Before I knew it, I was at the garden wall of number 23. It was a good few feet taller than I was. I looked around, reckoned I could scale it in one go if I took a quick running jump, and did just that before I could change my mind. I pulled myself up and as I swung my legs over the other side I thought, that's it now, there's no going back. I'd committed myself to it and I suddenly felt that what I was doing was completely fucking ridiculous and who the hell did I think I was kidding?

I dropped down when, from the corner of my eye, I saw the car headlights emerge from around a bend to my right, and just as I hit the deck, the sharp branches of the rhododendrons digging into my side, the car breathed past on the other side of the wall.

I winced and gritted my teeth, before finally exhaling and flicked on the torch. It was dark under the cover of the bushes, and when I waved the beam around - it was bright for such a small thing - I could see that I'd picked my spot almost perfectly. The Audi was no more than twenty feet or so away and it was the nearest vehicle to reach, so I guessed that was the one. Beyond, a light flicked on in one of the upstairs rooms. Fuck.

Fuck.

I turned the torch off and waited, suddenly feeling the chill of the night. I could see that the glass was frosted. There was a half-naked figure on the other side of it, casually moving around. I guessed it was probably a bathroom and someone had gotten up for a piss. I couldn't tell if it was a man or a woman, but just as I'd convinced myself it was Aisling up there, the figure moved out of sight and the light blinked out.

I waited another ten minutes just to be sure no one was lurking at a window and watching. No more lights flickered on. When I was finally convinced I could press on, I stepped out ever closer to the open space of the driveway and the Audi just feet away.

Fuck it. I stepped from the bushes, did a quick skip across the asphalt and dropped down on all fours just as a security lamp blinked on. With any luck, I'd be out of sight of the top window. I turned to face the road, just to make sure it was empty, before retrieving the tracking device and rolling myself around the front nearside wheel to clamp it in place. I strained my neck and kept one eye on the house while I felt around under the wheel arch and put the thing in place with a clunk. The whole process took moments, but it felt like hours. Felt like the entire street's eyes were on me.

I let out a breath, not realising I was holding one in, and scampered back into the bushes sharpish as the Audi's alarm went off.

Fuck, fuck, fuck.

Several lights came on in the top windows. The Audi's lights were flashing fast, and the alarm was piercing and loud enough to wake the whole neighbourhood. If I wasn't careful, I'd surely be fucked. I decided in a heartbeat to make my escape the same way I'd come in and scampered over that wall faster than I'd moved in years. I dropped down onto the pavement and ran to the car. Dived in and started her up just as the Audi's alarm went off and the downstairs lights blinked on. I sensed movement on the drive as I put the Volvo into gear and drove off as calm as I could allow myself. Glanced to my right as I passed the driveway gates. There was no one there. If the alarm had been switched off with a key fob from inside the house, I might've gotten away with it.

It was only when I reached the main A road beyond the street that I allowed myself to spark up. Took that shit in deep. I drove to the nearest street on the opposite side of where I'd come from and found a dark spot under a giant oak outside a large Victorian terrace. Killed the engine and finished my smoke. I was either mad or stupid. Probably both. I took out my phone and fired off a quick text to Dave, who assured me he'd still be up.

It's done.

A moment later, the equally succinct reply: OK.

Then I grabbed the brandy, took a hit and closed my eyes to try to take away the pain that was growing behind them.

After I'd sat there for the best part of an hour, trying hard to keep the brandy locked in the glove box, I figured it was probably safe to return to number 23 and park up again, but this time a bit further away. I had the binoculars - though was reluctant to use them - so I could see any movement if I needed to.

I took the car around, this time with the all night talk radio back on, which was somehow reassuring. Now that the worst part of this little operation was over, I could almost relax and just watch things unfold. At least, that's what I kept telling myself. I checked the time when I pulled over. It was just gone quarter past two and the night was deep with shadows. It was that hour where everyone's asleep and nothing much else was happening. I switched off the radio. The silence was foreboding. Watched a black cat cross my path several times, pacing back and forth across the street. Our eyes met. I wondered if she knew what I was up to. Stared back. Thought for a moment I might've finally lost it.

I kept my eyes trained on the house, mostly. And although a big part of me thought this was all a waste of my time, I knew it couldn't be once the GPS tracker was in place. At least I now knew that it definitely was, and Dave had sent me a thumbs up to confirm it once he'd set the program to track the vehicle. I just hoped it stayed that way or all of this would've been pointless. I'd have put myself at risk for nothing.

It wasn't lost on me that the house could've had CCTV and I'd be on it. The Badowskis were a criminal family that would always cover themselves with evidence they could trace. Lukasz could even be watching me watching him right now, somewhere deep in that massive house. Though I knew this was paranoia setting in. I didn't know anything for sure, was just letting my thoughts run away with me, which was easy to do when you were alone.

I ate the sandwich, feeling like some kind of pissed up weirdo train spotter, and followed it with a Galaxy and an almost hot coffee. Halfway through the coffee, just as I was getting down to the filter of my smoke, I saw movement up ahead, about fifty feet away. Tossed the cigarette and sank back into my seat. Watched as the figure emerged from the deep black shadows and walked slowly towards the car, head down. It was a man in a long black coat, hands in pockets, collar up. His steps were the only sound in the night, each footfall on the pavement loud and striking. I considered my options quickly. I could either start her up and casually drive off, like I did this kind of thing all the time. Or I could start her up and get the fuck out of here fast. Or I could stay where I was and act innocent, say I was locked out of my house, the wife had taken my keys, something shit like that.

He stepped closer and closer. By now, he was just twenty feet away and didn't look like he was going to stop. He wasn't going into a nearby house like I hoped he would. He wasn't a sixty something whisky drinking raconteur returning from a late night at the casino. I had to be as casual as possible. I relaxed into my seat and looked out of my window, but like a magnet, my eyes were drawn back to him.

Just a few feet away, he stopped. Looked directly at me.

I looked at him.

Waiting, eyes fixed.

He took his hands from his pockets and I thought for one horrifying moment that he was going to pull a gun or something, but he just cupped a hand over his eyes and leaned over, peering into the car. Either he was blind or intentionally intimidating. Whatever it was, I didn't like it.

I thought I saw a grin, no, was sure I saw a grin. Then he straightened back up and carried on walking at the same pace. I watched him in my mirror. He didn't look back.

But I did.

E ither he was just a guy trying to freak me out for some reason only he found amusing, or he knew why I was here and wanted to show me he knew. And although we didn't exchange words, we certainly exchanged a look. And it was a telling look. I didn't feel happy about it one bit, so started her up when he was out of sight and drove around the block, thinking that this whole thing was a madness I'd conjured in some nightmare. I naively thought it was a good idea to scope out Lukasz Badowski's place, and that was all it was initially, until I told Dave over the phone and he dropped by the office earlier this evening with the GPS device that would be ever so easy to plant in a discreet location in the target vehicle. I could see the benefit of this, easy. It was the risk I wasn't comfortable with and my instincts that had never lied to me turned out to be right once again.

So after the walking man episode that I knew would be on my mind for days, I drove to yet another vantage point, on the corner of the road. I edged the Volvo onto the pavement and let my window down. Sparked up and poured another barely hot coffee that I topped up with brandy, just to settle the nerves.

And waited. Occasionally, a car whispered past, or an out of service bus either leaving or on its way back to the depot. Besides the all night radio for company, I browsed the internet and smoked, thinking of what I was going to do with the cash Seamus was paying me. I'd already made two grand out of him for basically doing fuck all. There was no telling how long I could drag this out for. Maybe I'd book us a holiday once all this was over, just me and Laura. God knows we deserved a break.

I had no loyalty to Seamus, so didn't exactly feel great about putting myself in harm's way just so I could track his daughter. I knew the Badowskis were a shower of bastards and tonight's events might have put me at greater risk. I couldn't help but feel that someone was watching me as I was watching them. The old guy walking up to the car and peering in could've easily been connected to them some-how. I knew they weren't stupid. Maybe they'd sent him out to put the shits up me. Or maybe I was reading too much into things. I knew this was an easy trap to fall into on surveillance nights like this.

When I got bored with the Internet, I looked through those photographs again. The ones of my friend Bob Turner lying dead in his armchair, the blood spatter from the gunshot wound - only one to the head - sprayed across the wall. Thought about the suicide note I'd found wrapped in a plastic bag in that bottle of Bowmore he'd left me. Thought about the words that were left unsaid between us. I could've stopped it. I should've known better, should've seen it coming.

I could still smell that blood in the hot summer air.

Could still hear George Thornley sobbing on the back step.

Before long, I was drifting, and I had to jerk myself awake twice.

But the pull of sleep was strong.

I dreamt of playing cards and black cats, and a deep black hole that led, eventually, to the stars.

———

I jumped when I heard something bump onto my windscreen. It took me a brief moment to wake and realise where I was. I mustn't have been asleep for too long because there was still no one around. The pine cone had rolled onto the bonnet and was kicked off by a lone blackbird. Checked the time on the dashboard clock. It was almost half-past five. Still dark, but dawn, I knew, would come soon.

Beside me, the traffic, what little there still was of it, was slowly growing. I put the radio back on and got the morning news. It was all Russia, North Korea and the President of the United States. None of it belonged in my reality. The flask of coffee had long since gone cold, and the chill of the morning was uninviting. Yet I needed a brew to get me going again. There was a petrol station about a ten-minute walk away and I knew they did half decent coffee in one of those machines. I figured the walk would do me some good as well, so I decided to leave the car where it was. At this early hour, it wouldn't be in anyone's way.

I locked the Volvo and sparked up, letting my eye linger on number twenty-three, which I could see across the road. There was still no movement, and the house was still. I wrapped my coat around me and walked.

It felt a bit senseless, all of this, yet despite it I knew I'd rather be doing this than dealing with the usual mundane stuff my job tends to attract. I didn't mind surveillance. Didn't mind it at all in normal circumstances, but these circumstances weren't normal. If I wasn't careful, I could end up getting myself into serious trouble. So I kept looking over my shoulder as I walked, aware that the incident with the walking man earlier in the night was more than odd and I would be a fool if I didn't think there was someone following me.

I couldn't help but feel I'd made a mess of things tonight, and it would come back to haunt me later. Was planting a GPS tracking device really worth it? I mean, what good could it really do?

I reached the petrol station, a BP all lit up in green, and found the main entrance was still locked. Moved around to the window hatch and asked the Pakistani guy behind it to get me a coffee, black. He said he was about to open up, so I may as well get it myself. I did just that, lingering inside a few moments to warm up, and added a packet of smokes, too. When I left to make the short walk back, I stopped twenty yards or so down the road to spark up. I stepped back into the shadows when I clocked Lukasz Badowski's Audi drive past, heading towards the city, doing at least forty. The man himself was at the wheel in a blue tailored shirt. It was almost six o'clock. It was early for him to be up and about.

Thankfully, I didn't need to wonder where he was going.

I headed back to the Volvo, thinking about breakfast.

EIGHT

I'd returned to the office and crashed on the couch. By the time I woke, at around half-past eight, Monday morning was in full swing. Took me a few moments to compose myself and, given that a decent sleep was hard to come by lately, it was no surprise I was groggy. I hadn't felt like this since Nicole was a baby and I'd had to get up to do the night feed and settle her back down. Those days were long gone, but I longed for them again. I had to speak with her soon. I knew I had to make up for lost time before it was too late.

I fired up the Mac, by force of habit, and got myself a coffee, black. Sparked up for that just woken up morning hit of nicotine just as Laura walked through the door. Dave and Maya accompanied her, trailing behind with warm croissants from the artisan bakery a few streets away. Breakfast all round. Sometimes I had to remind myself how lucky I was.

"How did you find it?"

"In a word: a pain in the arse."

"That's five words," Maya said. "That bad, eh?"

I shook my head, sat down in a swivel chair. Dave sat at the computer, his fingers hovering over the keys with the speed of an expert magician. He brought up the program that would track the GPS device I'd planted under Badowski's Audi. A little map popped up with a red arrow in the middle of the screen. I assumed that was our vehicle. Dave confirmed it.

"Cold and quiet," I said. I decided not to mention the walking man. "And lonely."

"You could've phoned me," Laura said.

"Didn't want to wake you."

"I couldn't sleep."

And I couldn't stay awake. "I just wanted to get it done as quick as possible. Once I had, that was it. Goodnight, sleep tight."

"What, in the car?" Maya said.

"I made sure I was out of the way first. So, Dave. What are we looking at?"

"Speaks for itself," he said, grabbing the bag of croissants and sharing them out. Laura poured coffee and a herbal tea for Maya. I'd noticed our next-door neighbour had added two more tattoos to her rapidly expanding repertoire. The girl was basically a walking painting. I guessed she had to be, being a tattoo artist. Her bright red hair had now been dyed green. I wondered what it would be next week. Her boyfriend, Dave - who was quickly becoming my go to tech guy - had also added another ear piercing, a silver dagger in his right lobe. Suddenly, I felt very old. "The arrow is the vehicle, and it shows exactly where it is."

"And where our man is," Laura said, handing out the coffee.

I took a bite of my croissant - chocolate - and nodded.

"It's amazing what technology can do. Is that really him, Dave?"

"That's the car," he said. "Wherever Badowski is, it's probably nearby."

"So where is he?" Laura asked.

It was a good question.

"Waterloo Road," Dave said. "Cheetham Hill."

Maya was nodding. "Just off Cheetham Hill Road. I know it well, used to have a flat down there. Hated the bastard place."

I took a closer look at the map. I knew it too, but I had to wonder what he was doing there. "Why would he be there at this time of the morning?"

"On a dreary Monday," Laura said.

"Maybe he's gone shopping," Dave said. "There's a lot of Polish shops down that way."

"I doubt he's the shopping type. I might head down there, see for myself."

"He'll probably be gone by the time you get there."

"It's not far. And anyway, Dave can keep me updated on the phone. All he has to do is tell me where he's going."

"True," Dave nodded. "Sounds like a plan. But you might as well put your feet up for half an hour. As long as we can see where he's going, there's no need to rush around like a headless chicken."

I suppose he was right. And God knows I needed the rest. I saw by the way Laura was looking at me that she thought so, too.

"So tell me," she said. "Where did you end up Saturday night?"

"It was Hell."

"Not turning into the easy money job you thought it was, then?"

"No, I mean that's what the place was called. And a pretty appropriate name, if you ask me."

"Nightclub," Maya said. "I've been there. You said this guy's Polish, right?"

I nodded.

"That place is owned by the Poles," she said. "The top people, I mean."

"How do you know this?"

"One of my clients told me. Bloke called Fat Jay. Reckons the place is used for money laundering and drug running. Like something from a film, you know."

"What?"

She was nodding. "Really. Well, that's what he told me."

"And is this guy in the know or something?"

"I don't know, really. I suppose so."

"Did he say who, specifically, ran the place?"

"Nah, nothing like that. Just that it was the Poles, whatever that means."

"You think it could be the Badowskis?" Laura said.

"Don't see why not." I finished the rest of the croissant and sparked up, topped up my coffee, and paced the room.

"I reckon they're the obvious candidates," Dave said. "If the place is used for money laundering and drug running."

"No wonder they turn a blind eye to it."

"To what?" Laura asked.

"Well, everyone was at it," I said. "You could practically smell the chemicals."

"What else goes on in there, then?" Maya said.

It was a good point. If it was the Badowskis running the place, it could be anything. My mind drifted at the possibilities as I opened the window to the fire escape and looked out at the Northern Quarter. The Monday morning drizzle was quickly becoming a downpour.

Maya said she had business to attend to, and Dave polished off another croissant before heading off to his real job. He gave Laura simple instructions on how to use the GPS program and said to get in touch if we needed anything. I had a feeling I would be needing him again soon enough.

I felt Laura's arms circle my waist, and she turned me around to face her.

"I've been thinking about this all night," she said, kissing me. She cupped my balls and squeezed. "You kept me tossing and turning, Jim Locke."

Pushed me onto the couch and said it had been too long.

Then she lifted her top over her head and unhooked her bra.

It was turning out to be a pretty good morning so far.

Afterwards, when Laura had gone out to the shop and I had sparked up again, my phone rang.

"What have you got for me?"

There was a pause. "There's been a development," Fiona said. "Not a good one, I'm afraid."

"What do you mean?"

"Are you sitting down?"

"Just tell me, Fiona."

Massive sigh. I heard her spark up on the other end of the line. "They've found something. A body part."

"A body part? Well, whose bloody body part are we...? Oh shit, really?"

"We don't know, we don't know. There's a team heading out there now."

"Heading out where?"

"River Irwell. Lower Broughton. Just outside of town."

"And you think it could be him?"

"They'll have to do tests."

"Of course."

"It was called in about an hour ago. A couple of students saw it floating in the river as they made their way to Uni."

"What did they see, Fiona? What is it?"

"I finish my shift in a few hours. Can we meet?"

"Come to the office."

"I think I need a drink, Jim. It's not looking good."

"I've got plenty of brandy."

———

A body part? Could be anything. And, of course, it didn't mean it belonged to Robertson. Okay, so he'd been missing for a while. It didn't mean he'd turn up dead. Could be anyone. People were found dead all the time, especially in the rivers and canals of this city.

I watched from the window as Fiona approached. I'd taken her cash from my wallet - there was more than enough in there - and locked a good amount up in the safe, leaving the rest, about two hundred, in my pocket. She'd changed into her civilian gear, her handbag slung over her shoulder, her slim fit jeans glued to her legs, her waif like arms pale in the lunchtime sun. She could easily be a girl out shopping or meeting a friend. Instead, she was meeting her private investigator acquaintance for the money he owed her for confidential GMP data and a drink or two to absorb the news. I spotted her easily - you couldn't miss the way she walked, confident and sexy, dark secrets behind her eyes - a good two hundred yards before she made it to the street outside my window. Could see her marching beside the tram lines, head forward and keen to get here as quick as her feet would allow.

Robertson? Found dead?

Which body part?

I'd already hit the brandy, feeling that it wouldn't do any harm to give myself a taster before she got here.

I buzzed her up just as soon as she rang the bell. Half a minute later she was sitting on the battered old leather Chesterfield, sipping at the same brandy I'd refilled my glass with.

"Well?"

She took a breath and sparked up. I followed. "I've heard it's a foot. Naked. Cleanly cut at the ankle."

I let out a breath I didn't realise I was keeping in. "A foot?"

She nodded. "Left foot."

"Could be anyone's. What makes you think it's Robertson's?"

"I don't. But D.C.I. Crane's having the place scoured with a fine-toothed comb."

"If there's a foot..."

"Then there must be more. The place is sealed off. Traffic down there's a nightmare already, Jim."

"You said it was in the river?"

"Apparently, yeah. A couple of Spanish students saw it bobbing in the water at the bank."

"Only a matter of time before the rest of it turns up."

She nodded, blew out smoke. "Could be. Then again, there might be nothing and all we're left with is a bloody foot."

"Any indication as to how long it's been in the water?"

"No idea, but I'll no doubt find out on the grapevine. The good thing for you is that D.I. McKinnon wants me on his murder team. Not investigating this one, of course, but I'll hear what's going on. I'll keep my eyes and ears peeled."

"If it is Robertson, the press will be all over it."

"Probably. It'll be big news."

"Copper murdered in cold blood."

"We don't really know anything yet. It might not even be him. Everyone's hoping it isn't."

"And you?"

She looked up, took a drink. Grimaced. "If it does turn out to be him, after everything I know about him, after what he did to Isabella Burns, that poor girl - I hope the bastard suffered."

Can't say her feelings on the matter surprised me. I sat down, ran a hand through my quickly developing beard, and thought over events. If it turned out to be Robertson, who would want him dead? There were likely a number of candidates, people he'd locked up, people he'd done wrong. There was no shortage of those.

"And there's still been no word from him?"

She shook her head. "Neither of his wives have heard anything from him. Nor his two kids. Nor anyone in the force. This is completely out of character and not like him."

"The foot could well belong to anyone."

"But he's still missing, whether the foot turns out to be his or not. If it's not his, fine. But he's still out there, somewhere."

"What has his mood been like the past few weeks? You know, prior to him disappearing?"

"His usual smug, arsehole self. Guy's a prick."

"You said he'd recently been promoted."

She nodded. "To D.C.I. So there's no real motive for him to do himself in, despite what we had on him."

"But he didn't know all of what we had."

"No, but the doubt had been planted in his mind. He knew you had him over something."

"So he could've walked himself?"

"It's as strong a possibility as anything."

"What's your gut feeling, Fiona? What do you think's happened to him?"

She didn't hesitate. "I think he's dead. I think someone's caught up with him, whoever that is, and they've killed him."

"What makes you so convinced?"

"Because if what he's done to Isabella Burns has been done to others, it doesn't take long for someone to get so mad about it that they murder the bastard."

"So he had it coming?"

She nodded, took a final drink. "I don't think we're the only ones who knew, Jim."

I suppose it was easy to come up with where her ideas were going, but it was a brave stab in the dark to come to such a conclusion so quickly. I'd done my fair share of murder cases and I knew that a foot simply turning up from nowhere would in no way be conclusive for anything. It would need to be identified first. A simple DNA test would no doubt sort that out and before she left, Fiona had gotten on the phone to D.C.I. McKinnon to try to pick up some gossip. All she got, though, was a confirmation that tomorrow was her day off and she wasn't due in until Wednesday.

Which meant she was free to help me out, if required. I wasn't paying her for nothing.

She went home soon after that phone call - she said she

had to sleep - which gave me the rest of the day to delve back into my own case. Where was Aisling, and what the hell was she up to?

Laura came back with a bag of groceries - some for home, some for the office fridge - so I asked her to monitor the GPS program Dave had gotten up and running. The Audi was still parked up in Cheetham Hill and had been since early this morning. I had to wonder what he was up to. I considered driving but had downed three measures of the good stuff already. It would be unwise of me to think I could handle the wheel, and besides, I'd been sitting in the car all night. It was time for some fresh air and a break.

I walked out into the early afternoon sunshine and casually made my way to Lever Street, where I jumped on the 135 I knew would take me to Cheetham Hill. The bus was full, even at this time of day, and I watched as the driver, slumped bored and frustrated in his seat, ushered what seemed like the entire world onto the bus. I sat at the back, so I could people watch, something I was simply drawn to, and lazily looked out of the window as the bus moved through the city centre.

Cheetham Hill lay in the North of the city, just a mile or so out of town, sandwiched between Salford and Collyhurst. It had long been an industrial part of town, and it was traditionally where immigrants were dumped, going right back to the Irish and the Jews at the turn of the nineteenth century. These days, the place was occupied by a handful of different communities, from Pakistani to North African, to Indian to Eastern European, including the Polish, who were the most recent wave of migrants. The textile industries were long gone, except for one or two outlets on the main Cheetham Hill Road, and now, instead of producing cotton, the most likely export was the kebab or the box of fried chicken, since that was all I seemed to see as the bus moved through the heart of the district. That, and abandoned shopping trolleys, piles of fruit, and whole pallets of goods that were being unloaded into the nearby world food supermarkets that catered primarily for the communities living here.

It was easy to imagine that I'd been transported to some far-flung place in the east, such was the hustle and bustle of the traffic, not to mention the multicultural mix of people. Take a photograph of the bus stop I alighted from and you'd have a microcosm of the whole world right there in one frame.

I stepped out into the street at the junction with Waterloo Road, the place where Lukasz Badowski's Audi was parked. Took a look around, the place teeming with life, and shook my head at all the double-parked cars and vans blocking the road, their hazard lights on, their not giving a fuck attitude pissing me off no end, not to mention the trail of traffic queuing bumper to bumper behind.

I stumbled into one of the world food places in search of water and got lost amongst a sea of spices and halal chicken, sacks of onions and rice and coconuts and plantains, a cornucopia of noise and colour and rich, tantalising smells of vibrant and wholesome food. I got my water and stepped back out into the afternoon, and by now the sunshine had given way to a darkening cloud that was sure to bring rain.

Clocked a Polish deli right at the corner - European Foods, Polski Sklep - and figured that this was as good a place as any to poke around given that Lukasz was apparently nearby, unless he'd just left his car here and vanished elsewhere. I sparked up, took that shit in deep. Almost choked on exhaust fumes as I stood beside the road and observed the place for a few minutes. Took a little walk around and spotted the Audi about fifty feet away, parked on the pavement so no one could pass. That not giving a fuck attitude was everywhere around here. Just for the sake of it, I took some quick shots with my phone, mainly so I had something to show Seamus. There was no sign of Aisling, which didn't surprise me. She wouldn't be seen dead around here. And as for Lukasz, I wondered what brought him here, too. I tossed my smoke and marched towards the deli, figuring this was probably the place I'd find out.

I stepped in to the sound of boxing commentary coming from a tiny TV sitting on the counter. Two men were behind it, one relatively old, the other much younger and throwing punches, shadow boxing at what he was seeing on the screen. I listened in as I walked the aisles, pretending to browse - how much sauerkraut and pickled gherkins could you really choose from? - the shelves over-loaded with tins of cooked meats, the chiller full of conti-nental sausage, the fridge full of strong beer. Hung around for several minutes, trying to remain inconspicuous and listening in on their conversation, which was in Polish. Couldn't understand a single word. Another guy came in, slapped something down on the counter, then quickly left. Only two other customers came and went, one of whom bought a six-pack of Lech, which brought thoughts of a cheeky beer flooding in. Perhaps it was time to give myself a few hours off.

A moment later, the older one disappeared into the back and I heard footsteps thudding on the stairs. A distant yet audible conversation, several voices chipping in. Was hard to tell if it was an argument or a shared joke.

Grabbed myself a half litre bottle of Lech and stepped up to the counter, dropping a fiver down.

"Boxer, eh?"

He shrugged, turned the volume down. "Real boxing," he said. "Only fist."

I nodded and twisted the cap off the beer. He definitely had a boxer's nose. "You fight, then?"

He grinned. "Sometimes. For a little money, you know."

I took a drink and raised the bottle. Pocketed my change and left.

Just as I was walking out, the older guy came back and they were jabbering in Polish again, the volume back up. Took one last look, nodded, and skipped out the door, figuring a look around the back wouldn't do any harm.

I drained the beer in record time and poked my nose into the back way, ducking down an alley that smelt of piss, a layer of strange green slime coating the cobbles. I almost lost my footing when I spotted a fat rat, its tiny teeth sticking out of its mouth in a death grimace. Its fur was matted with cooking oil, the container discarded nearby, and its tail, pink and slim like a sick worm, trailed lazily among the chicken bones.

But it was the heavy stench of marijuana that hit me dead on like a slap to the face. Jesus, it was strong. Too strong. I looked up, saw that the windows were blacked out upstairs. A telltale sign if ever there was one. I kept close to the side wall of the building and shimmied along on cobbles that were a little bit drier, feeling caned from the fumes. I don't remember feeling so bowled over when I used to smoke the odd joint down at the spot with Lindsay Shaw-cross when I was sixteen. This was some super strong demon shit.

When I reached the end of the wall, I peeked around the corner, just in case. A wise move, given that there was a large white van parked up, its rear doors open to the narrow back entrance of the deli.

Clocked a pile of loaded bin bags sitting in the back, and movement, just the slightest touch, of someone's arm resting on the passenger door, reflected clearly in the van's near side mirror. Ducked my head back out of sight on instinct.

And voices too, coming from inside the deli. That Polish again. Laughter and back slapping. A radio blared from somewhere, either from the van or somewhere inside. The music had been turned up loud. Some kind of weird shit death metal ruined the vibes, and I peeked around the corner again as two hefty looking men jumped from the van and stepped inside. Took it as my opportunity to make a move.

I stepped out tentatively and went straight to the back of the van. The stench of marijuana was overpowering. I made a hole in one of the bags and stuck my hand in, acting quickly and with one eye keenly on the back door. The bag I ripped open was stuffed with selophaned packages of weed, taped up tight with brown masking tape and when I pulled a bundle of it out - it must have weighed at least a kilo - I quickly shoved it in my pocket, turned the bin bag around so it couldn't be seen, and quickly turned back toward the alley I'd come from.

Only to find one of the van's delivery men step out of the back of the deli. He clocked me straight away and went to grab me, shouting in Polish to his mates inside. I ran, nearly going over on my arse on that green slime and when I hit the main Cheetham Hill Road, taking a chance to look behind me, he was on my case, pounding the pavement just yards behind.

Fuck. I got my head down and ran, bumped into an old Pakistani guy near the bus stop, did a hop, skip and jump over an abandoned shopping trolley, belted it down a side road until when I reached the end and chanced to look back once again, my follower was gone. Vanished. And the package was still in my pocket.

I stood there on the corner, a couple of kids on bikes staring at me as I caught my breath. Looked around for any sign of him and sank back against someone's wall as I drank in great lungfuls of air.

"Are you all right, Mister?"

I held my hand up, nodding. "I'm okay, I'm okay. Do me a favour, will you, and ride up the street, see if you can see..."

But there was the van, turning down the road, two men glaring out at me from the front seat.

"Can I borrow your bike?"

Gunning it down the road.

The kids just pedalled off.

I didn't bother finishing the conversation. I ran, faster this time, and ducked down a street to my right, then crossed the road, then the next left, then straight down to the bottom. I looked back, saw the van pass the junction I'd just crossed, and then heard it skid to a halt before reversing.

I looked around, clocked an alleyway across the street, and took it. There was an old mattress and couch dumped against a wall and I had to decide, quickly, if this was a good place to hide. I didn't even have to think about it, hauling the couch away from the wall and crouching behind it. I pulled the mattress over to cover the gap and took in great breaths again, wheezing with the effort, a stitch in my side, beads of sweat lining my neck, my heart and head pounding. I hadn't had to run like this in years. I checked my pocket and the package was still there, heavy and stinking. I felt stoned just looking at it.

Heard the chug chug of a diesel engine nearby. Had to be the van, and it had to be close. Heard doors slam, the engine still running, those Polish voices again, loud and angry.

Looked through the narrow gap from where I was hiding and clocked them step into the alley, pacing up and down. Either I was about to get the biggest kicking of my life or I was about to hit the pub for a stiff drink. I hoped it was the latter. I peeked out, saw two pairs of legs wandering up and down. Held my breath and tried to be still. A dog barked from someone's backyard nearby. It would either be my saviour or give the game away. Heard the clack of a lock on a nearby back gate and the creak of the door as it opened. Shit, it was close. A voice in Pakistani as the Alsatian trotted out and sniffed around. Fuck, this was all I needed. Clocked the dog through the gap and saw it walking around in circles, its nose to the damp concrete. Felt something crawl down my neck and I stiffened. God knows what kind of bugs there were in this thing.

Finally let out a breath when the two Poles walked out of sight, back to the van. Heard it pull away and off into the distance as the dog was called back in. Moments later, the back gate locked again and I was alone in the silence. I gave it a few minutes, the only sounds being distant kids at play, an ice-cream van tinkling its tune, and the wail of a hungry baby coming from a bedroom window.

I moved the mattress and clambered out from my hiding hole, careful to keep my eyes peeled for the Poles or the Alsatian.

Stepped out towards the street itself as the clouds parted and a beam of sun blazed down like it was God himself confirming my escape. I sparked up, took that shit in deep. Felt the package again, heavy in my pocket. The drugs had to be worth a small fortune and I half expected the van to turn up again. I couldn't relax.

I made my way through the back streets, got lost until I asked an African woman where I was, then stumbled out to Queens Road via a run down estate littered with rubbish until I managed to flag down a dodgy private hire cab who agreed to take me into town.

Got him to drop me off at the office, where I stashed the weed in the safe. Laura talked at me like I was a teenager and demanded to know where I'd gotten it from. Ten minutes later I was propping up the bar of the Lower Turk's Head, a double whisky lined up beside a pint of good ale. The exotic aroma of ganja stuck to my clothes like thistles in autumn and I was getting some hard looks.

I retreated to the beer garden above and sparked up, the March afternoon turning grey, the clouds heavy with expected rain. When my phone rang, I took a moment to answer, somehow knowing it was bad news but inevitable given recent events.

I answered just before it could ring out.

"Fiona?"

NINE

"Jim. Where are you?"

"In the pub."

"Why does that not surprise me?"

"Because you know me too well." I finished the whisky in one go and moved onto the ale. "Any news?"

"Well, whichever way you look at it, there will be no justice now, not for Isabella Burns, not really."

"It's him."

I could hear her sigh down the line, then she sparked up. I took a long pull on my own smoke, filling my veins with beautiful nicotine.

"It's him. His foot, his DNA, which apparently is a match for his blood record on Police file."

"Jesus."

"I know, I know. But that's not all."

"I suppose they now need to find the rest of him. Have the press gotten wind of it?"

"Oh yeah," she said. "All the majors have been on the phone, so Derek tells me."

"Derek?"

"Desk Sergeant and Station Gossip."

"I see."

"Won't be long until they run with it. News will break tonight, no doubt. Anyway, as I was saying: they're trying to find the rest of him. They didn't need to look for long."

"Go on."

"A left hand turned up, just a few hundred metres from where his foot was found."

"Fuck me, they've chopped him into little pieces."

"There's a wedding ring still on his finger."

"Severed again?"

"Another clean cut, right through the bone."

Nothing the bastard didn't deserve. "Christ..."

"Tell me about it."

"What's gonna turn up next, his head?"

"Don't joke about it, Jim."

"A leg..."

"Maybe whoever did this cut his bloody clock off as well."

"If they did it for those reasons."

"Who knows?"

"Seems plausible. So what now?"

"What do you mean?"

"Well, what we had on him: what's the use of it now?"

"I suppose we left it too late. I don't know, Jim. I don't know anything anymore. I need to think. Think about it all, really. The last week has been fucking mental, tell you the truth."

"Why don't you join me?"

"What, now?"

"Sounds like you need a drink. And we've a lot to talk about."

"That's true. Where are you?"

"Lower Turk's Head." I checked the time on the clock inside. Almost half three. "Reckon I'll be here a few hours, at least."

"I'll get a taxi down. I could murder a Guinness."

"I'll get you one in."

"What, like, homegrown or something? Isn't that what it is?"

"I take it you've never done a drugs bust."

"Can't say I have."

"I'm telling you, this is some seriously strong shit."

"You're not wrong," she said, screwing her nose up. "It is strong. I don't know whether I like it or not. But what are you gonna do about it? About them?"

"Nothing," I said. "I mean, what can I do?"

"You could report it."

"Nah, what good would it do? No one at GMP will listen to me, anyway. Besides, it's more than a pain in the arse. It'd be better for me if I kept my mouth shut. Whoever followed me will know who I am now, no doubt."

"And you think it's connected to Badowski?"

"Without a shadow."

"You said you traced him to there, but you didn't see him?"

"He could've been inside, upstairs. We're tracing his Audi. A Q7. It was parked around the corner, on Waterloo Road."

"So they're in the drugs game?"

"Most probably. And anyway, it's just something I stumbled upon, I didn't mean to do what I did, I was just poking my nose around and the next minute I had a kilo of weed in my hands and a big Polish geezer chasing me through Cheetham Hill."

"The trouble you find yourself in never ceases to amaze me."

Nor me. I cursed my stupidity and pointed my empty pint pot at the door. "Another?"

She stood, crushing her roll up in the ashtray between us. "My round. Same again?"

I nodded and she left. I tried to stop myself from looking at her arse, but couldn't. Gotta admit, I was seriously confused. She was giving me some big signals and I was finding it hard to remain professional.

Did I fancy her? Yes.

Did I love Laura? Yes.

Did I think I could get away with it if it was offered to me on a plate?

Yes.

I forced myself to think of something else, namely Robertson and where the rest of him was going to turn up.

Fiona put another pint of ale in front of me.

"So, what happened?"

She took the head off her Guinness and continued. "Apparently, a dog walker found the hand and called it in. SOCO were already searching the area after the foot was found, so it was no surprise, really. They found his wallet just a few feet away from the hand."

"Weird."

"I know. And then they found his car parked around the back of a factory that makes plastic cartons and stuff. Just a ten-minute walk from the river. It had been sitting there a week and no one batted an eyelid, no one bothered to report it as abandoned."

"And was he the last person to drive it? Which would suggest he had a reason to be there..."

"We don't know, but Derek reckons they're pulling out everything they can for it. The divers will be out tonight and forensics are all over the car and the river bank where the limbs were found."

"You think he could be in the river?"

"I doubt it. Who in their right mind would dump body parts in the Irwell?"

"Who in their right mind would kill someone? For any reason?"

"Suppose."

"Does Isabella know?"

She shook her head. "Not yet. But when it's on the news..."

"You seen her recently?"

"No, not since she gave me her statement. She knows where I am if she needs me."

"I reckon her head will be all over the place."

"It already is."

"When she finds out he's dead." I stared off, trying to gather thoughts, sparked up again. "It could be the final straw for her."

"Because she won't ever get justice? She'd have never really gotten it anyway."

I nodded. "How's things at the station?"

"Not in until Wednesday, am I? I'll find out then. From what I'm hearing, though, a few of the detectives are in a mess. There's one or two more cracking open the champagne. Maybe a slight exaggeration, but..."

"Not surprised. He was a massive prick."

"Strange to be talking about him in the past tense."

I took a long drag on the smoke. Took that shit in deep.

My phone buzzed a text message from Seamus, which I put to one side. Not like him to text. "I wonder if they have any suspects yet?"

"Don't think so. It's early days."

"Yeah."

"Certainly no stand outs."

"I suppose so. Listen, keep me updated, will you?"

"You know I will."

"I am paying you, don't forget."

"Which reminds me," she said, her hand out. "You owe me."

I dug around in my pockets until I brought out her cash, rolled up in a bundle with an elastic band. "Five hundred. But don't think you can relax now."

"Funny how things end up, isn't it?"

"What do you mean?"

"Oh, you know. You getting thrown off the force, me getting my fingers dirty in the PNC and Robertson murdered in cold blood. It's a funny world."

"Hilarious."

"But I do wonder who else had it in for him."

"You'd think they were seriously fucked up in the head to cut him up like that."

"Like an animal."

"They must have really meant it, you know. It's not good enough to just kill him, they had to chop him up and scatter his body parts all over the place."

"Jesus."

"Doesn't bear thinking about."

"That is fucked up, isn't it?"

I nodded, took my pint halfway down. "The more I think about it, the stranger it feels."

We were quiet a moment, each of us content to smoke

and look out over Shudehill and the bus interchange and the hundreds of people milling around. Rush hour was looming.

"Any other news on Aisling Connolly? The young Badowski keeping her sweet?"

I shrugged. "Probably. I tracked them on Saturday night, then followed it up last night."

"How did the surveillance go?"

I told her. "I keep thinking I made a right tits up of it."

"But the tracking device works, right?"

"Oh, it works. Yeah. But this guy walking towards the car. He just stopped and peered through the window, obviously at me and obviously to freak me out, which he did."

"Any idea who it could've been?"

"Not a Scooby. Could be completely innocent, but I didn't get that feeling."

"Be careful, Jim. You know how things ended up the last time you started poking your nose in. How's the scar, by the way?"

I'd been conscious of it ever since I woke up on the operating table. That strange, ethereal pulse was always there, and it only really disappeared when I was focussed on something else. I occasionally felt a sharp pain, as if a ghostly knife was plunging in all over again. I was taken back, always, to the moment it happened every time I lifted my shirt and looked at it, seven inches long, pale white and raised from the flesh like a branding burn.

"Gives me gip every now and again, you know."

She nodded, unconvinced. Grabbed my hand in hers and looked me in the eye. "And you? You nearly died, Jim."

"Well, I didn't. Thanks to you. I'm still here to tell the tale and I'll still be here in another ten years, at least. If my liver doesn't pack in."

"But it was a terrible thing. A horrific event. It's bound to leave more scars than just that wound. You know you can talk to me anytime, yeah? About anything."

"I'm okay, Fi. Lucky to be alive, yeah, but I'm okay."

She smiled, let me go. I lifted my pint and drained it, thinking there was just enough time for one more - there's always time - and that my liver wasn't ready to pack in just yet.

"My round."

"Not for me."

"Come on, Fiona, don't you want to celebrate?"

"Can't say I feel like it. I don't think Isabella will feel like it, either. Besides, I'm meeting a mate for a curry."

God knows what was going through that poor kid's head. Then there was the small matter of Robertson's two wives and his double life. Things were about to blow and get very complicated. Was just like this fool to leave such a mess behind. Even in death, he was fucking things up.

Fiona drained her pint, said she had to go. I didn't try to stop her, though I wanted to bend her ear just a bit before she left.

"You heard of Hell?"

She looked at me blankly. "Fictional place where the devil lives. What about it?"

"No, the nightclub. In town."

She shook her head. "There's so many places popping up randomly every week, I can't keep up with it all."

"I know. Well, this place is apparently run and owned by the Polish. And by that I'm thinking it's the Badowski family and their lot."

"Go on."

"Just wanted you to run a check on it for me when you can. No rush. Just see what you can find out."

"It'll have to wait until Wednesday, though I probably won't find much."

"Fine."

"So what of it?"

"A little bird told me they were using it for drug running."

"What, as a front?"

"Don't know. I suppose. There's a lot of shit being snorted and dropped, I know that much."

"You speaking from experience?"

"That's where Lukasz and Aisling ended up on Saturday. My worst nightmare."

"It's definitely not you, is it?"

She grabbed her purse and her tobacco and slung her bag over her shoulder before standing. We exchanged a brief hug and she said she'd be in touch. I told her not if I needed her first.

I hung around on the roof garden and looked out over the area. Watched as she headed off down the hill to meet her friend. Felt the rain begin to drizzle from the quickly greying cloud and dug into my pocket to retrieve my phone and the text from Seamus.

GOT YOU A SPACE SORTED FOR THE FIGHT! GIVE ME A CALL.

Fight?

I figured I needed a drink before I spoke to him. The place was filling up with after work drinkers and the chink of glasses was making me thirsty. Maybe another brandy, just to keep that early spring cough at bay.

I moved downstairs to a quiet corner as the drizzle turned to a downpour and found Seamus's number. Dialled as I knocked back the brandy.

"Locke."

"Seamus. Got to say, your text came as a surprise."

"I thought I said I'd send you an invite?"

I thought back and he did, on his doorstep. "I remember now, just wasn't expecting one so soon. So, what's this fight? And when is it?"

"I'll send a car to pick you up. Are you free on Thursday?"

I didn't have to think for too long and knew it would be a mistake to say I wasn't. "Of course."

"Good man. Because weekends always begin on a Thursday in my family. Just yourself, mind. It's kind of complicated, but I'm sure you understand these things, you know. Best we keep the location under wraps, eh?"

"No problem."

"Good man. There'll be plenty of well known faces there, you know, just think of it as a bit of a break from

Aisling and her fucking boyfriend. How is my daughter, by the way?"

Well, the last time I saw her she was halfway to picking up her knickers.

"Hard to tell. She seems pretty happy, so far as I know."

"That's grand, but I'm not sure I believe you, Jim. You know, I haven't seen her in ages. I'm beginning to think she doesn't like me."

"Does she not even phone you?"

"Jesus, no. She was at Mulligan's on St. Pat's night, but she never even spoke to me. Never even looked at me, actually."

"She's young. She'll come round."

"I'm not so sure. I keep sending her money, have done for years. Maybe it's time to cut that off."

"I'm sure Badowski will be keeping her well."

"Shit, don't say that. You think this fling will last?"

"I don't know. Who's to say? So far, everything looks fine. You heard from Kian? Is he still speaking to her?"

"He's the only one she really speaks to. Doesn't bother with Shane and Connor."

"Has he any idea if she's got plans this week? If you want me to keep on her tail, I could do with the inside track on what she's up to."

"You'll have to speak to him, but I think he said something about her going out tomorrow."

"Tuesday's a strange night to be going out."

"Yeah, well, that girl of mine doesn't do normal. So, are you in?"

"What do you mean?"

"The fight night. We're running a book as well, like."

"I told you I don't gamble, Seamus. But yeah, count me in."

"Okay, I'll send a car on Thursday at six. They'll pick you up from your office. So until then, get back to work, eh?"

"I'm on it."

"I was only joking, Locke."

But I didn't find it funny.

I hung around for a few more, trying to find the space to go over some things in my head, alone. So far, there didn't seem to be much point in tailing Aisling. As far as I was concerned, she was just a young woman in a relationship with a young man. I knew Seamus didn't see it that way, though. I suppose he thought he could still dictate what she could and couldn't do. I reckoned he was wasting his time. And if he was stupid enough to pay me for following her around, so be it.

I thought about calling Kian, just to see if he'd heard what she was up to this week. If she really was going out tomorrow, I wanted to be nearby to record events, just so I could show Seamus I really was on the job. But I decided to leave that call for now.

And Lukasz Badowski. All signs pointed to some serious drug dealing. Not that I could do much about that. The only instruction I was given was to follow Aisling and report back. Easy enough. Yet already I was bending the truth, just a little. I only hoped the package of marijuana I'd nicked wasn't about to get me in the shit.

I thought about this fight night Seamus wanted me to attend and wondered if he had an ulterior motive of some kind. I mean, why the hell would he want me there? To keep tabs on me somehow? I had a feeling that there was something Seamus wasn't telling me about his daughter. It was a bit unusual for her to not be talking to her dad, yet still attend the party at Mulligan's. Not for the first time, I thought not all was right in the Connolly family. Families had deep secrets and dark lies. I knew that just from my own, yet here was a gangland boss and his sons that pretty much ran the lot. Perhaps they had the darkest secrets of all. Did Aisling have some serious dirt on her dad? What the fuck was really going on here? Aisling getting involved with the enemy, a Badowski of all people, would seriously rub them up the wrong way. Maybe all they needed was the tiniest detail on what Aisling was really up to just so they could justify kicking off another war.

I didn't want a part of it. I didn't want to be the one to give them that justification, whatever that may be.

Maybe nothing at all.

I'd have to be very careful about what I revealed down the line.

I figured it might be as well to keep a closer eye on the Connollys too, if only to protect myself. An insurance policy, should it be required. Already, a plan was brewing in my head. I wondered if Dave could get hold of another GPS tracker. Given Seamus was sending a car to pick me up, it would be like taking candy from a baby. Sometimes, the best ideas came when I was in the place I felt most at home. Trouble was, I knew it was slowly killing me at the same time.

By the time I left, it was pushing eight. I'd taken my time with the ale, spending most of the evening people watching. Toyed with the idea of getting my head down at the office, but I needed a proper bed to sleep in tonight. Last night's overnight surveillance was catching up with me. And the warm skin of a good woman was inviting, too. Laura had sent several texts asking where I was. But she was used to it now, these nights out drinking. She knew I had work to do.

When I got back to the flat, she was still up, lounging on the couch with her laptop and a gin and tonic poised on the armrest. I could see the rain had begun to come down hard now, so I'd made it home just in time.

"There's some shepherd's pie left. In the oven."

I was hungry and plated myself some, adding a cup of tea in a weak attempt to stop me from cracking open another beer.

"Connolly's invited me to something," I said. She was laughing at something on Facebook. "Some kind of boxing match."

"Hm?"

"What do you reckon?"

"What's that, babe?"

I told her, bringing my plate into the living room and crashing in front of the telly. Nothing on but cooking programmes and soaps.

"So are you gonna go?"

"I said I would. Can't really say no, to be honest."

"I suppose. How do you feel about it?"

"Not great, really. I don't like boxing and I'll be surrounded by arseholes."

"I could go with you."

"It has to be just me, I'm afraid."

"Well, where is it?"

"Well that's just it. I don't know yet. A car's picking me up at six on Thursday. From the office."

"Oh Jim, be careful. You know how dodgy they are."

I assured her I would and flicked over to the news. And there it was, suddenly real. I told Laura before she clocked it on the TV screen. It took her several moments to take it in.

"Oh my God. Dead?"

I nodded. "Murdered in cold blood. Something ain't right, kid, I can tell you that."

"Jesus. So what happens now?"

"They try to find out who killed him. A murdered copper isn't like other murders, love. Especially this one. They still have to find the rest of him."

"Fucking hell."

"I know. And this one isn't going away in a hurry."

I slept in late on Tuesday, finally crawling from my pit around eleven. Laura had left long ago and had sent several texts informing me that Dave needed me to call him. I'd told her what I had in mind for Thursday and all I needed to do was clear it with him as soon as possible, while I had the chance.

I took my time getting ready, spending twenty minutes in the shower and drinking several coffees before I could even think about venturing out. I stood at the window and smoked, looking out over the city at the steadily falling rain, wondering what the day would bring. With a hangover I needed rid of, I figured a hair of the dog wouldn't hurt. I settled for a dash of brandy with coffee number three and made the first of two phone calls right there by the window, which I'd opened to let the cold air wash over me.

"Yeah?"

"Morning, Kian. It's Jim Locke."

"I wondered when you'd come crawling back."

"Hardly crawling."

Heard him laugh. "I see one of your lot's turned up dead. Nasty that. You know him?"

"As a matter of fact, I do."

"There's hating pigs and there's hating pigs. I think killing one's a bit extreme, though."

I couldn't disagree. "You going to this boxing match your dad's putting on?"

"I'm expected to be there. So I suppose I'll have to be."

"Like that, is it?"

"Not really. I don't have to bother, but you know he can get stupid if we don't do what he wants."

"Aisling going?"

"What do you think?"

"I'd say no."

"Then you'd probably be right."

"But she's out tonight, apparently."

"You been talking to my dad, then?"

"Well, he said you'd know. She only speaks to you, I'm led to believe."

"It's true."

"She got beef with Connor?"

"Not that I'm aware of. There's a big age gap between them."

"So they don't really get on?"

"I never said that. Probably just got nothing in common. So anyway, what do you want to know?"

"Do you know where she's going tonight?"

"Not for certain. Only that she's going out around the Northern Quarter. Meeting some of her mates after work for a midweek drink."

"Weekend can't come soon enough, eh?"

"It's just one long party for us."

"I bet."

Not for the first time, I didn't like the kid's attitude much. He was smug. Self assured. A Connolly.

"Anyway, if that's all..."

"I won't keep you."

"I have got things to do."

Yeah, like smoke a few joints and count your money. "I'll leave you alone then. For now."

I hung up and thought, briefly, about getting some breakfast. But now it was pretty much lunchtime and I realised I hadn't eaten in quite a while. Got my shit together and stepped out, smoking my way to the cafe in the drizzling rain.

I parked myself in the far corner of the Koffee Pot, only pausing to observe the world outside once I'd gotten my head out of a large full English. By the time I was ready to move, it was pushing two. I slowly made my way towards the office, thinking things over, wasting my time. Tried to get myself a bit of head space to escape the current case, but it was always hard until there was a line drawn under it. There wasn't much chance of that just yet.

Laura was pretending to be busy, going through various files and tidying up the accounts. I knew she was hovering around on the Internet, though, browsing for shoes and books and wasting hours on Facebook.

"Well?"

"What?"

"Any news? Did you phone Dave?"

"I'll phone him now."

"He is expecting you. And I asked him and Maya if they wanted to help us out on Thursday."

"Thursday?"

"The fight? Jim, have you been drinking again?"

"No. Not yet, anyway."

"I'll brew up. Could do with a tea."

I thought about the three of them hanging around in Dave's car. Too many cooks and all that. "Listen, I think three might be a crowd."

"Hmm?"

"Thursday." I hovered around the window and watched the rain, a fine spray still cloaking the city. "Might be a problem."

"Nah. And anyway, we've sorted it. Thought you could do with some moral support. I thought you were phoning him?"

I took out the phone and dialled. He answered almost immediately and we spent five minutes discussing what I thought was a cunning plan. Dave suggested a few tweaks here and there, and by the time Laura had handed me a hot tea and a packet of bourbon creams, we were pretty much clear on a strategy.

In the meantime, I brought up the Lukasz Badowski GPS map and clocked the Audi moving slowly along Chester Road, heading toward Deansgate and into town. I wondered if he was dropping Aisling or whether she was driving it. Observed quietly while I drank and Laura rummaged around in the safe.

I could smell it when I walked in, but now it was super strong and was making me feel stoned just looking at it.

"Seriously, Jim," she said, grinning. "What on earth are we gonna do with it? We can't leave it here."

I shrugged. I supposed she was right. It was certainly a large amount of weed. I watched as Laura took the package out and felt the weight of it in her hands. "I don't know. Sell it, maybe."

"Sell it? To who?"

"There must be thousands out there who wouldn't mind a bag."

"Jim, you're naughty. You could get in serious trouble, especially being a private detective."

"Either that or dump it. I don't smoke that shit anymore. Those years have long gone."

"Never felt like rekindling the past?"

"I've got enough problems as it is. You do what you want with it. Get rid of it, throw it down the toilet, whatever. I'm sure you'll think of something."

I turned back to the Mac and the little window with the GPS. The Audi was still moving and was coming to the bottom end of Deansgate. It stopped at the junction with Bridge Street and sat for a moment.

I watched and waited.

Several minutes later, and right on cue as I was draining the tea, the little red arrow spun around and moved in the opposite direction. A drop off, perhaps?

I jumped when my phone rang out.

"Enjoying your day off?"

"Well, I was until ten minutes ago. Just got a call from Derek with the latest gossip. You've probably seen it's all over the news."

"Saw it last night. Have they kept the paparazzi at bay?"

"Have they fuck. I'm told there's a large crowd of the media camped on the lawn outside. It won't be long before the more grisly details hit the newsstands, so I thought I'd fill you in first. A lot of this won't come out in the mainstream media, but no doubt some of it could be leaked and could've leaked already."

"Sounds ominous."

"And the rest. Have you eaten?"

"No. You buying us dinner?"

"Not what I meant, Jim. Just giving you pre warning in case you puke all over your shoes."

I got up from my seat and absently paced the office. I settled at the window, looking out over the Northern Quarter. "Jesus, go on. What have they found now?"

"A few things. First off, a torso. A dog walker found it sitting in some bushes in Heaton Park. Not in a good condition, as you might expect."

"Christ."

"Organs all removed. Heart and lungs, as well as the liver, the pancreas and the small intestine."

"Fuck me..."

"The whole park's closed. They reckon the torso has been there at least four days but could've been disembowelled and all the rest several days prior."

"Have they any idea what's going on?"

"Other than the fact that he's been cut up, not really. So far as I can tell, anyway."

"More than cut up, though. I mean, why remove his organs?"

"It's like Jack the fucking Ripper all over again. Did he really deserve this, Jim? I mean, he was a total prick, but did he deserve this?"

"He must've died before... you know, before being cut up. Jesus, how many parts is that now?"

"Three. A hand, a foot and a full torso."

"Any news on his car? That been seen to yet?"

"It's a big job. They're going through it at the scene before taking it to the lab. Could be days before anything comes up, if at all."

"No doubt." I sparked up, took that shit in deep. "Any thoughts on what we do now? You know, with what we know."

"Not really. Just make sure the files are safe for now. I think I still want it to come out. When all this has died down."

"Seems only right."

"Definitely. It's too sensitive now, of course."

"You know, what we reveal may lead to a lot of unanswered questions about his murder."

"Like?"

"Well, did anyone else know besides us? And if anyone else knew, who would be crazy enough to kill him like that?"

"As a punishment, you mean?"

"Yeah."

She was silent a moment. A big sigh before I heard her spark up. "Time will tell, I suppose. But this doesn't feel like a revenge killing to me. But there we have it. And listen, don't be surprised if the media turn up at your office."

"Oh, please say they won't."

"You're an ex colleague, you know him well."

"Not anymore."

"They'll probably try it with everyone. But might be best to be aware. You don't want any dodgy hacks listening in to your conversations."

"I've got nothing to hide, Fi. And anyway, it's not as if I know anything. Does anyone know anything other than that it was one sick bastard that dealt the killing blow?"

"There are a lot of unknowns, yeah. And I don't need to tell you it's big news. It's not going away."

"Don't I know it. Anyway, listen. Have you dug anything up about the Connollys? And the Badowskis?"

"Gotta admit, it's been off my radar."

"You fancy coming out with me tonight? Could do with a bit of help with surveillance."

"Aisling the lucky girl, I expect?"

"Yeah, and her mates. Just thought you might come in handy, you know. Help me blend in."

"I'm on an early tomorrow, so I'm afraid you're on your own. Got to be up at four."

I was happy those days were long gone for me. Wondered how I ever coped with them, in fact. "Well, if you're sure..?"

"Without any doubt. How are things going with it?"

"Nothing happening, to be honest. I'm just doing what Connolly wants. I'll follow her around, see what turns up, report back. That's all I can do."

"Sounds like you've got it easy."

"As easy as it gets."

I hoped they wouldn't be the famous last words that would come back to haunt me. I let her go and turned to Laura, who had taken over my seat at the Mac.

"Did you hear that?"

She nodded. "Only the interesting bits. She gonna join you, then?"

"She's on an early."

"Well, I can help you blend in."

"I don't think that's such a good idea."

"Why not?" She left her seat and came over to me, putting her hands on my shoulders and her lips on mine. "Could do with a drink. It could be fun."

"But I'm meant to be working."

"So you work and I'll watch."

Maybe she would come in handy. I couldn't keep her locked up in the office all day and night. But we needed to know where Aisling was going to be, otherwise we'd be wandering around aimlessly until we were drunk.

"Okay, but on one condition. You do as I say and stay out of trouble."

She raised her fist to the air. "Yes."

"You'd better go and get yourself together, then. I'll close up in an hour."

ELEVEN

"So which one is Lynsey Byrne again?"

"The one with the brown hair behind the bar."

"And it's her place?"

"No, she just manages it as far as I know. The mixed race girl with the white wine is Lisa Browne. She's her cousin."

"So where's Aisling?"

"Not here yet. But that girl walking in right now is Kerry Ainsworth."

"What, the one with the muscles? Jesus, she's got bigger biceps than you."

"Her triceps are well defined, you can say that."

"Not hard to have bigger muscles than you, though."

We'd been in Grain a good hour already, nursing a pint in a dark corner and trying to be as inconspicuous as possible. Not so easy. It was busy, though, which meant we could blend in better than I thought. Was always better to remain natural in these situations, and if Aisling or anyone spotted us - not that her friends knew who we were - then so be it.

The girl herself walked in just as I was about to drain

my second beer - I'd promised Laura I'd take it easy, especially being on the job - and they all greeted each other with big girly hugs, Lynsey Byrne running from behind the bar area in her red high heels.

We watched as they chatted and giggled, each pulling up a stool as Lynsey instructed her bar staff to keep the drinks coming. Doing what a bunch of twenty something girls usually do - catching up on each other's business.

"So what's the betting on where they go next?"

"Could be anywhere. It's changed so much around here, I hardly recognise it."

"There's a new place every week."

It was true. Or at least it felt that way. If it wasn't some ultra cool eatery, it was a new bar with a new concept. One disguised as a launderette, maybe? Or how about the convenience store, where you could pick up a box of cereal with your trendy North American pale ale? The trouble was, hardly any of them really lasted the test of time, not like real boozers. Once the gimmick died off, so did the punters.

"They might go and eat somewhere. Which means we can't. It would be far too obvious."

"Shame, because I'm hungry."

But I didn't really hear her because Aisling turned from her Cuba Libre, a dainty straw hovering over those beautiful lips, and laid her big green eyes right upon me.

The girl had called my bluff already. Told myself it was only a matter of time. I was half expecting her to wave, but she turned back to the other girls and carried on the conversation, as if she wasn't bothered by me at all.

Fuck.

"Our cover is blown."

"What?"

I nodded in Aisling's direction. "She's clocked me. She's

not as daft as she seems. No doubt Kian's told her I'm onto her, which comes as no surprise."

"What, Aisling?"

"Yeah. Don't stare. She's the one with the black hair."

"Chocolate brown maxi dress?"

"Is that what you call it?"

"Wow, she is beautiful. Very curvaceous. But what do we do now?"

"Nothing. I mean, what can we do? She's seen me, so that's that. She must know what I'm doing here."

"She probably finds it funny."

"Not so sure about that. Anyway, it is what it is. We're just out having a few drinks. It's not like she can do much about that."

"About what?"

Then there was the tap on the shoulder I hoped wouldn't happen. I turned to see her standing there with her rum and coke, this beautiful young woman busy getting involved with the Badowskis, this daughter of one of the most notorious gangsters this city had ever known, a Connolly, an heir to the family fortune and the subject of my surveillance. I almost fell in love right there. Almost.

"Aisling," I said, standing to see her face to face. "Fancy seeing you here."

"You must think I'm fucking stupid, Jimmy. So how much is that daft cunt father of mine paying you?"

"I don't know what you're talking about. I don't even know your dad."

She laughed. Hard. Threw her head back and screeched. "Jesus, you're funny. Look, I know you've been following me, I know he's got you on my case for some bizarre fucking reason, like he thinks I'm gonna run off with the Poles or something, and that he thinks I don't know what I'm doing, like I'm some silly little girl, you know? Jesus, he's got bollocks for brains, that man."

"So you don't get on?"

"He's a fucking gobshite."

"Does he know how you feel?"

She took a sip of her drink, looked me directly in the eye. "We don't get along, no. Never have, really. Anyway, are you just gonna stand there looking like a gormless fuck or are you gonna be a real gentleman and introduce me to your lady friend? Poor Girl's standing there like a proper eejit."

I swallowed. Christ, this had really gone tits up. It was all wrong. "Yeah, uh, Laura. Laura, this is Aisling, Aisling meet Laura."

"So are you guys married?"

"No," Laura said. "He hasn't gotten around to asking me yet."

Aisling nodded. "Men, eh? Typical, useless bastards."

Like she knew? She was barely twenty-five. "Yeah, well we're not all the same." I had my eye on the bar. Needed a strong drink all of a sudden.

Laura made up an excuse about needing the ladies and vanished. I sat back down and gestured for Aisling to join me, which she did.

"This won't take long."

"I know it won't, Jimmy. I've come out to enjoy myself with the girls, not get into the boring, silly little details about what he wants from you."

"You mean your dad?"

"Who else?"

"He's only looking out for you."

"That's shite and you know it. He's never given the tiniest little fuck about me, ever."

"So why would he have me on your case if he didn't care?"

"You call that caring? Please..."

"You're his daughter. He's bound to be worried."

"About what? For fuck's sake, the man's insane. He lives in a fantasy world. You do know that, right?"

I suppose she had a point. "He is what he is, Aisling."

"What's that, a gangster? Don't make me laugh. He carries on like he's fucking Al Pacino or something. He's totally deluded."

"But, like it or not, he is a gangster. A well known one in this city, as you know, and when someone like him asks me to do some work for him, I kind of find it hard to say no."

She sniffed. "So you're saying you're only following me around because you're scared of him? Of what he might do if you refuse? Jesus..."

Something like that. "Not quite."

"So there must be a reason."

"It's just work to me."

"What's he paying you?"

"Good money."

"Easy money, I bet. Just to spy on me and my boyfriend."

"So you two are an item, then?"

She laughed. "An item? Jesus, you're full of it. By us two, I assume you mean Lukasz?"

"Lukasz Badowski, yeah."

"Yeah, I've got no secrets. Shout it from the fucking rooftops. I love him, and he loves me. That's just the way it is and my dad is just gonna have to suck it up."

"But you can see why he's not exactly over the moon about your relationship?"

"I couldn't give two fucks what he thinks."

"You know, the fact that you're sleeping with the enemy and all that..."

"Sleeping with the enemy? Ha! Jesus, it's like he thinks he's in Goodfellas or something. Sleeping with the enemy, my arse. Look, we're just two young people, a man and a woman, who have fallen for each other. We don't go in for any of that gangster bollocks. Times have changed. It's the older generation who go around playing silly little pricks."

"Is it the same for Lukasz's dad? You think he's an arsehole too?"

"What, Wiktor? He's a really lovely man."

"But you know he's done time for murder?"

She shrugged. "A long time ago. And it is what it is, no one can turn back time. He regrets it, I'm sure. My dad isn't exactly innocent."

"So at least you know they take this bullshit seriously, then. So you can understand why your dad wants me to keep an eye on you?"

"Not really, no. And I don't need looking after, Jimmy."

"Well, your father seems to think so and he's paying me for it so until that arrangement ends, I have to do my job."

"You can follow me all you want. I've got nothing to hide. I mean, what does he expect, exactly? That I'm gonna finish it with Lukasz and come running back to daddy? He can't control me. Not anymore."

"So you find him domineering, then? He find it hard to let go of the apron strings?"

"He just wants me to replace mum, especially now that Siobhan's in Ireland."

"In what way?"

"Do what he says and keep my mouth shut."

"What, he wants you to wait on him, you mean? Like an old school housewife?"

"More than just cook his fucking tea."

"What do you mean?"

"Use your imagination, Jimmy. You do have something between those ears, don't you?"

I saw Laura weaving her way back from the bar, juggling two pints. A drink I needed quickly. And did I just hear her right? What exactly was she implying here, and was she just making it up? I didn't want to probe further, not now. This shit was sensitive ground.

"They ran out of that Spanish beer so I got you an ale."

I took it and drank while Laura and Aisling commented on each other's outfits. Saw a picture in my mind of Seamus and his daughter that I didn't really want to see.

"So you tell him, Jimmy," she said. "Tell him I couldn't give the slightest fuck what he thinks. Lukasz is a good man, a bigger man than he'll ever be. If he's daft enough to pay you money to follow me around, so be it. But you're wasting your time because there's nothing to see. If I were you, I'd milk it for all you can get. I won't be going back home, not ever. He's the biggest cunt I know. There is no Aisling Connolly anymore."

"What about your brothers, Aisling? You not care about them either?"

"Connor is a massive wanker. He's just like my dad. Shane wouldn't say boo to a goose, and Kian's just a little turd in fancy pants. They say you can't choose your family, but you can choose your friends, Jimmy. Never a truer word spoken. I'll be seeing you around. Nice to meet you, Laura."

And then she turned away and went back to the girls, each of whom had been looking over in my direction.

It was only when I was thinking about a bourbon that it occurred to me Claire MacGowan was missing.

TWELVE

"So what else did she say?"

"Nothing, really. Just thought it was a bit cryptic, that's all."

"Creepy as well."

There was that too. The girls had left shortly after arriving and we finished our drinks quick in order to follow, though now that things had changed somewhat, I barely gave a second thought to keeping out of sight. Aisling knew I was following her. There was no point getting stressed about it, although I also knew that at some point she'd get seriously pissed off. I didn't believe her when she said her and Lukasz weren't the gangster type. I would have to tread carefully. I knew not all could be as it seems. I'd planted a GPS device under the wheel arch of Badowski's Audi. Was she aware of that as much of the fact that her dad had me on her tail? Probably not, though I couldn't know for sure. I'd had her down as the type to play games. So, maybe now I had to watch her even closer than I had been, but try to remain relaxed about it. It was easier said than done. I didn't trust her. I trusted the Badowskis even less.

We followed about a hundred metres behind, just far enough away to give her some space. I half expected her to suddenly vanish out of sight, especially when the group turned corners, but when we caught them up, they were always there.

We reached King Street and I caught them heading into The Botanist, a bar specialising in gin. Mother's ruin had definitely had a revival in recent years and there were gin bars popping up all over the place. I half considered setting up home at the craft beer place across the road but Laura wanted a gin too, so we followed them in and I took a seat behind a giant spider plant while she ordered two double Tanqueray.

When she returned, she parked herself comfortably with her head in her phone while I sipped the gin and kept one beady eye on Aisling.

I wondered why Claire MacGowan wasn't with them. Had she been invited and couldn't make it because of work or something? Was she not invited at all and if so, why? I remembered her implying that her friendship with Aisling would soon be over - that they'd outgrown each other - but so soon? I knew, of course, that friends outgrew each other all the time. It seemed just a little bit cruel that she'd been left out while all the others were here having a great time. I told myself that was the nature of the fairer sex. Bitchy as hell. I instinctively knew that Claire MacGowan didn't belong in this little clique, though. In a way, I was glad she wasn't here. While these four were getting lost in a wave of gin bliss and cutesy party girl stuff, Claire MacGowan could be pumping someone's heart or helping someone into the grief room.

I couldn't see her hanging around The Botanist on a Tuesday night.

I wouldn't say it was quiet, but it certainly wasn't busy, either. There was a fair bit of moving back and forth between the bar and the toilet, from Aisling and Lisa Browne in particular, and I felt it wasn't because they had weak bladders. Aisling gave me the occasional sarcastic wave as she sipped her drink, and the girls all laughed hard and whispered behind their hands with their eyes firmly fixed on me.

In the middle of our second gin, by which time I was feeling a bit drunk, I'd sent Laura to the ladies to see what the girls were up to. Laura confirmed they were busy powdering their nose with what she thought was a decent sized bag of the white stuff. At least from her vantage point in a nearby cubicle, the conversation, she told me, was guarded. The girls obviously knew I'd sent Laura in after them. Aisling, I already knew, was no fool. She'd said she had nothing to hide, and I guess she didn't. Recreational drugs like coke were very common these days. Even on quiet Tuesday nights. It was hardly big news to me and I guessed it wouldn't be for Seamus. Both the Connollys and the Badowskis were no strangers to drug dealing, that was for sure. Aisling had probably grown up watching her old man's crew ship the stuff in. No doubt young Lukasz had grown up with something similar. They would be no strangers to any of it, especially party drugs.

I stepped outside the back to smoke on several occasions, but it was only when I went out the front that Aisling joined me. A spraying rain had begun to fall. I supposed I should've expected this to happen. It was the dilemma I now found myself in, the price I was paying for doing Seamus's snooping. I was beginning to think I'd fucked up by taking this job on in the first place. Knowing Seamus, he'd probably have someone watch me as I watched his daughter. Some of his heavies could even be watching me right now. I felt a twinge of paranoia. I was stumbling through this like an amateur. As she stepped up next to me, her beauty mesmerising, I sparked up. Swallowed. Took that shit in deep. She was high. Not quite as high as a 747, but she was well on the way.

"You must be getting bored of this. You know, chasing me around."

I shrugged, took a lungful of my coffin nail. "Just doing my job, that's all."

"Would it be easier if I just called you to let you know where I am twenty-four seven?"

"Probably, yeah." I managed a smile, content that she was only half joking. "But I don't think there's much need for that."

"Confident in your abilities, then?"

"Something like that."

"You do realise this is pathetic, don't you?"

She was pushing it. "Got to earn a living somehow."

"Listen, you could just pretend to be following me. You know. He doesn't have to know the truth."

She was right about that, but I could never know for sure who was watching me. "I can't take that chance, Aisling."

She shook her head, took a long drag on her smoke. "Do you know how hard this is for me?"

"My heart bleeds..."

"I'm sorry...?"

I turned, stubbed my smoke out and crushed it with my boot. "With respect, love, I am only doing my job. You think I want to be following you around? Think I haven't got better things to do than chase up a pair of fucking tin pot gangsters? For another old cunt gangster that still thinks he matters?"

Her mouth formed a big O, but not for long. For the briefest moment, I saw something dark in her eyes. Perhaps it was the coke she'd blown up her nose, but likely not. I'd hit a nerve and she didn't like it one bit. She was about to show her true colours.

"Who do you think you're talking to?"

I looked around. "Don't see anyone else around here, do you?"

"Oh, fuck off."

I grabbed her arm before she could go back inside. I knew this was a mistake, but I'd already dug my hole. "Wait."

Got a fist to my face and a finger in my eye for it and I suppose it was the least I should've expected.

"Just who do you think you are, Jim Locke?"

"Look, if you'd just stay in one place for one fucking minute, I wouldn't have to..."

"You don't hurt women."

"Hurt? For fuck's sake, Aisling, I didn't hurt you."

"We'll see what my boyfriend thinks when I show him the marks on my arm."

I almost laughed. "Jesus..."

"And when I tell him you spat in my face."

"What?!"

"See, I can say anything I want, when I want, and you can't do a single thing about it."

"Now, come on, there's no need for this."

"Then maybe you'll fuck off and leave me alone, eh?"

"Aisling, you're making out I'm knocking you about. For fuck's sake, this is ridiculous."

"There's nothing stopping me from saying anything I

like." She pushed me in the chest. "So you'd better stay out of my way."

"Gladly."

"And if I see you hovering around me or anyone I know, I'll make sure you fucking pay for it."

"Aisling, be reasonable. You know why I'm here, you know I mean you no harm. I'm just doing what your dad wants, that's all. Just earning a living."

"It's a sad, evil little way of paying the bills. Following people around? That how you get your kicks?"

"You know it's not like that."

She pointed at me, sniffing the remnants of that coke up her nostrils. "If you know what's good for you, stay out of my way."

Then she stepped back inside as Laura stepped out, a line of blood on her lip.

"Laura, what the hell..."

"She punched me!"

"Who?"

"The mixed race girl, whatever her bloody name is." She was dabbing at her mouth with a tissue. "Let's just get out of here."

"Did you hit her back?"

"Threw my drink over her. Let's just go, Jim."

I went to step back inside, but she hauled me back onto the street. "Let me sort that silly little bitch out."

"I can fight my own battles, Jim Locke. We're going home."

"She needs a fucking word."

"I know what your words can turn into. We're going, before it gets worse."

THIRTEEN

"Some night out this is turning out to be."

"I did say to do as I say and stay out of trouble."

"She punched me, not the other way around."

"What actually happened?"

She was dabbing at the cut to her lip - Lisa Browne had caught her with her ring - and already a bruise was forming. I felt angry that this silly little girl had hurt Laura, who wouldn't hurt a fly, and yet I couldn't help but blame myself. I should never have brought her out with me.

"She just came over to the table and started demanding I leave, that I had no right to be there."

"What?"

"Exactly!"

"You've a right to be wherever you want."

"I know, exactly. Anyway, she said I had no right to be there, that I shouldn't be following them around - as if I'd be bothered about what that silly cow's doing - and went to grab my drink. Naturally, I threw it in her face."

"Brilliant."

"Yeah, except she then lamped me one. Fucking bitch."

"She can't just do that in a bar and get away with it. It'll be on CCTV, I can try and get her charged for assault."

"They'll have to charge me as well then, because I pushed her on her arse before she could come at me again."

"Then you left?"

"No, I kicked her in her perfect tits. Then I left. Ow!"

Great. Not only had I pissed Aisling off, but her mate had been kicked by a member of my staff while she was on the floor. I'd be surprised if this didn't have repercussions, somehow. The whole episode had given me second thoughts about pursuing the case. I was beginning to think I should just let Seamus know I wasn't up to it.

I grabbed a beer from the fridge and lay on the couch while Laura ran a bath. Flicked the TV on and surfed a few channels, somewhat dazed, and staggered at Aisling's behaviour. One minute she was fine, the next - admittedly after blowing that shit up her nose - a nasty little bitch. It was amazing what that drug could do to people, but I wasn't putting her behaviour down to that alone. A leopard never changes its spots. She was from a family of nutters, and now she was aligning herself with another one. It was nothing to do with me. She could make her own decisions, of course she could, but I knew her father wouldn't be best pleased with how things were going down. And now that she'd threatened me with what could happen if I ever touched her - not that I would - it had become my business to watch her closer than ever. Fuck Seamus. I had to make sure she wasn't messing me around and setting me up for something regrettable. An unnecessary confrontation would be the very last thing I needed.

Although I wasn't really watching it, the American fast food programme I was finding strangely addictive was making me hungry and I decided that ordering in a Vietnamese from the restaurant down the road would do just the job. With Laura splashing around, I phoned through a quick order and switched to the news. Immediately wished I hadn't.

There he was, staring right back at me. Robertson. A respected copper, dead. Murdered in cold blood and his limbs scattered about, his organs removed, his body torn apart. He wasn't just murdered; he was annihilated. Whoever wanted him dead wanted to humiliate him, show the world he was nothing. They wanted everyone to know he was dead. Look at what I did to your copper. This is what I think of the police.

It had all the hallmarks of a ritual killing. Not that I would be going anywhere near the investigation. But I knew they would pull all resources for this one. The killing of one of their own never went down very well, across the whole of the force. It was big news. The media circus had just begun, but it wasn't going away anytime soon.

I lay and thought about what poor Isabella Burns was feeling right now and whether she'd taken a blade to her arms again, all because of what he did to her. Dead or not, I'd make sure others found out about his crimes. It was the least she deserved, though the damage was already done, had already been done long ago.

I paced the flat, smoking. Grabbed another beer and drank slowly as I watched the night unfold outside and waited for the food to arrive.

Maybe it was time to pack this shit in. I mean, who was I kidding? I pulled off my shirt and examined the scar across my stomach. The knife wound I'd received for having the audacity to confront that far right prick, Jamie. I'd already gotten myself into trouble too many times doing this job. Was it really worth the risk just to pay the bills? Thought about knocking it on the head and closing the business down. Give it up as a bad idea.

Yet it paid well.

Sometimes too well.

"So what's for supper?" Laura said, wrapping her arms around me.

I turned and kissed her fat lip. "Vietnam's best."

"I'm starving."

"Me too, for a change."

She grabbed my beer and helped herself. "I'm sorry."

"What for?"

"For fucking up."

"She punched you. You were only standing up for yourself."

"But I've messed things up, haven't I?"

"They were already a mess. I've not exactly gone about things professionally."

"So what now?"

"I was thinking of phoning Seamus and calling it off."

"You can't do that. Not now you're so far in. And the money's good."

"I know, I know. I suppose I just plough on. But things have changed now. Aisling won't be so friendly anymore. She's already threatened me with consequences."

"What do you mean?"

I told her what she'd said outside the bar, how she claimed I'd hurt her when I grabbed her back from the door.

"I should kick her tits in as well."

I was about to suggest that would be a bad idea when the buzzer went off.

"I'll get it," she said. "You get us some plates ready."

We spent the night eating and watching TV, though nothing was on. When Laura fell asleep, I switched back to the news and caught up on events. Robertson was no longer top story, but he was still big news. I only hoped the reporters weren't about to knock on my door, like Fiona had suggested they would. And all that death and mystery had only brought home the death of my friend, Bob Turner, once more. I tried to stop myself from looking at those bloody photos again, but I couldn't. I just couldn't. They were haunting me, those images. I took them as a kind of insurance policy at the time. That was my instinct, good or bad. And now they haunted me. He haunted me.

I cleared up, thinking about recent events and trying not to. Tried hard, as Laura slept, to turn my thoughts to more domestic matters. It was about time I got in touch with mum, even if she was a nasty old cow. She wasn't getting any younger and neither was I. I scanned my phone, just to see if Bill's number was still there. It was still a number I hadn't once dialled from this phone. Perhaps I'd make that change soon enough.

Then there was my daughter, Nicole. It was high time I stopped promising her everything and not giving it.

Family first, the rest second, always. At least, that's what I told myself it should be.

I supposed Seamus Connolly knew all about family and bloodlines.

Bloodlines that ran deep.

FOURTEEN

I took Wednesday off. I thought it would be best to find a clear head to come to some decisions about how to proceed, given last night's events. Laura had developed a purplish bruise on her mouth overnight. Lisa Browne must've hit her hard. I only wish I'd been inside to witness my woman throw her drink in her face. She said it gave her great satisfaction and the punch was worth it. But looking at her now, I wasn't quite so sure.

After my last assignment, when I'd been stabbed in the middle of Albert Square during a riot, Laura had asked if we could just go back to the normal stuff like investigating insurance fraud and cheating spouses instead of investigating murders and other hardcore stuff that only led to trouble.

I was thinking she had the right idea. Except trouble seemed to follow me around like a debt hanging over my head. This time I intended to avoid it at all costs. I wanted to make that time I woke up in a hospital bed the last. I knew what these people were capable of, on both sides. It just wasn't worth the hassle, and I valued my life.

We spent the day doing domestic stuff. We went and did a weekly food shop, spending almost two hundred quid on groceries. The cupboards had been bare for ages, so it needed to be done. I could think of better things to do with my time, though. We settled a few bills and Laura cleaned the flat. In the afternoon, we took a walk out around the city, trying to treat our home like we were tourists. To be honest, I felt like one. I hardly recognised the place. It was currently going through a massive boom, with new high rises going up everywhere. The Northern Quarter seemed to have a new place every month. On the surface, Manchester was becoming a bohemian, cosmopolitan metropolis. But underneath, out in the dark places, bad shit happened all the time.

The Connollys and the Badowskis had their paws all over a lot of it.

I'd have to toe the line with Seamus and grit my teeth in the process. I felt my scar as we walked and told myself it would be easy.

Yeah, as if.

But I was in it now. I couldn't back out that easily.

It was early evening by the time we got home and, having gotten a taste for gin last night, Laura bought herself a fancy bottle and we both sat and ate a curry and drank while we watched TV, or rather Laura watched it and I dozed off. It was almost ten o'clock when my phone rang out of the blue, just before I was about to crack a beer open and watch the news.

"Hello?"

"Mr. Locke?"

"Yeah?" I recognised the voice, but there was something different about it.

"It's me. Claire."

Claire. I didn't know a Claire. "Say again?"

"We met the other day." I detected a hesitation in her, like she was scared. An anxious breath, a stifled sob. "You bought me a coffee at the museum...?"

I sat up. "Claire MacGowan? Aisling's friend?"

"Claire MacGowan, yeah. No longer Aisling's friend, though. Look, can I come and see you? As soon as possible, if that's okay."

"Of course you can. Yeah. Look, is everything okay? You all right?"

I wasn't prepared for the full on tears, but when she burst into a bout of extreme sobbing, I got worried.

"Not really," she said. She sounded in pain. "But I think I'll be okay tonight. I'll be all right. I've locked the doors. No one can get in."

"Hang on, Claire. Tell me what the problem is, tell me what's happened."

"I don't want to go to the police, I didn't want to make it worse."

"Make what worse? Claire?"

"I'll come to your office. I'll be there in the morning. At nine."

I didn't get much sleep, but instead found myself tossing and turning through the night as the rain tapped the windows and the wind blew down the street. I got up twice for a smoke. The second time, I added a brandy to the mix, just for medicinal purposes. Laura, on the other hand, slept soundly beside me, occasionally moaning from the depths of some wild dream. I suppose I must've fallen asleep sometime around four a.m., and I thought it must've been the rain that did it. My mind had grown tired of the racing thoughts, the anxiety of how to deal with the current mess and how best to approach the subject, if at all, with Seamus. In the end I ended up thinking, again, of mum and how the hell she was coping alone out there in the middle of nowhere. Soon after, sleep came. Unlike Laura, I dreamt of nothing.

I awoke to the sound of her hair dryer on full blast and the muffled voices of the breakfast news. Stirred and dosed for a while as she pottered about the flat, naked and lovely but with a lip that had swelled and turned purple. I watched as she slapped her face on, taking extra care around her mouth. I was thinking, as I lay there, that one day I should make an honest woman of her and give up this business for good. Start again in a new town where nobody knew me. Maybe, just maybe, have a kid of our own.

Or maybe that was a bad idea. I wasn't cut out for being a dad. I'd made a mess of the job already with Nicole. Maybe it was time I started to face up to my responsibilities. Again.

We were at the office by half eight and it took several coffees before I even felt half alive. Laura had grabbed us two bacon rolls, but I left mine. Perhaps it was the anxiety kicking in again, but I didn't feel like eating. Seamus's fight night was looming fast and I didn't fancy it at all. And now, after Tuesday night's events, I was even more cautious about how to proceed. It was clear the coke Aisling had blown up her nose had had a galvanising effect. She walked the walk and had gotten silly with her mouth. But I knew I'd have to tread carefully from now on. I knew the Badowskis brought bad shit wherever they went. I didn't want to be caught in the headlights.

When the bell went at five past nine, I knew it was

Claire MacGowan. Laura buzzed her up and poured us both another coffee and set one aside for our visitor. When I saw her face, though, I wasn't sure a hot drink would do her mouth much good.

There was a large gauze patch over her left cheek and one hell of a black eye on the opposite side. Like Laura, she had a fat lip too, except this looked like she'd been hit with more than just a fist - perhaps a sledgehammer or the rim of a porcelain toilet bowl. Whatever it was, it had changed her face dramatically. She had several stitches across a gash in her nose and a cut, like she'd gone a few rounds in the ring, above her left eye.

Her right arm was in a sling.

Laura helped her to a seat on the old leather chesterfield. She declined the coffee but asked for water. I grabbed her a cold one from the fridge.

"I suppose you're wondering why I'm here."

Her voice was slightly watery, like she was finding it hard to get her tongue to work properly.

"Jesus, love. What happened?"

I could've said the same myself. "Who was it?"

She looked away, then down at the carpet. Laura sat beside her and grabbed her good hand. "I don't know. They weren't English. They were speaking in a foreign accent."

"What do you think it was?" But I could hazard a good guess.

"Hard to say. They'd kicked my head in before I had a chance to recognise what it might be."

Laura and I exchanged a look. Poor Claire MacGowan had a tale to tell and I wasn't going to let her leave until we heard it.

"Start at the beginning," I said. "And try not to leave anything out."

FIFTEEN

"**I**'d finished work at five." She took a sip of water and I sparked up. Laura sat beside her, looking concerned. "I went out to Oxford Road to catch my bus - the 42 - into town. I went into the shop first. The little Tesco Express opposite the park, you know it?"

"Whitworth Park? I do."

She nodded. Sighed. She wasn't the same girl I'd met on Sunday. "I was looking to grab something quick for my tea, you know. But I just got myself a bar of chocolate and a drink. Love my chocolate."

"Go on."

"Anyway, it was quite busy in there. Rush hour, you know. There were a lot of people around. Anyway, I don't really know why, but... well, there were two girls who caught my eye as soon as I walked in. Women, not young, probably in their thirties or something. And they just kept hovering around me. Like, wherever I went, there they were, you know?"

"Yeah," Laura said. "Invading your space?"

"Not quite invading my space, but a bit too close for

comfort, if you know what I mean. I was just looking for some crappy microwave dinner and they were conveniently behind me all the time, you know. Right behind me in the queue as well."

"Seems odd," I said. "They make you feel uncomfortable?"

"I'd be lying if I said they didn't."

"Did they say anything?"

"Yeah. They sounded Russian. Or Polish. Eastern European. Sorry, but they all sound the same to me."

I was thinking of Lukasz Badowski. "Okay. Did you understand anything they said?"

She shook her head. "Nothing."

"They say anything in English?"

"No. Sorry."

"Carry on," Laura said. "Or if you don't feel up to it, it's fine."

"No, no. You were the only person I could think of to talk to after it happened. I didn't feel like I could go to the police."

"We'll come to that in a minute," I said. "And I'll make sure you're safe from now on. Just tell me what happened."

She nodded, wiped her eyes, sniffed, and took a drink of water. She was on the verge of breaking down. "So I was in the queue and I could feel them almost breathing down the back of my neck. They were that close. I think they were deliberately intimidating me."

"Sounds it."

"Anyway, I paid for my stuff and crossed the road to the bus stop. You know what it's like on Oxford Road. The place is full of buses, literally one a minute. I saw them cross the road after me and they stood at the opposite end of the stop. They could've got on any bus, but they got on the same one as me. That's when I thought they were definitely following me. I went upstairs and they followed. One of them gave me a look when I sat down, like a grin, you know? They went to the back and I could hear them jabbering away. I was right to feel paranoid. I thought about getting off but then I didn't want to have to mess around getting another bus and stuff and I didn't want to show them I was scared or anything."

"How scared were you?"

"Very. Enough to start feeling panicky, and I know it's daft, I know it's ridiculous, but the whole situation wasn't right. And as you can see, I was right to feel that way.

"Anyway, I was thinking I should maybe say something to someone, a passenger, the driver, anyone. So I got up and went downstairs, but it was really busy. I couldn't even see the doors and I could hardly breathe in there. It was so claustrophobic."

She was breathing now, reliving the experience. But if she wasn't careful, she'd start hyperventilating. Laura and I exchanged a look.

"Take your time," Laura said. "There's no rush."

She took a deep breath, another drink. "So I forced my way to the front and tried to attract the driver's attention, but he was having none of it. I'd just missed the stop at the bottom of Portland Street, so now I had to wait until Piccadilly, near enough. Then I heard them coming down the stairs. I looked around and everyone's got their head stuck in a bloody smartphone and no one can see what's happening."

"You could've called the police, Claire. They would've been able to deal with it."

"I couldn't! I felt such a fool because nothing was actually happening and it could've all just been in my head."

"Maybe so, but..."

"No. You weren't there. You don't know how I could've possibly felt."

"It's okay. Carry on. Take your time."

She was shaking her head, staring blankly. "I just kept my eyes focussed on the doors. It was so noisy, you know. I could feel the blood pounding in my head. And I knew they were watching me. The bus pulled into the stop outside that music shop, the one just before Piccadilly Gardens, so I jumped off and ran."

"I take it they followed?" Laura said.

She was nodding. And now the tears came, in a wave of emotion. "Yeah. I looked back as I was crossing the gardens and they were running after me. I couldn't believe it."

"What did they look like?" I said. "Can you give me a description?"

She sighed. "Not really. One had black hair in a pony-tail, the other was blonde. They were both wearing blue cagoule raincoats. Skinny jeans. God, I don't know."

"Okay," Laura said. "Go on."

She wiped her eyes and blew her nose on a handker-chief Laura gave her. "I just kept on running. I ran across the road and a bus almost hit me, but I just kept going and I believed I was losing them. I didn't know why they were chasing me, I just couldn't understand it. So I ran into Lever Street and went down an alley, one of those places you use as a cut through. Back Piccadilly, I think. I remember a pub ..."

"Mother Mac's."

"How did you know?"

"I know all the pubs."

She nodded, looking absently at me. "And just as I was thinking about running in there, to get away, I was dragged back and ended up on the floor. They were kicking me, I think. In the face. I think they might've had a weapon, but I can't say for sure because I passed out soon after. Or they knocked me out."

"Did they say anything?" Laura said. "You know, when they were kicking you?"

She nodded. Looked me in the eye. "You were right, Mr. Locke. About Aisling. About the danger she was getting involved in. I was really happy for her in the beginning, I really was. But now I don't care about her. She's bad news. He's even worse. It's the kid I feel sorry for."

"What do you mean? I don't understand. What did they say to you, Claire?"

"They told me to keep my mouth shut, but I can't do that now. Especially now."

"I still don't..." But then the penny dropped.

"She's pregnant. Aisling is pregnant with his child."

SIXTEEN

"Pregnant? Really? Well...how far gone is she? It can't be long."

"Three months," she said. "Give or take a week or two. She had the twelve week scan not that long ago. She's not showing yet, but she's having Lukasz Badowski's baby, Mr. Locke. How do you think her dad's gonna feel about it now?"

Not very well, I would've thought. If he found out, it'd send him over the edge. He told me himself he'd murder the bastard if he knew Badowski was fucking his daughter. Well, now we knew for sure that he was. It was only a matter of time before Seamus found out the happy news. And when he did...

"So this is why they beat you up?" Laura said. "Extreme, if you ask me."

But it made sense. No doubt Badowski had put them up to it, maybe even Aisling, too. Claire had said they weren't going to be friends for much longer. So what was going on between them? She'd said they'd just drifted apart, like friends do. Perhaps she was keeping something else quiet.

Something that would've caused Aisling to distrust her with such big news.

A baby. A child with both bloodlines. It didn't bear thinking about. Christ, things were about to get a whole lot more interesting.

"Why didn't you go to the police, Claire?"

"They told me to keep my mouth shut. I was scared. I thought they might still be following me and they'd do it again, you know?"

"So when you woke up, what happened?"

"There were two paramedics leaning over me. They broke my wrist. Slashed my face. I'll have a scar. I just... I just don't..."

I left Laura to do the comforting while I stepped away and looked out the office window at the city outside. Felt my own scar beneath my tee-shirt. I knew the damage it could do to her, psychologically. Finished my smoke and sparked up another as Laura poured more coffee. Women could be vicious, I knew, but a blade to another woman's face? They'd obviously taken orders to 'deal with her'. The poor girl would be lucky to have the confidence to travel on buses or be around Eastern Europeans ever again. Every time she looked in the mirror, she would be reminded of them and the anxiety that came with it. The memory of the event would haunt her for many years.

When the sobbing had calmed, I returned to her. Took her hand. "You need to go to the police, Claire. Forget what they said. Forget the threats, and I know it's hard to do, but they will make sure you're supported. This was a vicious and violent crime and you were targeted. They'll take it seriously. Laura will go with you, won't you, Laura?"

She gave me a look. "Of course I will."

"Would you? I mean, would it not get worse, Mr. Locke? Once they find out..."

"They won't find out. Not a chance. And you owe it to yourself, Claire. You'll regret it if you don't. Reporting it is the first step to recovery."

"Well, if you're sure?"

I nodded. "I'm sure. Trust me. There's a station on Bootle Street. If Laura goes with you now, you'll be done by twelve. Are there any friends that can help you at home? You know, keep an eye on you, make sure you're okay?"

She sniffed, shook her head. "No. I thought they were my friends. I thought Aisling was a friend."

"What happened to this friendship, Claire?"

She shook her head. "Nothing. When a man comes along, it can change everything, can't it? And we were going our separate ways anyway, up to that point. When she met him, I mean."

I left it there, thinking it could wait. I'd managed to persuade her to go to the police, I didn't want her thinking of anything other than that. I let go of her hand and took my coffee while Laura helped her to her feet and gathered some things together. Five minutes later, they were ready to leave.

"Thanks, Mr. Locke. For listening."

"Call me Jim. And Claire?"

She stopped at the door. "Yeah?"

"She's not worth it. If you need me for anything, my door's always open."

Laura blew me a kiss as they left.

Dave answered on the fourth time of trying. I'd been pacing the office with a shot of the good stuff, trying to mentally prepare myself for the fight night. I'd no clue what the evening would bring, had no clue where I was going, and I must admit, I had my reservations about the whole thing. Yet it was too late to back out. I knew my plan was risky, but it would be easy enough to pull off. Once we were tracking a Connolly vehicle, though, I could watch them as they watched me. Seamus had me down for a fool, I knew. But he was the bigger one for playing silly buggers and paying me a grand a week to watch his flesh and blood get up to mischief. There was nothing to report, aside from the big news Claire MacGowan had just told me. A few days ago, I was of the opinion that what Seamus didn't know wouldn't hurt him. But now I'd changed my mind. Because the baby Badowski changed everything. If Aisling wanted to threaten me with what the Badowskis could do for 'laying my hands on her', then I now had no qualms about going deep with this shit and telling the Irishman everything I knew. That was where she'd fucked up. She'd gotten cocky - largely down to the shit she'd blown up her nose - and she'd only have herself to blame. To hell with the consequences. It really was fuck all to do with me. Let the two families fight it out with each other. It was what they deserved.

"Yeah?"

"Dave, it's Jim."

"You don't say."

"Are you still dropping me off that device? Are we all clear and ready to go?"

"Yeah, I'll be on my way in half an hour. Finished work early for the weekend. You looking forward to tonight, then?"

Was that a laugh? "Can't say I am, to be honest. I'm no boxing fan and even less of a fan of the Connollys. Seamus had said there'll be a few well-known faces there. It'll no doubt be full of hard case twats from all over the place. It could be a long night."

"Can't say I envy you, Jim."

"Thanks for your moral support."

"Yeah, well. I'm sure everything will go smoothly. Listen, it's exactly the same as the GPS for the Audi. You still tracing that, by the way?"

I glanced at the Mac and saw that Badowski's Audi was currently moving southbound along the M56. "Oh yeah."

"So once it's in, that's it. Same programme, same everything. All you have to do is plant it. We'll get a good signal either inside or outside the vehicle. Should be easy enough."

"Piece of piss."

"Yeah. And don't worry about the set up. I'll have it all covered. In the meantime, I suppose you need to get your head together, eh?"

He wasn't wrong. It was still midmorning, but I'd not had much sleep. I was about ready to crash on the couch but figured there was nothing keeping me here, so I decided to lock up and head back to the flat. "I'm trying not to stress about it."

"Easier said than done, I expect. I'm sure it'll all be fine. It'll just be a load of blokes on the piss with a bit of boxing thrown in. What's the worst that can happen?"

"I get drunk and say something I regret."

"So keep your mouth shut. I'm sure you'll find a way of blending in."

"I don't even know why he's invited me, to be honest. I mean, he knows I couldn't give the slightest fuck about boxing."

"Probably his way of keeping tabs. You know what his type are like. Pretend they're your friend and all that until they've got you by the balls. Sometimes literally, I suppose, eh? You know, like the films."

"You're full of reassurance, Dave."

"I try my best. Anyway, I'm about to hit the road. You need anything else while I'm out and about?"

I thought about carrying some kind of weapon, just in case. Kept it ticking over in my head instead. "I'm gonna go back to the flat just as soon as you've been, so make it quick, will you? I need some sleep before I freshen up and get my shit together."

"I'm on it. What time's the target vehicle picking you up?"

"Six."

"So easy. It'll be like taking candy from a baby."

"Not so sure about that."

"You'll see. You know how small the device is, Jim. Just pop it under the front seat or something. As long as it's hidden, that's the main thing."

Maybe I was bigging all of this up to be something it wasn't. Maybe I was worrying over nothing. I let him go and fired off a quick text to Laura, just to let her know I would be going home to get some sleep as soon as possible. She said not to bother locking up as she expected to be back soon. Claire was making a statement right then and feeling much better for it.

I grabbed a water from the fridge and downed it. Quickly followed it up with another and opened the safe to grab some spare cash I might need for tonight. The kilo of weed I'd stashed in there hit me head on and I had to go for a lie down, it was that strong. Whoever the Poles were flogging this to must be high as fuck.

I was falling asleep until Laura tapped me on the shoulder. Dave had arrived and was sitting at the Mac. The GPS device was sitting on the desk beside him.

"You're all set, Jimbo. Shouldn't have any problems."

"If you say so."

Laura sat opposite me with a stern face. I was about to ask her how it went at the police station with Claire, but she stopped me.

"Just so you know," she said, "Dave and Maya and me are gonna follow where you go tonight."

"Laura..."

"No buts, Jim. You know these people can't be trusted. Just in case, that's all."

"Think of it as an insurance policy," Dave said. "Laura's right. Don't worry, we won't make it so obvious. And we'll stay well out of the way. The sooner you can hide the GPS device, the better. We'll easily find where you are."

"It's a free country, I suppose. But be careful and stay out of the way. I mean it. This kind of shit's far too delicate. I'll be surrounded by arseholes, as you know. If they clock anything, you could do me more harm than good."

"It won't come to any trouble, love. But after what happened last time, I want to make sure you're within my sights."

"Look, it's just a boxing match, that's all. They'll all be too busy watching the fight to care about me. Besides, I'm a guest of Seamus. The top man. No one's gonna fuck with me."

"Unless you're caught planting the tracker," Dave said. "Then they might be interested."

"Dave's right."

"I'll be careful and discreet. Trust me."

They didn't look so reassured, but I didn't care. All I cared about was some decent sleep and a shower. I told them as much.

"Get your head down," Laura said. "I'll give you a wake up call about five. You've got four hours."

***

"Come on, love. Jim, wake up." I'd been dreaming about whisky and blood and guns when Laura sat on the bed beside me. The sky outside was darkening and I could hear the rain beating down hard. Took a few moments to drag myself out of bed and spent twenty minutes in the shower, thinking that what I'd gotten myself involved in had been totally unprofessional. I mean, Seamus Connolly, a client? What the fuck was I thinking?

Laura had prepared my best suit, a three-piece charcoal grey affair that had been tailored by an independent place on King Street. It was the business. I only bought it to use for special occasions, for times when I needed to look the part. Tonight was one of those times. I particularly liked the waistcoat. Laura said I scrubbed up well and I couldn't disagree. I had to get mentally in the zone I needed to be in, a place where I could comfortably interact with Seamus's contemporaries. The suit helped me get in that zone nicely. I even looked hard. The brown leather brogues finished the look off. It was important I felt comfortable. I did.

"You look almost...sexy," she said. "Like a real man."

"Thanks."

"Can you wear it more often?"

But I was a jeans and tee-shirt guy, mostly. In this gear, I didn't quite feel myself.

"You could've shaved."

"Nah." I examined my stubble in the full-length mirror. "This'll do."

She handed me a beer and I downed it, getting into character. I needed alcohol to calm this mild anxiety I was carrying with me. There would surely be more to come. Sparked up with my new Zippo and took that shit in deep. Time to get my head together.

We walked back to the office in the rain, which I kind of liked. Laura insisted on using an umbrella to keep my suit dry. Like I even gave a fuck. It was busy out, the rush hour at full throttle, and we had to dodge the crowds all the way there. I clocked Dave's Porsche parked around the back, beside the fire escape. The man himself was waiting out the front with Maya.

"Right on time," Maya said. "Wow, Jim, you look... great."

"Gotta look the part, I suppose."

"Must've cost a fair bit," Dave said.

"Gangster clothes cost good money, so I thought I'd crack it out. We all set?"

"Pretty much," he said, as Laura opened up. "Just a case of logging in to the program and activating the device. As soon as it's in, it's ready to go."

Upstairs, Dave fired up the Mac. It was almost six. I waited at the window with the GPS device firmly in my waistcoat pocket. I made sure the metal cosh was still in the inside pocket of my jacket, too. Just in case I'd need it. There was no telling what could happen when a group of men gathered together to watch fists being thrown. Tempers could sometimes get the better of some people. I considered it my insurance policy. It was neatly stashed away and no one would see it unless I had to use it.

And then I saw it. An all black Bentley, wheel trims

included. Privacy glass all round. A sparkling chrome grille you could see your reflection in. It pulled up right outside the office. A persistent rain fell over the city, but the guy who opened the front passenger door and stepped out, his brown suit as sharp as a razor blade, didn't need no umbrella. I watched him approach my front door. A moment later, the bell went.

"Should we buzz him up?"

"No, love. Tell him I'll be straight down."

I made a quick check to make sure I had everything, grabbing Bob's fedora from the desk as a last-minute afterthought. It somehow reassured me and I felt like Bob himself was with me for some moral support. I had a feeling I'd be needing it.

"Remember," Dave said. "The sooner the tracker's in, the better. We can just watch where you're heading and follow."

"Just don't make it obvious."

"We won't," Laura said.

"We can connect to it on my iPad," Dave said. "Maya will be our navigator."

"The wonders of technology, eh?"

"Something like that. Now stop stressing and go and have a good time. Relax. If nothing else, it'll be an experience."

As I made my way down the stairs, I absently moved my hand to my scar. It was tingling, as if it knew I was heading straight into trouble.

ANIMALS

SEVENTEEN

I was met at the door by one of Seamus's heavies, a huge guy with broad shoulders and a neck so pumped I could see his veins popping out. He was dressed in a sharp brown suit and a tailored shirt with cuff links. He was drenched in aftershave and had a tan so brown he almost blended into his outfit. There was a gold chain around his neck, another around his wrist, a Rolex on the other, and a series of silver rings across his right hand.

"Mr. Locke." He shook my hand, gripping tight. It was clear this guy worked out. "Call me Dale."

"Jim. Nice car."

"Not mine though, mate. Wish it was. Drives like a dream. This is Connor's second favourite. Nice hat, by the way." He opened the back door and I jumped in while he returned to his seat in the front. The guy behind the wheel, much slimmer but just as well dressed, introduced himself as Declan. A proper Dublin accent. He had a few teeth missing that had been replaced with gold fillings.

"What's his number one favourite, then?"

Declan laughed. "You told him, then?"

"Just making conversation, eh Jimbo? Mind if I call you that?"

Actually, I do. "Call me Maggie if you want, I don't care."

"Well, his absolute favourite is his Maserati. Now that is a fucking good set of wheels."

"Which no one else drives but him," Declan said. He started her up and while the engine purred and they faced straight ahead, I dipped into the waistcoat for the GPS device. Removed it and discreetly kept it in my hand. "Anyway, shall we get going?"

"So where are you taking me?"

"You'll see," Dale said. "You'll see."

The privacy glass kept the outside world in darkness. I didn't mind. We drove in silence for several miles until we left the city, heading north. They asked if I was looking forward to making some money. I didn't know what they were talking about until I remembered that Seamus said he was planning on running a book. There would be a lot of gambling going on, and I would no doubt be expected to place bets. It was a good job I had a large wad of cash in my wallet.

"To be honest with you, I don't know the first thing about boxing."

"Is that what you call it?" Dale said. The two exchanged a smile.

"Well that's what Seamus said. Some boxing night he was putting on."

Declan laughed out loud. "That fucking gobshite will say anything to get you to do what he wants. Listen. It's not quite boxing, you get me? But I suppose it's boxing of a sort."

"Can't say I do." I had a feeling this wasn't quite what I had in mind. "So we're not going to a boxing match?"

"Oh, it's fighting, all right," Dale said. "But I wouldn't call it boxing."

"So what would you call it?"

"Two great fucking lumps of meat punching the shite out of each other," Declan said. "I think that's a bit closer to the truth, you know? But relax. It's just their way of letting off steam, you get me?"

All of a sudden, I wasn't feeling too good. Had I come overdressed for the occasion? Where was I being taken? And exactly what kind of scene was I going to find when I got there? What the fuck was I thinking?

As we drove, the chatter from the front seats continuing, like they'd been through this routine before, I took the GPS tracker and slipped it under the front passenger seat. Neither batted an eyelid. I instantly felt better, knowing it was hidden away. It was a good job it was there as well because I didn't trust the Connollys to make sure I got home in one piece. I just hoped Dave could pick it up. I needn't have worried because a moment later, my phone buzzed. I took it out and checked the text:

GOT IT! AND WE'RE ON OUR WAY

Dave had a great knack for making me feel better. He must've been just sitting there at the Mac, waiting for it to drop. I just hoped he had the common sense in that techie head of his to stay well back.

I watched as they chatted, clocking their reflections in the glass. Occasionally they asked me my opinion on some such thing, but I wasn't listening. Instead, my thoughts turned to Aisling and the growing foetus inside her. If I was to reveal all to Seamus, there was no telling what he would do. I could inadvertently put her in danger. The kid too. Did I want that kind of thing on my conscience? But then she'd threatened me with 'consequences' if I carried on following her around. Maybe I should just say to hell with it and let things work out for themselves. Wash my hands of it. Trouble was, an innocent baby was now involved. I supposed I had a duty to try to protect it.

I noticed, as I looked out the window at the houses and trees flying by, the industrial estates and the high rises, the suburbs slowly but surely giving way to hills that were climbing ever higher, that we seemed to be leaving civilisation behind. We'd been driving for over half an hour now, making small talk as the evening descended, and the city was long gone, way behind us. And although I was twitchy, as grim council estates turned to green and mud coloured hills, I had convinced myself that I had nothing to fear. After all, I was in effect working for Seamus Connolly, and no one could touch him.

"How much longer?"

"Not long now," Dale said, turning in his seat. "Seamus himself will be there to meet us, I believe. Then we'll leave you to it."

"You're not coming to this thing, then?"

"Yeah, we'll be there. But this kind of shit's nothing we haven't seen before."

"And once you've done it once..." Declan said. "We may hang around for a few drinks, but we've got work to do, isn't that right, Dale?"

"Oh, yeah."

The Bentley rose up through the hills until, when I looked out the window, the sky had darkened further. Now there was only moonlight where the streetlights once were, and the ground outside was a black scar, a wasteland. Wherever the fuck they were taking me, it was way out in the sticks. I half expected to pass a solitary road sign with NOWHERE written on it.

Declan put the headlights on full beam, the glow illuminating the barren fields beyond. I shifted in my seat to peer into the distance and saw the faraway silhouette of an enormous cattle shed, pitch black against the sky. As we got nearer, the wheels beneath us bumping over a dirt track, I could see that the cattle shed simply lay in the shadow of another enormous building with a high brick wall skirting the entire perimeter. The car came to a stop. Declan shut the engine down.

"Where are we?"

"We're here, Jimbo."

"Yeah, but where?"

"Scarbrook Abattoir," Declan said. "Up on the moors. Not been in use since the seventies."

"As a meat shed, that is," Dale added. "I can see Seamus now. So we'll leave you here, then."

"You're not coming with me?"

"Nah," Declan said. "Our work here is done. Have a good time, eh?"

My door unlocked and I stepped out, signalling to Seamus himself as he stepped through the muddying track towards the Bentley. I watched him give a thumbs up and Declan pulled away before doing a U-turn and heading back the way we came. Suddenly, I felt sick. The abattoir seemed to loom over me like a hell house.

"Glad you could make it, Jim," Seamus said. "Drink?"

Seamus put an arm around my shoulder as we walked through the muddying track towards a tall metal gate that was opened to a large car park occupied by expensive cars, pick-up trucks, ramshackle trailers and beaten up caravans. A bonfire burned wildly, its golden red embers blowing around the abattoir like sparkling confetti.

"Not quite what you expected, eh?"

"Can't say it is, if I'm honest."

He nodded and laughed. "It's not as bad as it looks."

I moved my eyes across the scene before me. There were groups of men chatting but not mixing and huddled around the fire, sharing spirits from bottles and passing various types of smokes between them. There was a faint smell of marijuana on the evening breeze and I flinched when the loud barking - coming from three dogs, two Rottweilers and a Pit Bull - filled the air, their snarling jaws echoing into the night.

"I can't help but feel you've played a trick on me, Seamus."

We stopped at the edge of the bonfire. I could feel the heat as eyes landed on me from all directions.

"No tricks, Jim."

"You said it was a boxing match. Gotta admit, I was expecting a warm auditorium, comfy seats, scantily clad women in the ring between rounds. A few pints and banter."

"Yeah, well maybe I bent the truth just a bit. But it is a fight night, of sorts."

"So where's the ring?"

"Inside. Come on. Let's get that drink. My boy Connor's looking forward to meeting you."

He patted my shoulder before leading the way, and I followed, nervously feeling around my jacket to make sure the cosh was still there. I'd made a sensible move by bringing it, but I hoped I didn't have to use it. Two big guys shone a torch in our direction and Seamus waved them off as a heavy metal door opened and we stepped into a brightly lit, white-tiled corridor. There were high walls, behind which were even higher ones, and steps on either side. Metal fencing separated the high ledges from the walkway itself.

"They brought the animals through here," he said, unbuttoning his overcoat. "Can you imagine the fucking noise? The smell?" He lifted his right hand and made a gun. "Bang. Bolt gun, right between the fucking eyes. They wouldn't have felt a thing, eh?"

"I suppose not."

"Connor!" He nudged my shoulder. "That's my eldest boy, about your age, eh? You'll probably get on like a house on fire."

But I begged to differ. Connor nodded and raised a small glass at me. "Scotch or Irish, Mr. Locke? Or are you gonna be adventurous and have both?"

God knows I could seriously do with both. I suddenly thought of my dad and I instantly had my choice. "I'll go with Scotch. Whatever you've got."

Seamus led me over to a wide circular area, a place that had presumably been to hoard cattle bodies once they'd been killed. It had a sloping floor with a lot of drains in it. I guessed this was to drain the blood of the animal once it was dead. A couple of old church pews had been lain against the back wall. Fixed to all the other walls were a series of hoses, probably no longer in use, and hanging down from the roof, a criss crossed ceiling of iron girders, were heavy chains, left hanging in loops. The place gave me the fucking creeps.

Connor put out a hand and we shook. His grip was firm as he looked right through me and handed me the dram. I took it and drank as I looked around, clocking the scene, picking up the vibes. I assumed all the other men that were milling about were Seamus's lot, or indeed Connor's for that matter. Most were big guys, gangster types laughing it up. But then I spotted Kian over in the far corner, talking to a well groomed Italian looking guy. Four heavy set metal heads in biker gear, their bodies covered in tattoos, each one handling a beer. Two nervous looking teenage kids smoking a joint. An old guy in a mack just minding his own business. It was like the weirdest bar I'd ever been in, except I had to remind myself it wasn't a bar. Far from it.

"We'll get started in about half an hour, dad," Connor said, winking. "Should be fun."

It was a pretty gruesome way to be having fun.

There was a makeshift 'bar', if you could call it that, where bottled beers were being handed out and spirits poured. Seemed all this was one big party. I tried to look casual, but felt like a vegan in a steakhouse. This was going to be one long night. Had to wonder what the hell was going on. What was the set up? Told myself I would take things cautiously as the night went on, which meant taking it easy with the whisky.

I was struck by all the pick-up trucks and caravans parked up outside. There were a lot of people here and I wanted to know why. I hovered around Seamus - I was his guest after all - and got to work at finding out what was really going on.

"So, Mr. Locke," Connor said.

"Call me Jim."

He nodded. "Jim. How's that sister of mine? Is she becoming a handful?"

Connor was a big lad, about my age, well built and good looking in a Tom Hardy kind of way. A Manc accent with a hint of Dublin. Sharply dressed and stylish, I could tell he carried himself like the wealthy man he surely was. But there was something wrong about him, something I couldn't put my finger on. Not that I needed to. He was a Connolly, and Connollys were well known to be bad bastards.

"I wouldn't go that far," I said, thinking about how she'd threatened to set the Badowskis on me.

"My dad's filled me in." The noise went up a notch around me as a nearby stereo kicked in. Fuck me, they really were having a party. "I believe she's smitten with this Lukasz Badowski."

That was one way of putting it. "It seems that she likes him, yeah."

"So are they together or what?"

"Looks that way."

He nodded. "And this Badowski kid. I believe you're keeping an eye on things. For dad, I mean. Found anything we should know about?"

I knew the opportunity would arise, but I didn't think this was the time or the place. There were a lot of prying eyes and open ears around and I guessed that such big news wouldn't exactly go down too well. Perhaps I should tell them together after tonight's events. I supposed a part of me didn't want to spoil their evening. Yet I also knew that they'd lose it big time. I guessed no time was a good time, but it definitely wouldn't be now. It was a relief when Seamus took me aside.

"Connor. I just thought that before we start, I should show Jim around. Just so he understands what this is all about, you know. You can bring your glass, Jim."

But I downed it instead, feeling the burn, and handed it back to his son.

"All right, dad. There'll be a beer waiting for you when you get back, Jim. You can tell me all about that sister of mine later."

I said that I would, thinking it would open up the gates

of hell, but that would be none of my doing and not my problem either.

We headed back out the way we came in, and there was movement, also, from some of the heavies that had been hanging around inside. I got the impression these people were more than used to all of this, and Seamus seemed to read my mind.

"We do this kind of thing every three or four months," he said, as the bodies moved in and out. "You know, it's a way for all these lads to relax and have a good time after all their hard work."

I wondered what kind of hard work he was talking about, but thought better of asking.

"We run a book," he said. "It's what they want. The guys tend to come to me with a fighter. You know, they have a kid wants to fight - for good money, you understand, they get paid very well - and they bring them to me to get booked in. Then we pair them off with a like for like weight, just like in real boxing, and we watch the blood fly. All fun and games. No one gets hurt unless they're intentionally being a cunt. You with me so far?"

Sounded like lots of fun. "Go on."

"So usually there's four or five fights, depending on who's turned up. And believe me, not all the fighters do. But if they're sensible, they put on a show. They get a couple of grand for just turning up and taking part, twenty grand if they win. As you can imagine, there's a lot of money floating around and that doesn't include the bets."

"And where do these fighters come from?"

"All over the place. Young or old, experienced or not, it doesn't matter. If they have a good fight and make a bit of a name for themselves, it all goes in their favour. A lot of these boys make a very tidy living from it, believe me."

We were walking back out into the car park. The bonfire was still raging and there were still a lot of men circled around it, chatting in groups. The whole thing struck me as primal. When the wind picked up, the sparks were thrown into the darkness. I supposed it was time to prepare for a lot of punches being thrown, too.

Towards the back of the car park, sitting silently in a darkened corner, was a huge trailer. There was a black Ford pick-up truck parked in front. As we approached, I could see there were two young men inside, probably still in their teens, passing a joint between them and sipping from a hip flask. They were playing hip hop through the truck's stereo, loud yet muffled. Beyond, the trailer was illuminated from the inside.

"So, what's with all the caravans and trailers?"

Seamus grinned. "Gypsies. Travellers, you know? They're really big on this stuff. I'd be careful what you say, Jim. Let me do the talking, eh?"

I nodded as we walked towards the steps. We stepped up and were greeted at the door by a barrel of a man called Patrick McMurphy. He and Seamus embraced like only big men could. I shook when he offered his hand and ducked when he ushered me in.

I counted four other men inside. I must admit, I felt a bit uneasy and out of my depth when they made room for us on the couch. Felt like I was sitting in a box. Seven men, all cramped in, and I was close enough to smell the sweat on their palms. One of them had a vest on and his fists were wrapped in bandages. I guessed this was one of the fighters.

"Don't mind Jim," Seamus said. He addressed the fighter, who was staring straight ahead, getting in the zone, six foot and 15 stone of muscle and flab. "He's with me. You ready for this one, Kieran?"

"He's ready," McMurphy said. "Ready to win, eh, son?"

Kieran said nothing, just sat there limbering up.

"We go in about twenty minutes," Seamus said. "You'll be third on the bill."

The other three men, two just as big as Kieran and the other much smaller and older than everyone, all sat nodding and drinking beer. The older one was looking right at me and I raised an eyebrow in acknowledgement, only for him to spark up and pass me a can. I obliged and sparked up, too. Took that shit in deep, wondering what the fuck I was really doing here. It felt wrong on all kinds of levels.

"Don't you let me down, now," Seamus said, wagging a fat finger in jest. The others laughed. Kieran grimaced. "I've got a hundred big ones on you."

"He won't let you down, Seamus," McMurphy said. "He's been training hard."

"I'm sure you won't, eh Kieran?"

Kieran shrugged. He wasn't much of a talker.

"I'm just showing Jim around. He's a friend of mine, a good man. He's doing some work for me but this is his night off, eh Jim?"

"I suppose so."

"So I expect you to put on a show for your man here."

Though I didn't need a show and I didn't exactly feel relaxed. I took a swig of beer, feeling like I was ready for a session, and thought about how the hell I was going to tell Seamus his daughter was having Badowski's kid.

I guessed there was no easy way. It would probably be better to just let it all out and let him deal with it. Maybe then I could wash my hands of the whole affair and give it up as a bad job. A mistake on my part. Go back to the usual rubbish and steer well clear of crime families in the future.

Or maybe that was just wishful thinking.

"You want to put some money on Kieran here, Jim? Show the kid some faith?"

"Me? I thought I told you I didn't gamble, Seamus?"

"You'll make yourself some easy money. Kieran's an outsider but he can punch with the best of them."

"What are the odds?"

"Sixty to one at the minute but it changes by the hour."

"Who decides these odds, Mr. Connolly?" It was the old guy, whom I guessed was an elder McMurphy.

"Connor," he said. "My son. That okay with you, big man?"

You could cut the atmosphere with a blunt knife. I decided to break the silence. "I think I'll pass tonight, Seamus. I wouldn't know where to start, to be honest with you."

"Just stick a tenner on, make yourself seventy quid."

"Maybe later." But I couldn't wait to get away from the place. Trouble was, I didn't quite know if I was getting a lift back or whether I was expected to make my own way. I gave Seamus a look and he took the hint.

"We'll leave you gents to it, then," he said. "Got a few more things to show your man here before we get started." He held out a huge hand and Kieran shook it. "Best of luck, young man. Don't let me down, eh?"

Kieran said nothing. Nothing at all.

EIGHTEEN

We stepped out into the breeze. Orange sparks blew in a whirlwind and the smell of the bonfire was biting at the back of my throat. The two kids that had been sitting in the front of the pick-up truck were now leaning on the bonnet. They must've been waiting for us to come out because they couldn't keep their eyes off me. I didn't know whether they were deliberately trying to intimidate me or whether that was just their usual appearance, but it was giving me the creeps. They were travelling kids, probably another pair of younger McMurphys, dressed in almost identical tracksuits and gold chains, like gypsy hip hop twins high on marijuana and violence.

"He's always been a quiet kid," Seamus said, and it took me a moment to realise he was talking about Kieran. "But he's a good fighter. Like his dad. Those two cunts in tracksuits are the younger ones. The eldest is a fighter as well, but he's not throwing his weight around tonight. Unless he has to, of course."

I nodded, feigning interest. I decided, instinctively, to tell him the news.

"Listen, Seamus, there's something I need to tell you. I'm not sure you're gonna like what I'm about to say, but there's no other way, to be honest with you, and I think you have a right to know, you know?"

He waved me away. "Maybe later. Can it wait?"

Given that the gestation period of a human pregnancy was nine months, I supposed it could. But I wanted to get it off my chest. "Okay, later."

He put a huge hand on my shoulder. "Good man. Let's have some fun first, eh? Come on, I'll introduce you to Kieran's opponent." He grinned, like he knew this was going to be funny. "So what do you think so far?"

Was he actually proud of this shit? Probably.

"Do you set this up, Seamus?"

"Always. The first was in ninety-two. We do it every year. It's very popular with the lads. And the fighters love it too. This is a damn good living for some of them. You have to remember that these are my guests, Jim. McMurphy hosts an event too. As do some of the other guys. It's a way to make a living. It's just like real boxing except, of course, it's real fist fighting. These are hard fuckers, Jim. I wouldn't want to be on the receiving end, you know what I mean?"

"Do you always hold it here?"

"At the abattoir? Shit, yeah. What better place for a bunch of fucking animals? Come on."

We skirted the bonfire, which had several fresh pallets burning on top, and he took me down into the shadows towards a tiny caravan that looked like it had been towed through a swamp to get here. There was a shabby looking Ford Focus parked outside it, and four black men standing around drinking and smoking.

"Gentlemen," Seamus said, as we approached. Four pairs of eyes stared back at us. "You all ready for this?"

"Yes, Mr. Connolly." An older looking guy shook Seamus's hand and nodded at me, his yellow teeth shining. He had a heavy South African accent, and I guessed the others did too. "Isaiah is inside. He is ready."

"Can I?"

"Of course," he said. "He is waiting for you."

We stepped into a tiny van barely six feet by twelve. Isaiah was shadow boxing, again with that strapping on his fists, and he was listening to some African music, presumably to get him in the zone he required.

"Looking dangerous, my man," Seamus said. We took a seat on the couch that smelled like half a million mothballs had been at it and Isaiah sat opposite, catching his breath. He drank from some kind of brown concoction in a flask - I instantly thought of Aisling's friend, the fitness fanatic Kerry Ainsworth - and eyeballed me. Felt like he was going to put some kind of hex on me for just being here, until Seamus put him straight.

"This is Jim Locke. He's a good friend of mine."

He nodded and we shook. This kid couldn't have been a day older than twenty-one, but he was fifteen stone of raw muscle. No flab on him, unlike Kieran, and a look in his eyes that said he'd have no qualms about murdering you and eating your giblets in a spicy soup.

"Training hard?" I said, figuring I should make the effort at conversation.

"I am ready," he nodded. "God willing."

I turned to Seamus, who was grinning that grin of his, and let him do the talking. He obliged, reaching out with his massive, spadelike hands and cradling Isaiah's rock hard jaw in them.

"I've got a hundred big ones riding on you tonight, my friend. You won't let me down, right?"

"No, Mr. Connolly."

"Good man. You'll make a lot of money from this, kid. I've been to see McMurphy already. A word to the wise. He's slow. Sloppy. Got a head full of feathers and a jaw like glass. You'll finish him in no time. Don't you worry."

He nodded, drank, sucked his teeth. "I am ready."

We stood and I stepped out, suddenly intrigued by how the two would match up. The March night had brought a new rain with it, but it was just a spray and not enough to cause the bonfire any problems.

"He's a rookie," he said, as we walked back towards the abattoir entrance. "This is only his third fight. I'm expecting it to be over quickly."

"Why, is he that good?"

He laughed out loud. "Jesus, no. Kieran will fucking kill him. Poor bastard's about to get a good kicking. But it's all right. He's made himself a couple of grand already and he'll be back for more next time, mark my words."

"So you've not got a hundred riding on him, then?"

"Fuck, no. Do I look like a dumb bastard? This is an easy punch up for Kieran. It'll be over before it even gets started."

We edged closer to the fire and he pointed out some faces. "That's Ivan Zinchenko. Ukrainian." I looked over and saw a tall, chisel faced blonde in a fur coat, keeping warm beside two accomplices. "With his brothers. A well-known face at these events. A champion, no less. Experienced. A hard bastard. Could take two men on at once, easily."

"He looks like he could do some damage."

"And the rest. And over there," he said, pointing to the other side of the bonfire to a group of greaseballs standing around in top coats, "Is Luca Faranelli. Was a champion once, back in the day. Had more fights than anyone. A dirty fighter, though. Breaks the rules. Fucks around. Fancies himself as some kind of entertainer. That's his father and brothers. They're generally good men but are full of mouth. You know? Cocky. Anyway, Faranelli's fighting Ivan tonight. They've been at each other's throats before, so it should be a good one. Wouldn't surprise me if Ivan actually killed him for real. They hate each other."

"Fucking hell..."

He laughed. "See, Jim, I told you it'd be entertaining."

Gotta admit, I was keen to see how events unfolded. I was beginning to relax, just a little bit. But the knowledge that I was about to bring bad news to the Connollys was tingling my nerves somewhat. I needed a drink to calm things. I finished the can the elder McMurphy had given me and tossed it aside, craving another.

We walked back in and it was clear the place had gotten that bit busier. Now I had to stand on tiptoes to see over the crowd, and Seamus pushed me from behind so that we could squeeze our way through. Everyone made room as soon as they saw Connolly. We made it to the bar, or what passed as a bar, and Connor passed me a cold bottle of ale. I was more than ready for it. The volume had gone up a few notches and the punters were gearing up for some action. Nothing like a bit of gratuitous violence to get the blood pumping. I reckoned a few were even aroused by it.

I clocked Connor sniff a good helping of white powder from his car key before turning to a companion to chat shit as I watched on. I wondered how much coke he'd had already. He was talking it up like words were his passion, eagerly pointing at the two fighters that were limbering up in the 'ring', that sloping tiled floor where the cattle were butchered.

"Seconds out, eh?" Seamus whispered in my ear. "First on the bill, Jim. Two kids. They're both mid twenties. A gypsy called Jimmy Joyce. No relation to the great man, by the way. And his opponent, a young Salford raconteur by the name of Paul Sullivan. Thinks himself a wee gangster, but we know better."

"You got money riding on this?"

He nodded. "Joyce in the third, by knockout. You heard it here first. Let's have a seat."

He pointed to one of the Church pews and nudged me over, a ringside seat at the heart of the action. I saw Connor wave as we sat down, indicating he would join us soon enough, yet his expression was unkind. Maybe it was the coke.

I sparked up. Took that shit in deep. Watched as the baying crowd lapped it up. There was money being waved around and bets being tendered over by the makeshift booth at a side wall at the back. Groups of the Connolly's heavies were scattered around, watching proceedings. I figured that not everyone was here to relax. There was work to be done and they'd been told, no doubt, to do it.

"Two minutes until it all kicks off," the Irishman said. He tipped his beer to mine. "Cheers."

I forced a smile, drank the neck of the ale, and got myself ready to see the blood fly.

"Come on, Jimmy!"

"Have him, Sully!"

They were baying for blood. The two fighters were limbering up, staring each other out, getting motivated to fuck their opponent up by various hangers on and friends.

Both had their tops off. No shorts, just jeans or tracksuit bottoms. Joyce was easily the fitter of the two, his torso ripped. Sullivan was slightly bigger, less trim, and flabby in all the wrong places. It was clear who took this shit seriously and who didn't. I didn't think Seamus was wrong when he said he thought Joyce would win by knockout in the third. That would be my bet too, if I actually gambled. I didn't know what the odds were, but you didn't need odds to see who was going to come out on top.

"Who are all these people, Seamus?"

"Hangers on, friends, family. Doesn't take much for word to get around."

"What, and they want to see them batter lumps of shit out of each other?"

"It takes all sorts, Jim. You'd be surprised. Here we go."

The guy standing between them, short and overweight and making a piss poor attempt at being some kind of referee, told them the rules. I wondered how long it would take for them to be broken. No kicking, no head butting, no biting, no gouging. No hidden weapons. Just good old-fashioned fists and nothing else. He rang a bell, one of those old things you'd see in a church or a schoolyard, and bounced out of the way. Several meatheads circled the crowd, facing away from the fight, presumably to act as some kind of security for the 'boxers'. Now that all the squaring up and bravado was done with, it was simply down to who could punch the hardest.

Joyce landed the first blow, catching Sullivan by surprise with a quick jab. The crowd erupted. Seamus shifted enthusiastically in his seat. Sullivan landed one back, a clumsy right hook on Joyce's cheekbone.

"How long are the rounds?"

"Two minutes. Ten rounds. If it lasts that long."

I spotted a few people filming the action on their smart-phones, perhaps to be uploaded onto some dark corner of the Internet. Thought it all a bit too much, but then it all was, the whole thing. Not for the first time, I had to question my sanity. What the hell was I doing here and what the hell was I doing working for the Connollys? As if by extra sensory perception, I glanced at Kian standing over near the edge of the baying circle. He was looking right at me, grinning. Was that a wink? I couldn't be sure because the flab of Paul Sullivan obstructed my view when he was put on his arse with an uppercut.

"Fuck me, did you see that punch!?"

It was Seamus, excited, nudging my shoulder. Sullivan was being helped up by a few hangers on. Blood leaked from his nose and he was forming a lump above his left eye.

"He caught him all right," I said, cringing. I realised I was out of my depth. The violence was making me nervous. I felt around to make sure the cosh was still in my jacket. I sensed something wasn't right and I could feel my scar tingling. Right on cue, my phone buzzed in my pocket. I took a quick look as the punches rained down.

PHONE ME

It was Fiona. There were several missed calls, too. I couldn't call her yet. It was far too loud in here. I expected there would be a break in proceedings soon enough and I'd get the opportunity then.

In the meantime, the bell rang out and the two fighters backed off. Sullivan was in a bad way. There wasn't much damage to Joyce. Two minutes in and I wasn't even sure Sullivan would make the third.

Various friends and acquaintances gathered around him, each one doing their best to motivate him, give him advice, big him up. Joyce just hopped around shadow boxing, waiting for round two so he could land another one on him.

There was movement beside me, and I turned to see Connor park himself a bit too close for comfort. He handed me a beer and punched my shoulder.

"Fancy going a few rounds with me in there?"

"What do you think?"

"Reckon you can handle yourself, Locke?"

"Gotta say, I don't really go in for this kind of thing."

He grinned as the bell rang out for round two.

"Joyce is gonna kill him any minute now. Would be better for Sullivan, to be honest with you. He's fucking clueless."

Even I could see that. Straight away, Joyce went in for the kill. He pummelled him with two fast ones to the nose. Blood sprayed out like water from a burst pipe. He followed it up with three swift punches to Sullivan's ribs. He fell to the deck like a heap of shit. The church pews around me leapt to their feet. Surely it was all over now? The kid couldn't possibly take any more.

But he was hauled to his feet for one last go. Anyone could see the guy was finished, but they wanted their monies worth. They wanted Joyce to put on a show.

"Finish him!" Seamus yelled beside me.

Sullivan staggered to his feet and stumbled into the middle, a splatter of red staining his face like it'd been dipped in paint, his nose flat. The ref backed off as Joyce stepped forward and swung a right hook. It connected with Sullivan's face like a hammer.

Put him on his arse.

Put him out of his misery.

I t was my cue to get a breather. Sullivan had been knocked out and was taken away from the pit - my name for that god forsaken ring - as quick as his mates could drag him out of there. Seamus had said they were taking a twenty-minute break before the second on the bill.

I made my way outside and pulled out my phone. Fiona answered almost immediately, as if she'd been waiting anxiously for my call.

"Jim. Where the hell have you been?"

She sounded worried. "There's not such a great reception up here, Fi. Sorry about that. I'm a bit busy."

"Busy doing what, exactly?"

"A bit of this, a bit of that."

"Come on, Jim. You're talking to a copper. You can't hide anything from me. Where the fuck are you?"

"Jesus, you sound pissed off, everything all right?"

"Well, as it happens, not really. Just answer the question, Jim."

"Well, the truth is, I'm not entirely sure where I am. But I'm with Seamus Connolly. And Connor. At a fight he's organised."

"A what?!"

"A fight, you know. Fist fighting."

"Fist fighting!"

"Just seen a kid gangster get his nose broken. Joyce really put him on his arse."

"Oh, for fuck's sake..."

"Calm down, calm down. It's not as bad as it sounds."

Except I didn't believe myself. I looked around and took it all in as she breathed heavily down the line. The bonfire, the dirty caravans and trailers, the fighters and their entourage. The hangers on getting pissed on cheap booze and the gypsy teenagers smoking devilish weed.

But Fiona sounded like she was outside somewhere and the wind was picking up. And she clearly wasn't impressed.

"You must be bloody stupid, Jim Locke. What the hell are you doing there?"

"Working."

"Yeah, sounds like it. You're drunk."

"I'm nowhere near drunk."

But I supposed I would be sooner rather than later, if this went on into the night. I quickly checked the clock on the phone. It was 20:58. The night was young.

"I'm on the moors somewhere, I think. Somewhere up near Oldham."

"Jim, are you sure you know what you're doing?"

"Yeah. Look, it's not a problem. I'll be fine. Dave knows where I am. He's tracking me. It's all cool."

"Tracking you? What do you mean, tracking you?"

"Not now, eh?" I clocked one of Seamus's heavies looking in my direction. I turned away and sparked up. "But listen, I'm gonna be telling Seamus some news he won't want to hear, so... I'll probably want to get myself out of here before too long."

"What kind of news?"

"His daughter's pregnant. To Badowski, obviously."

"Fuck, no way. They're not gonna like that, are they? Oh shit, you be careful, Jim. Are you sure this is the right time to break the news?"

I'd been giving it some thought during the first fight. I'd probably never get a better time. They wouldn't want to make a scene in front of all their guests. Seamus had put a lot of time into organising this event, as sad and brutal as it was. He wouldn't want to spoil it for everyone, would he?

The news would come as a shock, yeah. But he wouldn't let it spoil the night.

"It's as good a time as any. I'm only telling him the truth. It's what he wants. He might not like to hear it, but there you go. Anyway, is this a social call? Because I've got to be getting back inside for the next fight, you know."

There was a sigh, a crackle down the line. "It's Robertson again."

I closed my eyes and saw him behind my lids as the flames licked at the sky. "What now?"

She paused, but not for long. "They've found another body part, Jim. They found it this afternoon. A council worker dragged it out of a city centre bin. Wrapped up in a plastic shopping bag."

For a moment, I couldn't speak. "You're fucking kidding me. What this time?"

"Not about this. No. Another hand."

"I mean... fucking hell, are you serious?"

"I'm afraid so. A bin, Jim. A fucking bin. Whoever did this just threw his hand in a fucking bin like it was a bag of rubbish from a takeaway."

"It can't have been there long. Those bins get emptied regularly and the smell would've been noticed, surely."

"We reckon it's been dumped in the last forty-eight hours. Which means whoever's done this, whoever's killed him and chopped him up, might still have some body parts in the bloody freezer or something."

"What, so it had been frozen?"

"That's what everyone's saying."

Jesus. Obviously done after his death. Maybe...

"There's one other thing, but it's pretty major. You've got nothing to worry about, obviously."

"What do you mean? Should I be worried?"

"They've put a list of suspects together. Just a short list so far. I suppose that's a good thing. But you're on it, Jim. You're a suspect. I mean, how fucking funny is that?"

M e? A suspect?
    A murder suspect?
It would be funny if it was someone else, I suppose, and I knew where Fi was coming from, of course - it was pretty ridiculous, to say the least - but I had to wonder how they'd come to such a conclusion. Did they really think I was capable of murder? Capable of murdering and dismembering an ex colleague? Okay, we didn't get on and never had done. That was common knowledge at GMP.

But murder?

I managed a laugh, just a small one. But it wasn't funny at all. Fiona picked up my vibes and broke the silence.

"Jim? You still there?"

I swallowed. "Still here. Just trying to get my head around this. You sure you're not joking?"

"I'm afraid not. You're a suspect. You're on DCI Crane's hit list. Don't be surprised if they come knocking at your door."

"But this is fucking ridiculous! Of course I haven't killed him! I might've hated the bastard, but I'm not capable of that, Fi. Jesus."

"I know, I know. But I'm just telling you what I know, Jim. As daft as it sounds, they're taking this seriously."

"But what do they have on me to come to this point, Fi? It doesn't make sense, Christ..."

"I don't know. Probably not a lot. And as you know, no evidence, no charge. They're wasting their time, of course."

"Who else is a suspect?"

"I don't know, I don't know. But you're the talk of HQ, Jim. I should stress that there's only a handful of the top brass taking it seriously. Everyone else thinks it's just bollocks, obviously. Or that they're trying to fit you up, somehow."

I wasn't surprised by it. Yet this was an opportunity straight out of fantasy land. I suppose that, after all the corruption was exposed as a consequence of the Angel case, it was only a matter of time before they were out to get me.

But this was an extreme kind of revenge. It was doomed to fail.

"You've got nothing to fear," she said. "The worst they can do is have you in for questioning. Might waste your time, but that's about it."

"They can waste my time all they want. But listen. Can you get hold of my file? See if anything juicy comes up? That was part of our deal, after all."

"I knew you were going to ask me that. Which is why I'm lying on the couch right now with a glass of Malbec and your file on my lap."

"What?!"

She laughed. "I've finally decided, Jim. I'm handing in my notice tomorrow. So today was my only chance, really. To get your file, I mean. Before they try to go to town on you."

"What? Seriously?"

"Yep. I've had enough. You know that."

"But what are you gonna do? You realise this means I can't pay you for information, right?"

"I know. Don't worry. I've got a little plan up my sleeve. But I've had enough of playing coppers, Jim. The time has come."

"Bloody hell, Fi."

"Hey, you can help me celebrate one night if you're free? I could make you a curry or something?"

Was I hearing her right? Was she flirting again or just being a friend?

"Yeah. Of course. But listen, Fi..."

"I'm not going for a month. I'll have to work my notice. So there's still plenty of time to dig into whatever I can get. For you. I'll be checking my own file out as well, mark my words."

"Jesus, you're a piece of work, aren't you?"

"I aim to please."

"But you need a job, Fi."

"Don't worry, I've got something lined up. It's all in hand. I can't wait to see the look on their faces when I hand my notice in. And this bullshit is just the final straw, Jim. You know I've been planning this for a while. It seems a good time to jump ship."

I supposed it was. It was her life. They treated her like shit and she deserved better. I told her as much.

"I know," she said. "Gotta tell you, I feel so much better now that I've made the decision. I suppose it was always going to end this way."

I clocked Kian waving at me from over near the main entrance. Seems the second on the bill was about to start.

"Look, Fi, I've gotta go."

"If you'd rather spend your time with the Connollys than me, so be it."

"You know it's not like that."

"Glad to hear it. I'll speak to you soon, love."

"Let me know how it goes."

"I will. And remember. Don't shoot the messenger. It is

what it is. Now I'm gonna pour myself a wine and read all about your dirty history, Jim Locke. Enjoy your night."

I was trying to think of something to respond but she'd hung up.

I needed a drink.

A strong one.

NINETEEN

I made my way towards the doors and found Kian hovering in the shadows. He was smoking a joint and handed it to me. I declined, wisely. Sparked up my own and made conversation.

"Kian. How's things?"

"Oh, you know. I've had to drag myself up here just to please my dad and Connor." He took a drag and blew skunk smoke everywhere. His eyes were so bloodshot he looked like a vampire. "Not my bag, to be honest."

I nodded. "Me neither. I suppose you'd rather be out at some bar, eh? Picking up some girl..."

"Something like that. Did you catch my sister the other night?"

I hesitated. What did the kid know? Had Aisling said anything? Did he know he was going to be an uncle? And if he didn't, what would he do when he found out?

"Heard from your sister?"

He shook his head. "But I'm guessing you have. Did you find her Tuesday night?"

Oh, I found her all right. And she found me. "Yeah. She

was indeed out with a handful of her friends." I thought about how Laura had taken a punch from Lisa Browne. "And she's no fool. She knows I'm onto her. You wouldn't have anything to do with that now, would you?"

He took another hit on the joint. "Me? Whatever gives you that idea?"

"Well, you are her brother. The only brother she bothers to speak to, so I'm told."

He shuffled and took another toke. "She's not stupid. She wouldn't need me to tell her anything. And anyway, you know my feelings on this. It's all bullshit. Just a silly game my dad's playing. I'm surprised you're still following her at all."

I was too. Totally. And now that she was carrying Badowski's kid, I cared even less. It was really a waste of my time and I was beginning to see that revealing the truth would give me the opportunity to knock this shit on the head for good. Yet as much as I wanted to tell Kian he was going to be an uncle, I knew I had to tell his father first. I guessed that by the end of the night, none of the Connollys would be very happy. I'd love to say I hated to be the bearer of bad news, but this family deserved all the shit that was coming to them.

"You been putting money down on any fights?"

"I put a tenner on a few. Not arsed either way, to be honest."

I nodded. It's not like he needed the money. "Well, I reckon I'd better get back inside. Your dad will be wondering where I am."

He gave me a look - or was it a smirk? - and said he'd catch me later. But I had no doubt he wouldn't after I broke the news.

I made my way back inside, squeezing through the

bodies as the noise went up. The stereo was now playing Eye of the Tiger, loud and lively. There were a lot of laughs, a lot of bravado, a lot of powder being taken. A cloud of smoke hovered above the pit. Most seemed relaxed, but I was tense. It was the kind of atmosphere where things could fuck up quickly. I couldn't stop thinking about what Fiona had told me, but I knew I needed to focus on tonight and put it to the back of my mind. It was easier said than done. I searched the faces in the crowd - there had to be at least a hundred people crammed in here - and spotted Seamus laughing his bollocks off with his eldest son. Connor beckoned me over. I wondered just who was next on the bill and didn't have to wait too long to find out. The obese referee was back in the middle of the ring and the next two fighters, each with their tops off and strapping on their fists, limbered up as he shouted out the rules. No head butting, no kicking, no biting.

I reached two generations of Connollys and Seamus patted me on the back like I was some old friend. Made me feel queasy.

"Ivan Zinchenko against Luca Faranelli. Seconds out, round two."

The bell rang. A roar erupted. The two fighters met in the middle. Faranelli spat towards Zinchenko and laughed as he backed off and Zinchenko swung. Seamus had said the Italian was cocky. Looked like the type of guy whose bravado could quickly get him into trouble, and it did right away when Zinchenko landed one right on the Italian's big mouth. The Ukrainian followed it up with a quick one-two to both eyes. Faranelli rocked on his feet as Zinchenko bared down on him and pummelled his ribs. Connolly wasn't wrong when he said he could take two on at once. He really was a hard bastard. Faranelli hadn't even landed a single punch yet, but he was taking them like a pro.

The fat referee intervened and pushed Ivan away when he had a hold of the Italian's neck. He backed off, took his stance, and waited for Faranelli to respond. The Italian gritted his teeth, which by now had showed pinkish blood, and stepped towards the Ukrainian. These two had fought before, many times, and Seamus said Ivan had come off the better of the two. I was beginning to think that Ivan would kill him, like Connolly had said. The guy was heavy, muscly. Like a man who wasn't phased by an afternoon's log cutting or bear bating. Like a man who couldn't give a fuck.

"My money's on Luca," Connor said. He handed me a beer and I drank. "He might be an Italian prick, but he's a hard Italian prick. Here he comes."

He was right. Faranelli came right back at Zinchenko with a ruthless uppercut that almost cracked his jaw. The sound made me wince immediately and the blow almost knocked the Ukrainian off his feet. I clocked Faranelli's father and brothers applauding as the Italian laid into his opponent again and again, catching him with a left hook, a right hook, and two swift jabs that seemed to flatten his nose.

Zinchenko stood and took each punch like a man, flexing his bare shoulders and standing his ground as the punches rained down. Except the Italian didn't have enough to do much damage. Just as Zinchenko came back at him with several hard and fast thumps to the kidneys, the bell rang out and Faranelli slumped to the floor, totally winded. It was entertainment, of a kind. The punters were thrilled and the fighters were, too. As both stepped back, getting their backs slapped by various members of their entourage, both of them grinned widely, as if fist fighting was a special kind of drug. Blood leaked from Zinchenko's mouth, but he just downed a bottle of water and spat it out into the pit, unfazed. The violence was raw. Primal. There was an electricity in the air that felt like a storm was coming. The punters were baying for blood, demanded it even. These two would give them what they wanted, for sure.

I turned to Seamus. "This is mental. These people are nutters."

"Don't let them hear you say that, Jim."

"They'll punch your fucking lights out," Connor added, before acknowledging his little brother by waving over the crowd. Kian stepped out and made his way over. Great. As if two wasn't enough. I wondered where Shane, the middle of the brothers, was hiding. Perhaps this wasn't his thing, and who could blame him?

The bell went again and another roar erupted.

"This is gonna be good," Connor said. "Watch Ivan finish it."

The Ukrainian stepped out and the Italian met him in the middle of the pit. Faranelli swung, but Zinchenko dodged it. He swung again and lost his footing. Zinchenko landed a hard jab on his nose. Faranelli stumbled, and the Ukrainian followed it up with two more fast jabs and a hard right hook to the Italian's temple. He slumped to the floor and the Ukrainian backed off.

"Finish him!"

"He's on the floor, dad," Kian said. "He can't."

Faranelli staggered to his feet, with the help of his brothers, and shook off the blow. He was soaking with sweat and blood stained his mouth, making him look like a kid who'd eaten too many cherries. His eyes were wide, as if he was trying hard to focus, and his stance was unsteady. That right hook had almost ended it, but the silly bastard wanted more.

And he got it. Zinchenko struck with a hard left, then a right, and the Italian fell back, keeled over like a sack of 'OO' flour, knocked out. The back of his head hit the deck and his eyes rolled back.

The Ukrainian was quickly pronounced the winner.

Vodka all round.

"So, come on then," Connor said. "What's that sister of mine been up to?"

He handed me a shot of vodka to celebrate Zinchenko's knock out and I downed it, figuring I needed a shot of courage to let the truth out. Seamus was looking at me. His burning cigar reminded me of my old friend, Bob Turner. I wish he was here now to give me advice. No doubt he'd be telling me I was getting out of my depth or that I was playing with fire. And he would probably be right, but to hell with it. I promised Seamus I would tell him what I found, however unsavoury. They couldn't shoot the messenger.

"Is there somewhere a bit quieter we could go?" I said. They exchanged a look. "I've got some news you'll want to hear."

"What kind of news?"

"Let's hear it, Jim," Seamus said. "What's that daughter of mine been up to?"

What hadn't she been up to? "I really think somewhere a bit more private might be best."

They took me back outside. There would be another twenty-minute interlude before McMurphy faced Isiah.

Connor led the way and they opened up a black Mercedes that was parked up at the back wall, away from the bonfire. Connor ushered me into the back seat while the two Irishman took the front with Connor behind the wheel. I watched those flames burn as the dogs barked into the night. Most of the punters were inside, eager for the next fight at the pit, with just a handful hanging around.

Connor handed me a smoke, and I obliged. Sparked up. Took that shit in deep. It wasn't long before the car was filled with a fog. The night smelled like hell.

"So," Seamus said, turning in his seat. "What's going on?"

I took a deep breath, thinking that it was probably best out in the open. I was never good at keeping secrets and this was a dangerous one to keep. It would no doubt do more harm than good if I kept it to myself.

"She's pregnant. A few months, I think."

There was a stony silence and I could see the anger rise in Connor almost instantly. A terrible darkness suddenly came into his eyes, as if he was overcome by some demon. Seamus stared blankly at me, half drunk. His anger wasn't instant, and I could see he was trying to remain composed. He pursed his lips and took a drag on his cigar.

"She's what?" Connor said.

I nodded. Looked from father to son. "She's having a baby."

Seamus was shaking his head. It couldn't be true, I must have gotten it wrong.

"Tell me again," Seamus said, as Connor gritted his teeth and ran a manicured hand down his troubled face. He was just saying 'fuck fuck fuck' over and over again as Seamus breathed heavily until that same darkness swam in his eyes too, as if they were both possessed by the very same demon.

"Are you telling me," Seamus said, his fat shovel hands

shaking, "that he's been fucking my daughter? That Polish bastard's been fucking my daughter?!"

I knew there was no easy way of telling them. The only way was to be blunt and frank. To just let it out.

"Looks that way," I said. "I know you don't want to hear it, but it's the truth, Seamus. You're gonna be a grandad, though."

"Don't give me that fucking bullshit, Locke. How long have you known about this? How long have you known?"

"Since yesterday."

"Then why the fuck didn't you tell me straight away? You telling me you've come here as my guest, knowing that Polish cunt's been shagging my kid, and you wait until now to fucking tell me?"

"Look, I know it's not what you want to hear, Seamus, but I'm telling you now, I'm doing what you've asked of me. I found out what she's been up to and... and that's it."

Connor was biting his fist while his father bit his tongue.

"Then you're no longer required, Jim," Seamus said. He dug around in his coat pocket and pulled out a wad of cash. "Payment. A grand." He practically threw it at me. "That's your lot. We'll take it from here."

"Dad."

"Shut your fucking mouth, son."

"But dad..."

"I said fucking shut it!"

The rap on the window made me jump. Seamus let his window down to find Kian standing there blowing weed smoke into the night. The fog left the car in the March night breeze.

"What do you want, son?"

"They're gonna get started again soon," Kian said. "Just letting you know."

Seamus tossed his cigar and got his shit together. "Come on, Connor. Back inside. You too, Jim. You're still my guest, even though you are a spineless little cunt. I suppose we'd better wet the baby's head, eh?"

Father and son left the car and marched back into the abattoir, leaving Kian standing in the drizzle. I pocketed the cash and joined him. The Mercedes flashed and beeped as I closed the door.

"What's up with them? And what does he mean, wet the baby's head?"

I slapped him on the shoulder. My work was done and I felt relieved at getting it off my chest. "You're gonna be an uncle, Kian. How does that feel?"

TWENTY

Kieran McMurphy was being marched through to the pit by the McMurphy clan, his father on one side, his uncle on the other, brothers trailing back and the oldest one bringing up the rear. Isaiah stood, flanked by his tribe, punching air as the last chimes of Gonna Fly Now by Bill Conti rang out over the gathered crowd. There were bloodstains on the tiled, sloping floor, even though it had been sprayed clean by the hoses attached to the walls. Most of the crowd were now half pissed, and the Connolly heavies were suddenly keen on doing their work and keeping things under control.

I couldn't get to Seamus and Connor, so I hung back out of sight and watched from a spot at the back wall.

Was just as well. Seamus was seething. He stood rigid, staring straight ahead and occasionally nodding as Connor whispered in his ear. The news was sinking in. I didn't expect him to take it well. Perhaps it was my cue to leave. After all, my work was done. He'd said so himself.

"No head butting, no kicking, no biting, nothing but your fists, gentlemen. Are you ready!?"

Ready or not, if Connolly was right, Isaiah was about to take a beating. The African edged the traveller for fitness. McMurphy, although big, was flabby in all the wrong places, as if he'd rewarded his training regime with beer after every session. Isaiah was toned and muscly, with well-defined biceps and solid forearms that could pack a punch.

The bell rang out and they stepped into the pit, fists pumping the air all around them. I noticed that Seamus was now no longer even slightly interested in the fight, not at all like before. He said he had money riding on McMurphy and had fooled the African into thinking so too, so to see him now just staring straight ahead, his thoughts totally elsewhere, was just a bit disturbing. Connor was doing something similar, pulling hard on a beer and flexing his jaw.

I knew right then that Aisling had torn the family apart and had embarrassed her father, brought shame on the Connollys. I wasn't sure exactly how long Seamus could cope with that before exploding.

Isaiah lunged and landed a hard right to McMurphy's mouth. He stumbled for a moment before regaining balance and retaliated with two quick jabs, only one of which connected. The African barely flinched. He shuffled back on quick feet and circled the pit as McMurphy lazily followed. This, I thought, was like watching Ali in his time. Isaiah was far from the greatest. He couldn't float like a butterfly, but he could sting like a bee. Or a wasp.

When McMurphy swung a right hook, the African caught him with three uppercuts that broke his teeth and put him on his fat Gypsy arse.

This was not going according to plan.

The McMurphys quickly went in and pulled Kieran up, and I noticed the bell seemed to ring a little hastily.

They dragged him out of there like he was already half dead as Isaiah jogged on the spot, flanked by his entourage, who were busy with shoulder massages and words of wisdom.

"Fuck me, I wasn't expecting that."

I turned to see one of the heavy metal biker dudes standing a few feet higher than me and guzzling a bottle of ale. He had a God like beard and his face was darkened with tattoos that Maya would be proud of.

Which reminded me that Dave was supposed to be watching and waiting for me somewhere near.

I pulled out my phone, but there were no missed calls, no texts.

"Me neither," I said. Perhaps Connolly's lie that McMurphy had a jaw like glass and a head full of feathers was much closer to the truth than he thought. Going by what I'd just witnessed, McMurphy was no killer in the ring.

I clocked Kian, who was watching me closely rather than the fight. Maybe the news was about to hit home. He knew what his family was capable of. He denied they took any of that gangster shit seriously, but I knew that he knew he was the one in denial. They took it very seriously and always had. And now he knew that shit was gonna go down. He'd said Lukasz Badowski seemed okay, like any other kid his age. I guessed that now he was going to find out if that was still true.

I was beginning to think it was time for me to make my excuses and leave. I was no longer required, guest or otherwise. I looked around for any sign of Dale or Declan, the two of Connolly's men who'd brought me here in the Bentley. They'd said they'd seen all of this before and wouldn't be hanging around. Trouble was, I didn't fancy making my own way back. It would be a long walk to civilisation, and dark too. Gotta say, I didn't fancy it.

I supposed I could call Laura. Get Dave to pick me up. He was supposed to be tracking me, anyway...

"He'll finish this now," he said. I turned to find the biker guy still hovering at my shoulder, and a moment later, the bell went for round two.

I made my way over to Seamus, to tell him it was time I left. I didn't want to part company on bad terms. Yet something about his body language told me bad terms were inevitable.

I was no longer watching the fight, but the noise told me McMurphy was doing a grand job at making a comeback. I looked up just as he laid four or five hard body blows to the African. Isaiah slumped, winded. McMurphy hit him hard, to little effect. The African seemed to have a head like a medicine ball.

I fought my way through the crowd, which was mostly occupied by Connolly's men, in order to reach Connolly himself. I reached out, but just as I was about to tap his shoulder, he stepped away. I watched as he marched off to one of his men and whispered in his ear. I looked over to Connor, who was still flexing his jaw, his gaze lost. Suddenly, the fight night was no longer of interest.

I supposed I could just cut off without saying so, though I suspected Seamus would see that as disrespectful. Besides, I wanted a lift back to town.

There were still a few more fights to go, and there were still plenty of punters and hangers on around, too. The night had seemed to reach a plateau and everyone had reached the point of no return. All inhibitions had gone, and with the alcohol flowing, and the entertainment keeping them happy, I didn't expect an end to proceedings any time soon.

I was standing there thinking about my next move when McMurphy came flying through the crowd and fell right at my feet, his nose flattened and his teeth leaking blood. A mass of bodies swarmed around me and I quickly made room. I couldn't see the gypsy getting back up from this punch, which didn't bode well for Seamus's mood, or that of his family. Patrick McMurphy came barrelling through the bodies, demanding people get out of the fucking way. Most obliged. Meanwhile, Isaiah had been declared the winner by the fat referee, and a strange mood moved through the crowd. The Africans ushered the winner out of the action before things went tits up. Patrick McMurphy was looking angry. How dare his son be beaten. The younger McMurphy was flat out on the floor. It was now Seamus's turn to shout demands and he demanded the gypsies remove Kieran immediately.

No one argued.

For the time being, the noise abated somewhat. There would be a short interlude before the next and final fight. I checked the time on my phone. It was crawling towards eleven o'clock. Maybe it was time to phone Laura for an update. And seeing as a lift home wasn't exactly forthcoming, I thought it best to plan ahead.

I went to step out through the mess, finally resigned to forgetting the whole thing. Now that Seamus had made it clear I was no longer needed, I felt relieved. I was looking forward to spending the money he'd practically threw at me in the car. And now that I was a spineless cunt, for merely informing him of what I'd found out, I was glad to be rid of the silly old fool. Of all of them. It was time to walk away. I'd never work for these people again.

Just as I was leaving, I spotted the kid making his way back in, punching the air as he was accompanied by the older guy. It was the kid from the Polish shop, the one who'd been watching the boxing on the little TV behind the counter the morning I traced Lukasz to Waterloo Road and nicked a kilo of weed from the white van parked up behind it. He didn't clock me, but I definitely clocked him. He was limbering up like one of his heroes, his fists strapped and his gum shield already in.

I sensed things were about to get fucked up. I didn't know who he was fighting, but I didn't give him much chance.

"Locke."

I turned to find Seamus standing tall over me. Tried to read his expression but it was just blank and emotionless. Perhaps something in him had snapped.

"Yeah?"

"You're not going so soon, are you? You're my guest, would be good to have you around a bit longer."

I swallowed. I'd have liked nothing more than to get the fuck out of here right now. I didn't appreciate his attitude when I broke the news. Talk about shooting the messenger. But I also knew it was better to be on good-ish terms, even if he was a massive twat.

"Well, the thing is, I need to get back. Can't stay out here all night. I've no idea where I am..."

He waved it away. "It's all taken care of. And listen. Sorry about earlier, eh? You know my temper sometimes gets the better of me. But I still think you're a spineless cunt."

"Just doing my job, that's all."

He winked, slapped me on the shoulder and ushered me back for a quick brandy before the final bout on the bill.

My scar began to twitch as he walked beside me, and I instantly felt I was making a mistake.

"I can't deny it," he said. I sparked up, took that shit in deep. "It's left me upset. How could she do this, Jim? My own daughter! How could she?"

She'd told me herself that her father's generation had spent too long playing at gangsters and, as far as her and Lukasz were concerned, it was all nonsense. They just happened to be born into families that did take it seriously. Kian had said the same. The younger generation were never into it at all. Were even embarrassed by it. So the whole rivalry thing was never a part of them as far as they were concerned. It was just something regrettable from the past.

But that was not how Connor or his father saw it. I looked over at Connor, who was still gritting his teeth. I also noticed he kept looking at the fancy watch on his wrist. Something was afoot. I could feel it.

"You know what these kids are like these days, Seamus. She's just fallen for him, that's all. It happens."

"There's a lot of good lads I know, from good families, who'd make her very happy."

"But she makes her own choices, Seamus. Whether you like it or not. Maybe you have to get used to that."

He glared at me, and I instantly knew I should've kept my mouth shut. I zipped it before I dug a bigger hole for myself.

"It's the thought of it that gets me. The thought of them fucking. You know. I know she's a young woman and she can do what she likes, but she's still my daughter. The thought of that bastard in bed with my girl is fucking killing me."

"There's nothing you can do. Not now. What's done is done."

He was shaking his head, like none of this was real. "How did you find this out, Jim?"

I was about to tell him what Claire MacGowan had told me, but the noise suddenly went up again when the final two fighters entered the pit. I leaned in and told him anyway, but wasn't sure if he heard.

"Aisling's friend?"

"Not anymore."

"What, from college?"

"They go back a long way."

But then what he said next was lost as a mighty roar raged when the two fighters stood facing each other in the pit. The fat referee shouted out his usual before the bell rang out and Seamus had returned to his son, no doubt to share what I'd just said.

Not that it mattered. All that mattered to him now was that his daughter was pregnant with a Badowski's kid.

I turned back to the pit, but the Polish kid was busy getting battered to notice me, not that I expected to be recognised. The biker gang were going wild at their man, another long hair, who was busy knocking ten shades of shit out of the Pole. The poor kid couldn't even keep his guard up.

When the bell rang out again, he staggered back to the old guy and a few other hangers on and got busy wiping the blood off his face. I knocked back the brandy Seamus had given me and went over to a nearby bench to place the glass down. Clocked Kian eyeballing me as I did so, and shrugged. Didn't know what the kid's problem was.

Maybe he was blaming me too for finding out what I'd found out.

When I turned back, Connor was in the Polish kid's face, telling him to keep his guard up, to focus on getting out of the way. Showing him how it should be done. The kid was nodding between gobs of blood and swilling water out and around his mouth before spitting into a nearby bowl. Sweat coated him like he'd just been rained on. Meanwhile, the hairy biker guy had barely been touched and he was knocking back a decent bottle of beer for his refreshment and having a long blast on a thumb thick joint like it was some kind of party and the band was about to come on.

I looked around, suddenly feeling drunk, and saw that almost everyone else was drunk, too. Or high.

Jesus, this was getting strange.

The bell rang out for round two. I instinctively stepped back, not really knowing why, but keen to make a move. Seamus had said he'd sorted my lift back and I looked around for Dale or Declan. There was no sign.

"Throw a punch, for fuck's sake!"

It was Connor, and it was aimed at the Polish kid, who was now doing considerably worse than the last round. The biker put him on his arse with a blow to the jaw, and I heard a few people scream when Connor waded in and slung the biker through the crowd.

Then he went to the Pole, pulled him by his throat and started punching him himself. Hard. One, two, three, four, five. Connor's fist went down like a hammer and on the third punch, the kid's nose exploded. Clots of thick, dark red blood burst from his head as Connor rained down punch after punch.

"Someone fucking stop him!"

The biker returned to the pit and tried dragging Connor

off, but got a punch for his trouble. Luca Faranelli threw himself onto Connor's back, but Connor shook him off and threw him back into the crowd.

He wasn't done. He wanted to hurt the kid and he wanted to hurt him bad.

Bang, bang, bang, bang. I heard something break, like a heavy bone wet against the sticky blood, and the kid's head slumped back. Connor let him go and got back up, madness in his eyes, blood splatter on his face and slick over his fists. The kid's face had been caved in and the screams went up a notch as everyone ran for the exit. I was frozen to the spot, unable to move. Connor had killed him.

"That's right, fuck off! The lot of you!"

Seamus had pulled a machete from somewhere inside his overcoat and stumbled into the pit, swinging it around like it was nothing more than a bottle of fizz he was about to crack open.

Someone shouted out that Connor was a murdering bastard, and it was true. There was no doubting what we'd just witnessed. He'd just battered the kid to death, and I looked at him lying there on that cold tiled floor, his face painted crimson, his vest soaking wet with it, his mouth a gaping hole. He was dead all right. The kid was dead.

Seamus stepped forward, circling the pit and defending his son like the deranged father he was. "Everyone out! Get the fuck out!"

The abattoir emptied in minutes as Seamus bawled at everyone, his son included. My heart was pounding as I fought my way towards the doors. I heard the Connollys shouting after me to come back, but there was no fucking way I was going back. I felt for my cosh. It was still there and I removed it, holding it tight as I tried to disappear into the crowd.

"Locke! You come the fuck back here!"

I backed into an alcove and took out my phone. Opened the camera app and started filming the chaos. I could see Seamus still circling the pit through the departing crowd, swinging that machete like a fucking madman, his teeth bared, the knuckles on his massive hands bone white. Connor had by now slumped to the floor, head in his hands, no doubt knowing he was fucked and he'd just started a war that might never end. Seamus clocked me filming and ran after me on his knackered old legs. I pocketed the phone and ran for the darkness I hoped would swallow me.

I spun out into the night, dizzy and disoriented, and ran for the huge metal gates Seamus had led me through earlier. There was a lot of commotion. The air was filled with a certain kind of dread as numerous engines fired up and the punters scarpered in all directions, a selection of languages all saying the same thing: let's get the fuck away from here as fast as possible.

I understood their fears. I chanced a look back and recognised one of Seamus's heavies pounding his way through the muddied entrance, with Seamus in tow behind. He was still gripping that blade, still had that venom in his eyes. I didn't bother wasting any time wondering if it was me he was coming for, just turned back and pelted it on my pissed up legs.

I went on my arse twice but got straight back up when I heard the dogs barking. Someone had released them from the cages and fuck knows where they were right now. I wasn't hanging around to find out.

I made it to the gate, the bonfire still raging behind me, and saw the Bentley I'd arrived in speed right past. There were two figures in the car, probably Dale and Declan, though I couldn't be sure as they were just silhouettes in the already dark privacy glass. It meant nothing now, and my lift home was gone. The only option was to keep running until I was swallowed by the darkness out on the moors.

I reached the dirt track I was pretty certain brought me up here and headed west, downhill. Several expensive cars sped past me and I instinctively dived into a ditch at the side of the road. Kept my head down and waited as the vehicles followed each other into the night, their headlights on full beam, which was a blessing. I looked down into the valley in an effort to cement the image on my mind, to give me something to go off for the journey ahead. God knows where I was or where I was heading. I only hoped I'd be able to get a phone signal somewhere up here. I knew that being in the middle of nowhere had a tendency to fuck with your technology. It was times like this I wish I'd picked another career. If I could phone Laura, they'd be able to find me. I rummaged around in my jeans, but my phone wasn't there.

Let out a breath when I found it in the inside pocket of my suit jacket. The cosh was still there, too.

I composed myself, standing out there on the moors, the torch on my phone illuminating the ground at my feet. I sparked up. Took that shit in deep. I only had four smokes left and if I wanted more before morning, I knew I needed to get off this fucking mountain. As I stood, smoking and catching my breath, I heard voices tumbling down the hill after me. And engines too. I knew I needed to get away from this dirt track, get somewhere the average vehicle couldn't go.

I stumbled out into the pitch black, with nothing but the light from my phone to guide the way. I lifted it to my ear and dialled up Laura.

Didn't even fucking ring. No reception, no nothing.

The only thing I could do was keep walking into the night. It could be a long one, though I kept telling myself I'd make it to sunrise without fucking up even more. Was I a dumb bastard for filming Seamus with that machete? No doubt about it. I stood out there under that black sky and played it back as a few headlight beams moved down the hill. I figured I would stay as close as possible to that track without being seen, though I knew it would be difficult.

That old Irish bastard was swinging that blade like he meant it. Of what I captured, which was no more than ten seconds, maximum, I knew it was enough to fuck him up. His son had just battered a kid to death and there had been multiple witnesses. There was no way he could keep this quiet.

I thought about the kid, back there lying on that cold white floor, his blood soaking into the tiles or being washed away by those hoses as they bagged him up. Thought about the booze Seamus and Connor would be slinging down their necks or smashing in anger in that abattoir. That pit of hell. Death came cheap to these bastards. But now they would have to clean up the mess.

I shivered and pulled hard on my smoke when I spotted how much battery I had left. It was down to 7%. I turned it off and pocketed it, knowing I might need it eventually. But for now I stumbled into the black, with only the occasional glow of blue moonlight to guide my way.

BLOODLINES

TWENTY ONE

I didn't know how long I'd been walking, but it was long enough. Stumbling out into the darkness, I lost all sense of direction very quickly until it felt like I was in some wild dreamscape with no civilisation in sight. All I knew was that I was somewhere high above Oldham, out in the hills, where nothing grew and only ravens flew. Somewhere out there, the city thrived. But I was a long way from home and I knew I was vulnerable. The temperature had dropped quickly, and I'd spent the last ten minutes just focussing on moving to keep the chill at bay. At least it had sobered me up, but a warm fire and a large brandy would be more than welcome right now. I'd rationed the smokes I had left and stopped to spark up. Raised my gaze skywards and saw no stars. The cloud must've been heavy because I hadn't had that moonlight to guide me for a while now. I was out here alone. I had to keep my wits about me. I'd almost gone over on my ankle twice already and if I wasn't careful, an injury could keep me out here indefinitely.

I switched the phone on. It was well gone midnight but I still had just 7% battery. I knew I had to preserve it and if I needed to use it, to use it wisely. There was still no signal. So much for 5G. I looked around, but there was nothing but moorland as far as I could see, except the faint glow on the horizon of what I thought might be the city lights. I stepped towards it, figuring it was as good a choice as any. But it was the only realistic direction I could take. There was no other choice.

I went over the events of the night. The Polish kid. Had he been an acquaintance of the Badowskis? I'd traced Lukasz's Audi to Cheetham Hill, just within spitting distance of that shop with the cannabis farm upstairs. Had exchanged a few words with him as he shadow boxed to the action on that tiny TV. The kid had obviously had big dreams of one day being a fighter, like his heroes. And now it had all been taken away after Connor had brutally taken his life with his bare hands. Had I just witnessed the beginning of something big? The beginning of a new war between the families? When word got back to the Polish, as it surely would, it would only be a matter of time before it all kicked off.

I was glad I was out of it now.

Or maybe that was wishful thinking.

I was worried about what Connolly would do. What his son would do. I knew I had devastating material on my phone and it was like carrying a hot potato. I wanted rid of it before it brought me more than I bargained for.

I took it out and went to launch it into the peat surrounding me.

Then stopped.

It would be a foolish thing to get rid of now. Maybe I could just delete what was on it, the damning stuff, and forget about it. Forget I'd ever seen what I did. Forget I'd ever recorded it like the fucking Spielberg I stupidly thought I was.

What had been going through my mind to even think about taking that risk?

My breath fogged the air. I was losing the feeling in my feet. The only sound out here was the ever present wind and my footfalls on the earth. So it came as a shock when the explosion rocked that very earth I walked on and a fireball illuminated the sky, followed quickly by a massive plume of smoke. Distant voices echoed through the surrounding hills, and for the briefest of moments, the sky lit up. I was too far away to feel any heat, but whatever had sent the abattoir up must've been powerful enough to really blow it apart.

A second explosion tore through the night.

"Fucking hell."

There was nothing I could do, not that I would. Let it burn. It should've burnt long ago.

The question was, had anyone been left inside? Would they have left the body of the kid before they torched it? Maybe. More likely not. I could only guess that they let it blow to cover any evidence of a murder inside. There had been a lot of blood in that pit. They couldn't have just abandoned it and left it at that.

I expected the police had known about Seamus's place, anyway. They had to have known, surely. It was out in the middle of nowhere, sure, but nothing stayed out in the middle of nowhere for people to access unless it was being used for something. So GMP must've known about it and turned a blind eye. Let the Connollys get away with it like they'd gotten away with all the other shit over the years. The Connollys had stuff on the police, I knew. They scratched each other's back all the time. I just didn't know the detail. I was hoping Fiona could come up with something on that score, but so far, not. And now that she was resigning, any further information wasn't likely either.

I turned away from the smoke plume and walked on, noticing that I was gradually moving down a sloping hill. As I walked, I listened. Listened out for those voices I was hearing, faint in the distance. Couldn't make anything out except that they were animated and lively.

And then I heard engines. The thrum of powerful cars being revved up, getting ready to do their work.

And the dogs too.

The dogs were barking like they were keen to get running.

I tossed what was left of my smoke and picked up pace, hoping to fuck those Rottweilers couldn't smell me on the night breeze.

I ran out on uneven ground, wishing I'd never gotten involved in any of this shit in the first place. Thing was, my work was now done. But I knew I'd made a balls up of things back there. Seamus had wanted to know more details and I couldn't give him any. And now that he'd clocked me filming him swinging that machete around after his son had battered a Polish kid to death, I knew he'd come looking for me, or at least send his boys looking for me. Connolly, I knew, didn't believe in not shooting the messenger. And now that he was getting old, he cared less and less about the consequences. It was a dangerous mix.

I stumbled and tripped, and this time my ankle went. I must've twisted it on a knot in the ground and I almost ended up twisting my knee too. Instead, I fell face forward and tumbled into the earth. My knee caught a rock as I fell and I yelped in pain. I rolled over onto my back, feeling a shot of agony race up my leg as the world spun out of control and fell down a steep embankment that had seemed to spring up from nowhere. My face smacked the ground several times and I tasted wet soil as well as smelt it. I continued to roll until I hit a rock with a thud, which winded me like I'd just been kicked hard in the balls. When I came to, I rolled onto my side and saw a blur of lights ahead, down in the valley.

The city.

Home.

I saw headlights first, a beam rolling in like I dreamt it. A slam of car doors and then voices.

"Is it him?"

"I don't know. I don't know."

"Turn him over."

"But what if it's not?"

"Do it."

"What?"

"Do it now."

I could smell that powerful aroma of green weed with the sweet tang of warm brandy as a pair of arms dragged me up from the dirt. My head swam and I doubled over to get my breath, but expected a kicking.

It didn't come.

By now, I'd clocked there were two voices, gypsies if ever I heard them, but I couldn't see the faces because the headlights were shining right on me.

I didn't need to. The hip hop beats coming from the car - which I now guessed was the pick-up truck from earlier - were muffled despite the open doors. Maybe the kids thought they couldn't be too careful and had kept the sound deliberately low to avoid attention. Right on cue, the lights were dimmed and their faces were no longer silhouettes, but clear in the low light.

"We thought you'd get lost out here alone," one of them said. He had a thick gold chain choked around his throat, his voice a harsh Irish, the words tumbling from his mouth at a hundred miles an hour. "Not a good thing on a night like this, you know?"

"We wasn't sure it was you, but you'd better come with us now so we can get you off this fucking moor before someone else gets you off it, you know."

I nodded, a bit dazed and more than confused, and let them lead me into the back of the pick-up. I sat there, thinking that this was either going to be a monumental mistake and I'd be robbed, beaten and possibly buggered, or they'd take me to safety like two knights in shining armour and I'd be left owing them big time.

"Smoke?"

"Don't mind if I do." I sparked up. Took that shit in deep. The two got back in and turned the volume further down on the stereo. Judging by the smell in here, I figured they must spend most of their time caning weed. Maybe I'd found two willing customers for the kilo bag in my office safe.

"Connolly's a fucking nut job, eh?"

It was one way of putting it. "He's a loose cannon," I said. "You know him well?"

"Nah." He put her into gear and manoeuvred over half a dozen large potholes. "My dad knows him well enough, like."

"Your dad?"

"Patrick McMurphy. I'm his son, Shaun."

"Kieran your brother, then?"

He nodded. "This here is my cousin, Finian. Hope we didn't scare you there, man."

Finian, who had taken the passenger seat, had sparked

up a joint and filled the pick-up with potent blue smoke. "Did you see what we saw, Mr. Locke?"

"So you know me?"

"Know of you. And why you know Seamus Connolly."

"You can't keep anything a secret these days."

"Word gets around," Finian said. "Not that any of us lot give a fuck, you know?"

"You working for him, then?"

"Not anymore," I said. "Surplus to requirements."

"Any idea what happened back there? Connor went fucking mental for no reason, eh?"

I guessed he lost it because the kid was Polish, not because he was getting beaten in the fight with the biker. No doubt as he was smashing his face in, he imagined it was Lukasz Badowski's and not the kid's. I doubted Connor wanted to go as far as he did, but I supposed he didn't know his own strength, the power in his own punches. Punches that could kill a man easily. It was without question that, pound for pound, Connor outweighed the kid massively. Combined with the fact that he'd lost all sense completely, it was an accident waiting to happen. And now they had to clear up the mess, get rid of any evidence, and make sure everyone who witnessed it kept quiet.

Like that was going to happen.

"I suppose he's the mental type, eh?"

"I wouldn't let him hear you say that," Finian said.

"Know something I don't?"

"Just, you know... he's a massive prick."

"Right."

"Could go off his head again, like."

I nodded. These kids were smarter than they looked.

The pick up picked up and bounced over the clumpy ground, bouncing me with it. They were as good as their word and headed through the darkness, away from the plume of smoke and the chaos behind us and ever closer to those city lights. The truck dipped and dropped as Shaun spun the wheel like a pro and pretty soon we were back on some kind of road, albeit a rocky one, before gunning it downhill towards civilisation.

"We'll drop you on the edge of Oldham," Shaun said over the noise. The engine roared and the truck rattled so hard over the rocky track I thought I was gonna lose my teeth. "You should be safe enough from there."

"For now," Finian said. "You never can be sure."

I guessed he was right. But once I was near people and buildings, I could easily blend in. For the rest of the night, I could get myself home, even if it meant walking. Once I had a basic idea of where I was, the rest was easy.

I took out my phone and switched it back on. 5%. It was enough to make a call, but I still couldn't get a signal. It would hold out for an hour at least, for sure.

We dropped down into a forest of evergreens, the darkness claustrophobic, finally relieved at leaving the moor behind. The darkness in here was so deep it felt like the pick-up had been swallowed by a whale. The road veered to the right and we descended down a steep hill, smooth with tarmac, and as we reached the bottom, I could finally see streetlights and road paint through the trees.

We pulled a sharp left at the junction and Shaun brought the pick-up to a stop at the roadside just within spitting distance of the pub. The White Lion had closed up for the night. Shame. I could really murder that warm brandy.

He let the engine run as he turned and gave me the nod. "Will this do you?"

A lift into town would've been better, but I couldn't be

ungrateful. "That's great. Thanks. It's appreciated and I won't forget that."

Finian nodded. "It's not a problem. We couldn't have left you out there all night."

"You took a nasty fall there," Shaun said.

"You saw it?"

"Oh yeah," Finian said. "Understandable."

"You okay?"

I waved it away. "It's nothing." But I supposed I'd find out when I started walking. My ankle must've twisted, but I didn't think it was that bad. "I just need to get back home and rest, that's all."

"You'll make it okay?"

I checked my phone. Still no signal. "I think so."

"Nah, you'll be right," Finian said. "There's a tram stop about half a mile up the road. You might catch the last one."

I doubted it. The long walk would do me good.

I said my goodbyes and made sure they knew I was grateful. Told them I would return the favour and repay them someday. They shrugged it off and Finian sparked up his joint. Then they did a U-turn and drove off uphill, out towards the Moors again.

I stood in silence for a moment before turning back towards Oldham. Fuck knows exactly where I was. I took out my phone and tried to determine my location. There was still no signal, no 5G. I didn't recognise the area but guessed if I walked towards the town centre, it would all become clear.

I sparked up, down to my last two smokes, and started walking. I should've asked for something to tide me over in the pick-up but I guessed that would be taking the piss. A lift off that fucking moor was enough. My ankle felt sore and was probably swollen, but I reckoned I'd be okay if I put it out of my mind.

The night was cold and damp. There wasn't a soul around that I could see. The pubs were shut; the restaurants had kicked their patrons out hours ago. As I walked, aware of my breath and the shuffle of my feet, I knew I was getting tired. I just wanted my bed, preferably with Laura in it. It seemed like ages since I'd left my office. Checked my phone again and it was down to 3%. Still no signal. I'd surely never get in touch now and I'd decided that a walk would do me good. Clear my head and give me some long overdue exercise.

Yet my ankle wasn't allowing me to walk easily. The alcohol I'd drunk tonight had been a convenient anaesthetic, but I knew that once the booze had worn off, the pain would flare up.

I'd had worse injuries. I absently felt my scar and it tingled beneath my shirt. I still knew I was very lucky to be here. I couldn't complain.

But my decision making left a lot to be desired. I'd made the grave mistake of getting involved with the Connollys and I knew I would never really escape them now unless I gave up what I had. Perhaps I'd never escape them even then. But like the shit Fiona and I had on Robertson, the footage I had on my phone was gold - if it ever got into the right hands. Trouble was, I didn't know who those hands belonged to.

I shuddered at the thought of what Seamus would've done if I'd have returned to him in that abattoir. What he'd have done with that blade he was swinging around. Maybe I'd have ended up going out in flames too, right after he'd cut me up.

I wouldn't put anything past those bastards. What he'd

wanted from me was work, yes. Work I'd have been stupid to turn down. Easy money. But I should've known that it would come at a price.

And now that Aisling's secret was out, what would become of her and Lukasz Badowski? Of their unborn child? Seamus had relieved me of my duties, yeah, but I still had a duty. And a conscience.

Maybe that was where my own power lied.

I walked on into the early hours of Friday morning, in empty streets where shadows were long, making sure that with every step, there wasn't a Connolly following.

TWENTY TWO

I kept walking until I got tired and sat down on a bus stop bench, sheltered from the steady flow of rain that had come in from the east around three a.m. I figured I was near the town centre because the buildings had gotten steadily bigger as I'd approached, yet by now the night had quietened. It wasn't quite the weekend, but it was close enough and there would've been plenty of mostly full pubs and bars on a Thursday night in these parts. I sat and watched the odd group of late night revellers stumbling their way through the town centre, thankful that I was away from that moor. And I remembered sitting down and watching the rain, thinking it might be a good idea after all to have that one last smoke, and I'd checked my phone, which had finally died, before resting my head on that cold bench until I fell asleep and dreamt of blood and fire.

It was a school kid that woke me, a random little guy with NHS specs and a canvas satchel wrapped around his grey blazer. He'd been throwing monster munch in my face and when I sat up, letting out a breath I must've been keeping in like a member of the undead, he backed off a little scared, keeping me at a safe distance. His bus pulled up, its diesel fumes choking the morning, and I choked with it.

I watched the kid get on board, then sat upright and turned to face the sun breaking through the grey cloud. A young woman stepped in to the bus shelter moments later and I asked her the time. She looked at me like I'd just asked her if she fancied a quick fuck or something, before telling me, with a face liked a smacked arse, that it was nearly seven o'clock. I was going to ask her for a spare smoke but thought better of it and staggered off, my legs aching, to the nearest newsagents. Bought a pack of twenty and sparked up. Took that shit in deep. It was promising to be a long day.

My phone was still dead. There was nothing I could do but catch a bus myself, back into town and home.

I ended up on an 83 about ten minutes later, busy with commuters into work. It would be at least forty minutes into the city centre, so I sat at the back so the engine could keep me warm and allowed my gaze to get lost in the world outside and my thoughts to drift on an ocean of nothingness.

When we reached the final stop, some guy nudged me awake and I groggily alighted into the crowded streets, craving coffee. I fumbled around for change and grabbed an espresso and a bacon sandwich before making the short walk to the flat in Ancoats. I polished off the sandwich just as I unlocked the door. Found Laura lounging on the couch and she didn't look happy.

"Where the hell have you been? I've been worried bloody sick, Jim!" She jumped up off the couch and threw her arms around me. "Why haven't you been in touch? Why haven't you answered my calls? Jesus..."

"Phone's dead. Couldn't get a signal."

"Look at the state of you. You need a shower."

"I know, I know."

"But how did it go? Was it okay?"

"I'll tell you everything later," I said, making my way to the bathroom. "I need to sleep first. I'm so tired, love. So fucking tired..."

She let me go as the breakfast news chattered away on the TV. It was almost six hours later when I could finally summon the energy to talk.

I found her still sitting on the couch with a laptop across her legs and a half eaten cheese toastie on the arm. There was a steaming hot mug on the coffee table and there was still coffee in the pot on the kitchen side. I poured my own, then joined her.

I told her everything, from how I got home to what happened at the abattoir, fist fights included. If she was surprised, it didn't show. I'd come to expect this reaction. Laura had seen me get involved in worse situations and had no doubt become accustomed to it.

"So that's it, then? Job done?"

I shrugged. "Seamus told me my services were no longer required. A polite way of saying I was sacked."

"But none of it's your fault, is it? That she's pregnant, I mean?"

"I've only got eyes for you, love."

"You know what I mean. You just did your job. Gave him what he wanted. What's his problem?"

"I think he's pissed off because he reckons I should've told him sooner, like straight away."

"Not as easy as that though, eh?"

I shook my head. "I reckon he thinks I've been fucking him around, you know. Being selective with the truth..."

"And have you?"

Maybe just a bit. But it hardly mattered. Aisling had still gotten pregnant, and she was still having Lukasz Badowski's kid. Bloodlines on both sides had now been compromised and corrupted. I knew that's what bothered the Connollys more than anything. They weren't happy she was seeing him in the first place, but this?

It was their worst nightmare.

"So what happens now?"

"Well, nothing. Case closed. We're no longer required."

"I meant with the footage. That's evidence of some serious wrongdoing, Jim."

"Don't I know it."

"It could get you in trouble."

"I know that too."

"Get rid of it, Jim. I don't like it. It's making me nervous already."

But I didn't think it was a good idea - yet. The least I could do was get a copy of it before I made any rash decisions. As much as I wanted it out of sight and out of mind, to launch it into the abyss, I knew it was important I kept hold of it as an insurance policy. I'd acted on instinct, just like I always do, when I took that phone from my pocket and filmed. I must've subconsciously known there was an important reason for doing so. I mean, Connor Connolly had practically killed a man with his bare hands and there had been lots of witnesses to it. I didn't believe I was the only one with footage of the aftermath - the punters fleeing, Seamus swinging that machete - but I guessed I must've been the only one with a deep connection to the Connollys. Fuck, I was even on the payroll, although technically speaking, I hadn't been at that point. Seamus wouldn't have seen it that way, though. He'd have seen it as a betrayal, a kick in the teeth.

Fuck him.

"Has he paid you?"

I dropped a grand on the table and told her to take her share. Her eyes practically lit up.

"I suppose we'd better get back to work," I said. "Proper work, I mean."

"There's been a few enquiries. The usual, you know."

I could do without it. "Put them on the waiting list."

"What waiting list, Jim?"

I waved it off. "Never mind. But listen, let's scrap work for a while. I'm taking some time off."

"Can we afford it?"

"Gonna have to. I reckon I need a break, love."

"Me too?"

I nodded. "You too."

She counted out half the money and kissed it. "Thanks, love." Her eyes dropped. "But I'm worried, Jim. I mean, what happens now? The Connollys will want to make sure you keep this quiet."

"I know, but it'll come out anyway. It's only a matter of time before someone else spills what went on in that shithole."

"Was it really that bad?"

I sparked up, took that shit in deep. "Worse. A place for animals, love."

"I'm just glad you're okay."

"Yeah, for now."

"Are you not worried? You know, that they might come looking for you?"

I sighed and ran a hand through my stubble. Was fucked if I was having a shave. "What can they do, really?"

"Well, shut you up. Batter you, kill you, throw you off a fucking cliff. I wish you'd take this seriously."

"I am taking it seriously," I said, opening the footage on my phone. I played it one more time, cringing as I did so, then sent it via email to Fiona. It was time I spoke to her anyway. "This is my insurance, love. And Connolly's not stupid, although he might appear so."

"You could've fooled me."

"He knows this is my ace card. He'd be a fool to threaten me with anything."

She left the couch and poured more coffee. I watched her pocket the cash I'd just given her and she said she was going out. Might as well treat herself to a nice new pair of shoes.

"And besides," I said, "he's got bigger things on his mind now, like becoming a grandfather again."

"Talk about taking the happy news badly."

"It's just the start of it."

She came back to the couch. "I wonder if there's anything on the news about the fire."

"What, the abattoir going up? I doubt it."

"Do you think the kid's body's been left in there?"

I shrugged. "Who knows? But I doubt that as well. Not the way they work."

"It's probably gonna kick off, isn't it?"

"The kid being Polish won't help the Connollys one bit. As soon as this gets back to the Badowskis, I expect things to go more than tits up."

She rolled her eyes. "They're all a bunch of stupid bastards if you ask me."

I couldn't disagree. "True. But this is the world they live

in. It's a completely separate reality to everyone else. Gang-sters playing dangerous games. Believing they're untouch-able. Playing by their own rules."

She was shaking her head as she pulled on her shoes. I threw my jacket on, thinking I might as well leave the flat too. I needed to keep my ear to the ground and my eyes peeled. I wouldn't do much of that between these walls. Before we left, I asked her what they did last night after I left.

"We followed you," she said. "For a while. Dave hung back in the traffic, and Maya kept her eye on things. Once the tracking device was in, it was plain sailing."

"But you didn't follow us up to the hills, did you? I would've clocked and they would have as well."

"We're not that stupid, Jim. Dave left you once the tracker was in place and we could just follow you on his iPad. Piece of piss."

Yet the tracker was left in the Bentley and I assumed it was still there. "Still tracking?"

"As far as I'm aware, yeah. But you'll have to speak to Dave to get any sense. You know I'm useless with this kind of stuff."

"You in the office today?"

"I thought you said we were taking some time off."

"Yeah, no worries. Just wondered, that's all. But listen, I spoke to Fiona last night. She said I'm on the hit list."

"Hit list? What hit list?"

"I'm a suspect. In the Robertson case."

She paused a moment and did a double take. "What, Robertson? The copper? The one they found dead...?"

I nodded. "I don't believe for a minute they think I killed him."

"So why are you a suspect?"

"Fuck knows. But I'm just letting you know in case something happens."

"Like what?"

"They might pull me in for questioning."

"You are joking, right?"

I wish I was. "Afraid not."

"But they can't... I mean, what the fuck are they actually... Jim, what's going on?"

I almost laughed. Almost. "Not a Scooby, honest. I need to see Fiona to know more. She told me they were onto me last night."

I told Laura about Fiona's plans to pack the job in. She said it was probably a good thing for us. Maybe she could help out more.

We left the flat and split up. I watched her walk into town and thought about my next move, though I didn't have any ideas. But there was a nagging feeling that I had to warn Aisling about her father and brothers. I'd be doing that unborn child a serious injustice if I didn't at least let her know what was potentially going down.

Then there was the small matter of the Robertson murder. I was more than intrigued. It was big news, all over the papers and TV, even the nationals. I didn't want to be a part of that news, if I could help it. Though I knew I had nothing to fear - I was as innocent as a newborn baby - I also knew these scumbags couldn't wait to drag me in, especially after Bob had blown the police corruption wide open during the Angel case.

They couldn't be trusted. I knew it, Fiona knew it. Whoever had killed him and left his body parts scattered around the city must have had good reason to do so.

I sparked up and took out my phone. Dialled Fiona up. She answered on the first ring.

TWENTY THREE

"Please tell me you're still in one piece."

"Come on, Fi. You underestimate me."

"Maybe so, but I don't underestimate the Connollys, Jim. Or the sick bastards they mix with. So how was it?"

"Well, you got my email just now, yeah?"

"Not checked. Anything important?"

"You can look at the footage when we finish this call. But in a nutshell, it went seriously pear shaped when Connor decided to batter one of the fighters to death. A Polish kid, probably in his early twenties. I don't know his name, but he works - or worked - in one of those European shops in Cheetham Hill. Seems to have gotten involved in the fist fighting game and ended up paying for it with his life, poor bastard."

"Killed a man...?"

"With his bare hands."

She was silent for a moment while she took it in. "And this footage? You filmed it?"

"Not the actual murder, but the aftermath. Seamus

went fucking nuts and demanded everyone leave when it became obvious the kid wasn't just unconscious. Started swinging a blade around."

"Anyone else hurt?"

"Not that I know of. Yet."

"Yet seems about right for these twats."

I took a long drag on my smoke and headed towards the office, figuring I may as well check in. I wanted to check on Lukasz Badowski's whereabouts and call Dave, if I could get hold of him. "Thing is, Seamus saw me filming it all on my phone. So obviously I fucking legged it and got out of there as quick as I could."

"Christ, Jim. Are you actually mental?"

"Got lost on the moors until two gypsy kids rescued me and took me down into Oldham. If it wasn't for them I'd still be out there now, probably."

"Gypsy kids?"

"Family of one of the fighters. The father is a longtime acquaintance of the Connollys. Patrick McMurphy. He holds these events as well, according to Seamus. Anyway, the main thing is I told Seamus the news about Aisling falling pregnant. That's when the mood changed."

"I'm hardly surprised. I mean, to have you even following the poor girl around tells anyone what a sad old bastard he is. He was bound to take this badly."

"I think Connor took it the worst."

"Evidently. Anyone else get footage of what happened?"

"No doubt. I guess we'll know for certain if the bodies start piling up."

"So what happens now?"

"Well, I don't know. But I think I should warn Aisling."

"But she won't like that, Jim. How has word gotten out

about her pregnancy? Have you given that any thought? She'll want to know why the hell you told him."

"Just doing my job, that's all. And anyway, one of her oldest friends was beaten up by Badowski's women, to warn her off opening her mouth. Bad move on their part because it only made her want to come straight to me. Claire MacGowan's already made a statement about that at Bloom Street station."

"This will only end in tears, Jim. Hers, theirs. Everyone's."

"Maybe. Probably. But there's an innocent baby in all of this, Fi. Don't you think the kid deserves a bit of protection?"

"Well yeah, but what exactly do you expect the Connollys to do? Seamus isn't about to do in his unborn grandchild."

"I wouldn't put it past him."

"But the kid's his blood..."

"Badowski's too. You're forgetting that. You think Seamus is gonna want the kid round for Christmas dinner? Think he's gonna want to treat him or her for their birthday? No, he's not. Not when he knows the kid has Badowski blood too."

"So you're saying he'd rather cut the kid out of his life completely?"

"Or cut the life out of the kid."

"Jim, don't."

"Don't what?"

"Don't go there."

"You know what these people are capable of, Fi."

"So what about the Badowskis?"

"What about them?"

"Well, what do they think about all this? You think Wiktor is as unhappy as Seamus about it all?"

She had a point. "Who knows? Not that I care."

"See, you say that, Jim, but I think you do care."

"I care about the unborn baby, Fi. But that's all. Aisling's still a silly little girl, and I couldn't give the slightest toss about pretty boy Lukasz. They're made for each other."

"So walk away. What's the point now?"

"Well, Seamus did relieve me of my duties..."

"So there you go. Not your problem."

"Maybe you're right."

"You know I am. But this footage, Jim. Either get rid of it or go back to Seamus and hand it over. Apologise for your actions. Beg if you have to."

I laughed out loud and got some funny looks as I made my way through the Northern Quarter. "Are you serious? No chance of that happening. You weren't there, love. There's no going back now."

"If he knows you've got footage, he'll want it erased from history."

"Not happening."

"He'll see it as a betrayal, Jim."

"So fuck him. It's his own stupid fault."

"When has Seamus Connolly taken the blame for anything?"

"Never. And I guess he's not about to start now."

"So you can't really walk away, can you? Not until that footage is gone."

She was right. I couldn't erase the footage and I couldn't turn back the clock. The damage was done.

"I suppose it comes down to what he fears, Fi. Which isn't much. He's got the police and the politicians in his pocket. He won't get into trouble, he knows that. He knows too many people at the top and he's using them as pawns.

The only thing this footage does is make him look like a total cunt. Which he is."

"He probably wouldn't deny that."

"He'd give it a good go."

"It's a badge of honour for him. He's nothing but a big fucking kid."

"I know, I know. But anyway, talking of the police. You handed your notice in yet?"

"I'm about to do it now."

"Do me a favour and record it. I'd love to see the look on their faces."

"Yeah, right. But there's no going back now, Jim. Once it's done, it's done. I can feel the weight lifting off my shoulders already."

"Do you think they've seen this coming?"

"Not a chance. But they won't care, anyway. I'm just another copper, nothing more. I don't mean shit to them."

"So a month from now, that's it?"

"That's it. Sayonara, Auf Weidersen, arrivederci. It was never really me, if I'm honest."

"So what's next?"

"I'll let you know when you come around mine to celebrate. I'm doing you a curry, remember?"

I'd forgotten, but now that she'd mentioned it again, I felt a twinge of anxiety. I mean, what did she want, exactly? I'd seen the way she looked at me. And I must admit, I kind of fancied her.

"You just say when, love."

"I will. But listen, I'm gonna get going now. Need to hand it in to the chief while I've got my chance."

"Okay, but just one more thing."

"Go on."

"My file. I assumed you were engrossed in it last night. Interesting reading?"

There was a pause. "To say the least. I'll fill you in on what I found soon enough. Speak to you later."

"Let me know when it's done."

But she'd hung up. I pocketed the phone and made my way to the office, head down. The afternoon was busy; the streets crowded. A darkening sky was threatening a downpour. I was looking forward to a pick me up but when I turned onto High Street, there was a pool car parked outside my office and two coppers flanking one of the twats I recognised as a former colleague. DCI Crane was leaning on my door and talking into his phone. It wasn't difficult to guess exactly what they were doing here. I was about to be pulled in for questioning. I could only hope they had a good reason for it, or they would be seriously wasting my time. I ducked into a bar doorway, the smell of booze taunting me, and brought up the footage I'd recorded last night. Now that it had been sent to Fiona, I deleted it. I also sent her the footage and images I'd had of Bob Turner's living room, too. I had no time to explain that one away. I knew I had to delete that too, or I'd have a mess to explain if I didn't. The last thing I wanted was all that shit still on my phone when they took it away. I returned the phone to my pocket and approached. Crane clocked me and ended the call quickly. The two uniformed coppers blocked my way to the door.

"Mr. Locke," Crane said. "We meet again."

He was balding and had put on more than a few pounds since I last saw him, but he still had that smug expression I'd always despised. I always knew he'd end up a DCI. The question was when. The bloke was practically married to the job. "Dennis," I said, holding out my hand. He chose not to shake. "Been a while. To what do I owe the pleasure?"

"James Locke, I am arresting you on suspicion of murder..."

"Please, for fuck's sake, save me that shite..."

"Although what you do say may be..."

I laughed as the two coppers cuffed me and ducked my head into the back of the car. "You do know this is a load of bollocks, Dennis. Don't you?"

He got in beside me and one uniformed copper the other side as the last one took the wheel. "Let the professionals be the judge of that, Mr. Locke."

"Call me Jim."

But he said nothing as the police car moved away from my office.

TWENTY FOUR

We'd continued to say nothing as the pool car moved through the city and out to the place I once called my own HQ. The GMP headquarters was in the north and occupied a massive patch of land that had lain dormant and disused for so long. A railway yard in the sixties, then empty through the next three decades until two enormous buildings were built to house Greater Manchester's coppers, myself included, until I'd been shown the door.

We rolled down a ramp and into the basement car park of the main building, and there were numerous glances through the glass from various detectives, constables and non entities, each keen to get a look at the latest suspect on Crane's radar. No doubt I was the gossip of the station, not that I gave a fuck.

Or maybe I did. It wouldn't have been the first time I was the talk of the station. There were different reasons back then, of course, and coming back here had brought it all to the surface once again. But I'd moved on. At least that's what I kept telling myself. I wondered if I'd get a glimpse of Fiona, the only copper who wouldn't have been surprised to see me. But then we ducked out of sight completely and came to a stop in a parking bay just beyond the lift.

"So, are you gonna tell me what this is all about? Who am I supposed to have done in?"

Crane kept his mouth shut as I was led down a long corridor to be booked in. The guy behind the counter had clearly been expecting me. I'd never seen him before and was taken aback by how tall he was, his beaky nose and glaring expression making him look like a pissed off giraffe. They confiscated my private items - phone, smokes, cash - and sealed them in a blue plastic bag.

Then I was taken down to Interview Room 4 and made to sit in a rock hard chair, cuffed to the desk through a hole at one corner. There was no heating in the room, a common trick. They left and made me wait until the sky was darkening outside. I was sitting there for almost an hour before Crane came back in with two coffees. One for him and one for the observing DS. That would've been one of my roles, back in the day. Instead, I was finding myself on the other side of the desk. It was a good job I knew what to expect.

"I'm saying nothing without a solicitor and a phone call. I know my rights."

"You've been brought in as a suspect in a murder case, Locke. You don't get anything easy."

"We can sit here all night, then."

Crane rolled his eyes and left the room. Ten minutes later, he was back with a duty solicitor and a hand held phone. I insisted the call was a private one, even though I knew they'd be listening to every word. When Crane and the DS left the room again, and the duty solicitor left me to make the call while she made some notes, I dialled up the only person I knew who might be able to get me out of here as soon as possible.

It rang for several long moments before he picked up. "Hello?"

"George?"

"Who is this?"

"George, it's Jim Locke. You remember me?"

"Of course I remember you, Jim," he laughed. "You know I do. How are you? What can I do for you?"

"Well, it's kind of a long story but..."

"When is it ever a short one with you?"

George Thornley, former editor of the Manchester Evening Chronicle, now retired. An old and great mutual friend of Bob Turner, my mate who'd done himself in with a shotgun in his living room. We'd found him together and said little of that day to each other since, but it went round and round in my mind every single day.

"I'll get straight to the point. I've been arrested."

"Arrested?"

"For murder."

"Murder!"

"Yeah, but listen, it's bollocks. The lot of it. They've got it in for me, you know. Won't let it lie. So they're now wasting my time and their own with fucking me about, you know."

"Murder...?"

"Yeah. Look, you must know about DCI Rob Robertson? Copper found cut up across the city."

"It's not exactly easy to avoid it."

"Yeah, well... him."

"What, they're trying to say you've killed him? That's what they trying to say?"

"Yeah. I know. It's ridiculous."

"Please tell me you haven't, Jim."

"Have I fuck!"

"Because if you have..."

"For fuck's sake, George, as if..."

"Calm down, calm down. I'm joking. Right, okay. Where are you now?"

I told him. The duty solicitor was pointing at her watch and raising her eyebrows, like this was a complete waste of her time. Which it was.

"Leave it with me."

"I don't expect to be here long."

"These things can drag out though, Jim."

"I know, I know. But look, I only get one call. Can you let Laura know where I am?"

"Of course."

"And as soon as I'm out of here, we need a catch up. You owe me a pint."

"Let's get this dealt with first. You got representation?"

"She's sitting right here."

"Good. Innocent people don't get sent down, Jim. Are they trying to charge you?"

"Routine questioning. They won't be able to charge me because they'll have fuck all on me. They're living in a fantasy world, George."

"Always were, kid. Okay, hang in there. I'll try to pull a few strings. See you soon."

He hung up then. I turned to the solicitor and gave her the nod. "Let's get this done. I'm innocent. And they know it."

"I hope, for your sake, that's true."

Not gonna lie, she was cute.

"Things have changed a lot since you were last here, Locke. There's no more walking on eggshells trying to avoid the pissed up twat in the corner, for a start."

"That's original, Crane."

"And true."

"Not how I remember it."

"Can we get to more important matters, please?" the solicitor said. Emma Harrison was hardly a rookie, but I got the impression she hadn't been on the job too long, which didn't bode well for me.

Crane shifted in his seat, glanced at the DS - a young guy called Sean McKenzie who reminded me of myself before things went tits up - and cleared his throat. He pressed record on the machine beside us and glanced up at the camera I knew was recording video footage too. I saw him grin and nod before launching into his pre interview spiel.

I needed a smoke. They couldn't keep me here indefinitely. I'd have to be charged to be kept in any longer than the legal period for questioning a suspect. They had nothing on me, and this was a waste of time and resources. The chief wouldn't let it drag on. They had to have some kind of ulterior motive for bringing me in. I suspected this had nothing to do with the Robertson murder and everything to do with trying to intimidate me into complying with them and the things they wanted. But it wasn't going to work.

"Interview approximately timed at seventeen hundred hours. Present are myself, DCI Dennis Crane, DS Sean McKenzie, duty solicitor Emma Harrison, and the suspect in question, Mr. James Locke."

"Jim."

A sigh. "Jim Locke."

"That's me."

"For the benefit of the tape, Mr. Locke, can you please state your full name, address and date of birth?"

"Do you want my shoe size as well?"

Another sigh. "Just state your name, address and date of birth please, Mr. Locke."

I did. I gave them both the flat and office address. I had nothing to hide. I had to question whether their resources would stretch to turning my office upside down. They wouldn't find anything incriminating in there if they did.

And then I thought about that kilo of weed in the office safe.

"So I'm guessing you know why we've brought you in..."

"Well, I'm guessing the real reason is so you can look like you're actually doing some work. You must be living in a separate reality if you think I've done Robertson in."

"We just want you to help us with our enquiries, that's all. Just a few simple questions."

"You're wasting your time, clearly. I've not seen Robertson since I left."

"Oh, I beg to differ."

"Tell a lie, I saw him hanging around Lower Broughton when my friend Lloyd was shot at point blank range through the windscreen of his car."

"We both know you've seen him after that, Locke. Salford Royal ring any bells?"

"Can't say it does, to be honest."

"Well then, let me refresh your memory. We have a statement from PC Colin Fletcher that you viciously assaulted DCI Robertson in an uncontrollable and frenzied rage. This was just outside the hospital grounds. Can you confirm or deny that, Mr. Locke?"

Fuckety fuck. I remembered it well. "You got evidence of that?"

"Well since you ask..."

The bastard had me. DS McKenzie handed him a blue folder. He reached in and brought out a handful of photographs. I could feel my palms getting that little bit sweaty. I'd have to think on my feet but could hardly deny the fact that I'd knocked Robertson about a bit and may have knocked his teeth out too one night near Salford Royal. I'd just been to see Shannon Kennedy on the burns unit and left to find Robertson and a scrawny, straight out of school, face like a baby rookie copper in PC Colin Fletcher. Robertson had been goading me, taking the piss about the death of my friend Bob Turner, and so I gave him a piece of my mind, not to mention informed him of what I knew he'd been up to with the kid, Isabella Burns.

Punching him repeatedly made me feel good for a while. I should've known it would come back to haunt me.

Crane placed a photo before me. It was hard, at first, to make it out, but then I realised I was looking at myself pummelling Robertson around the chops from a vantage point I couldn't have known at the time of the event.

"CCTV from the cafe. Simple, really. It was the first thing they looked at when Robert decided to proceed with assault charges."

I didn't know what he wanted me to say. "Go on."

"And this one," he said, sliding another print onto the table, this one in full colour. "DCI Robertson's face when he came back in."

A mouth that looked like it had been rollered onto hot tarmac. Bashed in, battered, bruised. Had to admire my handiwork. The guy looked like he'd never kiss a good woman ever again. Maybe his killing had been bad karma of the very worst kind, given what he'd done to Isabella Burns.

And then it occurred to me that what we knew about him, what Fiona and I had documented on him, could be my winning hand. So I'd assaulted him. Fair enough, guilty as charged.

But what he had done was far, far worse. Maybe now was the time to reveal it all, to really throw a spanner into their murder investigation. Could his behaviour with an underage girl - at least the one that we knew of - be the real motive for his murder?

"Well?"

I shifted in my seat. I knew that if I admitted it, I'd be up for assault charges. I shrugged. "Well, what?"

"Is it you?"

"Isn't it your job to find that out, Dennis?"

"Jim, just do us all a favour and tell us if that is you or not."

He held his finger on the grainy print of my enlarged face. It was definitely me, right down to the hollow cheekbones.

"Even if it is," I said, "I don't see what connection this has with his murder."

"Nor can I," Emma said. "Got to be honest."

Crane rolled his eyes and then glared at me. I held his gaze. "What beef did you have with him?"

"None, really. We didn't get on but there's no secret in that, as you know."

"The footage I saw shows you battering his face in like it was a punch bag. We see PC Colin Fletcher retreat and then return with a truncheon, and you disarmed him and punched him too. You broke his nose, Locke."

It was just an instinctive reaction, from what I remember. But I kept my mouth shut.

"Why did you do it, Locke?"

"Do what?"

"Batter him."

"It wasn't me. I don't know what you're talking about."

"This is ridiculous," Emma said. "This has nothing to do with the murder of DCI Robertson."

"Just wanting to paint a picture, that's all."

"A picture of what, exactly? Your suspect isn't a suspect at all at the moment because you don't have any evidence whatsoever related to the murder of DCI Robertson. This event you're referring to - and may I suggest the footage is dubious at best - bears no relation to his death. And if you can find a connection, I invite you to do so. As far as I can see so far, Detective Crane, all you have are flimsy assault charges."

Crane reddened and shuffled in his seat. "Interview paused at approximately seventeen thirteen p.m."

TWENTY FIVE

They made me wait another half an hour at least. Emma Harrison disappeared for a coffee and never even bothered to ask if I wanted one. Before she left, she told me she'd have me out of here in no time and that I shouldn't be too worried. I didn't realise that was the look I was carrying. It was probably because I was dying for a smoke.

It was almost six o'clock when Crane came back in to resume the interview, which was hardly a resumption of it at all. He said he was charging me with assault and that because of my well known relationship with Robertson, I had automatically become a suspect for his murder given that I must've had a good reason to beat him up. It was some jump they were taking. Emma said they would need more evidence in order to proceed and that without that evidence, I was free to go.

They made me wait another two hours before a release document could be signed off, by which time Emma had long gone.

They had wasted everyone's time, not least their own. I

could've held my hands up and admitted that yes, I had been the one to give him a smack or two around the face, but where's the fun in that? They'd have to come up with better footage than they had before attempting to charge me. Robertson's statement, however exaggerated it was, could not be changed now. And come to think of it, now that he was dead, could they proceed with it at all?

But I knew that none of this was about Robertson, or the alleged assault. It was a silly game they were playing, a desperate attempt to pin me down for something, anything. They were clutching at straws, yet bold enough to try, shambolically, to nail me for something far worse than assault.

They dragged out the whole process of checking me out of the place and made sure it was a real pain in the arse. The tall, beaky copper eventually handed over my belongings - phone, wallet, smokes - and said I was free to go, for now. Crane hovered around me like a bad smell as I marched towards the exit and freedom, insisting that I'd gotten off it very lightly and that my time would be up sooner or later. Had to really try hard to not laugh.

"I've got my eye on you, Locke. You might've gotten away with taking the piss out of me in there, but don't think you've won because you've not. You'll be back, mark my words. The truth will come out."

"I'm sure it will, Dennis. Robertson went to the grave with secrets. And they're pretty damning."

"What?"

"The truth will out. You'll see." I'd reached the door now, the air flowing into my lungs like nectar. "Only a matter of time."

He grabbed my shoulder. "What did you say?"

I pushed his arm away. "Get the fuck off me, cunt."

The word was like a slap to the face as I practically jumped down the steps to the car park.

"I'm watching you, Locke. This isn't the end of it. Keep looking over your shoulder because we're coming for you, and when we get you where we want you, the game is up."

Threw him the finger and walked into the night, in need of a drink.

TWENTY SIX

I started walking towards the city centre, my collars turned up in a vain effort to shelter from the wind and rain, and smoked hard on several coffin nails, one after the other, taking that shit in deep. I'd gone over the absurdity of it all as I walked, wondering what their next move would be. Even though I had been the one to give him a good kicking, which he deserved, I wasn't about to admit it. They'd have to work harder to pin that on me, and I guessed their heads were busy with more important matters, like finding the psycho who'd actually killed him.

I dug out my phone and went to call Laura. She answered immediately.

"Well?"

"Tried charging me with assault but the solicitor was having none of it."

"Assault?"

"I'll tell you when I see you, but it's nothing to worry about."

"But Jim..."

"Later. Listen, I'm gonna walk. Could do with some fresh air."

"A likely story. Stay out of the pub, Jim. I know what can become of you when you've got a drink inside you."

"I can handle myself. And besides, I deserve one after being sat in that shithole all night. The good news is that they've done nothing but waste their own time. They've got fuck all on me, love."

"But will it stay that way? Just get home, Jim."

"I'm on my way."

I hung up, suddenly having the feeling that they might be tapping my phone. Either I was being paranoid or I was totally in tune with their thinking. I checked it, just to make sure it hadn't been tampered with. I knew that acting on my gut instinct by sending Fiona that footage of Seamus Connolly was probably the right thing to do, not to mention those images of Bob Turner lying dead in his living room.

All my other photographs had disappeared. There wasn't much, just the usual stuff from the odd day out Laura and I had had, a handful of Charlie and Nicole. But they were gone. Wiped. Stolen. I went into my emails and they'd been wiped clean, too.

Fuck.

It meant they had the emails I'd sent to Fiona as well. Shit, how could I have been so bloody stupid? I should've tossed the phone or hidden it somewhere the minute I laid eyes on Crane standing outside my office.

Fuck, shit, bollocks!

I'd been lazy and stupid and shortsighted. I should've encrypted it all somehow. Yet I didn't know for certain that they had anything.

Except all my emails were gone. My inbox, my sent items, everything. These things don't just vanish.

My texts were all gone, too. My contacts were all still there, still intact, but all texts had been deleted.

Fiona. Fiona Watson, WPC employed by GMP. My contact on the inside. There had been lots of calls and text messages that had gone back and forth to her. No doubt they'd want to know why.

I'd just dropped us in it, big time. I knew I had to call her.

I found her number and called. Got a dead line. Tried again as I looked over my shoulder. This was all I needed. This was another example of my inability to think before acting. Of course they were gonna rifle through my phone.

I thought about the night I'd battered Robertson and how I'd filmed him begging on his knees. Filmed him using the app on my phone.

I was done. Bang to rights. Emma Harrison had got me off this time, but I wouldn't get away with it forever. And now I was half expecting blues and twos to pull up right beside me. Those assault charges were coming my way. On the night in question, I thought I was being clever.

I couldn't have been more stupid.

"Jim?"

"Please tell me you've resigned."

She laughed. "All done."

"Good, because we're now in some deep shit, love. You at home?"

"Yeah, but... Jim, what's up?"

"Not now, not on the phone. I can come to yours?"

"What, now?"

"Yeah, now. That okay?"

"Yeah, but. Jim, are you okay?"

"It's been one of those days. Where do you live?"

She told me. I told her I'd be with her within an hour,

that I'd flag a taxi as soon as I made it to town. But almost as soon as I'd hung up, a silver BMW pulled up beside me. High end, with tinted windows all round. Had a feeling I'd seen this car somewhere before and then realised I had, outside The Ivy. Lukasz Badowski had seemed to be friends with whoever was inside the night I followed him and Aisling straight to Hell.

The driver's window dropped down and I was confronted with a familiar looking man at the wheel. The old guy who'd walked past my Volvo the night I'd staked out the young Badowski residence.

"Mr. Locke." Unmistakeably Polish. I looked beyond him and saw another old guy in the passenger seat. "Get in."

The gun pointing straight at me told me I had no choice in the matter.

I reached for the rear passenger door, feeling like my guts had fallen out and knowing this could be very bad news indeed.

TWENTY SEVEN

My fears were eased almost as soon as I stepped inside and crashed into the plush leather, but I knew I'd need my wits about me. The old guy in the passenger seat introduced himself as Wiktor Badowski and put the gun away inside his heavy overcoat. Told me he only showed it to me so I'd get in and not fuck off like a squealing pig.

He held his massive hand out, and I knew I'd be a fool if I didn't shake it. Like Seamus Connolly, he gripped like a vice. "So good to meet you at last, my friend. Jerzy, drive."

The other guy, the one who'd looked straight through my windscreen that night outside Lukasz Badowski's, put her into gear and moved off with ease towards the city.

"Jerzy here came to this country with me back in nineteen seventy. We were just twenty-six. About the same age as my youngest son, Lukasz. You'll know all about him, won't you?"

Actually, I knew next to nothing. How to play this? I didn't honestly know, but figured it would be best to crack on like a nodding dog and give him the answers I thought he wanted. But I had to be honest, too.

"I... I don't really know anything, Mr. Badowski."

"I didn't know I still had it in me," he grinned, cupping his hands. "When we had him. You know, I must have good balls. But they say a man can produce children all his life, huh? But I draw the line at any more little brothers and sisters for him. You want a drink? I know you need one."

I couldn't say no, for several reasons. Wiktor opened the glove box and took out a small bottle of vodka. He handed it over and I twisted the cap and drank. The hit of alcohol instantly made me want more. I needed a beer. I took another lengthy sip and handed it back, but he waved it away, told me to keep it. I replaced the cap and pocketed it, wondering where the hell they were taking me.

"I got a phone call," he said. "From someone you know. He said you were being harassed by the police. Talked about some nonsense to do with the murder of that detective. Robertson, am I right?"

"Who called you?" But I guessed there was really only one man who could have. "Thornley?"

He smiled and nodded. "George Thornley. Did you know we went back a long way?"

"No."

"Old friend. More of an acquaintance. I told him I'd be more than willing to offer my assistance. Give you a lift home, you know."

But I detected an ulterior motive. And the gun worried me. "Thanks."

"You're welcome. And to be honest, we've been meaning to speak with you, haven't we, Jerzy?"

The driver nodded, silent, eyes fixed on the road. It was putting the shits up me.

"Mind if I smoke?"

"Go ahead."

I took the lighter he was handing me and sparked up. Took that shit in deep. "So what can I do for you?" Trying to sound cool and calm and failing.

"I'll be honest with you, Mr. Locke."

"Call me Jim."

"Jim, then. It's good to know we are friends. I like that. And I can see that you're a good man. But something has been troubling me, I admit."

Oh, fuck. "What's that?"

A smile that was more like a grimace. "I understand you've been working for the Connollys."

And there it was, like a punch to the guts. "I wouldn't quite put it like that."

"Well then, how would you put it?"

Outside my darkened window, the world rushed by as the car picked up speed. Jerzy was a natural.

I had nothing to hide. "Seamus Connolly approached me. Asked me to keep track of his daughter."

"Aisling?"

"Aisling."

"And?"

"And report back to him on what I found."

"And what did you find, Jim?"

"Not much, I'll be honest. And Seamus already knew she was seeing Lukasz."

"I see. But this troubled him, huh?"

"You could say that."

He was shaking his head. "I don't understand this. We have disagreements in the past, of course, but the union of our children - of our bloodlines - puts an end to that. You agree?"

Gotta admit, I didn't. "It's not the way he sees it."

"Well then, that's a shame. How do you feel about it, Jim?"

"It's none of my business. Why should I care?"

I got a feeling he didn't quite like that response. He turned to face the road, nodding at Jerzy to continue ahead. "Yes, why should you care? I can see that. It's none of your business, that's true. It didn't stop you from following my son and Aisling around, though. You seemed quite interested last week."

"Just doing my job, that's all."

"You know she is pregnant?" Was that a smile in his eyes? "I'm going to be a grandfather again! And Lukasz is very much looking forward to being a father. I think this will finally be the making of him."

I nodded. Recalled that that's what my mum said when Karen and I found out Nicole was on the way. She couldn't have been more wrong.

"Look, Mr. Badowski. If you don't mind me asking, what exactly do you want me for? It's just I've got to go see someone and I'm just wasting your time, tell you the truth. Seamus Connolly isn't a client anymore, he told me I was no longer required. So I just want to go home and forget all about this. I wish your son and Aisling well."

He held his arm up to stop the words spilling from my mouth. "We're going to have a long discussion, Jim. A long talk. So you just relax. Everything will be fine."

I could see him in the rear-view mirror and he didn't look happy. A silence descended and I wanted something, anything, to break it.

After several long minutes, as we moved through the ever busy city centre, he carried on. "Aisling is a good girl. And I am aware, of course, that she is Mr. Connolly's daughter. And that is not her fault. You can choose your friends but you cannot choose your family, am I right? So she has chosen my son as her partner. Her husband, no doubt. Her best friend. For this, I am happy. They have my blessing. But you can see that I am a little unhappy too. Do you know why, Jim?"

"I'm sorry, I don't."

"I sense a certain dissatisfaction from the Connollys. You could say there has to be given that Seamus Connolly has been paying you to follow Aisling and Lukasz around. It's as if he doesn't want his daughter going around with my son. Would you agree?"

He was pretty good at pointing out the obvious. "I suppose so."

"I can't possibly think why. He's a good boy. Treats her well. And do you know, I believe, from the bottom of my heart, that Seamus would warm to my son, if they gave him a chance. Seems a real shame. I bet we all have a lot in common, you know."

They did. Loan sharking, drug dealing, prostitution. Murder. I'm pretty sure they'd all get on like a house on fire. "Probably."

"But this business of hiring private detectives to snoop around. A stupid and silly game. Not a wise thing, if you ask me. I mean, that's just asking for trouble, isn't it?"

"I suppose so."

"No suppose about it."

"Yes."

"And being a private detective, Mr. Locke..."

"Jim."

"Jim, of course. Being a private detective, my guess is that in your line of work you'll know all about the Connollys and the games they play."

And the games you play, I thought. "To a certain extent. I'm hardly privy to their every move."

"Maybe not. But you're no stranger to their activities, huh?"

"I suppose."

"And no doubt, in your line of work, you have contacts. Am I right? People on the inside? Friends who remain loyal."

"I'm not following."

"You're an ex police, Jim. You know and I know that you know people on the inside who sometimes maybe help you from time to time."

Was he referring to Fiona? And were his words a veiled threat? "Maybe. It's true I have a few individuals who help me now and again. There's nothing unusual about that."

"Indeed not. And we have our mutual acquaintance in George Thornley, of course. And George and I have a mutual dislike of the police. The 'top brass', as you call it."

I nodded. "Yes."

"And given your past and the way you were treated, it seems we have a hatred in common too."

Jesus, seemed like everyone knew my history.

Wiktor picked up on this. "It's common knowledge in my circles, Jim. Ex copper turned private detective. You're bound to have some feelings of bitterness towards your former employers."

"You could say that."

I saw a hint of a smile as the BMW moved out towards the Mancunian Way. Wherever they were taking me, it was too far from where I wanted to be. Outside, the night was black, the city cold. A fog was descending rapidly, skirting the canals like the ghosts were gathering.

I had to wonder where all of this was going.

"You have nothing to fear. In terms of what the police wanted. Consider it already taken care of. They won't bother you again. You have my word. But I would like something in return for my good nature, I'm sure you understand."

"Thank you," I said, though I was apprehensive about returning any favours. I supposed, though, that if I wanted Crane off my back, and Wiktor was offering to help, I should accept it and be glad about it. But it would come at a cost. And even then, I wasn't entirely sure I could take him at his word. "What can I do for you?"

I saw a flicker of a smile again as Jerzy took us south down the Princess Parkway. Gotta say, I wasn't getting good vibes.

"A number of things. I won't beat around the bush. Obviously, I know you've been following my son and Aisling around. The reasons I don't understand. But I want to pay you for your services too. We'll come to payment soon enough, but I want to outline what I want from you first."

Whatever it was, I knew I couldn't turn it down. "Go on."

"I hear someone close to us is gone. Beaten to death by someone connected to Connolly. How do I know this? I have contacts, Jim. I know about the abattoir, I know about the fist fighting. And I know one of our boys has been killed. This makes me very upset."

"I understand."

"I suspect you know who is responsible. But there is no need to hide it because I know Connor Connolly has blood on his hands too."

I wanted to ask him how he knew Connor was responsible for the death of the kid, but I guessed he probably had his insiders present on the night in question, perhaps even with the kid himself. I knew Lukasz Badowski had been in the area, probably even upstairs in the shop, the day I took a look around. Whatever operation they were running from there - a cannabis farm was my best guess given I had a kilo of their weed in my office safe - it seemed the kid would've been involved. Maybe they'd even groomed him long ago to get involved in the fighting game just so they could keep tabs on the Connollys.

Maybe.

"I want you to follow them. Find out what they're up to and report back to me."

Great. The same old shit. Surveillance and more surveillance, except this time I was watching the people who were probably watching me for the people who were probably watching them, anyway. I couldn't see the point and told Wiktor as much, but he shrugged it off.

"Just think of yourself as a decoy," he said. "They'll probably know you're keeping tabs on them and they might not care. But I wouldn't fear them. I offer you our protection in exchange for your information."

"So basically, you want me to give you the works on them. Grass them up."

"But you have no loyalty."

"No," I said, but I wasn't entirely sure I felt it, even after all that had happened. "No, I don't. I'm loyal to no one, Wiktor. Even you."

He looked right through me and, for the briefest of moments, I thought he was gonna throttle me. But then he just laughed, like some devilish old weasel who knew all the jokes. Perhaps the joke really was on me.

"You'll be paid handsomely, Mr. Locke. You can even have it tonight."

"And if I say no?"

He shrugged. "Your loss."

Outside, the world moved by. The BMW took a right onto Barlow Moor Road, heading in the direction of the crematorium, where we said goodbye to Lloyd. But before we reached there, it turned into the Southern Cemetery, the largest in the city, its gates still open to the public, which I found unusual at this hour. I wondered what the hell we were doing here.

We rolled beside grand mausoleums and extravagant headstones, the war dead and city founders. Perhaps even Wiktor saw himself being buried here. I knew there were one or two Connollys six feet under around these parts. What's good enough for them...

But I admit, I was a tad nervy. A cemetery may be quiet, but it was filled with dead people. I didn't want to join them.

Jerzy took us down a long track, buried beneath giant oaks and sycamores, and brought it to a halt beside a pile of earth.

"Some fresh air," Wiktor said, and left the car. I guessed he wanted me to get out too, so I went for the handle but the door already opened for me. Jerzy ushered me out. The air was thick with the smell of rain and fog crept across the graves at the Princess Road side.

The boot opened and Wiktor urged me to take a look. Sitting there alone was a grey hold-all. Nothing else.

"One hundred grand," he said. "Yours, tonight, no questions asked, if you do what I'm asking."

I looked at it. Felt an incredible urge to run. But the urge to take it was stronger. "All of it?"

"A hundred grand. You can do what you want with it. All I want in return is for you to follow the Connollys and let me know what's going on. If you can find out what they've done with that poor boy's body, all the better. That's all."

"And you can ensure the police stay off my back?"

"I said so, didn't I?"

"But how? How can you keep them away?"

"I'm calling in some favours of my own. It's on a need to know basis. You have nothing to worry about. DCI Robertson's not coming back. They know it."

"Sounds like you know something."

"More than them. And more than you. That's how it stays."

"So if I say no?"

"You can walk away. Leave now, if you want. But your help will be gladly received and, as I said, the money is yours, right now. You could do a lot with that money."

"There's a catch here somewhere, Mr. Badowski."

"You don't trust me, fine. It's been nice talking with you. Jerzy."

Jerzy hovered in the darkness with that gun Wiktor was waving at me to get me in the car. He was pointing it right at me.

"Wait," I said, my arms up. "I'll take it, I'll take it. I'll do the job."

"Good boy."

"I'll start straight away."

"Even better. Look inside the bag."

I stepped forward to unzip it. Sure enough, it was packed with cash in bundles of tens and twenties.

"You'll see beside us, Mr. Locke, that we've arranged to have a grave dug. For a special, private funeral. Take us to Connor Connolly and you can stand here and read the eulogy as we pile on the earth. Will you do it?"

"You saying you're going to kill him? And you want me to help you lure him in? You want me to be complicit in a murder?"

Wiktor smiled. "You won't be the one doing the killing, Locke. You don't have to witness the burial if you don't want to. I understand it might seem a bit... macabre. But for what he's done, we want to make sure the bastard is dead."

He wasn't one to mince words. Neither was I. I was going to take the money, no doubt about it. I wasn't stupid. But I had some questions of my own first.

"I have some questions, Mr. Badowski. I hope you don't mind."

"Go ahead. I would be no gentleman to deny you this."

I took a deep breath. "See, I'm a bit upset, too. About a few things. Nothing major, it's just... well, the last time I saw Aisling, she was threatening to have me dealt with by your son. And then soon after that, her friend Claire turned up at my office, beaten and battered. She'd been jumped by two girls. Polish girls, I'm told. Claire seems to think it was because she knew about Aisling's pregnancy and she was silenced because of it. Would you know anything about that? And can you ensure that I come to no harm?"

In the darkness, I could only see his silhouette. So it was hard to tell what he was thinking, couldn't read the expression on his face. And the silence that deadened the air between us seemed to last a lifetime. If I'd hit a nerve, I didn't know it.

"Her friend? Claire MacGowan?"

"Yes."

"I can assure that I didn't know about this, but now that I do, I will deal with it. When did this happen?"

"A few days ago."

"Leave it to me. I can understand your concern. And let

me say that none of my sons deals with anything without my say so. If Aisling has said something, then I can only apologise. My future daughter-in-law has a way with words."

"She's Irish, they all do."

"And a woman. A lethal combination." He stepped toward me and the light from the boot interior illuminated his face again as Jerzy hung around. "Do we have a deal? The money appeal to you?"

I didn't need to think about it much, but I let it drag out. Zipped up the bag and grabbed the handles, picturing in my mind what I could do with the cash. What I could do very soon. But I had one more question.

"It sounds to me like you know a lot more than you're letting on about Robertson's murder. And to be honest, I couldn't care less about him. My only regret is that he's left this world without facing justice. But I'd be a liar if I said I didn't want to know who was responsible for taking him out. Seeing as I'm doing you a favour - and let's face it, I need this job like I need a firework up my arse - care to elaborate on what you know?"

That smile again, like he knew all the jokes. "You're bold, Locke. I'll give you that. And maybe, just maybe - if you deliver what I want - I will tell you more. But until that time comes, take the money and run. This will be the easiest pay day you've ever had."

I slung the bag over my shoulder and he slapped my back before placing a folded up piece of paper in my shirt pocket. "Have a lovely evening. You can contact me anytime."

Wiktor and Jerzy stepped back into the car and started her up. I watched it roll away slowly down the narrow track.

Watched it until it disappeared behind the chapel and out onto the main road.

I took out my phone and pressed STOP on the dictaphone app. It always paid to be prepared, to gather evidence. You couldn't trust any of these bastards.

I thought about whether I could make it to Fiona's. It was getting late and Laura would be wondering where the hell I was.

I turned up my collar and sparked up. Took that shit in deep. It wasn't the first time I'd been left alone in a cemetery, but I had to admit; it was giving me the willies.

I slung the cash over my shoulder and picked up pace, eager to get away, to get away from it all.

TWENTY EIGHT

I found Fiona's house, a small two up two down end terrace, out in the east of the city. The street itself was pretty nice, clean and gated at one end, and there were brand new fruit trees that had looked recently planted lining each pavement. I felt a bit uneasy as I stood there on the step in the little front garden. Tried to tell myself that I was only here for professional purposes, that there was no other reason at all. But I knew that I was lying to myself. Knew that once I crossed the threshold that, metaphorically speaking, I had crossed a certain line. And there would be no going back.

The door opened and she was standing there in her silk pyjamas, a glass of red wine in her hand, her perfume delicate and inviting, her body a mystery beneath. Music filtered from the back room and she stepped aside so that I could step in.

"Planning on staying the night?"

"What?"

She nodded at the bag over my shoulder.

"Oh...no. Long story. Don't know if I've got the energy, to be honest."

"Try me."

Her living room was messy with papers that had been scattered around, a laptop perched on the edge of the couch, several empty glasses on the mantelpiece, and a few bottles - some opened and some not - on the coffee table. There was a wood burner glowing and the TV was on, muted. A pile of vinyl records occupied an armchair.

"The Slow Readers Club," she said. "Saw them at the Ritz a few years ago."

"What you mean?"

"The band, silly."

I pictured a handful of goons sitting around with copies of Biff, Chip, and Kipper and struggling over the phonics. But I noticed my feet tapping as I crashed into the couch, one eye on her top half.

"So, where've you been? I was expecting you earlier."

"Got a bit sidetracked. Wiktor Badowski gave me a ride in his BMW."

"Fuck off..."

"It's true."

And then I told her all about it, starting with how Crane was waiting for me outside my office and how they tried to pin an assault on Robertson on me. How I'd realised I'd fucked up when I clocked they'd wiped all my emails and texts and how they'd by now probably realised Fiona was doing a number on them and had been for a while. She looked bloody worried about that for all of two minutes until I told her that Wiktor Badowski assured me he'd handle the police. Maybe that was enough to convince her it would all be okay. Either that or she couldn't give the slightest. She was out of it now. They couldn't discipline her. But they could probably bring charges against her, if they found out anything concrete.

"And how is Badowski keeping the police off your back? Did he say?"

"Not exactly, but I believe him. Not many fuck with him."

"Try telling that to the Connollys."

"I know. Which brings me to why I'm carrying this bag around."

"Oh?"

"Can I trust you?"

"A bit late for that, isn't it?"

She poured herself another glass of wine and handed me a cold beer from the fridge. By now we were standing in the kitchen after she insisted I eat with her, even though it was getting late. She had a homemade curry bubbling away nicely. We hovered around the back door to smoke.

"There's a hundred grand in cash in that bag," I said. "For me. He wants me to follow the Connollys and give him the dirt. He knows about the kid Connor battered to death and he wants Connor. Wants me to find out where he is, all that."

She was open-mouthed, perhaps lost for words. She took a long drag on her smoke and put her hand on my chest. "A hundred grand? What for?"

"It's a lot of money, I know."

"But why?"

"He wants Connor dead. He wants retribution."

"And he's paying you that so you can...so you can bring Connor to him? That right?"

"Something like that."

"Jim, that's blood money! You'll be complicit in a murder. You'll be involved."

"But I won't be the one pulling the trigger." I downed the beer, needing it badly.

"It's too bloody risky."

"But it's a hundred grand, Fi. I'm fucking loaded."

"Yeah, right, and what are you gonna do with it all? Jesus..."

"They'll only end up killing each other anyway. If the daft cunt wants to pay me that kind of money, let him."

"Jim..."

"I was thinking of helping you out as well, you know..."

She finished her wine and went to top up. Cracked open another beer for me. "Are you out of your mind?"

"No, but they are."

"And what does Laura think of this?"

"I haven't told her yet."

"And does she know you're here?"

"No."

There was a pause as she sipped her wine, giving me a look. "Good."

I gave her a look back, thinking this was all too dangerous.

"Curry's nearly ready. I hope you're hungry."

There was a song about temptation running around my head. Tried to shake it off as we ate the Madras she'd knocked up.

"I wasn't expecting you tonight."

"I thought I should see you in person after I realised they'd wiped my phone. Didn't want to speak over the phone in case they were listening in."

"Are you getting paranoid, Jim?"

"Maybe. You think I'm overreacting?"

She shook her head, took a drink. "I'd have made myself look nice for you if I'd have known you were coming. I mean, if you gave me plenty of notice."

"You look nice anyway."

She looked down and smiled coyly. I let it hang in the air and launched my beer back, thinking all the time that this was crazy, madness. But I couldn't help it.

"So are you gonna go ahead with it?"

"Well, not quite. Yes and no. I mean, there's not much I can give them. But because he said he's keeping the police off my back, I felt obliged to do what he asked."

"So he's conned you into it."

"I must admit, the cash had a lot to do with it. Look, I couldn't just let that go."

"No doubt. It's a lot of money. A bit too much, if you ask me. Which tells me he knows you'll be complicit in what he wants to do with Connor. Reeling you into their games with hard cash. Jim, are you really capable of this?"

"It's not as if I'm pulling the trigger, like I said. They'll end up killing each other anyway. Might as well take the money and run, while I can."

She was shaking her head. "You'll end up in deep shit."

But I felt knee deep in it already. Did it really matter anymore?

"There's something else," I said. "About Robertson. Wiktor seemed to imply that he knew what happened to him."

"What, who killed him?"

"I think so. Said he knew more than the police and that's how it would stay."

"Do you think they had anything to do with it?"

"The Badowskis? No."

"Did he give you any clue?"

I took a long drink. "No. I asked, but he didn't reveal anything. But then he said he might let me know more afterwards."

"Afterwards?"

"After I did what he asked."

"So he's blackmailing you as well. Could be a massive bluff, Jim. He probably knows nothing."

"Maybe. But then again, being who he is, he might know everything."

"Do you trust him?"

It was one of those questions that hit like a slap to the face. Did I trust him? Not one bit. I couldn't trust any of these bastards. The one hundred grand he'd given me could be Monopoly money, for all I knew.

"Not as far as I can throw him."

She raised her eyebrows. Either she was asking me to go to bed with her or she was telling me I was a stupid cunt. "There you go, then. I'll clear up."

I watched her keenly as she pottered about the kitchen, loading up the dishwasher and binning the leftovers. She cracked me open another drink and I quickly checked the time on my phone. It had just turned eleven. Laura would be getting anxious, wondering where the hell I was. She told me to have a seat on the couch, so I did, a little apprehensive about where this was going. I was feeling drunk, too. It was a deadly combination.

Moments later, she came in and took a seat beside me. Leaned in and whacked a blue folder on my lap.

"What's this?"

She grinned and sparked up. Took it as my cue to spark up too. Took that shit in deep and let a cloud gather in the room above us.

"It's your file. Most of it, anyway."

"You're kidding me. Have you been poking around?"

"You can't blame me, it is partly what our agreement was."

"Yeah, get the file. But not to read it."

"Come on, Jim. You can't blame me. There's not much of any interest in there anyway, so don't flatter yourself. But what is interesting, as I'm sure you'll find, is that they were keeping close tabs on you. For several months."

"What?"

She nodded, touched my shoulder. "They were watching you closely."

"I fucking knew it."

"Yeah."

"Wouldn't surprise me if they still were. In fact, I'm pretty sure they are."

She moved a little closer as I leafed through the contents of the folder. Close enough so I could feel her press against me. Close enough for me to feel her breath on my face. It didn't matter what was in the file right then. I couldn't concentrate on it. I turned to her as she leaned in closer, close enough to kiss.

I spilt my beer across the couch when my phone blared into life. The phone fell to the floor too, and I stumbled to retrieve it before it died as Fiona disappeared back into the kitchen for a cloth.

"Laura." I'd dropped my smoke so scrambled for it before it burnt a hole in the cream carpet. "You okay?"

"I'm okay, yeah. I'm just checking up on you because I know how you can sometimes misbehave. Are you still in the pub?"

"Yeah, I'll... I'll be home soon."

"You'd better. I'm keeping the bed warm for you. I've been really missing you all day."

"I'm on my way, love."

While Fiona mopped up the spillage, I gathered the papers together, feeling a little guilty.

"I'll phone you a taxi," she said.

"Look, Fi, I'm sorry but I should really go, you know."

She waved it away, pressed her fingers on my lips. "Save it. Another time."

"Fi..."

The taxi turned up within five minutes. It was all kinds of awkward. She told me to read as much as I could and to let her know what was happening with the Connollys. I assured her I would.

TWENTY NINE

I awoke with the morning sun blazing through the window. Turned to face Laura, naked and sleeping soundly beside me. I realised I loved her and I couldn't be with anyone else and didn't really want to.

On the bedside table was the blue Manila folder with my files in it. I'd resisted the temptation to dive into it when I got home, and Laura had me preoccupied, anyway. I let her lie in while I pottered about the flat and made a good coffee, black. The hold-all was sitting on the kitchen floor, stuffed full of cash. I took a much closer look, rifling through the bundles and smelling it, just to make sure it was real.

I was one hundred percent certain that it was.

But not one hundred percent certain I wanted any involvement in this.

I sat on the couch and sparked up. Drank the coffee as the morning came to life. Outside, the city buzzed. The nine to five was calling to thousands of people on their way into work. It was a lifestyle I could never go back to.

I tiptoed around for a while, groggy from recent events

and keen to draw a line under it, before finally grabbing the folder from the bedside table and delving in.

Everything was on GMP headed paper, some of it photocopied, some of it not. There was a lot to get through, not that I'd be getting through it all any time soon. And as far as I could make out, none of it was in any kind of order but rather a jumbled up, out of sync mess.

A bit like me, then.

I took the two inch thick ream of paper out and started at the top.

2 1st February 2012.
        Detective Chief Inspector Rodri McCleod.
Greater Manchester Police
Central Division
Our Ref: DCI_McCleod111438921

Dear Sirs,
        As you may be aware, it has come to our attention that DS James Anthony Locke has recently been the subject of several internal complaints regarding being intoxicated on duty and being verbally abusive and suggestive to several colleagues, again whilst on duty. While an internal investigation is ongoing, please be assured that DS Locke will not be given any role that may require him to work with the colleagues in question. At this stage, we will take the opportunity to discuss the matter informally with DS Locke and will therefore notify you of any outcome. In the meantime, a request has been made by Detective Inspector Dennis Crane to formally launch a covert operation on the

matter. I am therefore passing this request to you, Professional Standards, for consideration.

Please find a memo attached, which contains the original complaints.

Yours,

DCI Rodri McCleod.

B astards.

The lying, two faced bastards.

I might've known Crane had been up to no good. It was in his makeup, written under his conniving skin.

Okay, I may have been a bit drunk on duty, once, but it was certainly not something I made a habit of. Who hadn't been?

And yeah, I may have made a few off-the-cuff remarks now and then, but I was never abusive. Suggestive was taking the piss...

I let the papers scatter across the coffee table when my phone buzzed into life.

It was a number I didn't recognise.

I hesitated, tried to think logically. Could be anyone. PPI, life insurance, or someone wanted for murder.

"Are you gonna answer that, or what?"

Laura, naked and half awake, standing in the doorway.

I grabbed it before it rang out. "Hello?"

Silence. Silence except for someone breathing and then, "Mr. Locke?"

"Yeah...?"

"Mr. Locke?"

A voice I recognised, for sure. Irish, too.

"It's Finian."

"Who?"

"Finian. Shaun's cousin."

"What?"

"Shaun McMurphy. We picked you up off that fucking moor, Jesus, you must remember us, like..."

The two gypsy kids, high on weed and hip hop and driving that pick-up truck over those moors like it was a tank.

"Finian."

"That's me."

"So what can I do for you?" I said, wondering if they'd gotten wind, somehow, of the stash of weed in my office safe.

"It's not good. I'll put Shaun on."

I felt a twinge and absently felt my scar. Prepared myself for bad news.

"Mr. Locke?"

"Go on."

"Right, it's Shaun. Shaun McMurphy."

"I know, Patrick's son, yeah?"

"Listen, we thought it best to give you warning, you know?"

"I'm listening." I was already on my feet, scrambling for my jeans.

"After we dropped you off, we went back up there to find my dad. Except we didn't get close. The place was swarming with the fucking cops and fire brigade. So we turned around and drove back. Got on the road to Halifax."

"Halifax?"

"Got a camp there. Anyway, we saw them bundling a body into the back of a Bentley. I won't forget it because we could see them at the side of the road and this car was the bollocks. They must've thought they were in the middle of nowhere, like, and they were, and one of Connolly's bastards looked right at me. So we put our foot down, you know."

Can't say I was surprised. "What did they look like? And how many?"

"One of them was a big guy, muscly. The other not so much."

So Dale and Declan had been assigned the job of disposing of the Polish kid.

"How do you know it was a body?"

"Saw his feet as they slung him in. Wrapped in a fucking bin bag. It was dark, like, but we know what we saw. Anyway, that's not really what I wanted to warn you about."

I had that feeling of dread and impending doom. Told him to hit me with it as I took the end of the smoke and Laura hovered in the kitchen.

"When we got back, dad was already there. He told us that Connor Connolly was fucking pissed off, big style, and had declared to Seamus that he'd kill Aisling as soon as he got hold of her."

It was what I expected. The guy was a mental case. "Can't say I'm surprised, to be honest."

"I mean, who the fuck would murder their own sister?"

"Wouldn't put it past them."

"Me neither, man. Does she know, do you think?"

"Hard to say. Maybe. I doubt she'd believe he was capable."

There was a pause as what sounded like a stiff wind blew down the phone.

"Where are you, by the way?"

He had to shout over the noise as a truck went past. "Salford! It's a fucking shithole around here!"

Laura was mouthing something to me and waving wads

of cash in my direction, a mix of concern and joy across her face.

The sound went dead again, as if he'd been sucked up into some vacuum. "Sounds noisy."

"Just ducked into a cafe," he said, his voice now down to a whisper. "Listen, I'm just passing on what I heard. What my dad said, you know."

"Thanks."

"I'm guessing you know this already, like, but... well, my dad's pretty much well in with Seamus Connolly. They go way back, you know. And even he didn't believe they'd be mad enough to do one of their own in."

"But now she's a Badowski, pretty much."

"And having Seamus's grandkid. But I'm told she hasn't got long, Mr. Locke. Jesus, I'd go to the police myself, like, if I thought it'd do any good. Thing is, I think someone's been following us. We're trying to lose them, you know?"

"They following you now?"

"Not seen them for an hour."

"You recognise them?"

"Some of Connolly's boys."

"I suggest you get well out of the way, Shaun. Disappear into the countryside, fucking anywhere."

"But what are you gonna do?"

I eyed the cash in the bag and Laura dancing around the kitchen, her eyes alight. Figured now would be a good time for a long holiday. "I don't know, I don't know."

"I've got a bad feeling."

I had that feeling too.

Yet I felt I had to protect that unborn child.

"Keep in touch, Shaun. Let me know if anything happens. Anything at all."

"We will. And Mr. Locke?"

"Call me Jim."

"Jim." He sounded out of breath but relieved he'd called me. "My dad phoned ten minutes ago. Said the Connollys are heading into Manchester. I'd keep out of the way if I were you. Something's going down."

Yet I knew I was going right into the fire.

THIRTY

"Jim, where the hell have you got all this?"

I hadn't had time to think of an excuse, and I knew she'd go mental when she found out the truth. I braced myself and told her.

"What?!"

"I knew you'd react like this."

"Oh, and can you blame me? For fuck's sake, Jim! Have you lost your fucking mind?"

I told her what I'd told Fiona. That I thought they'd end up killing each other anyway, so I might as well take the cash and run.

"Run to where, exactly?"

"Just... I don't know. Somewhere. Anywhere. Somewhere nice until all this blows over."

"Somewhere nice? Jesus..."

"Come on, love."

"You're unbelievable."

"But think of all that money, love. Think of what we can do with it!"

"Do you not think this could go tits up? Nothing is straightforward with you, Jim."

"But that's why you love me. Admit it."

She disappeared in a huff, then re-emerged ten minutes later, pulling a pair of jeans on and stuffing cash in her pockets.

"What're you doing?"

"You've twisted my arm. I'm going to book us a holiday. It's been ages since we had a break."

"A holiday? To where?"

"Somewhere nice. Until all this blows over? Isn't that what you said?"

"Yeah, but..."

She shushed me as she stuffed handfuls of twenties in her bag. "You said so yourself, love. Just leave it to me."

"Well, I didn't expect to win you round this easily."

"Yeah, well if that prick wants to give you this much money, I'm damn sure I'm gonna enjoy it. But I want you to be extra careful, love. I don't want you dying on me. You know what these people are like, on both sides. You're in deep, Jim. Time to swim out of the shit."

"Trust me. I've got it under control."

"But have you?"

She had a point. And Shaun's phone call had made things a little bit more immediate.

I went to shower and when I came back out, Laura was counting out the cash into two grand bundles. Said she was going to visit several banks.

"Between us, we have six separate accounts. The business has two. I'm gonna split fifteen grand between them. You'll have to decide what to do with the rest of it. Oh, and I'll take five grand to pay for the holiday."

"Well, what can I do with it?"

"I don't know. Sara's, maybe? It can't stay here. I don't think we can, either."

"Laura..."

"No, Jim. I don't trust the Connollys and I don't trust the Badowskis. What if some heavies turn up at our door? I don't need this. You don't need it. You've got us in this mess. I'll stay at our Sara's tonight. You can join me there if you like, if you bother to come home."

"We'll take the cash there now. Will she ask questions, you think?"

"She doesn't know what day it is half the time, so I doubt it. We can stuff it in the loft or something."

"God, I love you."

She told me to stop fannying around and get my shit together. I didn't need telling twice.

There was barely any traffic, so we made good time. There was no need to explain anything to Sara, not that she would've cared. She was strung out on antipsychotics most of the time, the stronger kind that had taken away all her personality, so all that was left of her was just a barely functioning meat suit. Her eyes were often glazed over, her attention elsewhere, most likely on the voices or dwelling on the bad thoughts in her head.

It was tragic, watching her like this. She was vastly different from the woman I met just a few years back, the close friend of Angel, the missing girl I'd been roped into finding. When Angel finally turned up dead, a part of Sara died, too. Her latest suicide attempt had prompted a long stay in hospital under the mental health act, and she wasn't the same woman when she came out.

Laura spent a lot of time here, chipping in to help with Charlie, Sara's son, when he wasn't with his father. It wasn't strange at all for her to stay in the spare room to look after her sister. When Laura told Sara we were both staying for a while, she even perked up. I was beginning to think this was a brilliant idea.

Laura persuaded me to get the cash in the loft while she made a pot of tea. It took me twenty minutes to get it safely tucked away behind a fake Christmas tree and an ancient rocking chair. By the time I was descending the rickety ladders, a thick wad of hard cash burning a hole in my pocket, I felt a lot better about taking it.

But I felt less great about the circumstances surrounding it. I knew I couldn't renege on my deal with Wiktor Badowski. If I could find Connor and, better still, find the Polish kid he'd beaten to death, my work was done. Yeah, it'd probably start world war three, but that was always going to happen now, anyway. And If Shaun McMurphy had been telling me the truth about what he and Finian saw on the high road to Halifax, my job was half done. I wondered if the kid was still in that Bentley somewhere, somehow.

I brought up Dave's number and called.

"Jim. You made it out alive, then? I was getting worried there for a while."

"You busy?"

"Well, theoretically, I'm at work. But I'm about to nail Call of Duty."

"Call of what?"

"Never mind. What can I do for you?"

"Can you still trace that GPS device I planted the other night?"

"The one in Connolly's car?"

"That's it."

"Give me a couple of hours and I'll phone you. Everything okay, by the way?"

I filled him in on events, skipping the details. The 'boxing' wasn't what I thought it was going to be, Connor had probably started a new gang war, they wanted Aisling dead and a Polish kid had been battered to death. Multiple witnesses.

"Just another day at the office, then?"

"Something like that."

And then I told him what Shaun McMurphy had told me. About the body in the boot of that Bentley.

"You think they might've dumped it?"

"Maybe. Probably."

"Maybe you should just get the police involved, Jim. This sounds fucking crazy."

"Well, it's not exactly normal, I'll give you that. But no police. That's why I want you to try to trace it for me."

"And then what?"

"We'll cross that bridge when we come to it."

"Could be a long bridge..."

"Get back to me as soon as you can."

"I'm on it, Chief."

I returned to the living room and we all shared that pot of tea with a tray of biscuits. I confirmed with Laura that the money was safely hidden away and we'd simply dip into it whenever we liked. Her mood had seriously brightened at this news. We didn't stay long and I'd been itching to get back on the streets as soon as possible, knowing that this money hadn't yet been earned. I didn't want two families onto me, so figured I'd better get back to it before anyone had the chance to stop me.

Laura promised Sara we'd all have a slap up tea tonight,

and would be back this afternoon with supplies. Knowing Laura, those supplies would be the luxurious kind. Something told me she was ready to celebrate our new found wealth. As long as it brightened Sara, it was fine with me.

Laura dropped me back in Piccadilly and I spent some time just hanging around while I thought about my next move. Dropped into one of the new bars in the Northern Quarter and sank a cold one, watching the world drift by as I pieced all this shit together in my head. Considered calling into the office after Crane had been hanging around outside it before my arrest, figuring they'd probably done more than a little noseying around. It could wait. I now had a more immediate situation to contend with. If the Connollys were really heading back into town, as McMurphy had said, it was only a matter of time before trouble reared its ugly head.

I was suddenly hit with the notion that Aisling was in immediate danger. Could I give her fair warning? Would she even listen to me after our last conversation?

I needed a plan of action, something to drag me away from this bar. Yeah, I could let things take their course and wait for the blood to fly, but there was an innocent unborn kid to think about. I didn't need to examine my conscience. I knew I just had to do whatever I could to help prevent a nasty outcome.

Connor's development was an old mill down Ancoats way, around a mile or so from Laura's flat. It had stood derelict for years and had seen plenty of changes in the vicinity around it, but it had taken until just this year for Connor to take over. New Islington had been built up in the past decade, attracting professionals from all over the place. The Connollys had no doubt seen the area as a sound investment and the purchase of the mill was made. It was big news at the time, and Connor had become the face of the operation. Everyone knew he'd acquired the building in circumstances that were hardly legit, but no one was willing to question it, least of all the media.

The place had become a building site overnight and nothing would be done in a hurry. The mill would get more than just a lick of paint. Luxury apartments were springing up everywhere these days. Connor had ambitions to outdo everyone else.

I made my way over there, crossing the busy traffic of Great Ancoats Street and heading into the shadows of the old brick mills beside the canal. Now it was the old retail park's turn to lie derelict as, beyond, brand new high-rise apartments loomed.

When I reached the building itself, most of which was protected by metal fencing, there wasn't a soul around. There was no work being done, no drills drilling, no hammers banging. Nothing. Not a single hard hat in sight. Perhaps the work had been put on hold for some reason. The Connollys certainly didn't seem in such a great rush to see the project finished and the apartments occupied. Tools had been downed and I had to admit, I was finding the vibe quite spooky. I looked up, the scaffolding skirting the perimeter right to the top. Looked like the exterior would be getting sandblasted anytime now.

Wondered if I could scale those heights.

Instead, I walked around, keeping my eyes peeled for anyone I recognised. Didn't see a soul, but I caught a couple of high end cars, a Mercedes and a Jaguar, parked up together down a side street. The Mercedes, I knew, could've been Connor's, the same one I'd sat in to deliver the good news to the Connollys about Aisling's forthcoming birth. I couldn't be sure, but it was likely given this place was his new toy.

I found an entrance into the building behind a narrow, curtained off door. I slipped inside, prising open a sheet of plasterboard and shimmying through the gap. Made a mental note of my escape route, should the need arise. There was enough natural light shining through the gaps for me to see, which was a blessing. Coming here in the dark would be a different story, though. All the lighting on this floor at least still needed wiring in. Looked like the job was half complete and then they'd just downed tools and left. I guessed there had to be a good reason for that.

Mooched inside and found myself in an enormous room, bits of rubble scattered around, heavy industrial equipment parked in the middle, power saws and sledge-hammers left lying against the far wall and a large work-bench occupying the centre of the room. Above, the ceiling had been in the middle of being re-plastered, and there was a vast collection of barely unboxed window frames stacked against the western wall.

The room was deathly silent.

I jumped when my phone rang out.

"Fi," I said, my voice echoing through the room. "You made me jump."

"How so?"

"Wasn't expecting your call, you know."

"Where are you?"

"Connor's place."

"Connor Connolly's?"

"The development, you know."

"Ah, right. Well, be careful."

"I don't think anyone's here."

"Probably not. The Connollys have an unexpected death on their hands. They're probably tied up elsewhere."

"Hang on, back up. What unexpected death?"

There was a pause. Took the opportunity to spark up, instinctively feeling I'd need it.

"Kian Connolly is dead, Jim. She found him this morning, at home."

"Kian? What, Kian Connolly?"

"Kian."

"Who found him?"

"His girlfriend."

Took that shit in deep. "What happened?"

"He'd been bludgeoned to death. Serious head injuries. She found him in a pool of blood in the kitchen. She's obviously in a state but..."

"Fuck..."

"It's being treated as a murder, obviously."

"Any suspects?"

"Not immediately, so I'm told. There was no weapon found on the scene. I believe it was a bit of a mess."

"Not surprising."

I thought I heard something upstairs, a loud thud like something heavy had been dropped.

"The scene will be cordoned off for a while. I don't know if the Connollys even know yet. I mean, he was only found this morning. Jim?"

"I'll call you back."

I pocketed the phone, suddenly aware that I was holding my breath. Stepped on, cringing at the sound of my boots on the marbled floor. The building was empty, I was sure of it. Perhaps my mind was simply playing tricks on me. I crept on and found an old stone stairway behind a set of double swing doors. The air was cool. I looked up and saw the staircase went all the way to the top, which was at least seven storeys. I must've been crazy to think going up there was a good idea, but nevertheless found myself ascending.

But I stopped when I heard voices. Couldn't make out how many there were or what was being said, but it was clear they were pissed off. I realised I had to get out of here.

But I stepped up again, knowing it was stupid.

Something went clattering against metal, and the voices were raised a notch.

Time to get out.

I retraced my steps and escaped into the early afternoon sun, shimmying through the gap and carefully closing it behind me.

The two sports cars were still there, which hinted that they did indeed belong to whoever was in the building.

I moved across the street to another mill that had been renovated and found a little hiding place in the crevice of a wall, just a few yards from the main entrance into the apartments. There was no one around, which was just as well, and I made sure I was out of sight in case Connor and his boys appeared. It was a good vantage point.

I needed to call Aisling, to try and warn her somehow that she could be in trouble. At least if I tried, my conscience would be clear.

I knew this game was getting silly. Whoever was responsible for Kian's death - and I suspected the Badowski's were involved somehow - had probably started something that would end in major tears. The Connollys wouldn't take kindly to one of their own being taken out like that. It was only a matter of time before the response came. Perhaps it was a reaction to the Polish kid killed at the hands of Connor himself.

I took out my phone and found Aisling's number.

"Hello?"

"Aisling?"

A pause. "Yeah....?"

"It's Jim Locke. Look, don't hang up."

"The private detective guy? The one doing my dad's dirty work? What the fuck do you want?"

"Well, I didn't exactly expect the best of welcomes."

"I thought I told you to stay away from me."

"You did."

"And I'm telling you again. Now fuck off!"

"No! No, wait. Aisling, please. Please, you need to hear what I'm about to say. It's important."

"My dad put you up to this, has he?"

"He knows you're pregnant. I know. We all know. Everyone knows you're pregnant, Aisling, and it doesn't look good for you, I'm afraid."

Another pause, this time longer. A half laugh, but I knew there was anxiety in it. I kept one eye on Connor's building opposite as she breathed down the phone.

"What do you mean? What do you mean, you know?"

"There's no need to know how. But I know."

"It was her, wasn't it? It was Claire, that fucking bitch!"

"Aisling."

"I'm gonna fucking kill her."

"Yeah, if they don't kill you first. Listen, they know. Your dad, Connor, everyone. And they're not too happy about it, love, I can tell you that."

"Jesus Christ, for fuck's sake!"

"I think you're in danger. All right? So consider this a warning. The cat's out of the bag, love. And they're coming for you."

They were coming for me, too. I almost dropped my

phone when I saw Connor march around the corner and come straight for me.

Fuck.

I had two seconds to think about running.

I ran, clutching the phone tight as boots thumped on the pavement behind me. There must've been more than one of them and I couldn't chance a look back. I sprinted out to the left, winging it completely as I ran out onto Great Ancoats Street. Dodged the traffic as I skipped across the road and almost got hit by a van. I looked back when I reached the other side and saw that they were gone. Ducked into a Brazilian restaurant, just across from the old Express News building, and hovered near the window so I could see the traffic flow from relative safety.

There was no sign of them.

"Can I help you, sir?"

I caught my breath. "Sorry. Sorry, I'm gonna go. Just... sorry."

Jumped out of the door, back to the pavement. Traffic streamed past and for a moment, I thought I saw Connor over on the other opposite side. It wasn't.

But then his Mercedes rolled out, pulling up on to the pavement opposite like he couldn't give a fuck. I watched as two of his boys followed on foot from a side street and got in the back.

A black cab pulled up behind a bus that was blocking my view. Flagged that bastard down before he had other ideas. Got in, caught my breath again, took out my phone.

"Where to?"

"See that Mercedes over there? The black one, on the pavement."

"Nice..."

"Follow it," I said, feeling the wad of cash in my pocket. "I'll pay you whatever it takes, just follow it."

"What are you, a copper or something? Going under-cover, like?"

"Just shut the fuck up and drive."

THIRTY ONE

He took a U turn at the first opportunity and fell in behind the Mercedes as it joined the traffic. He was babbling some shit or other as he dropped back a few vehicles behind our target car. I thought about calling Wiktor Badowski, to let him know I was following his man right now and have done with it all, but I wasn't sure I was ready for that yet. If Connor was on his way to Aisling, I had to make that my priority. After I'd witnessed him kill that Polish kid with his bare hands, I knew he was capable of anything. I couldn't let him get to his sister.

We picked up speed as we headed down Great Ancoats Street towards the Mancunian Way. I took out my phone and opened up the camera app. Started filming. I zoomed in on the Mercedes as best I could, but it was hard keeping the car in shot. The taxi was bouncing from lane to lane and, to be fair, the driver was doing a decent job of keeping on Connor's tail, but it didn't make for good footage. Nevertheless, I had something, and I considered using it to send to Badowski, just so he knew I was doing the job he'd asked.

"And so it's bloody annoying, you know...?"

"What?"

"I said it's bloody annoying! You know, the council doesn't give us enough places to..."

Like I gave a fuck. "Try to stay back a bit. I don't want him to clock me."

"You really are a copper, aren't you? You know, I should've been a copper myself. Back in the day. Too late now."

The phone rang. "Yeah."

"What do you mean, I'm in danger? What's my dad got planned?"

Her voice sounded broken, like she'd been crying. Did she know about her brother?

"Look, Aisling. I'm sorry about... Well, I'm so sorry to hear about your brother."

"My brother? What about my brother?"

"You don't know? About Kian?"

"What about him? You're not making any sense!"

It was my turn to be silent as the wheels rolled beneath me. I watched as Connor's Mercedes crossed the junction at Ashton Old Road and went straight onto the Mancunian Way flyover. The cab picked up speed.

"Well?"

"He was found dead this morning. At home. I suggest you contact the police, for two reasons: to learn about your brother and to ask them for protection."

But she'd gone already. Perhaps it had finally hit home that she was in trouble. I'd done what I could for now.

"So the way I see it is, they just don't give a fuck, you know what I mean?"

"Yeah."

The Mercedes was speeding, easily doing way over the fifty limit on here. I told him to keep up.

"It's alright, I've got my eye on it."

"You're gonna lose it."

"Not to worry."

As the cab dropped down towards the Regent Road roundabout, I was relieved to see the traffic had come to a standstill in a gridlock. The roadworks ahead had brought the Mercedes to a stop, a few cars ahead of us. With horns blaring as the Mercedes manoeuvred and blatantly forced its way through on an outside lane, encroaching onto a traffic island to squeeze past, I was certain we'd lost them as they went speeding up towards Deansgate.

The cab went to do the same, squeezing in through a narrow gap between two lanes. He ran a red light and we almost got taken out by an eighteen wheeler, but he slammed on before screeching over the cordoned off section of tarmac and crashing through the barriers.

"Woah, what the fuck are you doing?!"

"There they are!"

"You'll get us both killed!"

But he was intent on catching up, a crazed look in his eyes as I caught his reflection in the rearview. I went sliding across the seats as he weaved across lanes, suddenly feeling sick and dizzy. I wasn't entirely sure this day was going well so far, but fuck it.

He ran another red light before putting his foot down some more as we passed the Hilton, then Spinningfields, before he cut a bus up and spun a hard left down Bridge Street. The Mercedes was down the bottom end. Seemed like Connor and his boys needed to get somewhere in a hurry.

"Where the fuck are they going?"

He didn't answer, just kept the taxi on its tail, his foot on the floor. We crossed the bridge, passed the courts and the People's History Museum, gunned it past the Salford rail station and under the bridge before taking a sharp right onto Chapel Street. The Mercedes pulled into Dearman's Place, which was a one-way street, but I knew where it led.

He pulled up on the left, under another rail bridge.

"Looks like they're going to the Lowry. I guess they've got the money."

I threw him a twenty and headed for the hotel entrance.

The hotel was busy. I did my best to stay out of sight, but it wasn't so easy when I didn't know what I was hiding from. Wandered over to the check-in desk, wishing I was invisible. There was no sign of Connor, which told me he must have had a room booked in. I spun around, my eyes scanning the foyer. Then I clocked him and two of his boys - one of whom I recognised as Declan, the Dubliner - hovering near the lift.

"Can I help you, sir?"

I turned to see a pretty blonde awaiting my response. I stumbled over a quick decision and took out my wallet, digging around for my business credit card.

"Room for one. Basic."

"For how many nights?"

"Just tonight. For now. I might want to extend my stay if that's ok?"

"Of course." She took my card. "I'll just need some details."

I willed her to hurry the fuck up as I kept one eye on Connor. Thankfully, he didn't see me, which was reassuring. I was clearly the last thing on his mind. I watched as the lift doors opened and they stepped in. Tried to clock which floor they were headed to, but it was useless.

I gave her my details, skipping over the niceties. She handed me a key card and I thanked her, heading for the lift. Pressed the button and waited. Moments later, it pinged open and I stepped in, alone. Pressed the button for the third floor, wary of what might await me when I landed.

I was swept up in seconds. When the doors swished open again, I stepped out into an empty corridor, but there were voices nearby. I didn't recognise them. I warily tip toed on as the voices got louder. When I turned the corner, I was relieved to see a handful of people who had nothing to do with this whole shit show.

I found my room at the bottom end. Pressed the keycard against the handle as my phone went off again.

"Dave."

"Jim. So I've been doing a bit of digging. That GPS device is still giving a signal. I've tracked the location and I reckon it'd be a tough one to find, but not entirely impossible. You might have to do a bit on foot."

I slipped into my room and crashed on the bed. "Where is it?"

"There's a forest in Darwen. Blackburn way. Looks like it's there."

"You think the car's there or just the device? Could they have tossed it?"

"If they found it, yeah. But have they found it? Probably not. Where did you hide it?"

"Under the front passenger seat."

"Whether the car's there or not, the signal is still active. Only one way to find out."

"Are you free tonight? Could probably do with your help."

There was a pause. "I'll pick you up at seven. That okay?"

"I'll see you then."

I sparked up and called Laura. It took several efforts but I got her in the end. She was obviously busy out shopping because all I could hear was noise.

"Where are you?"

"Kendals. I've just bought the most amazing dress, you'll love it."

"Do me a favour. I need you to go to the office and check everything. I'm gonna need the camera and my walking boots. I've got a nasty feeling the police have been rummaging around with my stuff but I'm trying not to worry about that now."

"Everything's backed up on the hard drive. And that's in the safe. Even if they've got anything, we've got copies. Blackmail's a very useful tool."

"Just don't be out all day. And let me know the state of the office as soon as possible."

"Okay, but where are you?"

I told her. She told me to be careful. Easier said than done.

"I've got a surprise for you when you get home. And remember we're having steak for tea."

"I might not be home tonight, love. I might not make it."

"Oh, Jim! Come on..."

"Got stuff to do."

"And why do you need the camera?"

"I think there's a body in a forest in Darwen. The Polish kid. I'll need to record any evidence we find."

"Who's we?"

"Dave's coming with me. He picks me up at seven."

I checked the room out quickly while I gathered my thoughts and considered my options. I realised I didn't have many. I'd told myself that as long as I'd warned Aisling of the danger she was in, my job was done. And even though she'd treated me as an enemy, I hoped she could see that all I wanted was her best interests, which was protecting that unborn child of hers.

I didn't need to think twice about my next call. Though before I did, I went through the footage I had on my phone of the pursuit in that taxi of Connor's Mercedes. The footage was pretty crappy, but I sent it via text message anyway, just so he had it. Then I dialled Wiktor up.

"Mr. Locke."

"Mr. Badowski. Connor Connolly is in the Lowry hotel. I'm here now. And by tonight, I may have news about the kid. The one from the abattoir. I'll keep you informed."

"I'm happy you're not wasting any time, Locke."

"Never."

"This pleases me a lot."

I bet it did, but I wanted nothing more of it. I was getting twitchy with the curtains while he spoke.

"Listen, I'm gonna hang around here."

"There's really no need."

"Maybe not, but I feel I need to. And listen, about Aisling. Things aren't looking good for her."

"I'll make sure she's safe."

"You can't trust these bastards."

And I knew full well that the Badowskis couldn't be

trusted either. This shit somehow needed to come to an end. I felt I could only relax once Connor was taken care of.

"We thank you for your efforts, Locke. But there is no need to hang around. We'll take over from here. Your work is done. Relax. Take time out. Enjoy the money."

"I will." But I would hang around, just to see for myself what kind of shit would go down. "I'll leave all this in your capable hands."

There was a pause as I heard him breathing down the line. "We may require your services another time. I trust we have a professional relationship."

"Of course."

"Good. Good. Then I thank you again. I will be in touch should I require those services."

I was about to say that was absolutely fine, but he'd already hung up.

I stepped to the door and turned the handle slowly. I had to be careful now that I knew Connor was in the same building. Perhaps Seamus would join him soon enough. One of his sons was dead. He wouldn't take that lightly.

I peeked out into the corridor, which was empty and quiet. I could hear the traffic outside, but that was all. Made sure I had everything I needed before venturing out of the room. Put my phone on silent and allowed the door to shut behind me. I figured I could play this two ways: I could either creep around wherever I went or I could move around casually and take things as they came. I'd do my best to avoid them wherever possible, of course, and I couldn't be too relaxed. I had to be on my toes, just in case. But creeping around would only draw unwanted attention to myself and could end up doing more harm than good. So I put a bold foot in front of the other and made my way down to the bar. A drink was long overdue.

The bar was dotted with patrons, no more than twenty, scattered around the room and enjoying an early Friday drink. I knew I had to be careful not to get carried away, especially if I was to go trudging through a forest tonight.

I stepped up and got myself a pint, then settled in the far corner, in an empty booth beside the window. That way I could keep an eye on outside too.

I sat back in the shadows and drank, savouring every mouthful. Tried hard to not down the fucker, but it was proving difficult. Now that I had a taste, I was ready to go all in. I knew it would be a mistake, so I sat on my hands until I could take it no more, then got myself another. This could be a long afternoon.

I was relatively satisfied that I was inconspicuous enough, and I soon found my thoughts drifting. I thought about my work file that Fiona had gotten for me. And I thought about our close encounter, too. I mean, what the fuck was I playing at? God help me if Laura found out... and I loved her. I didn't want to hurt her.

But temptation had almost gotten the better of me.

I had to remain professional.

I took out my phone and dialled her up.

"Jim?"

"Fi. Look, love, I..."

"Go on."

"I was... I was wondering if there's any news on Kian. On what happened."

There was a pause, and I heard her breathing down the line. "He was bludgeoned to death. And that's really all there is to it. Apparently, he had CCTV on the house and it had picked up the attacker. They're going through it as we speak."

"I take it the Connollys know."

"Oh yeah. Seamus is angry, to say the least. Look, where are you, Jim?"

I told her.

"You think that's a good idea? You should get out of there."

"I've got a bad feeling something's gonna go down."

"All the more reason to leave. Are you drinking?"

"Just the one," I lied.

"Then just leave it now. You've done your bit, let them bloody kill each other."

"I suppose I want to enjoy the view. I need to see what Connor's up to. I'd like to see the bastard get what's coming."

"You think they'll get to him?"

"I've no doubt about it," I said, knowing that I'd already told Badowski where he was. "Only a matter of time."

"You're crazy, you know that?"

"You wouldn't be the first to say that."

There was another pause. "Look, what's the real reason for this phone call? Is it about last night? Because you don't have to hide anything, Jim."

Was she picking up on my vibes somehow? No doubt about it, but I couldn't go there, not now. "No. I just wanted to check in, that's all."

"Save it. Another time. And do yourself a favour and get out of there. Leave it all behind you. It's done. Take the money and run. Disappear for a while, now that you can."

"And what will you do?"

"There's not much else left for me to do, to be honest. My notice has gone in and I'm just counting down the days. I should probably get busy looking for a job, but I'm gonna give myself a break. Think I need one."

"You do that, love."

The sight of Lukasz Badowski caught my eye then and I

instinctively sank into my seat and the shadows. He'd walked into the room with a keen stride and stepped up to the bar. Two heavy looking men followed him. All three were dressed as sharp as they come.

"I will. For now, I'm just biding my time."

"Listen, Fi, I've got to go."

"Okay..."

"Lukasz Badowski's just walked in. I think it's about to go down."

"Get the fuck out of there now, Jim."

I hung up. Sank my pint. Kept my head down. I was feeling jumpy, so I did what any self respecting private investigator would do and started taking photos. I was far enough away to be irrelevant to them, but also close enough to take a bullet in the head if one was to come my way. Would I put it past them? I didn't think any of them could be that stupid, but I couldn't be too certain. Yet I felt an urgent need to get moving.

THIRTY TWO

I left my seat and headed over to a space beyond the entrance to the bar. The foyer was quite busy with people leaving and entering the building, so I mingled with them, standing out of sight of Lukasz Badowski and his hangers on.

I looked around for Connor, but there was no sign of him or his entourage. I suppose it was to be expected. Perhaps they'd had an inkling that the Badowskis would show up - after all, he'd killed one of their own countrymen with his bare hands - but perhaps they'd not expected them to show up here. They had me to blame for that, of course, and in that regard, my debt to Wiktor had been done. It was all easy enough. Now I could leave it all well alone. And it would be a long time before I let either of these two families entice me into their silly games again.

I kept one eye on the exit. Out there, sanity beckoned, and I was keen to get moving, but something was holding me here. I watched Lukasz Badowski lift a drink and sip. Clocked the reflection of his crew in the full length bar mirror. I was conscious that the back of my neck was prickling with sweat. Swallowed hard when I realised I was holding my breath.

I backed off into the shadows and kept out of sight behind an enormous plant as Declan ran into the bar. The screams went up before I could realise what the fuck was happening. He was holding a blade, a machete, a slab of steel that gleamed in the afternoon light as he lunged at Badowski. One of his men got in the way and took it across his forearm, and the blade went down like a cleaver smashing into animal bones on the butcher's block. I could almost hear it chop through the flesh over the screams as the crowd scattered and I scattered with it.

An alarm was raised and it echoed through the hotel as more of Connor's entourage steamed in, and Connor too, fists flying as the bar area erupted into a mass brawl. I took photos as randomly and as fast as I could before I finally got the sense to get the fuck out of there. Clocked a pool of blood on the marble floor and one of Badowski's men lying in it, his arm a red and white mess of flesh and bone.

Things had gone tits up, big style. Glasses and chairs flew, gunshots cracked against the mirror as bodies scarpered.

I ran out into the street, hoping the chaos behind would be swallowed up. It wasn't, but instead spilled out with me. A metallic gold high end BMW spun across the road, wheels spinning, and its back end slammed into a lamppost, smashing the tail lights.

I chanced a look back into the foyer and saw Lukasz Badowski sprawled facedown across the floor, a bloom of crimson sparkling with broken glass on his back. But there was no sign of Connor Connolly. There were a few others out of it too, though I couldn't be sure whose side they were on.

I staggered out, almost blind, as the chaos went up a notch. Stumbled into the road, eager to get the fuck out of dodge before I got caught in the crossfire. Already, sirens were blaring somewhere nearby. It had all happened so quickly, and I could only hope this shit was over.

I stumbled into the road, the sound of gunshots piercing the day. The entire world swam, and I turned to see Aisling Connolly running, tears streaming down her pretty face. She was running towards me, and at first I thought she was running for me, but she couldn't have been. I was insignificant to her, an accomplice of her father, the bastard who'd delivered nothing but bad news.

I turned back around and realised she was running for her lover, the father of their unborn child. Lukasz Badowski, I realised, was already dead. The pool of blood soaked the hotel foyer and the glass sparkled around him. He was gone.

When I turned back to Aisling, I watched her stumble. Then her eyes seemed to glaze over and burst wide as her stomach exploded, which sent her falling face forward. She reached her arms out to cushion the fall, but failed. When she landed, she lay flat out on the road. Behind her, Connor pocketed the gun in his suit jacket as he ran for the Mercedes, its rear passenger door open and ready. He dived inside and the Mercedes sped off, leaving Aisling dying there on the city street, her copper dress stained.

When it was clear the violence was over and the atmosphere had become a strange, eerie silence, which was only disturbed by an army of blue flashing lights and sirens, I got to my feet and went to her, along with others. We turned her over and she was still alive. My hands got covered in her blood as her eyes glazed over and she looked right at me. She didn't say a word, couldn't say a thing. When she tried to speak, she coughed blood, and then the crowd was dispersed by police and paramedics and before I knew it, darkness seemed to fall. A storm had gathered and it was about to pour.

The next few minutes went by in a blur. My only instinct was to get out of there, figuring the police would have something to say. I backed off amid all the commotion and ran blindly into the city. Before long I was on Deansgate, conscious of my bloody hands with my phone to my ear.

"Fi? You there?"

"Please tell me you've left the hotel, Jim."

"I've left. In a hurry. Listen, I think Badowski's dead."

"Wiktor?"

I shook my head, swallowed, aware of my bloody hands. "Lukasz. It all went off in there. Gunshots, blades. I think Aisling's dead too."

"Aisling?"

I swallowed, out of breath. "Yeah. Connor shot her. I saw it all."

"Where's Connor?"

"Fucked off fast, in a Mercedes. I don't know where. It's a bloodbath, Fi."

"Jim, you sound in a panic. Stop and take a deep breath."

"I can't, there's no time. I've gotta... I've gotta..."

"So what happens now?"

"Police have got it surrounded. Maybe they've got it under control, I don't know. There was a lot involved. There could be a few dead."

"Where are you now?"

I told her. I was aware my heart was pounding, my head dizzy with it all. "I need a drink."

"I think that's the last thing you need."

But it was the only thing I needed. "Listen, this'll probably be on the news, along with all the other shit. Can you keep your ear to the ground and keep me posted?"

"Yeah, but what now, Jim? You need to walk away once and for all."

"There's something else I need to do, Fi."

"Whatever it is, do it quick and keep yourself in one piece."

Easier said than done, though I'd do my best and she was right. That holiday couldn't come soon enough. I was reminded of Laura then, and I knew I needed to call her.

I took the backstreets to the office, conscious of the blood on my hands, and dialled her up. Got some funny looks as I tried to keep my hands out of sight. Aisling's blood was staining them pink, and it occurred to me that the baby's blood might be there too.

"I promise I won't spend too much, love," she said. "Just wait until you see this dress I just bought."

"Listen, love, you might've heard the sirens through town. It's all gone off. I think Aisling Connolly is dead. Probably her baby, too. Connor couldn't live with a Badowski in the family."

"Aisling? Dead? Oh, Jesus..."

"I know. Though I'm not one hundred percent. Look, it's complicated. But I'm heading back to the office. I think things might get worse before they get better."

"Ah. Look, there might be a problem."

I paused, waiting for traffic. "You haven't actually been back to the office, have you?"

"Kind of got laid up."

Which made sense, of course. In a way, it suited me.

"Fine. That's where I'll be until Dave comes for me. I'm hoping everything's still in one piece."

"Okay, but please be careful, love. A forest in the middle of nowhere isn't exactly filling me with confidence."

"It's not the middle of nowhere. It's in Darwen. Blackburn. Lancashire? Hardly a million miles away."

"But if something went wrong, Jim. What then?"

"Don't you worry your little head."

There was a pause and I had to strain to hear her, but when a bus went past, it drowned her out.

"Say again, love?"

"I said I love you!"

I found my office key in my back pocket, along with the keycard for my room at the Lowry. I doubted I'd need that again and almost tossed it, but kept it, just in case. I could almost taste the silence as I stepped inside. I climbed the stairs, satisfied the place was how I'd left it, and when I crossed the threshold, it was as I'd thought. I'd been just a little paranoid, maybe, that Crane had been rooting around in here. I wouldn't put it past him, but maybe that was for another day.

I stepped over to the safe and opened up. The kilo of weed I'd nicked from that van in Cheetham Hill was still sitting there, stinking the place out. On the shelf below, my camera. A Nikon D5300, which was more than good enough for the job.

I crashed onto the couch and sparked up. Took that shit in deep.

My temples throbbed and my head felt blocked, like all

the stuff inside it - my thoughts, my ability to think straight - had been messed up. I lazily packed up the camera and finished my smoke, going over events as best I could without allowing it to take over. When all this was over, I'd take a long break from it all. I didn't deserve any of this shit. I didn't deserve Crane on my case, didn't deserve to be standing in between two of the biggest crime families in the city, putting myself at risk like I was. But then, I wasn't entirely blameless. I was the one who'd got involved. I was the one who took the business. Told myself it was easy money and I suppose it was, but even easy money has its consequences.

I thought about the money I'd hidden in Sara's loft. It would certainly keep us well and keep us going for a while. I was even satisfied that it was in a safe place and I could relax about it, at least for now.

Kian's face came into my mind then. The last time I'd spoken to him was at the abattoir and he was high on weed. Said he'd never wanted any part of his father's gangster empire and was almost embarrassed by it. How sad that he had now fallen victim to what the Connolly family had brought upon him. A violent death, the worst kind. Fiona had said there had been CCTV at the property and the police were checking it out. We knew it was highly likely to be one of Wiktor's men, but which one?

I lay back and tried to empty my mind, but it was no use. With my eyes heavy and my body weary, I dozed until I eventually fell into a deep and disturbing sleep.

I dreamt of being buried alive and only woke, gasping for breath and mercy, when I found my hands were covered in blood.

THIRTY THREE

The buzzer sparked me to life and I jumped off the couch, spilling a drop of brandy. Felt like I'd only slept for ten minutes, but it must've been more. I clocked the time on my phone. It was gone seven.

Dave.

The body in the forest. Time to move.

I stumbled over to the intercom and let him up, knowing I had to get my shit together. Crashed over to the sink and scrubbed my hands in month old soap, watching the sink turn pink with Aisling's blood. Saw her stunned, dying face in my mind and felt her pregnant bump in my hands as I swilled my face in freezing water.

"Jesus..."

Heard Dave on the landing. "Been a long day, Jim? You ready?"

I couldn't say I was. I needed two things; a cold beer and a hard smoke. I could only muster one. I sparked up and asked him to give me a minute. I grabbed the camera and some other things, not forgetting my clunky walking boots, and five minutes later we were in Dave's black Porsche and leaving the city centre.

"So, what's the plan?"

"Well, you tell me. This was your idea."

"You said you could trace this tracking device to that forest," I said. "So we find it... and maybe find him."

"Am I gonna end up in trouble, Jim? Because I don't think I could handle that right now."

"No," I said. "Not if you stick with me."

I saw him laughing from the corner of my eye and sunk back into the plush leather beneath my arse.

"Come on, man. You and I both know you've been playing a dangerous game. If some of my mates knew I was doing this right now, they'd either piss themselves laughing or hand me straight into Park House. So which is it?"

"Come on, Dave. We're only going to find a dead body. It's not as if this is totally out of the ordinary in this city."

"Oh yeah, completely normal."

"You've not seen what I've seen."

This time I clocked him gripping the wheel. We were heading out of town, up Rochdale Road and down to the motorway. Pretty soon, we'd be far away and out in the sticks. If Dave could still pick up the tracker, who knows where we'd end up.

"Mind if I smoke?"

He answered by dropping the passenger window. I sparked up and blew smoke into the night. A deep dark had descended and there was still plenty of traffic about. It occurred to me now that perhaps this was just a bit crazy.

Even if we found the forest, it could take ages to find the actual spot in this darkness. And there would be even less light beneath those trees. It was a good job I hadn't forgotten the torch.

I'd quickly gathered up some essentials to bring along while Dave had waited. A large torch, the camera, a bottle of water, spare smokes, a heavy raincoat and some nitrile gloves. I made a quick check to make sure I hadn't forgotten anything. Wished I'd brought some food too. I realised I was bloody hungry.

Dave asked me what I'd been up to, so I filled him in as best I could. I didn't leave anything out. When I got around to the dead Connollys - although I wasn't entirely certain Aisling was dead - his face changed. The nervous laughter had gone and he now looked worried.

"Jim, I mean it. I hope this isn't gonna get me in trouble. I'm not quite ready to die just yet."

"You're not gonna die," I said. "Not even close. Look, I know this must seem crazy and looking for a body in the woods is straight out of some horror novel, but if we can find it and find evidence the Connollys are involved, then we hand it over to the police and our work is done."

"It might come back to haunt you, though. You know these people don't fuck about."

"True. But now that Lukasz Badowski is dead, I expect them to kill each other long before anyone gets around to me."

"So Kian's a definite. What about Aisling? Do we even know for sure she's joined him?"

"No. But I can't see her surviving that."

He was silent for a moment and I detected a sudden reluctance as he pulled onto the M60 at Victoria Avenue and I tossed my smoke. "What kind of person would murder their own sister?"

"Look no further than Connor Connolly. Psychopathy runs in the family. You know, I wish I'd never gotten involved in any of it. I should've known better. Perhaps I really have lost all sense."

"He sounds like a massive prick."

It was an understatement. And God only knew what other kind of hell had gone down since this afternoon. No doubt I'd find out soon enough, but I didn't expect the killing to stop.

Dave put his foot down once we moved onto the M66. I guessed we'd be there in about half an hour, though getting to the actual place might prove difficult. And we didn't know what kind of terrain we'd find.

"I take it you know where we're heading?"

"I've got a good idea," he said. "But we'll need the sat nav the closer we get."

"And is this device still giving off a signal?"

He nodded. "Grab that iPad on the back seat. It's all on that."

After some messing around, I opened up an app and saw a beacon icon flashing in red in the middle of what appeared to be a forest. The wonders of technology never ceased to amaze me.

"That it?"

"That's it," he said. "The signal's not great. To be expected given where it is. But it's still there."

"Does it say anything else?"

"Like what?"

"What kind of terrain. How can we access it?"

"The terrain will be earthy and spongy underfoot. Maybe rocky in places. It's a forest, Jim."

"I know that, but ..."

"I think there's a two hundred metre elevation. Something like that. There's a major road on the outside edge of it and probably a few dirt tracks leading into the forest itself. It's all pine. What you'd expect, I suppose. The nearest village is two miles away."

"Is the place managed by anyone?"

He shrugged. "Local council? Forestry Commission? Don't know. Never thought of that."

That would be my guess. There was probably a ranger involved, maybe even a team. How often they were there, I had no idea.

We soon left the boundary of Greater Manchester shortly after we passed the exit for Bury, and carried on towards Rawtenstall and, beyond that, Blackburn. Dave said we'd be leaving the motorway soon to take an A road to our destination. As he drove, I thought about my next move.

There was nothing I could do about much of this now except watch it all play out. These two families had it in for each other, so why should anyone care, least of all me? A long time feud was about to reach a conclusion and no one gave a toss except those involved. I thought about Aisling's baby, the innocent one in all of this. Surely it couldn't survive. I'd seen the horror of that gun blast with my own eyes, watched Aisling crash to the deck. Maybe they were at peace now, joining young Kian. I thought about my first encounter with the kid. He was full of bravado, a little bit cocky. A bit of a fool. But he didn't deserve the kind of death he'd had to endure.

And Lukasz Badowski. Gunned down in cold blood. Connor hadn't fucked around. He wanted them dead. He wanted them all dead. But I knew Wiktor wouldn't stand for that. He'd take them all down and no doubt go down with them. They were fucked up people and the city would be a much better place without them.

My phone rang just as we left the illuminated section of the motorway. Ahead of us was pure black, and Dave put the lights on full beam to guide the way.

I expected her to call, but maybe not so soon. I looked out at the rolling hills and answered.

"Jim, where are you?"

"Heading for the hills, Fi. In the heart of darkness."

She sounded out of breath. "Be careful. Though I'm not entirely sure why you're bothering, but... I'm ringing to update you."

"Aisling's dead."

"You know?"

"I saw it all, Fi. Held her in my arms."

"She died about an hour ago. The baby was only in the second trimester. It was a boy. Gone too."

"Fuck."

"She had no chance."

"I know. Any news on Connor?"

"Nothing. He could be anywhere right now. Wouldn't surprise me if someone's got to him before us, to be honest."

"Where are you now?"

"At home. You know it's all over the news?"

"I guessed it might be. Haven't had chance to catch up."

"This is still ongoing, Jim. Top brass are expecting major repercussions. There's armed units at the Lowry and around town. There's no sign of Seamus or Wiktor. Do you know where they are?"

"Not a clue, but why would I know, anyway? This has nothing to do with me."

Except I took that money from Wiktor without any hesitation. Told him where Connor was and then it all went down. Perhaps this really was all my fault.

"Maybe not, but you're in the thick of it. You must have some idea."

"Not at all. You know what these old bastards are like, Fi. They've seen it all before. Old hands at evading the law. They'll be keeping low, no doubt. Waiting for the next opportunity."

"An opportunity that might never come. And I don't think it will now. It's over. According to the news, half of them are dead. I'd be surprised if any of them turn up alive."

"Let's hope so, eh?"

There was a moment of silence on the line as the Porsche purred over the asphalt beneath us. Dave took the exit ahead, and there was a sudden warmth as the heated seats kicked in. The stereo was on low, playing something by The Fall.

"Look. I don't need to tell you to be careful, Jim. I want you home in one piece."

"We'll be fine."

The line went dead. But my thumb hovered over Wiktor Badowski's number.

G ot a dead line.

Tried him again. Same thing. Either he didn't

want to be contacted or he'd simply switched his phone off. I guessed he wouldn't want to speak to me, anyway. The same went for Seamus. I'd have been the last thing on their minds. I wondered how Seamus was taking the death of his daughter and unborn grandson. Kian, too. And how was Wiktor feeling about his son's murder?

The tragedy, as is usually the way with these things, is that they'd very much brought it all on themselves. And maybe both old men always knew it was gonna end this way.

"Maybe it doesn't matter anymore," Dave said. "You know. This."

"I'm not following you."

"Well, if they're all basically killing each other, is there really any point in us being here trying to find this dead kid?"

I could understand where he was coming from. Maybe there was no point. But I felt we had to find him. And if we were lucky, find the Bentley too. The kid had a family somewhere. He'd gotten himself tied up in fanciful dreams of being a fighter and lost his life right there in the pit. Murdered in cold blood like the animals once were in that abattoir. No one deserved to go that way. There had to be some kind of justice for him. As far as we knew, his killer was still out there somewhere. Still alive, though for how long was anybody's guess.

Dave took the Porsche up through some rolling hills that stood black against the starlight. Tonight was a full moon, the sky clear. We passed through a quiet little village before heading downhill on a long B road. There were parts of the road that were very narrow. It was a country lane, pretty much, and Dave had fun showing off his driving skills.

We almost missed it, but finally came to a stop about twenty metres from a gated entrance hidden back from the road. Dave backed up with precision and parked it snug beside the gate. It was dark enough here that any passing cars - and I guessed it was a rarity because we hadn't seen one for miles - would miss it.

"So I reckon this is it," he said. "This is the forest. One entrance, at least. It's a small one, size wise, compared to most."

"But big enough to dump a body?"

He nodded. "I suppose so."

"Are you ready, then?"

"I've come prepared," he said, pulling out a foot long torch and a couple of joints. He winked. "Nice night for it, eh?"

"You can keep that shit away from me. Let's go."

I made sure I had the rucksack on and everything I'd packed was there. Maybe I wouldn't need it at all, but it was there if I did. The torch I'd definitely need. It was pitch black. A dense darkness that was putting the shits up me. We jumped the gate - nothing more than an average farm gate - and stepped cautiously at first. It was spongy under foot, the floor carpeted with fallen branches and bracken. When the ground levelled out and we got more used to it, we found our eyes adjusted to the gloom and the pitch black faded away to a milky white, with only the light of the full moon peeking through the high canopy of evergreens surrounding us.

Dave had his iPad open to a sophisticated GPS app, and he was double checking it against a similar app on his android phone. He explained how it was all linked up to the tracker I'd planted in the Bentley the night Dale and Declan took me up to the abattoir. I was amazed it was still giving off a signal. Dave reckoned the device had an excellent shelf life and was designed to survive the elements for a long time. Unlike humans. The clear sky had brought a chill with it. Spring was around the corner, but it still felt like winter out here.

"According to this," he said, "it should be somewhere east of where we're standing. I reckon we can find it in less than an hour if we keep our wits about us. Can't be that hard to find."

I shone my torch into the depths and caught my breath when something rustled and sprang away out of sight. "Jesus, what was that?"

He shrugged. "Don't know. Pine Marten, maybe?"

"Who do you think you are, Chris Packham?"

"All right then, a bat."

"A bat?"

"Plenty of bats in here, I think."

"It had legs and ran."

"Whatever. Anyway, if we go east for a few hundred metres, we should be there. It won't be entirely accurate, but I think it'll be close."

I sighed and fastened up my jacket. Maybe I'd come under prepared. It was cold. What I needed right now was a cosy log fire in a quiet pub.

"We'd better get on with it," I said. "I don't want to be out here all night."

We fought our way through the spongy earth. There was a deep smell of pine around us, which wasn't unpleasant, but it soon mixed with Dave's weed. He couldn't resist sparking up as we walked. Offered me some, which I declined. I sparked up my own, though. Took that shit in deep.

Out here, the air was cold and pure. A far cry from the city. And as we walked, the sound of the forest floor - all pine branches and ferns - cracked under our feet. Wherever I shone the torch, and Dave his, there was another fallen tree, another rotting stump, to negotiate. I fell on my arse a few times, much to Dave's amusement. I was a bit worried that, should he drop his joint, the whole forest would go up in flames, the place was that dry.

"Are we any closer?"

He checked out the iPad, running his finger across the screen. Showed me the flashing red spot and the blue one to indicate where we were standing. It was hard to judge just how far, but it was close. Probably no more than another ten minutes' walk if we got a move on.

"You sure you don't want a blast of this? It's good stuff."

"No, thanks," I said. Wondered where it had come from and considered that maybe it had come from the cannabis farm I stumbled upon. The premises where the very kid we were looking for was shadow boxing to some old school boxing hero on that portable T.V. I also considered that I'd finally found someone to palm off that kilo of weed onto. It had been stinking my office out for days now.

He stubbed it out on a nearby trunk. "I'll save it for later."

I nodded. "Probably just as well."

We carried on. Dave led the way while I tried to keep my balance. We reached a clearing, empty and quiet. Something whizzed past us - probably one of those bats - and then dived at Dave's head before whooshing off again.

Dave shone his torch and pointed out the dirt track that

seemed to cut through the trees. "Are they tyre tracks or have I smoked too much?"

I took a closer look with my own light. "It's possible, I suppose."

"Nah, they're definitely tyre tracks." He shone the torch into the darkness beyond, but could see nothing. What were we looking for? Could be nothing at all. Maybe they'd found the tracker and tossed it, but why was it here? Strange place to get rid of it unless someone launched it from the road. They'd have to be good to throw it from there.

No, the only possible explanation was that they'd dumped the car here.

Or maybe they'd driven it here up this dirt track and buried the kid in a shallow grave before tossing the device - which they'd found beneath that passenger seat - somewhere nearby.

"Come on," I said. "We won't get anywhere standing here."

We wrestled our way through the trees, with nothing but a couple of spotlights illuminating the way ahead. We both stumbled a few more times until the darkness got that little bit darker and the Bentley, hidden away in a thicket of tall pines that seemed to go right up into space, came into view, its front end crushed against the trunk of a pine. The car was still in one piece and hadn't been burnt out like I thought it might've been. I supposed that would explain why we could still pick up the tracker. Fire damage would've surely knocked that out for good.

We edged closer and circled the car. Couldn't see anything inside through the privacy glass. I rummaged around in the rucksack for the gloves. Slung Dave a pair and we put them on. Then I tried the handle on the driver's side and was met with a foul stench that turned my stomach and I had to turn away while I retched up bile all over my boots.

"Fuck, man," Dave said. "Jesus, that's awful."

He wasn't wrong. I retrieved the camera from the rucksack and attached a flash gun. Fired her up and started shooting all around the vehicle. Got as many photos as I could before it was time to open her up and photograph inside.

Dave opened the passenger side and almost threw up himself. I was getting nervous about what was in that boot. He felt around beneath the seats and pulled out the tracker, holding it aloft like a trophy before pocketing it. The flash buzzed and whirred, the bright light showing up the horror in our faces every time.

"You ready?"

"Can't say I am," I said, "but I suppose we'd better get this done."

Dave lifted the boot and staggered back, his mouth gaping as he moaned in disgust and terror, his eyes wide in fear, his body tense and frozen. "Fuck!"

"What is it?"

"Look," he said, and promptly staggered away. This time he did throw up, splashing it all over the floor. He coughed and screamed and booted the nearest tree. "Oh, Jesus Christ..."

It was my turn. I'd seen dead bodies before and the stench was strong on this one. I knew it was bad without even looking. I stepped towards the boot, the smell getting stronger, and peered in.

Almost sank to my knees but kept it together. I could feel the vomit rising too, but kept a lid on it, covering my mouth. Shone the torch as Dave crept up behind me and shone his in, too.

The kid had been cut up. Into pieces. His head was sitting between his legs, eyes wide and mouth gaping. Blood pooled all around him, and the bugs and maggots were getting busy on a feast. His skin was almost blue.

He was looking right at me.

THIRTY FOUR

"So what now?"

A stupid question, I suppose. But I knew where he was coming from. "We report it to the police," I said. "After I get some photos."

"Jesus, Jim. Why the hell would you want photos of this?"

He had a point. Why indeed? Well, I suppose it was just to satisfy something in me, to bring some kind of closure, to get my own evidence before it had a chance to be corrupted or hidden by the police. The camera never lies. My thoughts spun to Bob Turner then, my old friend who'd blown a shotgun into his own head. Or had he? I still had those photos of the scene in his front room that I might one day return to. I felt the same way about this poor kid. Macabre, yes. Of course it was. But I was always a stickler for detail. You never knew, in my trade, when something was gonna come back to haunt you. I considered it an insurance policy, and an insurance policy was always handy in my line of work. So before I did anything else, I got to taking those photographs, as many as I could, before I took out my phone and called Fiona.

"Jim."

I caught my breath in the cold. "We found him. The Polish kid. They cut him up into pieces, Fi. Decapitated too. This is not a pretty sight, as you can imagine. I'm just letting you know first because I'll have to ring it through. They'll have to launch a murder inquiry, though it's pretty obvious to me who's responsible. Any news on Connor yet?"

"Chopped him up? Jim, are any of his limbs missing?"

"What do you mean?"

"It's a pretty straightforward question."

I turned to look at the corpse. Dave had wandered off into the darkness, but hadn't strayed too far. Just far enough so he didn't have to look at the body. Were there? As far as I could tell, all body parts were there, though he was still clothed and the bugs moved around his flesh so hungrily it was hard to decipher what the hell was intact and what wasn't, especially in this light.

"Hard to say. Why do you ask?"

"Well isn't it obvious?"

"Not sure where you're going with this, Fi, but..." And then it hit me. "Shit, you don't think...?"

"It's possible, I reckon. A similar killing. Dismemberment. Car involved. If they'd taken any parts to scatter around the city as some kind of mark, some kind of warning..."

"Are you saying what I think you're saying?"

"Connor Connolly's just become a suspect in the murder of DCI Robertson."

I swallowed hard, and this time I did sink to my knees. I sparked up. Took that shit in deep. Fi was silent on the other end of the line for a moment, and I guessed she was just as stunned as I was. Though nothing was concrete just yet - no evidence, no nothing - I had to admit that this was the closest anyone had come to a suspect in Robertson's murder since it all began. And I'd just happened to stumble upon it. The question was, what would've been Connor's motive - if indeed it was Connor - to kill Robertson? With the young kid in that boot behind me, his motive was anger, pure and simple. But with Robertson? Nothing added up.

"Jim, you still there?"

"I'm here."

"Listen. You're forgetting you're at a crime scene. If you're not careful, you could put yourself at major risk, so you need to get out of there immediately. Don't leave any trace."

"Yeah."

"And don't ring it in. I will."

"What!?"

"I'll say I'd had an anonymous call or something."

"Fi."

"Just leave it to me. Please. But get out of there now, Jim. You have a knack of making things go tits up. Please don't fuck this one up."

"I won't. We're going right now."

"Send me a text when you're back on the road."

"I will."

"And Jim?"

"Yeah?"

There was a pause. Heard her breathing down the line. "Doesn't matter."

I packed up the camera and we retraced our steps as best we could, leaving the body of the kid behind. There was nothing we could do. Even a few words seemed useless. Getting out of the place seemed even harder than getting in, though we put that down to feeling that little bit more tired. The cold had more of a bite, too. We were silent as we walked and stumbled. The poor kid was on my mind, God rest his soul.

The Porsche was still in good shape where we'd left it. Still in one piece and hidden from the road. I guessed there hadn't been many passing vehicles since we'd ventured into the forest - probably none - and it was a relief to get inside. Dave fired her up and got the heating on full, including the one beneath my arse. We hit the road quickly, Dave expertly manoeuvring the car through the winding country lane. He couldn't get away quick enough and I could hardly blame him.

"That was some fucked up shit, Jim. Please don't ask me to do that again."

"I knew it was gonna be bad, but even I didn't expect that. I'm sorry, Dave. Sorry to have put you through that."

He shrugged, put a brave face on it. "It's okay. No, really, it's okay. Just never seen anything like that before, you know? Don't think it'll leave my mind any time soon."

"Me too."

"So what now?"

"Do you mind dropping me at the office?"

"Of course not. But I meant with the body."

I nodded and sparked up. Dave took the cue and found it appropriate to spark up the joint again. I guessed he needed something. "Fi said she'd sort it. Take it off my hands. I just want to get back to Laura now. I'm sick of the whole thing."

"So they'll have all those forensic guys up here soon?"

"As soon as they get the call," I said. "I just hope we left the scene as we found it. You get the tracker?"

"Yeah," he said. "You know, next time, I think we'll use a recording device as well. Imagine we had done with this? They would've been bang to rights."

You live and learn. I took out the camera and went through the photos. I'd upload them to the Mac as soon as I got back to the office. They weren't pretty and the folder would need a secure password. I sat back as Dave drove and thought about what I would do with them. Perhaps not much, but I had them before the police did, and that meant something.

Pulled out my phone and called Laura. Told her I was on my way back.

"Well?"

"It was him. It mustn't have been good for him in the end. They really made a mess of him."

Dave said that was an understatement.

"So what happens now?"

"For us? Nothing. It's over. The two families are no doubt busy killing each other. Suits me just fine."

"It's all over the news, love. And are you coming home? We've all eaten. I can warm yours in the oven if you want."

"Maybe later. I need to stop by the office."

"Is everything okay? Sorry I couldn't call in earlier."

"Seems to be."

"When can I expect you back? Because I've got a surprise for you."

I was intrigued. She'd gotten giddy, no doubt, with our new found wealth. "I don't know. But soon. Sooner than you think. Just got to get some photos on the Mac, then I'm done with it all. Do me a favour and keep the beer on ice. I could do with a cold one."

She said she would, told me she loved me, and hung up.

I looked out at the passing traffic when Dave finally reached the motorway. A convoy of blue lights swept past us moments later. Fi had made the call.

W hen we got back to the office, I insisted Dave come up. He said he had to go, but I persuaded him when I mentioned the weed. When I opened up the safe, he almost dropped to the floor.

"All that?"

"Well, I don't need it. I don't smoke that shit. Call it a little thank you for helping me out. Now if you don't mind, I need a stiff one."

"If I wasn't driving, I'd join you."

"Didn't let that joint stop you," I said, tossing him the kilo. He caught it like an expert. "All yours. Take it off my bloody hands."

"My pleasure. Cheers, man."

"Don't cane it in a week, though."

"As if."

I grabbed my brandy from the filing cabinet, usually only reserved for special occasions, and poured a good measure before slumping on the couch. Outside, the night was lively.

"That was some experience, wasn't it? Not sure I want to repeat that in a hurry."

"Fuck, no."

I didn't want to repeat the rest of the day, either. I could see that Dave was the same. "You want a beer?"

He thought about it. "Better not, eh? As much as I'd like to. But it's my shout next weekend. When all this is done with."

"It's a date."

Dave got his shit together and said he'd be in touch. I saw him to the door and watched him speed off from the window moments later. Brought the brandy to my lips and drank. It was good. Sparked up. Took that shit in deep. Then I spent the next hour looking out over the street and the city beyond. Thought about the dead, stacking up like dominoes. Aisling and her baby. The father of her child, Lukasz Badowski. Kian, bludgeoned to death in his house. The Polish kid in that forest. Surely it was only a matter of time before there were more. These families were fucked up, all right. Worse than that. Bloodlines ran deep. And the blood ran like a river.

I kept coming back to something Fiona had said as I sat and poured more brandy and let the shadows wash over me.

Could it be?

Robertson's body parts had been scattered across the city. We knew that much. Wiktor had hinted that he knew something, too.

And then a memory came to me. Got shivers.

Could be nothing.

But maybe it wasn't.

THIRTY FIVE

"Come on, come on. Answer the bloody phone..."

She did, but only after I'd tried it several times. She wasn't in the best of moods and told me I was a useless, drunken arsehole, which I guessed wasn't that far from the truth.

"I've been thinking. About Robertson."

"Jim, you woke me up, you selfish bastard."

"Did they find his legs? I mean, you know... have they turned up?"

"What? No." There was a pause and I heard her scrambling around. "No, I don't think so. Why? Why?"

"Have you been drinking?"

"What? Just some wine. What do you want, Jim?"

"I need you to drive us. I'm coming over."

"What?! Drive us where?"

"I'll explain when I get to yours. Look, sorry for waking you, but this could be important. I'll be there as soon as I can."

The taxi pulled in down Fiona's street, and by now, it was pissing down. I stumbled out of the cab and dashed it to her door. Knocked three times and didn't have to wait too long before she was in my face.

"So, do you want to explain what the fuck you're playing at?"

I stepped out of the rain and into the hallway. "Look, I know this might sound way out there, but I think I might know where the rest of him is."

"The rest of who? Jim, start making sense."

"Robertson. Look, call it a hunch, a wild stab in the dark, whatever, I couldn't give a fuck anymore. But I think Seamus Connolly killed him. Or at least had him killed, for reasons we don't know. Fi, why are you looking at me like that?"

She laughed. "Christ, you don't know?"

"No."

"You sound like a crazy man."

"Look, I know it sounds crazy but hear me out...."

I stepped into the front living room and crashed onto the couch. The ticker on the mute news channel told me it was approaching midnight. I didn't expect her to exactly be happy about my sudden appearance. I'd be pissed off, too. But this mattered.

"So what brings you to this wild conclusion?"

She was putting her coat on, which was encouraging. Grabbed her keys off the mantelpiece.

"Like I say, I don't know. Just a feeling."

"You've gotta do better than that, Jim."

"Okay, something Wiktor said. He implied he knew what had happened to Robertson. And given the circles he moves in, it wouldn't surprise me if he knew."

"So why not ask him?"

"Come on, Fi. When all this is going on? I don't think so.
I don't think he'd tell me anyway. And maybe he'd just been
bullshitting me. But there's something else as well."

"Something to make you so sure?"

"I could never be certain, but if I don't check it out, I'll
never know."

"So, where are we going? What's so urgent?"

"We're going to Macclesfield."

"Macclesfield?! What the fuck for?"

"Connolly's house."

"Now I know you really have lost your mind."

"He won't be home."

"What makes you so certain?"

"His youngest son is dead. Murdered by the Badowskis.
He'll be out smelling blood."

"You don't know that."

"No, but the odds are against him being home. And
that's perfect for what I want to check out. Are you ready?"

She turned and headed for the door, calling me an arsehole as she went.

"One other thing. You got any meat in the fridge?"

Five minutes later she started up her Fiesta and we
headed out towards the M60 with a butchers wrap of good
steak sitting on my lap. Part of me accepted that this was
probably madness. Like a man willingly walking to his own
death. But I had to know. Needed to know.

As she drove, we caught up on events. She told me what
she knew about Kian's murder. The kid had probably been
whacked around the head with a baseball bat a few times. It
wouldn't have been a pretty way to die at all. The scene was
still in the hands of GMP SOCO, and it would be for some
time. His sister, of course, was dead too. Yet she'd died at the

hands of her own brother. Had he taken it upon himself or had his old man given the order? It didn't matter. She was dead and her unborn son was, too.

"Are you gonna tell me why we're on our way to his house? This doesn't feel like it's a good idea, Jim."

I shrugged. Took out my phone. Opened my contacts and found his number. "It might be nothing at all. But there's something I can't get out of my head and I need to check it out, just for my own sanity. Something I remember from when I visited him at home. From when I first took on this stupid job."

"Care to be more specific?"

"You'll see. Or maybe you won't. What did you say when you rang it in? The Polish kid, I mean..."

"Said I'd had an anonymous call. I rang it straight through to DI McKinnon's desk. They'll probably want to trace that call, but it won't exist."

"No."

"Which might eventually get me into trouble, but I don't care."

"You should've left it to me. I'd have taken the hit."

"Doesn't matter now. Like all this stuff. Robertson's dead and will never face any justice for what he did to Isabella Burns."

"You heard from her recently?"

She shook her head. "No. Last time I saw her, her arms had just been bandaged up again. The emotional scars will last much longer, I'm sure."

We were quiet for a moment. "You got bluetooth?"

"I can just put the radio on if -"

"It's for a phone call. I want you to listen in. Do me a favour and dial up this number from your phone."

"My phone? Why mine?"

I showed her the dictaphone app. It was already recording. "Ah. Okay." She fumbled for her phone and handed it to me. I dialled and hovered my thumb over the green call button. It was worth a try.

Ringing.

THIRTY SIX

"Mr. Locke. I thought you'd had enough of all this nonsense. I thought I told you we'd take it from here."

"Wiktor," I said. Fi mouthed an Oh Fuck! "You did. But I keep thinking about something and I can't get it off my mind. I was hoping you'd be able to help."

There was a long pause, and we could hear him breathing through the speakers as the wheels rolled beneath us. "Enlighten me, Mr. Locke."

"I'll get straight to the point. You said you might tell me more about Robertson. How he died. Who was responsible. You said if I brought Connor to you, you'd tell me more. I suppose you could've been bluffing, but I can't help but be intrigued. About what you know. Just wondered if it matched up with what I thought myself, you know. So, tell me. What do you know, Wiktor? Who killed Robertson?"

"I said I might tell you more," he said. "There is a stark difference between a maybe and a definite, Mr. Locke. As you know. But you did what I asked of you and I must admit, it surprised me. I recall our conversation. In the cemetery, yes?"

"That's right."

"Well now. Tell me. Where are you?"

"Travelling. On the M60."

"Are you driving?"

I glanced at Fi, who was making a cut throat sign across her neck. "Yes."

"Then I hope you will pay attention to the road instead of to me."

This seemed to tickle him. "Of course, Wiktor."

"You may realise that my son is dead, Mr. Locke. Killed by a single bullet. From one of Connolly's men. His wife is dead too. And their baby boy."

"I'm sorry, Wiktor. I truly am. Did you say wife?"

"They were married last month in London. It was beautiful. A shame her father couldn't be there, but..."

"Married?"

"Why so surprised?"

"No, it's just..."

"They loved each other, Mr. Locke. I'm sure you're a man who understands love."

"Of course."

He said something else, but I let it fly over my head as I turned to Fi, who was looking as equally perplexed.

"I'm happy they cemented their relationship before all of this," he said. "Now they can rest in peace together."

For someone who'd just lost his son, his unborn grandson and his daughter-in-law, Wiktor didn't seem too upset. Perhaps that was a sign he really was mad, like the rest of them. Perhaps he'd known that all of this was inevitable. It was a part of their life. Bloodlines like theirs had seen murders and dying with 'honour' as just the way it was. But then I heard him sobbing.

"Wiktor...? Look, I'm sorry. This was clearly wrong of me to call you at such a bad time. I don't know what I was thinking."

I turned to Fi, who was open-mouthed, as we listened to him crying through the speakers.

"This is all my fault, Locke."

"No."

"Yes, all of it. My son would never have been killed if it wasn't for me, my past, the life we lived. It's over now. I will join my son soon. You can be sure that when they find me, they will find me with a smile on my face."

Was he saying he was going to do himself in? "Wiktor, are you saying what I think you're saying?"

There was silence for a moment as he sniffed and sobbed. I could imagine him sitting in some leather armchair with a large brandy - or vodka - alone and heart-broken, ready to do away with the world entirely.

"What does it matter anymore? I tell you, Locke, that I have wasted my life. Wasted everything. Yes, I have money, more than most could imagine. I have all the material things, everything anyone could want or need, and yet I have nothing if my grandson is dead. And I am to blame. I am to blame."

"Wiktor, don't do this. Please."

Yet I knew I couldn't stop him and he was probably right. Although he wasn't directly at fault for his son falling in love with Aisling, Lukasz had been raised in a bad family and Aisling likewise. Maybe the way they had died had been coming. Just a matter of time.

"I'm holding my gun to Connor Connolly's head, Mr.

Locke. Right now. Soon, I will pull the trigger. And then I will turn the gun on myself."

"Wiktor, where are you?"

"It doesn't matter. Nothing matters now."

Yet I wanted to know the truth. "Wiktor, who killed DCI Robertson? Please tell me what you know."

There was some commotion, like a struggle, and several voices in the background. I couldn't make out what they were saying, but I recognised Polish. I glanced at Fi, who was still driving on autopilot as we listened. A loud bang, but not a gunshot, then a familiar voice, slurred like he was extremely drunk.

"It's me."

"Who?"

"It's me. Connor. My dad killed that fucking copper. The great Seamus Connolly killed your paedo fucking copper bastard." Spitting down the phone like a drunken fucker. "That paedo bastard got what he deserved."

We exchanged looks again and Fi wrestled with the wheel at the last minute, so we didn't miss our exit.

"I saw you kill your own sister, Connor. I hope you're proud of yourself."

"Fuck you."

More commotion. Then the sound of a man being beaten hard. Screams that made my blood run cold.

"We're keeping him in a cage for now," Wiktor said. Was that a laugh? I was pretty sure it was. "His death will not be quick, I can assure you of that. But I will be the one to take him out at the end. First, we make it hurt."

"Jesus..."

"Trust that this is true justice, Locke. Our bloodlines shall end here. Goodbye."

The line went dead.

THIRTY SEVEN

"Well, what the fuck have we just heard?"

She was right. What the fuck indeed. By now I was past caring what happened to any of them. Connor getting a bullet in the head was everything he deserved. And if Wiktor Badowski wanted to do himself in, it would be one less cunt on the face of the earth. Between them, both families had done the city a huge favour. I wasn't the slightest bit concerned or bothered because a lot of people had been hurt at the hands of these bastards. And now all that was over. But I also knew it would only be a matter of time before others took their place.

"Was that really Connor?"

I shrugged. "Sounded like it. They got to him. I suppose I knew they would in the end."

"What should we do, Jim?"

"What do you mean?"

"Well, we should do something. Shouldn't we? A man is going to die by the sounds of it and we're doing nothing. We're police, Jim. I'm gonna call it in."

I grabbed her arm. "We're police no more," I said. "You'll do no such thing. Let them die. It's what they want. It's the only thing these arseholes know."

We pulled off the slip road and I opened up the sat nav on my phone. We were ten minutes away. I sparked up. Took that shit in deep. Fi did the same. I needed a strong drink and when this was finally done, I'd be having several.

"So why the steak?"

"For the dog. Hopefully, it'll keep it busy while we look around."

She gave me a look. "Oh no. Don't expect me to come in with you. I brought you here, you do the dirty work yourself."

"I'll need you with me, Fi. Just in case."

"Just in case of what?"

"In case it all goes tits up."

"What exactly do you have planned?"

I shrugged. "I just want to have a look around, that's all."

She shook her head, kept her eyes on the road. It was dark out. The streetlights seemed to have vanished. I turned around and saw the last of them fading away like distant stars.

"Are you sure you know what you're doing, Jim?"

I thought about that question he'd asked me on St. Patrick's night at Mulligan's. Are you a gambling man, Mr. Locke? Was I?

Not really, I'd said. I took risks, plenty of them, the dangerous kind that could get me in deep shit. And I realised I was gambling now.

"It'll be fine. Like I said. I don't believe he'll be home and if there's any sign that he is, we turn right around and go."

This seemed to settle it. We were quiet as the sat nav

voice delivered instructions. Fi gripped the wheel tight, nervous and showing it.

"Do you believe him?"

"Who, Wiktor? About taking Connor out?"

"No, Connor. About Seamus taking Robertson out. And the reason why."

"They must've known he'd been messing around with Isabella Burns."

"Which suggests there were others we don't know about."

I thought about it. It was all just a big definitely maybe. Perhaps there were others. I wouldn't have put it past him. And maybe the Connollys knew about it and didn't like it and wanted him out of the picture. Perhaps they knew more about Robertson than any of us. And not just the Connollys, but the Badowskis too. Is that how Wiktor got me out of police hands last night? Because he knew more than the police did? And if he did get me out of Crane's way, did he give Crane more to think about given Robertson was a murder victim? In short, had he let on to GMP that he knew more and would tell more, just like he'd implied with me? I suppose now I'll never know.

"It's just up here, I reckon. I feel sick, Jim."

"Don't be silly. We'll be out of here in no time at all."

"I should be in bed now. You pick your moments, don't you?"

I gave her a look I thought was reassuring.

Fi slowed the car down and took a right into a pitch black country lane. The walls were high and dark on either side, and I knew I couldn't even open the door to get out. God help us if another vehicle was coming towards us. But then as we edged further on, the road widened and I realised we'd just driven up a driveway and not a narrow road. Suddenly we were out the front of Seamus Connolly's house, a little unfamiliar in the darkness, but the unmistakable size of it, stark in silhouette against the midnight blue sky, made me almost forget I was holding my breath.

"This the place?"

I nodded. "This is it. Come on."

"Jim, wait. You really want me in there with you? Wouldn't it be best if I just wait here? You know, we don't really want to draw attention to ourselves, do we?"

"Fi, there's nothing to worry about." I turned to look at the house. There wasn't a single light on. "It's obvious there's no one home. Now come on. The sooner we get in, the sooner we get out."

Besides the massive sigh, I could tell she was more than nervous. I felt a touch of guilt for dragging her out here with me. But I needed to be sure of something and I needed her assistance to get this done. Maybe I'd turned a corner and had really gone beyond any sensible thinking. The lights were on, but no one was home. Maybe. But then I reminded myself of what Connor had said just minutes ago. That the great Seamus Connolly had killed our paedo copper bastard. Perhaps I wasn't so crazy after all.

"Can we just do whatever it is you dragged me here to do, then fuck off as soon as possible? And you owe me one, Jim."

"Let's go."

"Aren't you forgetting something?"

Maybe I wouldn't need it, and I hoped I wouldn't. But I wasn't a huge fan of dogs, especially ones that wouldn't have a problem ripping your fingers or balls off. The steak was an insurance policy, perhaps a silly one, but I felt it was a wise move. I grabbed it before pulling the door and approaching the front of the house.

Even out here in the dark, it was imposing. And you could see the wealth it must've taken to build the place. Seamus had never been short of money, of course. It had an impressive mix of old and new. It was a grade two listed building, no less, with the added addition of ultra contemporary modern architecture, all white-washed walls and privacy glass, as if the several wings that had been built onto the original house had been designed for the very purpose; to hide what was behind the walls.

The perimeter was illuminated with hidden lamps in the gardens. There were no vehicles parked on the drive except for Fiona's fiesta. Didn't mean there weren't any in the garages. Everywhere else was in shadow. If it wasn't for the light of the moon, I'd be thinking about turning back myself. I took out my phone and flicked on the torch. Urged Fi to do the same.

"I don't like it, Jim. I want to go."

"Jesus, it's not like you haven't done this kind of thing before, being a copper."

"One of the things I hated, to be honest. We can't just go snooping around someone's house, can we?"

"Technically, no. But this is for the greater good."

"Exactly what are you hoping to find, Jim?"

"Let's keep going and see, eh?"

"Have you thought about how we're gonna get in? You haven't, have you?"

I shrugged, but she was right. There had to be some rocks scattered around the garden, though.

"Look, Fi," I said. "We've come this far. Pretty pointless backing out now when we're here. In and out, that's it. Then we're done."

"You really think that dog will be arsed about a steak?"

"Why not?"

"You look a right prick, Jim."

I tuned her out and stepped on into the darkness. We headed for the far eastern side, and into a large side garden I assumed led to around the back. The darkness got thicker beneath the trees and overgrown privets. It occurred to me then that we could be all over the CCTV. To hell with it.

"Shh," Fi said. She stopped and whispered. "Did you hear that?"

"Hear what?"

"Keep your voice down."

"I didn't hear anything."

We made our way to the steps around the back and crept up them. Everything was in darkness. The entire wall was made of glass, flanked by huge plant pots on either side. I stepped closer to check out the sliding doors and stopped when I heard the whine. I shone the torch to my right and spotted the large mound moving in the shadows.

"That's what I heard, Jim. You heard it, yeah?"

"I heard it."

The dog was lying in a pool of blood, its huge belly rising swiftly as it struggled for breath. Its glassy eyes vacant, its solid muscles frozen and stiff as it clung on.

"Oh, fucking hell..."

"Poor thing."

"It's been shot, Fi." I knelt down beside him, careful to avoid the blood, and stroked his head. "Or stabbed. Shit, there's a lot of blood. I want to put him out of his misery but..."

"You can't, Jim. That's horrible. Let's just sit with him."

"... I don't know how. Fucking hell."

"What do you think's happened?"

"I don't know. But we can't stay with him. He hasn't got long, love."

I realised the steak was pointless and slung it onto the lawn. Got my hands wet from the animal's blood. It was bad. Really bad. There was nothing we could do but leave him to die. I gave him a gentle stroke, then stepped back and wiped my hands on my jeans, saw the bloodlines flow across the flagstones under the moonlight. Fi struggled to tear herself away, but I managed to persuade her. As hard as it was to leave it, we knew we had to.

The question now, though, was why and how the dog had been butchered. Bullet or blade, either way, it was the animal's downfall. No creature deserved that. I wondered, not for the first time, that what I was doing - what we were doing - was madness.

I stepped up to the glass doors and peered inside. Darkness. Not a soul around. No lights, no sounds, no flickering T.V. Tried the handle, but it didn't budge. That was no surprise. I saw a tear roll down Fi's cheek when we both heard the last breath of the dog, like air being punched from a wet bag.

When I shone the torch back at the body, the pool had gotten bigger and blacker under the moonlight. He was gone now.

"Let's go, Jim. We're wasting our time."

"We've come this far," I said. "Not yet. Not now."

I was annoyed with myself for being so blind, so stupid as to not bring some kind of weapon. Whoever had hurt this dog could still be here to hurt us. I shone the torch and scrambled around, looking for something I could use as a cosh. There were plenty of rocks in the shrubbery, but my eye caught a glance of something much better. A bone that no doubt the dog had been busy chewing on before he met his end. I grabbed it in the darkness, surprised at its weight. I could still feel the grains of meat and gristle attached, flesh that had been gnawed on in the dead beast's jaws for hours.

"Let's go."

"Jim."

But I'd already lifted the bone and got ready to smash the glass.

"For fuck's sake, Jim, no!"

She'd gripped my arm. "There's no other way in."

"Let's look around first."

I supposed she was right, and I'd been just a little too hasty. She led the way around the perimeter once more and I followed. We left the dog behind us and skirted the wall, the moonlight just enough to see. Shadows danced around us, and I suddenly wished I was somewhere else. Made a quick mental note to not do this again any time soon.

We took our time around the edge of the wall and peeked through every window we came across. With each one, I was more convinced the property was empty. Fiona clung to me like a frightened child. We stepped over a small knee height fence and onto a large wooden decking area. Peering through the gloom, I could see a huge barbecue that had been covered up, a garden hose, several picnic style benches. And beyond the glass sliding doors to our left, a shimmering blue light rippled through a gap somewhere deep inside. I peered in, face to the glass, careful to keep the heavy bone from smashing into it, and could see now that the blue light was the rippling water of an indoor pool, the bright white glint dancing like electric snakes.

Tried the handle on the sliding doors.

This time it opened easily, swishing away from the latch. I realised I was holding my breath as it opened up and we tentatively stepped across the threshold into a large rest area. The phone's torch picked up a bench, an exercise bike, a couple of loungers with towels draped over them. Beyond that, what looked like a sauna. The glossy tiled floor shone creamy white in the moonlight. Fiona hovered warily behind me as we stepped towards the open partition door and the pool beyond.

The water reflected cleanly off the glass. The pool was about a half size, enough to swim a few widths and laze on a blow up lounger. But it was big enough and about twelve feet deep. Over on the other side lay a handful of empty bottles and beer cans, a couple on their side. Perhaps we weren't alone after all.

"Let's just do what you dragged me here to do and go."

My thoughts exactly. Gripping the bone, I stepped on towards a narrow door in the far corner. It was open ajar, and dark beyond it, but I guessed it led into the belly of the house. Had a bad feeling that we weren't alone after all in here. The empty beers only added to my paranoia. I supposed they could've been there a few days, but... the sliding door to get in here was unlocked too. Told myself that it was nothing. I was being overly cautious, which was to be expected. But I also kept telling myself that we'd come this far. Backing out now seemed pointless. It was do or die.

"Jim," she whispered. I could sense her shaking and put it down to the cold. "Don't leave me on my own."

"I won't. Just stay behind me. Keep shining your torch."

But then it blinked off. "Shit. I think my battery's gone." She messed around with her phone but the screen wouldn't light up. "Ah, bollocks."

"I'm still good for a while yet. Let's get through and find a light switch. You take my phone and I'll go ahead. But make sure you give me plenty of light."

She did, and we shuffled along, our breath the only sound

to break the silence. There was a heaviness to the air, the energy in here somehow dense. It felt like sheer dread. As we left the pool area behind us, we moved on through a utility room, a washing machine and a dryer plumbed against the wall, a collection of clothes and other stuff that had been dumped here, and a scattering of plastic storage boxes along the floor. Fi almost tripped over one and we stumbled for a moment. I found a light switch beside the doorframe as we reached the exit and switched on. It gave no light. I looked up, saw a halogen flickering. Seemed the bulb needed replacing.

And then we heard a clatter and a thud coming from a room above us. We caught our breath and Fi was ready to run, but I stopped her before she could.

"Fuck, Jim. Let's get out of here."

"It was probably a cat or something, that's all."

"That was no bloody cat."

"We'll go soon."

"We might not have that long."

"Just hold on for now. We'll be out of here in no time."

"Two minutes, then I'm gone."

I tuned her out and stepped through the next door, into a room so dark and cold. Got her to swing the torch around for some kind of light switch, but we couldn't see one and instead stumbled around again.

I couldn't exactly tell what kind of room we were in - perhaps a kitchen, as there was a large porcelain sink on the left wall and a couple of cabinets against the opposite one. Fi shone the light, but it still wasn't clear. I listened to the hum and whir for a moment, then realised that the two cabinets were chest freezers. I took the torch and got a closer look. They had padlocks to keep prying eyes out, and I couldn't help but wonder why.

"Shine the torch, Fi," I said, handing the phone back. "Right on the padlock."

"But are you sure that's -"

Before she could finish, I brought the bone crashing down hard, splitting the lock, which went spinning across the floor. Then I brought it down on the second one. I lifted the first freezer and looked in.

THIRTY EIGHT

My first instinct was to run, but my legs were frozen rigid. Staring back up at me were a pair of eyes. A gaping, hollow mouth as dark as a black hole. Mottled skin, the flesh almost rubbery and pure grey, like a lost alien. Black hair that clung to the scalp in thin wisps.

Her breathing was rapid and sickening. I wanted out as much as her, but instead I reached out to touch that face I knew so well.

"Oh fuck, oh fuck, Jesus, Jim... we've gotta go, Jim, we gotta go right now."

I touched it. Touched him. Flinched and pulled my hand back like I'd been electrocuted. Felt a hard shiver run down my spine and when we heard the thud from above, Fi bolted the fuck out, dropping my phone. I quickly retrieved it and started filming through the camera app.

"Fi!"

Turned back to the horror in the freezer and filmed it all, the light from the phone illuminating limbs and other monstrous things wrapped in cellophane and plastic bags.

"What the fuck..."

A thud again, followed by footfalls.

I grabbed one and got a closer look. It was meat. Flesh. Offal. I realised I was still holding the bone and wondered if it had come out of this freezer too. Examined it close in the stark light, the gnawed bits of flesh still clinging to it, the gristle attached slimy and putrid. It was easily big enough to be a human femur bone. I almost let it slip from my fingers, but instead swung it wildly at the figure that had darkened the doorway.

I whacked him around the head, letting it fall hard on his temple, but he muscled me away and pushed me back, my phone going clattering across the floor. I fumbled for it, but felt something severe hit me in the guts. I cried out and panicked in the darkness. The bone vanished too and I prepared myself for it falling down upon my own head.

But it didn't come. I stumbled blindly through the door, halfway to my feet, my phone left behind and half expecting a rugby tackle any second. I shouted for Fiona, but there came no answer.

"Basa. Fuckin basa..."

Seamus. Heavy, wheezing breaths as he stumbled after me. Even in this madness, I knew that voice.

"Ya fuckin... scum... bastard!"

I felt him grip my ankle as I scrambled across the floor like a toddler chasing a ball, and kicked out, my boot connecting with what I thought might be his face. I kicked out twice, then a third time, until he let go and I got to my feet and ran. Something flew over my head in the darkness and crashed into a doorframe while I crashed through that door, knowing that somewhere on the other side would be the pool and somewhere beyond that, Fiona, and freedom.

Yet I knew he was right behind me. I'd dropped my weapon in the madness - the bone - and now I had nothing but my bare hands. Up against Seamus, I knew I couldn't put up much of a fight, even against a man of his age. He was a monster.

"Locke! You drunken bastard cunt! You come for me, eh?"

I spun around, hoping to God that Fiona would return, but there was just me and him in the swirling blue light of the pool, a strip light above us flickering. I backed off, holding my arms out in a vain effort to calm him down, but I knew it was useless. He let that machete he'd used at the abattoir swing beside him. There was blood on the blade. I knew then that he'd used it time and time again on the poor victim - or victims - that lay dead in those freezers just metres away.

"Seamus, it's not like that," I said, knowing I sounded completely ridiculous. Here I was snooping around his house while his dog lay dead in a pool of blood outside. His son Connor was probably dead now too, off to join Kian in the next world. And Robertson chopped up in the freezer. Seamus Connolly had killed that paedo copper bastard. And if I wasn't careful, I knew he'd do the same to me.

"You should've told me about Aisling sooner, Locke," he said. "I could've done something about it. I could've stopped it. I hired you to follow her around so that this wouldn't fucking happen. And look what happened!"

"You couldn't have done anything to change it, Seamus," I said. He was drunk. Not paralytic, but drunk enough to let himself do something silly. I saw movement from the corner of my eye. "You couldn't have stopped anything."

"Bollocks. I should've put a stop to it fucking years ago. If I had, none of this would've happened. Aisling wouldn't have gotten pregnant. Our bloodlines wouldn't have mixed. Now they're fucked up, Locke. Don't you see that?"

"She didn't deserve or need to die, Seamus. Killing her was completely unnecessary and you know it."

Wrong move, because he lunged for me then with that blade raised. I stumbled back as he stepped towards me and again saw movement from somewhere nearby to my right. A blur of a figure, a haze of motion.

"I couldn't let that fucking baby live," he said, and those words almost cut me in half. Almost.

"He was your grandson, Seamus. An innocent child. You must be so proud of yourself."

"You fucking little cunt, how dare you speak to me like -"

"Jim!"

Fiona. I turned to her as he swung the machete at me. The momentum of his swing sent him clattering across the tiled floor, which was slick with pool water, and he crashed face down, just avoiding falling into the pool itself. The blade fell from his grasp and Fi went to grab it, but he found it again and lashed out, cutting her arm. The blade connected and she winced, shocked. She lost her balance and fell into the water. A cloud of crimson ballooned from her slashed wrist, and she held it with her other hand as the blood leaked from her like oil. Jesus, the wound must've been deep. The water around her was turning a velvet pink as her lips were turning blue and she glared at me, open-mouthed and panicking.

"Fiona! Fuck. What have you done to her, you sick bastard!"

He was writhing around on the floor, laughing. Or crying. Or maybe both. His massive head was pressed against the cold wet tiles, his fat fingers still clutching the blade. I went to grab it, but he rolled over and lashed out at me. I dropped a bottle on his fat fucking nose and stamped hard, almost losing my balance in the wet. I was aware more than ever that Fiona was losing it, dropping beneath the water.

I got on top of him, my hands at his bastard throat as he swung the machete one more time. I managed to bat it away and it went skidding across the floor. Seamus planted a fist to the side of my head. My temple thudded and my brain buzzed. I saw stars and blacked out, but only for the briefest of moments.

I scrambled away from him, knowing I might've lost her, and dragged myself across the floor. I felt a grip on my ankle as the neon blue flickered, and then I caught sight of the empty beer bottle. Reached out and grabbed it, swinging it back and landing it right in the bastard's eye.

I hit him three times before I smashed it on the tiles and pushed the shard into his face. My screams were all I heard until the gunshot came and I fell into the water and blacked out.

***

Drifting...
    Drifting...
In a deep blue dream. Her crimson skin. Her velvet eyes...

When I came to, I was lying on my side, shivering. Fiona was lying next to me, as white as a ghost, her eyes staring blankly at the ceiling. Someone was hovering over her, over both of us, and I flinched when I saw him, but he reassured us that it was okay, that he wasn't like them, he just had to live with the name.

He barely said two words to anyone, was the butt of all the usual jokes, but right now I could've kissed Shane Connolly. The last time I saw him, he'd handed me a Guinness on St. Patrick's night at Mulligan's. Now he was handing me his open hand and lifting me to my knees as the room spun.

"Shane?"

He said nothing, just smiled. I glanced over at the other side of the pool. Outside, the night was quiet, but the air was cold. I thought I could hear faint sirens echoing in the night. Seamus lay dead, a gunshot wound to his head and his face shredded. There was a pool of blood beneath him and he looked like a bloated wildebeest that had been hunted down.

"Fiona."

"It's okay," he said, the water dripping off him. "She'll be okay."

But she didn't look it. I went to her then, cupped her face in my hands, kissed her cheek. She was breathing, but cold. Deathly cold.

"Fiona, come on, love..."

Shane must've pulled us both out. He was soaked. He'd wrapped a towel around her arm in a vain effort to stop the bleeding. It was just enough. She was conscious, but only just. I was about to ask him what had happened, but the flashing blue lights caught my eye and the sirens cut the silence from the night.

"I'm gone," he said. "I wasn't here. You understand me, Mr. Locke?"

I nodded, spaced out. I'd need a drink after this.

When I looked to catch his eye again, he wasn't there, and only the creaking door beyond left any sign he was here at all.

THIRTY NINE

I felt arms go under me and lift me to my feet. The crackling airwave radios blared all around us as the blue lights flashed from somewhere beyond the glass. Jumbled voices chattered, men and women, paramedics and police as I was put into a chair and a light shone in my eyes. I flinched and looked away, looked away at Fiona on a stretcher. It had all been my fault. They had an oxygen mask over her face, a blanket and a drip on her chest. I saw her arm all bandaged up. A paramedic carefully held a bag of blood that had been pumping into her body as they carried her out.

It was all my fault.

My head was pounding hard. My eyes swam as I peered into the blur, saw Seamus Connolly covered in a black plastic blanket. There was a familiar figure - Crane - standing over the body. He was holding my phone. Our eyes met for the briefest of moments. Then he nodded and looked away.

I told him about the body parts in the freezer. About the face of DCI Rob Robertson that had stared back at me as I'd opened it to peer in. About the leg bone - probably <u>his</u> leg bone - that I'd used as a weapon.

But he wasn't listening. Or he couldn't hear me.

Or maybe I was just talking to myself.

L ater, though not much later, I was travelling in the back of a police car. There had been a time, a long time ago, when I'd be the one sitting in the front. I'd be the one quizzing the suspect in handcuffs as we brought him in. But they hadn't cuffed me. Crane glanced back occasionally, usually through the interior mirror. I told him that I was the one that cut him up with that beer bottle and I didn't regret doing it. He was going to kill me, it was in self defence.

All that.

Though I wasn't sure he was listening. Or even cared.

The silence hung between us for what seemed like forever.

FORTY

"So what time's the flight again?"

"Eleven. It's a few hours off before we even head to the gate. There's plenty of time for breakfast."

But I wasn't thinking about food. The airport was buzzing, even at this hour. 'Is it too early for a pint?'

"Well, I suppose the holiday starts here," she said, leading us over to the bar. A full English and a few pints would be just enough to settle the nerves before take off. "But let's just take it easy, eh? Forget about all this for a while."

I had no arguments there. "So you still not telling me where we're going?"

She tapped her handbag beside her with all the necessary paperwork inside. "Thought it would be better to keep it a surprise. It's the kind of thing you need, Jim. A bit of normality for a change. A nice surprise instead of a nasty one. You've been through a lot. We've been through a lot. Time to relax, take your mind off all the... shite. For once. Let's just enjoy ourselves for a bit. Look after us, you know."

"Do I not get a clue?"

She shook her head, handed me a twenty. "It's too early for me, but what the fuck. I'll have a lager."

She was right, of course. I needed some normality. Craved it. At the bar, I looked around at all the people who were readying themselves for a holiday. A casual morning coffee. A few alcoholic ones to kick it all off. And most of them without a care in the world.

I looked back at Laura, who was busy ordering our breakfast through the restaurant's app. The woman I'd fallen in love with. I felt a pang of guilt for what I'd almost done with Fiona. Told myself it wouldn't happen again. Maybe it was time I made an honest woman of her. Made that final commitment and took the plunge. I knew she'd been waiting for me to ask her. Maybe I'd make that decision on our break away from it all. Maybe the break away would finally help me discover who I really was again.

Then there was Fiona. Three weeks ago, I thought we'd lost her for good. But she pulled through. She'd lost a lot of blood, but after several hasty transfusions, she managed a full recovery. Well, almost. Physically, she was well on the mend. Mentally, not so much. I wasn't exactly her favourite person right now. And maybe that was just as well. I owed her. Big time. And while she went off and took herself away to heal her own mind, we agreed to steer clear of even discussing what went down at Seamus Connolly's until we'd both came out the other side mentally restored. I wasn't sure how long that was going to take. For both of us.

Then there was Robertson, of course. Robertson, found dead and mutilated in that freezer. I could still see his face now, staring up at me. I could only hope that he wouldn't come to haunt my dreams.

The police had turned Connolly's place upside down and had retrieved body parts from an estimated seven victims. Robertson had merely been a small part of it. They were still trying to find a motive for his murder. Why did Seamus Connolly want him dead? I guessed that there could be many reasons, but in the end, it didn't matter. The man was gone. He wouldn't face justice for his abuse of Isabella Burns. And maybe Seamus had known what he was really about all along. Maybe that had been enough motivation for Seamus to take him out. The other victims they found in that house - and they were still digging up evidence all over the Connolly properties, of which there were many - told a different story. And it would no doubt take GMP many years to get to the real truth. Perhaps the thing that surprised me most was that there were body parts belonging to women, too. I'd heard from a good source, my old police acquaintance Anton Maddox, that Aisling's own mother could've been one of them.

Crane had made it clear to me that this was not the end. They'd taken my phone and stripped it of everything they wanted. Photos, emails, texts, video, all the data they could find. They owed me one for bringing them to Robertson - and they had Fiona to thank for the Polish kid - and even though that chapter had ended a gruesome one, they at least had some closure. But they hadn't closed on me. And I didn't expect them to anytime soon.

Aisling had been gunned down in the street, of course, and I'd heard on the grapevine that one of her friends - Lisa Browne - had been knifed to death in the neck by her trader boyfriend, who had been sentenced to life in Strangeways prison. Lisa Browne hadn't deserved to die, especially in such a brutal manner. Not like that. But she'd now joined her friend on the other side and left their inner circle behind. As far as I knew, the other girls - Kerry Ainsworth and Lynsey Byrne - had returned to mere normal lives.

Claire MacGowan had called me to say she felt the whole thing was all her fault. She wouldn't listen to reason and no doubt had her own demons to conquer. I suppose getting beaten up the way she had been had done more damage to hear head than just bruises.

That's the thing about this business. You see the damage in all its ugly forms. As the barman handed me two pints, I took the head off and clocked myself in the mirror as he went fishing for change.

Time to rest, Locke, I told myself. Time to recuperate.

We ate breakfast and read the papers - sleaze, pandemic, project fear and the forthcoming end of the world - and got mildly merry until it was time to make our way to the gate. Laura had made sure I also had a few coffees before we boarded the flight, which was unfortunate as I wanted to catch up on lost sleep. And maybe this time I'd dream of something other than what was haunting my mind.

Thailand was a pleasant surprise indeed. A month far away in a hot climate could do wonders for the soul. Perhaps I could find the time to re-energise and refocus between bottles of Chang and Singha and finally escape the world with a tropical storm on the horizon to get lost in.

I'd seen enough death to last me a lifetime. I'd come to realise that it haunted my every move, but I knew I had to accept that it came with the territory.

As we reached altitude and the in-flight food and entertainment kicked in, I turned to Laura and watched her sleep instead of drifting into my own reverie. It was time to see some life again, to find Jim Locke once more. Somewhere along the line, I'd lost him.

But I'd be back.

ACKNOWLEDGMENTS

Special thanks to my better half, Kelly-Ann, for the Punch Publishing logo design, and also for putting up with my expert procrastination again. Thanks and appreciation must also go to Stuart Bache and Books Covered for the awesome cover. And a node to a few others who've helped along the way, most notably fellow author Andrew Lowe

ABOUT THE AUTHOR

P.F. Hughes was born in Manchester in 1976. He's worked in many jobs over the years - which has contributed strongly to his writing - and continues to work on the Jim Locke series, among other forthcoming projects.

He currently lives in Ramsbottom, somewhere between the city and the countryside, with his partner Kelly-Ann, their two children and his guitar. He is currently trying to escape the real world.

Join the author's mailing list for regular updates on forthcoming releases and more.

PLEASE LEAVE A REVIEW

If you enjoyed this novel, or any of the novels in the series, I'd be eternally grateful if you could leave a rating or review!